Groundwood Books is grateful for the opportunity
... books on the Traditional
... including the Anishinabeg,
... It is also the Treaty
... the Credit. In publishing
... illustrators, editors and
translators, we commit to publishing stories that reflect
the experiences of Indigenous Peoples. For more about
our work and values, visit us at groundwoodbooks.com

I0823611

Groundwood Books is grateful for the opportunity to share stories and make books on the Traditional Territory of many Nations, including the Anishinabeg, the Wendat and the Haudenosaunee. It is also the Treaty Lands of the Mississaugas of the Credit. In partnership with Indigenous writers, illustrators, editors and translators, we commit to publishing stories that reflect the experiences of Indigenous Peoples. For more about our work and values, visit us at groundwoodbooks.com.

WAVELENGTH

WAVELENGTH

CALE PLETT

Groundwood Books
House of Anansi Press
Toronto / Berkeley

Copyright © 2025 by Cale Plett

All rights reserved. No part of this publication may be reproduced, stored in a retrieval system or transmitted, in any form or by any means, without the prior written consent of the publisher or a license from The Canadian Copyright Licensing Agency (Access Copyright). For an Access Copyright license, visit www.accesscopyright.ca or call toll free to 1-800-893-5777.

Published in 2025 by Groundwood Books / House of Anansi Press
groundwoodbooks.com

We gratefully acknowledge for their financial support of our publishing program the Canada Council for the Arts, the Ontario Arts Council and the Government of Canada.

With the participation of the Government of Canada
Avec la participation du gouvernement du Canada | Canadä

This project was funded by the Manitoba Arts Council and the Canada Council for the Arts.

Library and Archives Canada Cataloguing in Publication
Title: Wavelength / Cale Plett.
Names: Plett, Cale, author.
Identifiers: Canadiana (print) 20250136511 | Canadiana (ebook) 20250136538
ISBN 9781779460295 (softcover) | ISBN 9781779460301 (EPUB)
Subjects: LCGFT: Novels.
Classification: LCC PS8631.L477 W38 2025 | DDC jC813/.6—dc23

Edited by Emma Sakamoto
Designed by Greg Tabor
Cover illustration by Bhavna Madan

Printed and bound in Canada

Groundwood Books is a Global Certified Accessible™ (GCA by Benetech) publisher. An ebook version of this book that meets stringent accessibility standards is available to students and readers with print disabilities.

Groundwood Books is committed to protecting our natural environment. This book is made of material from well-managed FSC®-certified forests, recycled materials, and other controlled sources.

To Mom, for always listening to my stories

To Dad, for reading with all the voices

Every time I hear your voice
I'm bent around the sound
— Lillian Finley, "Beneath Vacancy"

SASHA

I text Isabelle with all the caution the stars at the Channel take when we've got a secret. Like someone is looking over my shoulder or hers. It takes distrust and encrypted apps to keep plans from the Channel and the paparazzi. Or to hide our sex lives. Mostly that, I'm told.

For me and Isabelle, it's just the opposite. Though with the way Isabelle talks about our "relationship" in interviews, I know it looks like there's a spark burning between us. She can laugh at gossipy questions and blush when it's the perfect time to blush and keep everything PG-13 like the Channel says she must.

Alexander
I need a big favor
A huge favor, actually
Are you alone?

Isabelle
Well
That depends why you're asking

She's like this in our messages. At this point, softly flirty is a state of being for her. It's a brand, and Isabelle is nothing if not an expert at marketing herself. She's worked ten times as hard as me, clawing her way from background character to lead role to being practically her own manager. But the Channel wouldn't like that image, so she has a way of disguising her relentless drive underneath a persona of being relatable and fun and bumbling. I've seen her plan charmingly relatable social blunders, practice tripping while walking onstage and write twenty drafts of an acceptance speech that will seem genuinely shocked.

She's exactly what the Channel wants her to be. Exactly what they made her, or what she turned herself into. Eventually, you can't tell. People might feel deceived, but it's just acting. In the end, that's what we signed up for.

Our overlapping fandoms would die to scroll through me and Isabelle's private conversations. They'd see backstage. They'd see before the camera starts rolling. And they'd be disappointed.

Because the romance is acting too. Most people don't want to see us exchange an endless parade of entertaining nonsense. They don't want friendly, warm messages interspersed with complaining about talk show appearances. They're not interested in the pictures of Isabelle making faces that reveal she isn't quite as young as the characters she plays.

Isabelle
Ok I'm by myself now
You alright?

If anyone could scroll back, they wouldn't find a single picture of my face. I'm scared of those.

The helmet I wear in any public setting is iconic now, an

instantly identifiable brand, but it also lets me keep my visual anonymity. As much as putting it on every day is hell, I've been able to hold on to that one thing for myself.

I'm not sure if wearing it is in my contract. That's not something I've ever been shown. And anyway, Heather Erin, who manages me and my brother, Augustus, has never needed to order me to wear it. I've saved my face from the spotlight in case I ever reached a moment like this.

Alexander
I need to disappear
And I can't do it by myself

Isabelle
You want me to come with you?
That's a big move
I feel like it could be a good stunt in a couple years
17 is too young
Later we could disappear, get engaged
Then it's wedding speculations and I can make headlines just by being seen with a ring
Or without it (gasp)

There's this too — the professional side. Between touring with my brother and Isabelle's shooting schedules, we're relentlessly busy. Some of our communication is to make sure we're keeping our timelines straight when we're pretending to be in the same place and we're not. Our messages are full of candid-seeming videos and pictures of us together with my face out of view. They're paired with adoring captions, all pending approval from the other person before becoming public.

Alexander
Why don't I get a ring?

Isabelle
Your helmet is your famous prop
Don't be selfish

Alexander
I'm serious though

Isabelle
You can have a ring if you want
Should I propose to you?
It's the lightly feminist thing to do

We've been at this for years. Dream couple, actress and popstar, teenage sweethearts.

We're the result of an algorithm the Channel ran. Fake lovers planned by marketing teams and pushed together in a meeting that wasn't a request. I'm lucky it was her.

I was supposed to be in TV shows and movies too. My brother and I were first brought on as Channel actors when I was ten and he was twelve. Heather Erin got ahold of us not long after and transformed us into the pop duo Admirer. She was the one who told us what our job really is.

Heather Erin said, "You know when you have a good dream and lie in bed for a minute with your eyes closed pretending it's real? You want to believe in it. It's easy to sell a dream people want to believe in. You just have to keep it up. You can't do anything that opens their eyes."

Alexander
I mean I'm serious I have to disappear
Just me
I have to do it tomorrow night
And I need your help

Isabelle
Why now?

2

LILLIAN

As soon as Emelia's gone, I go downstairs. Quickly, before I have time to consider what just happened. I disinfect a big safety pin. I'm going to give myself another ear piercing just to prove to myself I'm still tough. Fierce, unbeaten. As soon as my hands stop shaking. I focus on my body, waiting a few minutes until my hands are as steady as they're going to get tonight.

When I leave the bathroom, the pin is through my earlobe, angled and hanging heavy on the new damage.

My mom asks if Emelia's staying over. I keep the bright red irritation of my ear turned away from her and try to sound casual. "No, Emelia actually left a few minutes ago." It's Friday night. Emelia stays over every Friday night.

"She has to get up early tomorrow," I say, "for soccer practice."

I avoid eye contact with my mom as we both silently remember that Emelia quit playing soccer at the start of sophomore year. My mom allows the lie to stand, but I feel her concern follow me up the stairs and through my bedroom door.

Then I call Cyprus, since she always answers. Except this time. It cuts me off early, so I know she declined the call. I'm not sure what I'll do if she's angry at me. Having one friend angry at me is already more than I can take tonight. Though I'm not sure Emelia and I have ever been friends. We went from strangers to love to tonight.

That's not right.

It's the wrong order.

There shouldn't be another stop after love.

Then I call Quinn, who I would have called first except he's not as good at answering his phone. He picks up right away.

I've decided not to cry. My bedroom is already awash in tears. Any more and the salt water will start to pool at my feet. It'll start to drip through the ceiling onto the main floor, into my brother's room below mine. Any more tears and the people around me will start to drown. And without them, I'll be the one to drown.

"You don't have to tell me what happened," he says. "Cyprus already texted me." Quinn preempts my next question. "Emelia's at Cyprus's place."

I lie down on my bed facing the wall with my legs tucked up to my stomach. "That's good," I say. It's only a few blocks from my house to Cyprus's. "Cyprus will look out for her."

"Exactly," says Quinn, "and I'm here to look out for you. Want me to come over?"

"Emelia was a mess. It scared me how much of a mess she was." The fight I had in me has switched off and left me with anxiety and emptiness. "She shouldn't have biked in the dark when she's this upset."

"She's safe at Cyprus's," says Quinn. "What about you, Lillian?"

I rest my forehead against the wall. "I mean, I'm sad."

What a cute, useless word. From when I was a kid, lots of emotion words felt too small. Things that could get resolved by the end of picture books.

The weight of what I felt, I found in music.

I press my forehead into the wall a little harder, willing the house to support me.

"Mostly, I'm worried about the band," I say. "If Emelia quits, there's no bass. And she's our best singer too."

"Don't sell yourself sho —"

"She hits notes I can't, all the harmonies. It's like half our set we can't do. You want to sing?"

"Hell no."

"I really like your voice," I say. "It's calming."

"Not when it keeps breaking," says Quinn. He makes it crack on purpose to try to make me laugh.

"Give the testosterone a couple months," I say, while the word *breaking* settles in the center of my chest.

"My dad just got home. I can take the car. I can be there in five."

Quinn's making it easy for me. He knows I have trouble asking for help. It's so goddamn kind. It makes my throat have to clench harder to keep the sadness from hitting my eyes. If Quinn comes over, I'll fall apart. He's friends with Emelia too. This isn't his to carry. This isn't his fault.

This is Emelia's fault.

It might be my fault.

Normally she's in bed with me by now. Her head on my arm and her back pressed up against me. It's my favorite thing in the world. This summer, we started skipping the performance of setting up a bed for her on my couch. That was for my mom, and she doesn't care if me and Emelia sleep together. She's always adored Emelia.

Me too.

"Don't bother coming," I say. "I'm too tired." And I am. I feel like I might be tired from here on out. "What should we do about the band?"

"Cyprus can program the bass parts," says Quinn, "or play them on her synth. We'll change some melodies and write some new stuff."

"Emelia might stay, though."

"Yeah, or that." Quinn tries to sound hopeful. I can hear the effort.

We talk awhile longer about what covers we can insert into the set for our next gig at Initialism. A band of three feels so small, even though that's what we used to be. Emelia joined early on, after her and I started dating. People break up and get back together, though Emelia and I have never even been close to breaking up. Cyprus and her old boyfriend did a bunch of times. Now they don't speak to each other. But people do get back together.

Quinn is saying something encouraging and distracting. I think he's asking if I like a band's new EP, trying to make me smile by making a ridiculous comparison to another album. My mind is a screaming feedback loop. What if I never hear Emelia's voice again?

"Lillian?"

"I'm falling asleep here," I lie. "I've got to go. We'll talk tomorrow." I hang up before he can respond.

Well, that was a nonsensical thing to do. It's a very Lillian move. As soon as there's no small voice beside my ear, I want to call him back and say please, please come over. Or can I go and stay at your house? I'm holding my phone tightly, flicking back and forth between numbers. I start writing a message to Cyprus to ask how Emelia's doing even though I could just text Emelia.

Though Emelia did say, "Don't text me."

Before that, she said, "I just wanted a break. *You* made it into this."

I asked, "What is 'this'?"

She said, "Don't be naive."

Emelia was the one being naive. Everyone knows taking a break is the beginning of the end. I was just making sure it didn't drag on.

"When I'm with you, I can barely breathe," she said. "This turmoil you're always in doesn't work for me. I never know what to expect."

I thought I knew what to expect. We talked about living together after graduating. Getting a tiny apartment with more amplifiers than furniture. Where guitars and posters were hung on the walls before we bought a bed frame. Last week, we talked about it. She brought it up.

Emelia, whose book is still on my nightstand. I bought it for her at a thrift store and pressed it into her hands. She was telling me about it as she went, but I got impatient and read the shattering last page after she fell asleep.

At least I saw that one coming.

I delete the unsent message to Cyprus.

Below me, I hear my brother put on an album by Packing Boxes. I recommended it to him. When I ask him how it is, he'll tell me, meh, it's alright. But I can hear him humming along tunelessly. I could go downstairs and see if he wants to watch something. He'd joke, "You've got something on your ear," like I hadn't noticed the safety pin. I'd let him pick and we'd wind up watching some fantasy show. All I have to do is roll over, find some air to breathe and walk down the stairs. I'm going to do it.

I glance at my phone one more time, looking for responses to texts I didn't send. Then I fumble it and it falls into the gap between my bed and the wall, out of reach. Which is too much. If I don't move, nothing else will change. There will be nothing to push me to tears. I lie on top of my covers with my forehead against the wall, listening to the soft sound of the music coming up through my floor.

I'll hold on to that.

3

SASHA

Alexander

In 2 days I'm supposed to appear on a talk show and publicly defend Augustus

Heather says it will "create a groundswell of public support" for him so he's less likely to get charged

She made me memorize a statement

Isabelle

Is Admirer broken up if your brother gets charged?

Alexander

I'm not sure

I'm signed until I'm 21. I'm worth too much to let go even if Augustus is done

Heather Erin talks about rebranding me as a solo artist

But it doesn't matter

I think what Augustus did was wrong

I'm not going to go on a show and say it's alright

Isabelle

With the Channel's lawyers, he'll walk anyway
Your statement probably won't make any difference
And he's your brother
Maybe see if you can leverage a more neutral statement and just survive this one?

Alexander

I'm supposed to appear without the helmet

Isabelle

Well shit

Alexander

This is my last chance to leave before everyone knows my face
My last chance ever

Isabelle

What's your plan?

When I lay out the steps, Isabelle doesn't say I'm being paranoid. With the Channel, there's no such thing. Instead, she asks me not to tell her where I'm going.

After four years of wearing the helmet, I'm not going to go out into the world without a plan. Escape will become impossible if I just step out the front door of the beach house with no visor covering my face and get photographed.

But if I leave wearing the helmet, I'll be recognizable, creating my own media frenzy. Since Augustus is on trial, there are even more photographers around than usual. Paparazzi who will follow me if they see me leave. If I get past them, Isabelle knows the fans and media will try to figure out where I am and what I'm doing. They'll know something's up when my accounts go silent, even though I'll leave them active to buy me some time. The Channel will panic. Any star they're not monitoring is a massive liability. We get into trouble, shatter the image.

See: Augustus.

He tore the fans out of their good dreams.

In the evening, Isabelle arrives alone, driving a sleek silver sports car that is somehow her most subtle vehicle. She parks in the garage underneath the beach house. We lie on my bed and take cute photos of ourselves. Get changed, go to a different part of the house, take more, repeat. Practiced angles and poses to keep the details of my face just out of view. Isabelle's hair, fake kisses, our bodies curled close together. Isabelle will post a few later tonight to make it look like she doesn't know I'm gone. Write little words about looking forward to seeing me every day to disguise that we have no idea when we'll see each other again. She's got enough saved to make it look like we're still together regularly if she has to.

We load everything I'm bringing with me into a plain backpack. There isn't much besides bundles of cash I withdrew from my personal accounts weeks ago. We reset my phone, crush the SIM card and flush the remains. More a gesture than anything, but I'm not making some big getaway just so they can track my phone or open it up and learn any secret I've failed to hide. Contacts and contents gone with no intention of retrieving them or reaching out to anyone.

Isabelle says I should at least write down Augustus's number in case there's an emergency.

I write down hers instead.

Because along with being my accomplice, ally and associate,

she's my friend. She's the only person I need to give a hug to before I disappear off the face of the earth. We hold each other for a long time in a posture that isn't fun enough or sexy enough for anyone else to care about. Touch for us, not the cameras. We don't say much. We know I'll come back to the Channel eventually. I'm simply too valuable for them to let go.

And in a way, my seclusion at the beach house with only my security team for company already had me missing the crowds. I'm hooked on it. It's why bands go on multiple farewell tours.

I leave a small note on my bathroom counter. By tomorrow afternoon, someone will get worried, check my room, find the note.

I'm safe. I'm gone.

It feels rushed, but if I'd taken more than twenty-four hours to plan this, I wouldn't be doing it. Someone would have caught on to me, or I would have considered the consequences.

That's how the Channel keeps its stars. They give us what everyone imagines they want. And whenever the fame and the pressure become too much, someone's on hand, reminding me.

You have what everyone desires. You are what everyone desires. Where can you go that's better than this?

And if that doesn't work, there's always the contract.

Isabelle is her friendly self, chatting with one of my security guards to give me a chance to sneak down to the garage. I should have added *don't fire my security team* to my note. They've never failed to keep me safe. A couple of them lost their jobs when Augustus was arrested, since they were supposed to be with him. But it wasn't fair. What my brother did was no one's fault but his.

I wedge myself into the crammed darkness of Isabelle's trunk and feel her driving away. Soon, she ditches the paparazzi by going into a twenty-four-hour car wash.

When I hear the car wash door close, I slip out before the next car comes in. I take a side door into the gas station and wait for the cameras to follow Isabelle. Then I use a pay phone to call a taxi to the airport.

4

LILLIAN

Teacher told us
Most of the universe
Is just
Empty space
So I believed I was
Cosmic vacancy
Atoms, molecules
The absence in between

Until I saw you singing
Under the night sky
Where your breath in the air
Tangled with mine
I knew I needed
Your face beneath mine
I knew all the emptiness
Would be alright

Because every time I hear your voice
I'm bent around the sound
Time bends, for a second I'm fine
While I'm bent around the sound

That's a true story.

Though even when Emelia was there, there were still times I could feel the edge of the nothingness. Now she's gone, it presses down on me, crushes me, and I panic about being dead. Not the dying, the being dead. I try to drive off the dread with anything I can.

Noise.

Comfort.

Chaos.

Pleasure.

If none of those work, I try to go numb. Irony is fighting a fear of being dead by finding a way to feel nothing at all.

Darling, I'm still bent around that sound
Even now

5

SASHA

People look different when they're not looking at me.

At the terminal, I watch them in profile. I haven't shown my real face in public since I was thirteen. With the helmet on, all eyes are on me. Arenas full of faces turned upward with just Augustus and me looking back at them. Together, we're Admirer, and Admirer is always the center of attention. Always the headliner.

Focused on their phones and departure times, the faces in the airport look different.

They aren't adoring.

They aren't frantic.

They aren't singing along.

I always tell the crowd they look beautiful tonight, and it's true. I point to different parts of the venue and say, "You, and you, and you." Pretty soon everyone thinks I pointed at them. And they act like they're beautiful because I told them they are, because I looked at them. That's the lie. It's the music that makes them beautiful, not me. Sometimes I believed it was me. I should have taken that as a sign I needed to leave.

The people in this airport — tired, rushed, each intent on a point in the future — their beauty is tucked away. I take out my empty phone, put my earbuds in and find a Monochrome Stoplight album. Hit play. There's a wash of heavy synths, thick and reverberant. The high, clear voice of Liv James comes cutting through. Soon, the guitars will rampage in.

And just like that, all around me, I start to be able to see people's stories. The music draws them out. Lovely, fragmented, shattering. This is my lens on the world. The sound pairs with the faces to become the heartbeat of the whole damn thing, and I can't explain what it's like except to say I'm in love with it all.

LILLIAN

"I wasn't trying to end things with you," Emelia said. "I really wasn't. I hope you know that."

But she'd already opened my bedroom door to leave. All our intentions and hopes shouldn't add up to that moment. I've counted them and it can't be right.

I should have torn out the final page of her book and shown it to her.

I should have pressed the crumpled paper into her hands and said this ending isn't for you, it isn't for us.

All the words I've written about her. When I needed them, I had none.

She said, "Why is it when you think you're in trouble, you always go out of your way to make it worse?"

Then she put the door between her tears and mine.

It's a strange thing, how we make our fears come true.

SASHA

When they call boarding for my flight, I feel the same rush as when I'm about to step onstage. I stand in line clutching my ticket and ID. My body is unlearning the panic of people seeing my face. It's getting drawn out of me. My hands are shaking.

I'm tensed from years of moments when someone would yell, "It's Admirer!" and suddenly Augustus and I would get swarmed. People screaming and pressing toward us. Augustus and I trying to be charming while trying not to get crushed. We would sign things and take pictures while our security struggled to get us out of there.

I was hidden behind the helmet's reflective visor then, playing a part. I don't know how I'd survive it if I was out in the open.

But the man checks my ID like it's boring and moves on to the next person in line. The name Alexander Moore isn't as famous as Alexander Ash, thank god.

I settle into a window seat in the second-last row. Right before we start taxiing out, this lanky guy whose look screams strung-out middle-aged rocker sits next to me, knees against the seat in front of him. His white T-shirt has the badly stitched edges of something very expensive.

He introduces himself with a pair of names like they're always said together. He says he's an actor, but he hasn't been in anything I would have seen. That's how it is out here.

"I'm Sasha," I say. I'll have to think of a last name.

"Loved flying when I was a kid," he says as he tries to stretch out. "Now you know they keep moving these fucking seats closer together. Acclimatizing us until it's standing room only. Screwing over people like me and you."

Admirer has a private jet.

I realize this is a chance to test-run my stories. He'll bluff his fame and I'll bluff my lack of it.

"So what's got you flying from paradise to nowhere?" he asks. He doesn't know that once we land, I'm going even farther, taking a bus ride to a small city in case the Channel manages to track where I flew.

"My family just moved," I lie, then balance it with truth. "I'm going to finish high school."

8

LILLIAN

Up until two weeks ago, senior year felt like a barrier between me and the rest of my life. I knew what was next. The band, Emelia, gap year/s. Now school is something familiar I'm clinging to before a giant uncertainty.

Admittedly, it's familiar shit, but it offers a day-to-day distraction. Since mid-August, since the breakup, I've been rattling around inside myself. Even my summer job at the drop-in center ended last week, so no more paid distraction of hanging out with "troubled youth" (the program's words). A summer of answering questions about being queer from kids pretending it's pure theory for them, listening to whatever music keeps them alive and crushing them at foosball. I'm not going to lose on purpose just because they're kids. I'm not a saint.

Before school started today, I made a list of things to do, mostly music related. That was in one of my upswings. It was an inspired and ambitious moment where I ignored the evidence and decided that without my relationship, I'd dedicate all my extra time to productivity and self-improvement instead of despair.

Reorganize guitar pedalboard
New setlist
Pick rehearsal nights / band meeting
Restring Butler
Daily run / strength train (pact with Cyprus)
Get merch logos from Quinn / band beanies?
Fix bike brakes
Call Christensen
Write ~~two~~ three songs (naive/breathe?)

As my brother and I ride up to the bike racks in front of school, I have to start slowing down before he does. Jasper makes a big show of rushing in, slamming on his working brakes and skidding to a stop. He's riding a bulky old mountain bike. It's things like this that make him perpetually my little brother even though he's sixteen now.

"I'll loosen your tires and watch you die!" I call after him, squeezing my brakes harder like the force will make up for my lack of bike maintenance. I'll pick up new brake pads on the way home. I'll definitely do it tonight.

By the time I coast to a stop, Jasper's already on his way inside. He's greeting people and being effortless with his impossibly tall group of friends. I swear straight cis guys make friends just by being tall, or maybe that's how they make teams, or maybe that's just Jasper having an easy time living. I might be having a moment of envy about his whole breezy existence.

He's forgotten to lock up his bike, so I snap my U-lock around his frame and the frame of my single-speed. Hopefully stealing two attached bikes is more effort than it's worth.

Now where are my people? I have people too. One less than before, but there's still Cyprus and Quinn and some others who are friendly faces even if they aren't much beyond that. Though most of them are Emelia's friends. We'll see how they treat me. I don't think Emelia will have talked shit about me since she's generally kind and sweet. Sometimes to her own detriment.

But then, I did break up with her.

And we haven't talked since.

Possibly I now have only two friends at school.

Beside me, there's a loud clang as someone hits the rack with his bike frame. He's really struggling to lock up his bike, making every part of it seem weirdly difficult. Eventually, he clips his U-lock through just the front tire.

He's got excellently styled hair with a few pieces that have fallen out in the attractive way they're supposed to. It looks deliberate, like someone on set did his hair. It's very first-day-of-school intentional, which might cut down on the attractiveness. I haven't decided yet. If my hair was like his, I'd do something like that. For now, I'm trapped with a partially grown-out undercut.

I have no business giving him advice, but I don't see Cyprus or Quinn and I'm stalling on going inside alone. If I run into Emelia, I want one of my friends by my side.

"They'll steal the rest of your bike and leave the front tire," I say.

He looks up at me, all embarrassed and frazzled. It's deeply cute. "Really? Don't they kind of need that?"

He's white, wearing a plain gray shirt knotted in the front to show a sliver of his stomach, cutoff jean shorts that are shorter than any other guy here wears and the littlest bit of sky-blue eyeshadow. Not drastic, but it's noticeable. This is not a school where guys do any of that. This is a school where they play hockey. When they go out, they wear a denim jacket, a hoodie underneath and a baseball hat. Possibly with the hood over the hat. Call it business casual, because this is endless horizon country.

And it's occurring to me that I should definitely hold off on "guy" and pronoun assumptions until we've introduced ourselves. Shit. I know I'm preoccupied if I lose track of something that's usually so automatic for me.

They're not quite meeting my eyes. I've been told I have a very intense, direct way of looking at people. I never lose staring contests.

"They'll reuse the parts," I say, "or they'll put another tire on the front." I point at a different bike. "You should put it through the frame and at least one of the tires."

They unclip the lock, and I desperately want to step in and do it for them. It just all seems so awkward for them. They've gotten grease from the chain on their shin.

"I was picturing some thief riding around in an endless wheelie," they say. "Thanks to you I can banish that image from my mind."

"Lillian!" I see Cyprus waving at me from the front steps.

I say, "The pleasure was all mine," but in trying to make the phrase ironic I manage to make the whole thing come across as mean. This happens to me a lot.

I make a beeline for Cyprus before they can respond or seem confused. Cyprus has her camera pointed at me, collecting a million pictures and hours of video. Even during shows, she has it on her laptop or her keyboard. From being her friend for so long, I've learned I'm best off if I don't respond or pose. It's my only hope of being digitally intriguing when Cyprus works promotional magic for the band.

She hugs me when I reach her. It's all elbows, and she smells like a whole store of bath bombs. She's wearing sunglasses that are so big they must either be a joke or Cyprus's new favorite accessory. By twelve, she responded to insults about her clothes by saying, "Trends are just companies creating new ways to feel bad about yourself so they can sell you the solution." Statements like that made me worship her a bit back then.

"Who's your new friend?" she asks before she's even let me go. "They seem like your type."

I brought this on myself. I may have bemoaned my lack of romance and physical touch in moments of making light of things. Maybe Cyprus plans to pair Emelia and I off with other people or hopes the two of us will make up. Maybe she just wants what we all do — our group back to normal.

"They've got a pretty face," I say. "That's everyone's type."

"Trust me, it is *not*."

The person at the bike racks finally gets their lock through the frame and the front tire, and clicks it closed. As they walk toward the front steps, Cyprus whispers to me, "I can get their name for you. Number, address, social security number, whatever you need." Her send-the-first-text, cross-the-room attitude kept me alive through years of childhood shyness.

"Don't you dare."

"I juuuust might dare." Cyprus probably raises her eyebrows at me. I can't tell behind her glasses.

Softly, I say, "Cyprus, I can't."

They walk by. They've got this energy that's nervous without shying away. I wouldn't call it confidence, but it's standing tall. It seemed like going through those doors was brave for them. I suppose they're new to the school, and they look like a senior. Not the best time to join. And our school (named after one of those colonizing demon-men) is this categorically unwelcoming square brick thing from back when they used essentially the same design for prisons and schools. I used to think that was very edgy, representing how schools imprison young minds. Wrote a song about it. Really, it just means the windows are small and all the hallways look the same.

"Sorry," says Cyprus. Then, "I'm sorry, Lillian. I'm just not sure how to act right now."

I tell her it was nothing, when actually I feel like throwing up. Trying to work my brain around being attracted to someone else and wanting them and that being a real possibility … it washes over me. My body gets overloaded. I suddenly miss Emelia so much that I can't get enough oxygen. My heart can't decide between activated and shut down.

What the hell is that? That's not moving on. I can do better than that. Today started better than that. I can still reel it back in.

As Cyprus and I go through the doors, I try to stand tall too. Today, I'll be friendly. I'll get moving, and moving on from Emelia. I've already bested potential bike thieves. Twice. I'll fix my brakes and get started on all my music things. At lunch, we'll make band plans.

I've got some lyrics bouncing around my head. I can be brave and stand tall too. Let's go let's go, I tell myself.

It's possible to be
Better than heartbreak
Coughing out my lungs
From the tear gas grenades
Don't mistake me for dead
I'm coughing up blood
But I'm not
Bleeding out yet

SASHA

So about the mythology of high school the Channel perpetuates. That shiny version of adolescence Isabelle acts in.

Yeah, it's a scam.

That sounds bitter, but I didn't expect it to be true. I think I would have been disappointed if it had felt like a Channel show. As much as day one was very disorienting, it was also profoundly nothing much. Mostly, people were fully preoccupied with their own lives. I had classes, none of them hard. I've been educated by tutors for most of my life, though technically I haven't graduated yet. If I make it through this year, I'll graduate from this school. Here, in this nowhere city. This is based on the doubtful proposition that I manage to stay here for an entire year.

Without the Channel tracking me down.

Without accidentally revealing my identity.

Without the fans finding me.

Without missing my old life too much.

Without wanting to be famous again.

Without Heather Erin kicking down my door.

Even getting registered without being exposed involved some maneuvering. I don't have a parent or guardian around to sign anything. Since our dad passed away last year, Augustus has been my legal guardian, but he's otherwise occupied. And he's not exactly nurturing or involved. Or aware of where I am. Ultimately, it took a large anonymous donation from my "family," aka me, to get in. I chose to be called Sasha Weaver, not Alexander Ash. I picked new names that felt like I could wear them around me while I made something beautiful out of my life.

Yet more ways I could blow my cover.

The theory of my escape is this: since Augustus is on trial and Admirer is on hiatus, the Channel won't really miss me. It's not like we'd be touring or releasing music. And the Channel can't afford more scandal, so they can't reveal that I've gone missing. They'll want to handle everything quietly. I'm counting on it.

Then again, the Channel could have already unveiled my real face and be combing the nation for me.

One way or another, I'll be back. I'm too famous for it to be any other way. And then it's fifty-fifty whether they claim it was all a promotional stunt OR they take the breach of contract very personally and ruin the rest of my life (I've seen them do it before). They're looking for me, either to destroy me or to make a lot of money, and they're not choosy about how those two things overlap.

I try not to think about it. I've been ignoring the trial, the news, everything since I left the beach house in Isabelle's trunk. The shift feels like when a storm knocks the power out and suddenly the hum around you is gone. At first it's anxious, then peaceful, in a way.

I've escaped the buzz of every person I meet wanting something from me.

I had a lab partner today named Quinn. The teacher said to find a friend to work with. I didn't know anyone. This situation is objectively a more frightening moment than stepping out onto the biggest stages in the world.

Then Quinn pointed at me from across the room. I thought he was pointing to someone behind me until he walked straight for me. Brown skin, curly dark hair, wearing this beautiful baggy hoodie with sound waves that turned into whitecaps on the front. It was subtle, but the fabric paint formed the color pattern of the trans pride flag.

He doesn't even know who I am. He chose me just because, not to try to climb a ladder to fame.

"Quinn," he said. He clasped my hand in that way that feels like it's right between some light arm wrestling and a hug. I made a mess out of it. I've always been hopeless at stuff like that, possibly because Isabelle is my only friend. "Amateur chemist, expert judge of people, he/him," Quinn said.

At which point I had a small-to-medium-sized panic, because I realized I could say my pronouns too. I could introduce myself however I want. But for all the school forms, there were just two boxes, and I knew which one I was supposed to check. The box that confirms how most people initially code me. I was going to say he/him like I had on the forms or on the plane when I was making my backstory. But I immediately felt safe with Quinn, even though he had started flicking the burner on and off. Emotionally safe.

"Sasha. They/them. I think?"

Out loud, it felt strange. Though I already knew it belonged. I've flipped the language around and around in my head for a couple years. I've followed all sorts of queer people on my private accounts and watched a lot of videos of them explaining things and found the words that feel like they fit me right now.

Queer. Nonbinary. Pan. They/them. Sasha.

I'm not sure I understand all of them, not sure it's possible to, but they've helped me put the pieces together into a picture of me. I no longer need to come out to myself. I only put a question mark after my pronouns in a moment of insecurity.

Because those words almost always stayed in my head at the Channel. The one time I spoke them to Augustus, they weren't really heard. I could have tried with Isabelle too. I trust her, but it felt like there was no point. I would have gotten her to treat me the same way so our romantic act remained undisrupted. At the Channel, I knew who I was supposed to be.

"Nice," said Quinn. "Called it."

I suppose trying to guess pronouns isn't ideal, but I definitely try to figure people out in my head too. And to have someone guess right? It simultaneously made me feel unsettled and like I was glowing.

"Was it the eyeshadow?"

"There's no linguistic requirements to wearing anything." Quinn pushed up his sleeves. "And yeah, the eyeshadow helped. But also like, eight other things."

I very much wanted to know what the eight other things were. I could only think of maybe four.

The teacher had finished giving instructions (indiscernible scrawls on the blackboard and a textbook page shown with an overhead projector). He made a comment about how life wasn't going to hold your hand, turned on some seventies pop, and started working on his laptop.

"What a class act," I said. "What an educator."

Quinn nodded agreement. "True true. I've taught myself science for years. But at least ..." He gestured vaguely to the speakers on the teacher's desk.

Then we chatted about the music for the rest of the class and taught ourselves science. A new song would come on, and Quinn would say, "They could replace that drummer with an actual metronome and no one would know the difference. In a bad way." Or I would say, "If they start with this much excess, where do they think they're going to go?"

Quinn: "Key change. Two if we're lucky."

Me: "Two key changes is lucky?"

When the big choruses hit, I wanted to sing along, full voice, but of course no one else was. It's not a musical.

After class, Quinn said, "I'd love to give you a tour-of-the-high-school-and-its-social-dynamics montage sequence, but I've got a band meeting. Top tip: sit outside while the weather's good."

I'd gotten too relaxed with Quinn. Two weeks after making a break for it, and I spoke without thinking. "I used to sing in a band."

Quinn's face immediately showed a concerning level of interest, and he generally had an eager face. He stopped packing up his bag, no longer rushing to get to his meeting. He wanted to know what band.

When you're a performer, you lie all the time. I told every second city how it was one of my favorite cities. Sometimes I had to write the first letters of the city on my hand in tiny letters to make sure I got the name right. I'd say it was great to be there even on nights when I felt too exhausted to stand. You look straight out at the crowd, and you lie.

"Just a local thing where I used to live." In my conversation on the plane, I'd chosen an extremely mundane west coast city. People recognize the name, but no one visits it. And it's from a climate I don't have to fake being from. "We kept changing names. Sasha's Crew, Sasha and the Rest." What was I talking about? Those were terrible names.

And I felt like twice the liar, because the real band that played with Admirer was never really ours — just industry veterans on risers at the back of the stage lifelessly playing music that bored them and cashing checks while me and Augustus soaked in the attention.

I slung my backpack over one shoulder and started for the door, still talking. "But what's your band meeting about?" Give a little, redirect.

"Well, our bass player and our guitarist broke up." He glances down at his phone, where I can see new messages coming in. "Aaaaand the bass player has just sent a message with paragraph breaks. This will go *great.*"

LILLIAN

Emelia texts our band group right before we're supposed to meet.

I'm sitting at the picnic table across from Cyprus, still hoping Emelia will show up. Even though rehearsal was one of the only places Emelia and I fought. But there was space for it there because it was about sound, not love. Or all our love was aimed at the sound. Those fights didn't really count. I used to be certain of it. I still believe it enough to think maybe she'll come to the band meeting and maybe she'll softly ask to talk to me after.

Instead, this long message appears.

There are no typing bubbles. It has the deliberateness of something written elsewhere and copied in. I can picture how she might have looked looked writing it, leaning against her locker, tired, frowning at her phone. Just thinking about it makes me want to comfort her.

I know if it was just Quinn and Cyprus, she would have talked to them face-to-face. It's me she's avoiding. The caution and formality is all for me.

The gutting opposite of everything we were.

Emelia

I still don't know exactly how to talk about this, but I'm trying to be fair and let you guys know as soon as possible.

I know the band's really important to all of you. It's important to me too. We've all put a lot of work into it. Right now, though, I need to step away from it. Making music together can be so intense even when there's nothing else complicating it and we're all getting along well. I've thought about it a lot, and in this moment, it's not a good idea for me emotionally.

Please please please don't take this as me stepping away from any of you. If I could have friends or have a band, I'd pick friends every time. I know in this moment it doesn't work for all four of us to hang out together, but I hope it will again. It's just going to take some time.

Rock on. Love, Emelia

Quinn joins me and Cyprus as we're silently reading it. He puts his arm around my shoulder and gives me a quick side hug squeeze. It's the first time I've heard from Emelia in two weeks. I can't stop myself reading it over again.

The message is very her. I've helped her write things like this to other people before, and I always want her to be meaner or show more bite. Sometimes I think she's being passive-aggressive or unnecessarily gentle when she's actually being sincere. She says she's never snapped at someone and had it leave her feeling good. That I just don't believe. When we broke up, she cried when she said hard things to me. She still said them, though she tried to start out with soft phrases. I wouldn't let her stay there. I pushed her to her biting words. And it figures — by doing that, I managed to hurt both of us.

At the picnic table, I set down my phone and say, "Seems a little late for 'as soon as possible.'" To which Quinn says nothing and Cyprus keeps looking at her phone. I keep going anyway, picking up momentum. "And she's intense about making music too. It's not like it's just me. There's nothing 'fair' about this. Do you think it's fair for her to bail when —"

"Lillian Finley." Cyprus cuts me off sharply, with authority. She's wearing her big sunglasses again, but I can tell she's looking right at me. "Don't think just because I've been friends with you longer than I've been friends with Emelia that I'll sit here and let you drag her through the mud. If you think I'm going to take anyone's side on this, then you clearly haven't been paying attention to who I am."

I try to jump in at that, but there's no interrupting her before she's finished.

"I know you're heartbroken. So is she. You were pretty shitty to her. I'm always here if you need to talk about it or eat ice cream and watch *Supernatural* until four in the morning or even get someone's number. But I'm gone if you expect me to team up against my friend."

"Ditto," says Quinn. "Except for the *Supernatural*. You'll have to be in way worse shape before I'll watch *Supernatural*. If you get cancer, possibly. If it's one of the really gruesome ones."

To his perpetual credit, we all laugh. He's always had a way of taking all the tension out of situations. He told me he only learned to play drums to do the ba-ba-tish at the end of jokes. I once saw him notice his parents fighting, say, "Watch this," and pratfall in the kitchen to defuse the tension. He helps unclench the knot of guilt in my stomach.

I say I understand. I say I'm sorry.

Cyprus says it's part of the process. That we're all figuring this out. She says, "You'll heal eventually, I'm sure of it."

Then we talk about the band and make plans to see if we can sneak into the Packing Boxes show at the Mercury this weekend, and I don't tell Cyprus what I think. That I'm not sure everyone can heal. Some of us may just accumulate scar tissue until we die.

SASHA

I feel like I need to catch my breath after the morning, so I follow Quinn's advice to eat lunch outside. I sit alone with my back against a tree, facing away from the school. It's the start of September, and there's already a hint of autumn here. The school is in a neighborhood of old two-storey houses and trees that have been here even longer. Some of them have flecks of gold leaves starting to show. It's a calming area with a lot of cats that no one seems to own but aren't strays and occasional pride flags in windows. It moves at a slow pace. At least, that's why I picked it.

I need to catch my breath after my entire life.

Last year, Admirer played 162 shows.

In most cities, we went straight from the jet to the hotel to the venue to the hotel to the jet. It was one of the highest-grossing tours ever. With all the travel and publicity, I wore the helmet constantly. It made being outside without it almost impossible.

I was behind the reflective visor when I tried to tell Augustus that I'm queer. We were about to go onstage.

I said when I think of myself, I think Sasha. I said I'm pretty sure I'm nonbinary.

He barely glanced at me. "That's trendy of you."

I wanted to tell him that there have always been nonbinary people. New language for an ancient feeling. Then the lights went down, and it was time to sing. Time to be Augustus and Alexander Ash.

Brothers.

Princes.

Admirer.

At the end of the night, we waved goodbye to the crowd with our arms around each other's shoulders. That was last winter.

We never talked about my queerness again. We never talked about the snowballing crisis he was creating for himself or how some nights I wanted to take the helmet off and make a break for it. We didn't talk much at all. We haven't for a long time.

If we did, I can't imagine him listening to me for long enough for me to feel like I'd been heard. He'd nod along and then suddenly he'd need to go, and I'd know his mind had been elsewhere the whole time. His charisma and charm wear thin eventually.

That year on the road, I needed someone to talk to about a hundred different things. I was lonely and run-down. I could have really used an older brother. If he'd been paying any attention, he would have seen that. That's the part that hurts.

After the encores were done and we were back at the hotel, I locked my door, took off my helmet and sat among the big plants in the corner. But when I let them brush my face, they were plastic.

Outside the school, I place my hand in the grass and lean my head against the bark of the tree. I can feel the sun on my closed eyelids, the wind on my skin. There's nothing between me and any of it.

When I first moved into the second-floor walk-up I'm renting, I asked the owners (who are also my downstairs neighbors) where I could buy some plants. Ever since, they keep knocking on my door to offer me foliage. They're this group of three friends in their thirties who I'm pretty sure are all together romantically. They have a six-year-old named Chrysanthemum who interacts with all of them like parents.

They've given me cacti, three aloe plants in various moments of their life cycles, a vine that I swear grows if I look away from it for too long, something with big leaves and a name I can't pronounce, and a herb-filled window box (decorated by Chrysanthemum and an entire box of markers).

After I get home and once again try and fail to figure out a graceful way to carry my bike up the stairs, I decide to ask my neighbors about the music scene. As I was talking to Quinn, I realized I've never truly been in the audience. Occasionally in box seats, up and removed from the actual press of people and the full volume. I've been backstage at huge aid concerts and hung out with all the people with number-one hits. But I've never stood up close to the stage in the midst of it all.

I'm going to find a concert to go to this weekend. I'm going to become part of the crowd like I've never been before, and I'm just going to listen.

12

LILLIAN

"Why did you park so far away?" asks Quinn as we approach the Mercury. There's a warm night wind blowing through the city, which feels soft against my skin even though it carries the smell of overflowing dumpsters.

"Next time, *you* parallel park the station wagon," says Cyprus.

Quinn kicks a loose piece of concrete into the street. "You know I can't do that. Plus it's *your* land yacht."

I'm trying to visualize me, Quinn and Cyprus from a third-person perspective, as a passerby might see us. It's a dangerous exercise. I might disassociate and have an anxiety attack.

Racing heart.

Tunnel vision.

Catastrophizing mind.

The feeling that nothing is real.

A desperate need to somehow prove to myself that I exist here, right now.

It's the same as the fear of being dead, really. It's a fear of non-existence. Of nothing and aloneness. It's odd how rationally I think about it when it's not happening. But most times it's not that bad, better than when I was younger. Instead of buckling under the weight, I slip out from under it by distracting myself or outlasting it.

From the outside, the three of us look like a full complement of friends going out for the night. From the inside, it feels like there's a string that's snapped. Unreplaced. Unreplaceable. We're still a chord, but there's a gap in the middle.

I've been analyzing Emelia's message. I try to take it at face value, not coded to hurt me. I'm failing. Because who is the "Love, Emelia" meant for? When she kept saying "friends," was that Cyprus and Quinn, or was that me too? How much time is "some time"? She said she needed "some space" right before we broke up, and look what that became.

One part makes me smile. "Rock on." It was so cheesy, cringey, what-have-you. I was always trying to get her not to say things like that, but she couldn't see why they're awful. And she doesn't even say them cynically. From that, there's the grief, washing over me and threatening to sweep me away from my friends, off the sidewalk, into the street where I hope the cars will swerve around me.

Cyprus is gossiping about some big pop band. "I'm not saying what Augustus Ash did was *right*, just that it was consensual."

"Also, statutory rape," says Quinn. "Which if you're not famous, is, you know, a crime."

I chime in even though I only peripherally know what they're talking about. "Maybe age gaps in relationships that make us uncomfortable now are the next sexual barrier to be broken down? Like how there were 'anti-sodomy' laws against anal sex in half the country until like twenty years ago. And now it's normal."

Cyprus stops to take a picture of an alcove between buildings with a bright piece of trash in the middle. "Older men with younger women isn't exactly a sexual barrier that needs breaking down."

"I was thinking more like younger people in sexual relationships with each other," I say. "Our lines around adulthood are arbitrary. Like there's no magic age when you're suddenly mature enough to not hurt people and not get yourself into toxic sexual relationships."

"Do you know what we're actually talking about?" asks Quinn.

"I just saw an opportunity for controversy and seized it," I say. "But we were talking about the Admiration trial, right?"

"Admirer." Cyprus crouches down to get a more cinematic angle on the trash. "And strictly speaking, only Augustus is on trial. Alexander has been mysteriously quiet about it."

"What was the age gap?" I ask.

Quinn pulls Cyprus away from the alcove. "Four years. What they've released says it started when she was thirteen and he was seventeen. Last year he turned eighteen, she was only fourteen, and that's what's known as stat rape."

"I'd like to retract my heedless argument," I say. "That's sleazy. That will never not be sleazy."

"*Predatory* is the word." Quinn's got ahold of Cyprus's sleeve, and she's switched over to taking video of him.

"Send help," she says to the camera. "My friends no longer want me to produce artsy promotional content that's also personal and makes us seem more interesting than the friends you already have."

Truly, Cyprus is a genius at it. She says you have to believe publicity is a lie to play the game right. I get fed up too quickly, and Quinn's mostly excited about designing logos and befriending people, less on the turning connections into opportunities. My eternal gratitude for Cyprus's work goes somewhat under-expressed. In my defense, she once tried to make me dance on camera in middle school. It almost ended our friendship.

"Am I going to have to take your device away from you?" I try to grab her phone, but she moves it just out of my reach, almost stumbling on some steps jutting out into the street to dodge me. She'd run into a burning building for it, I swear.

"Because Augustus is a celebrity," continues Quinn. "They say she was a normal fan. Power imbalances." With him pulling her along and me trying to reach the phone, we've devolved into a six-legged stagger down the sidewalk.

"My name is Cyprus. If this is my last entry, know that I was killed by my bandmates in a heartless —"

"That's not a short line." Quinn finally lets Cyprus's arm drop.

We've rounded a corner to see people outside the entrance to the Mercury. We've arrived between the opener and the main act. There's a mix of people trying and failing to get tickets along with some standing around smoking and chatting before Packing Boxes hits the stage. People are dressed in their own individual ideas of what indie rock should look like. So randomly. So self-consciously. They're mostly older than us, which is typical. If industry-crafted pop bands like Admirer who play recycled-sounding songs with all the lyrical complexity of corn puffs are trying to target my demographic, they're fully missing me.

"That's why we're *sneaking* in," I say.

Cyprus ends her video with, "As you can see, Lillian has a long history of getting her perfectly innocent friends into trouble. Just one aspect of the badass allure you've come to know and love."

Sneaking into shows is an art form. Emelia never wanted to, because rules and supporting musicians and venues and getting caught, et cetera, et cetera. Is it an art form I've perfected? No. But one time when I was fifteen, I managed to see the second half of a sold-out Fluorescent concert. I'm just chasing that high, baby.

Here are some sample methods:

A — Fake digital ticket. Sometimes it works if you have an old ticket from the same venue and you do a little bit of editing. And if it won't scan you in, people do tend to jump to blaming technology.

B — Slip in with a larger group between the opener and main act. Whoever's watching is usually relying on remembering faces.

C — Get ahold of the same stamp the venue uses, if it's a venue where they stamp your hand (though some change theirs). Can also work if you're underage but look older and you've just *got* to drink.

D — Bluff that you forgot your tickets or your phone's dead. Possibly Emelia was less concerned about getting caught and more embarrassed about the time I tried to pull this off with her. I figured we'd have a better shot at it if we played the really adorable, incredibly in love sapphic couple. It almost worked too.

E — Find a back entrance or side door, and hopefully if you accidentally wind up in the greenroom the musicians will at least sign your shirt before someone kicks you out.

Initialism is one venue I've never tried to sneak into. I respect Christensen way too much, and I'm always up to date enough to get tickets. Though he did once pay me twenty dollars to try some of my methods out and see how effective his door people were at recognizing the tricks. One hundred percent effective, unfortunately.

Tonight, we're aiming for option E. I don't know of a back/side entry for the Mercury, so if that fails, we'll try to merge with a larger group going back in, using the classic option B.

The Mercury's only a few years old, built in what used to be an incredibly dingy club called Cock Rock. I think the new owners took one look around and gutted it rather than cleaning it. It's on the lower two floors of an old brick building in a neighborhood that's in the midst of the transition from run-down to hip. The interior has artfully exposed ductwork and pipes.

I call it gentrification. Emelia said if she had a beautiful apartment with an exposed brick wall, she'd know that she'd made it in life. She'd die happy, gentrification be damned.

And someday, I could see myself there with her. It was a rare thought of getting older that didn't fill me with dread. Thinking about it now is just another missing string.

Sometimes you need a win. Sneaking into a sold-out Packing Boxes concert would be an emotional win. For a moment, I could forget three is the wrong number for this group, for the band, for everything. It's an iffy thing to hang my hope on, but you take what you can get.

Me, Quinn and Cyprus skip the crowd and go around to the back of the building, where there's someone standing on a garbage can trying to reach the bottom of the fire escape. They're facing away from us, standing on their tiptoes. Short haircut, black suit jacket with a subtle white paisley design weaving around it, knee-length black pleated skirt, fuzzy calves.

"Sasha?" asks Quinn.

The person on the garbage can turns around, and their face jumps straight to a sense of familiarity. They skip or hide that flicker of confusion and disorientation from running into people where you did not remotely expect to run into them.

Meanwhile, my brain grinds for a second before I realize they're the one from the bike racks. I blame the great outfit. Even standing on a trash can, they look classier than I ever have in my life. Their impossibly white shirt buttoned all the way up and tucked loosely into their skirt really clinches it.

It's all pointing toward my initial distracted gender assumption being one hundred percent wrong. Though Quinn does always tell me my radar for queerness is broken.

I'd counter that maybe I'm just incredibly open-minded about the relationship between gender expression, sexual orientation and gender identity. More likely, I'm destined for a life of inadvertently hitting on people who aren't oriented to me.

As if I needed any help generating awkward social situations.

13

SASHA

Quinn grins up at me. "Can I give you a boost?"

I think he's serious for a second, though he's easily half a foot shorter than me and not exactly built like a powerlifter. I'm used to doing this thing with fans and industry people where I treat everyone as if I know and like them, since they all recognize me and I meet way too many people to conceivably keep track of. I've been working at switching it off, at not performing all the time. It's in progress.

Then I laugh and jump down from the trash can. The skirt does a bit of a billowy thing that feels great, like I'm a cute heroine. This skirt is my absolute new favorite garment, though all of my clothes are new right now and most are my favorites on one day or another.

I'm genuinely happy to see Quinn, so my automatic response is correct. And he introduces me with, "This is my friend Sasha." Which is pretty generous given that our relationship so far consists of sitting beside each other and chatting in chemistry class during the first week of school.

Or, oh my god, I've made a real friend. Sasha has, not my

celebrity self. I mean, Quinn befriended me, but I haven't messed it up. My heart goes through a sensation I'd describe as fluttering.

Quinn introduces the other people as his bandmates.

There's Cyprus (she/her), who's lanky in a way that seems like she must knock over a lot of glasses and has platinum hair in a way that seems very dyed over top of a different color. She's white, wearing a purple Rosie the Riveter–style bandanna along with bandannas on both of her wrists like sweatbands and somehow making it all work. Lillian's also white and she/her, though Quinn introduces her as sad/sadness. She gives him a push and corrects him.

"You trying to sneak in too?" Lillian asks.

"That's the general idea."

Of all the concerts my downstairs neighbors recommended, I chose the one that's sold out. I've never encountered this problem before in my life. Normally things like a show being sold out just miraculously don't apply to me.

I point to what I was trying to reach. "It looks like it's fire escape or bust."

Lillian's already moved past me. She's skipped the garbage can and gone to inspecting the wall. "There are other ways."

"Please spare Sasha the methodology," says Quinn. "No letters, I'm begging you."

"We could wait to see if a band member goes through a locked back door and use gum to jam the latch, so we can slip in after them, for example. Or or or." She pulls hard on a pipe on the wall. By my assessment, the amount it shifts indicates that under no circumstances should anyone climb it.

Her assessment differs. Lillian grabs the pipe and digs her boots into the brick wall and climbs way higher up than she should.

"Lillian …" begins Cyprus, and then lets her be and films her.

I don't love the camera being out so close to me. I make a point of being out of the frame.

Lillian jumps to the side of the fire escape. She takes an overshot approach, first crashing into it and then grabbing on. The whole thing creaks. It's not graceful, but it works. The door's unlocked and with Lillian up there to help us, the rest of us manage to climb up from on top of the trash can.

At this point, I should mention that Lillian is one of the scariest-looking people I've ever met. I talked to her for a few distracted seconds at the bike racks, and I'd already recognize her anywhere. She looks like the bad kid who went to juvenile detention in an eighties high school movie. And it does not seem like an act.

There's the cutoff Packing Boxes T-shirt with a chunk missing from one side that seems ... burnt off? Her undercut looks very worse for wear, though disheveled is pretty much her whole vibe. It's too comprehensive to be accidental. There are a couple braids in her dark hair that seem to have been there for a long time, including one that has an old fabric wristband from a festival woven into it. She's got a scarred tattoo of a game of hangman on her calf, though I can't make out what word was being spelled. Throw in a lot of plain silver rings on her hands and through her earlobes and nose, a big safety pin hanging from her ear, a septum piercing, and two eyebrow piercings. Top it all off with actual black lipstick but no other makeup, and frankly I don't want to mess with her. Or anyone with that much metal in their head who looks like they haven't slept for a week.

I doubt the people in charge of the Mercury share my feeling. They run a music venue and have therefore seen everything and fear no one.

We wind up at the back of the upper tier of seats, but as

soon as we're there, I see people right in front of the stage and I can't resist.

"We have to get there," I whisper. The band's going to be onstage any minute.

"Why?" asks Cyprus.

"Kind of comfy here at the back of the balcony," says Quinn.

But Lillian nods at me, scoping it out. "Obviously close is the place to be."

Cyprus is posting something, which seems to require about as much attention for her as walking does for most of us. "It never sounds good close to the stage."

"For sound, I put on my headphones," I say. "Live, I want the crush."

I've seen all my concerts with my helmet on. Or far removed, from behind reflective glass in a private box with only the few people who were allowed to see my face. Augustus, Isabelle, Heather Erin, my security team. That's the full list.

"See, Sasha *gets* it." Lillian looks a bit obsessed, excited, and I feel it too.

Packing Boxes steps onstage with tattoo sleeves, grungy jackets and a vibe that promises a guitar-heavy show that will be considerably less mellow than their recordings. The crowd on the floor presses forward, creating a window for us to join them. Despite their protests, Cyprus and Quinn follow Lillian and me into the fray.

It only takes two songs to get me hooked.

For half of the first song, all I can see is the act.

They sound nothing like Admirer's upbeat catalog of love songs, but I've done everything the lead singer for Packing Boxes does. All the gesture and show and revving up the crowd. Then the singer holds out his microphone to us, and I let myself go. I'm immersed in uncontrolled sound and the energy pouring off the crowd. Lillian is shoulder to shoulder with me and we've gotten right to the front of the stage. We're in a pocket between the speakers where I can feel the drums live off the stage. Everywhere is sweat and noise and joy.

We're applauding the second song when suddenly Quinn's at my ear yelling over the music that we've got to go. I see venue security coming toward us and Cyprus is already weaving upstream through the crowd and Lillian's grabbing my hand and I like how that feels and I barely have any time to consider it because she's pulling me away and still singing along.

So am I.

We aren't exactly the most visually sneaky group, but we probably could have stuck it out longer if we'd stayed at the balcony level. Still, it was worth it to get into the midst of it all.

I keep glancing back at the stage as it disappears behind swaying shoulders and hair. I want to be in front of that stage. I want to be on it.

I know I belong there, but maybe not in the way I've always been told I did.

14

LILLIAN

We scatter through the lobby, through the doors, and we're all running and laughing as we hit the night air. We keep up the pace for half a block before turning down an alleyway, not that anyone chasing us could be bothered to leave the venue in pursuit.

I realize I'm still holding Sasha's hand.

Since we reached the fire escape, all I've been is alive. For a moment, not shattered. Now we're catching our breath and I let go of Sasha's hand. The thought hits me that Emelia's the only person I've ever really held hands with, and I'm full of memories of how she'd feel next to me. How her laughter would reverberate through her body and into mine.

Eventually, I'll be home. I'll be in bed by myself. I need tonight. It can't end until I'm dead on my feet. It's all more confusing because Sasha's face is the brightest I've ever seen. They're pulling me in with the smile lines around their mouth. They've taken off their suit jacket and rolled up the sleeves of their white shirt. Just like me, they picked the fire escape and wanted the crush.

And.

My desire has felt shut down for three weeks. For me, that's an absence. Normally it's never gone that long. When I'm angry or I'm sad, it's always there some of the time, spiking up and down. Now three weeks of nothing. Flat. None of the audio porn I usually prefer or touching myself or wanting anything or anyone.

Sasha's saying it was worth it to go into the crowd. Two songs like that rather than a set from the back row. There's a flicker inside me. Not some sort of wave of desire, but a small grab in my stomach waking up again. It reconnects me with my body and disperses panic even though it only lasts a second.

Cyprus says we should go to Falafel 'Til Dawn. Quinn tells Sasha they have to tag along, which is good. Now we're a different group, not one that's missing Emelia. We're walking to Cyprus's car, singing occasional Packing Boxes lines. Sasha picks out moments of harmony, but their voice sounds tentative.

In the station wagon, I grab shotgun and hit play on the last of the cassette players. This car is that kind of ancient. Music leaps in mid-song.

"Did you know," says Sasha from the back seat, "that some soulless people drive with *no* music at all?"

Cyprus gasps dramatically and pulls into the street. "It can't be true!"

"Let's take a vow." Quinn's still talking loud like his ears haven't stopped buzzing yet. "May the music never die."

"Hallelujah," I say, though I don't believe in god.

15

SASHA

At the Channel, people worshipped Heather Erin. Not adoringly, but fearfully and hopefully, the way some people pray. There was a tiny opportunity to ascend, though you were much more likely to be damned.

Meet the person who raised me.

Heather Erin, who's currently embroiled in defending her client, the international pop star Augustus Ash, on the world stage in a celebrity trial. Presumably, she's also perturbed by my absence, maybe infuriated, but Augustus tends to require a little more maintenance. Usually, I'm the good child. The ignorable one. And my note said I was fine. Though I doubt her concern is for my well-being so much as my image.

As Admirer, Augustus and I have made Heather Erin wealthy and powerful, and she's made us famous (and wealthy and powerful). She wasn't the one who scouted me and my brother and signed us to the Channel, but she was the one who switched us over to the music side of things. She got us the contract that goes until I'm twenty-one. I owe her, because I was dying on the soundstages in the Channel's warehouses. I'm not good with my face on camera. I can't lip-sync. The helmet absolutely saved me in music videos.

Now I sit in the back seat of Cyprus's station wagon with no helmet on, windows down, going to someplace called Falafel 'Til Dawn.

"It's an absolute staple," says Lillian.

"Oi, and you're an expert on that, eh?" says Quinn in an incredibly iffy approximation of a British accent. "Bloody fuckin' 'ell, your wanker ancestors can't cook a wee bit."

Lillian pretends to look offended. "You can't just say British expressions and call it an accent."

"Bullocks," says Quinn.

It takes me a second to get the courage to join in. "Loosely Australian at best."

Quinn laughs. "My point exactly. But this place is open late. It has falafel. That's all you can dream of. My dad orders it for every occasion."

"That's because it suits every occasion," says Cyprus. She changes lanes without glancing at a mirror. "Can you bug him to send me those grant forms?"

"My dad's an arts council grant person," says Quinn for my benefit, which I appreciate. He talk-sings, "I got all the connections / connections / really just the one con-nec-tion," not really answering Cyprus.

That's the sort of talk my own dad would have liked. He cared most about art when it intersected with business. He was sick and fading out during Admirer's ascension, but he got to witness some of it. He died just after Augustus turned eighteen. I'm glad he didn't live to see the charges and trial. My mom too, though she died when I was baby — before I remembered her well enough for it to be tragic to me. The fans still like to frame my life that way. My alleged sorrow is very alluring, apparently.

My dad would have made an uproar about the career implications of my absence. Now I wonder if Heather Erin has even told Augustus that I'm gone. Since he's my guardian, she might be obligated by the law, though I've seen her step right over that red tape a lot of times. After all, the more people know, the higher the chance of the world finding out. Which would endanger me. So she'd claim she simply *couldn't* tell Augustus, for my safety.

Heather Erin is fabulous at seeming like the good guy. Here's her trick: she tells you what to do and makes it seem like it was your own choice. If things go badly, she blames you. If they go well, it was her, and now you're in her debt. When she cues you to laugh, you laugh. More importantly, when she cues people to buy, they buy. When you say something seems wrong, she says, "It's just business." And if you want something different, she says, "Why aren't you grateful?" She was always trying to shape how I saw the world.

To her, Quinn, Cyprus, Lillian and me would be a collection of amorphous promotional problems to be solved. These are the same thoughts that go through my head, like trash you can't ignore floating in a stream.

Lillian's going to have to have a tidier, prettier, more feminine look if she's going to continue that punk thing. Got to make sure she's appealing to some statistical concept of average straight men. Male gaze and such. Sexy punk girls should wear dark eye makeup and the remnants of tights. As the conversation goes on, it sounds like Lillian's dad is British. Heather Erin would like that, but she'd be less happy with someone who won't follow orders. Who might call out problems. Heather Erin only gives voices to people she thinks she can control.

Cyprus is white and skinny, which to Heather Erin looks like possibility. Except for Cyprus is too tall. Tall enough to make a male co-star look short. The way she moves isn't right, not seductive enough, and Heather Erin would want to unteach Cyprus's fashion. Incorrect proportions and facial asymmetry. Heather Erin thinks Cyprus could maybe die early in a B movie, but she's not the final girl.

Quinn's got so many marketing problems that he'd have trouble getting hired as an extra. He's not a person the Channel elevates. At best, Heather Erin gives Quinn sitcom potential, side character, only if he passes within the Channel's frameworks of masculinity. She'd use words like *complexion* and *commercial potential* to mean her actual thoughts of *not white enough* and *looks Middle Eastern*.

Then she'd say, "That's just the numbers talking, not me. If he was Latinx the way Isabelle is, we could use him as an ethnic wild card." As in relatively fair skinned, as in colorism. So she'd be sure to add, "Christ, this industry's a cesspool, but what can you do?"

These things are usually said by the people who have the power to do something.

Instead, she's the one who made Isabelle change her name to a "classier" spelling, aka more French.

Oh yes, and we'd all meet the latest in absurd body standards. In a TV show, we'd still be eating at Falafel 'Til Dawn, but after each shot, we'd spit out our food instead of ingesting it.

Last, Sasha.

See here, I catch myself. Better late than never. Even when you know the way someone views the world is wrong, it takes a while to unlearn what you're surrounded by. A lifetime, maybe. There are tendrils of intruding thoughts, irrational prejudices, disgust toward yourself and everyone who doesn't check an improbable list of boxes that shouldn't need to be checked.

I've been working on recognizing the trash and cleaning it up. On not trusting the thoughts or using them to define value. Even if what happens in my head was put there by someone else, it's still my responsibility. It's selfish, but I didn't seriously start throwing away what Heather Erin had handed me until I sorted out the nonbinary thing and started directing some of the hate I'd learned at myself.

I felt repelled by me.

I guess it was the first time in my life I'd experienced any of the internalized prejudice I had against other people. Now, I'm not pretending I couldn't have been nonbinary at the Channel at this point in my career. I'm an extremely wealthy, powerful white superstar. Layers of unearned advantages. But every fragment of yourself you give to someone like Heather Erin is a fragment she tries to turn into money. She's Queen Midas. Sometimes the gold touch kills, but at least you're rich.

I will not have my gender and sexuality picked apart by a marketing team.

I had to leave. To ditch the lies and learn who I am, and most importantly to grab a few precious moments like this.

We're piling out of the car in front of the busy glow of Falafel 'Til Dawn. I'm trying to absorb everything about these people and this night. To start out open, start out listening. That's how they're treating me.

Pop music is about being able to be understood very quickly. Hear the song for the first time, and by the second chorus you know the words. Stardom is the same. You see a celebrity in one movie, and you'll recognize them in everything else they're in. There has to be continuity, rigidity.

Well fuck that.

Okay, actually I love pop music, but it's a metaphor.

The restaurant's built in the style of a diner. There's a long counter with tall stools and a huge menu above it written in Arabic and English. There's music playing tinnily from a speaker somewhere toward the back of the room. Cyprus is bobbing her head to it.

We head toward one of the cracked red booths. Quinn and Cyprus take one side and leave the other for me and Lillian. She gets there first but doesn't seem to want the inside seat. Instead, she makes a sweeping, exaggerated bow and says, "Why please, after you."

"Such chivalry," I say.

"I would *never* be chivalrous. It's a patriarchal long con." She sits next to me and immediately starts fiddling with the saltshaker, screwing the lid on and off. "But since you're our esteemed guest, let us do the ordering."

"You do look esteemed," says Quinn to me. "Does anyone ever look at you and say, them-there's a sharp dresser?" asks Quinn. "They/them, them-there? Anyone?"

We all groan, but I like how comfortable they are with my queerness. Lillian asks whether I'm "punk enough to be vegan." I shake my head and she orders what sounds like a ridiculous amount of food.

Quinn puts his head on the table. "My puns are utterly wasted on you three."

Cyprus pats Quinn on the head. "There, there."

Lillian turns to me with a serious mouth but smiling eyes. "If you make a dad joke too, I will *end* you." She slams the saltshaker down for emphasis and the lid flies off, sending salt everywhere. A couple people at the counter glance over. Lillian's laughing too loudly and apologizing and brushing salt off the table and the booth and me but then apologizing for that too.

"It's not the first time," I say without thinking. Suddenly, I find myself halfway through a revamped story about how Augustus, who I just call my older sister, dumped an entire one of those big things of diner sugar on my head as a kid.

"Where are you from?" asks Cyprus, and as soon as I say, she goes, "Oh, you're the music one. Quinn said he met an excellent music person. Okay, weigh in on something here. Do you listen to Admirer?"

16

LILLIAN

Sasha brushes some remaining salt off their skirt and then folds their hands tightly under the table. I didn't mean to spill it, but then using it as an excuse to touch them? I am not being subtle. I've been with Emelia for so long that I've forgotten how to be attracted to other people in a non-hypothetical way. Though I was never the best at flirting, so it's not like I had skills to forget.

"I mean, who doesn't?" says Sasha. "Admirer's kind of everywhere."

"I don't," I say. "They're just shimmery trash."

Curating my musical tastes is a matter of pride for me. There's more listening to do than there is life. Can't waste it on Top 40. Though the world doesn't share this approach, so I certainly know my fair share of Admirer choruses. And for all the inane predictability of their earworm hits, I can't help but begrudgingly hear how they can both sing their peers into the dirt. At least in a youthful, over-produced sort of way. Just because I know it doesn't mean I'll admit it.

"Snob," says Quinn.

"Thank you kindly."

"A-ny-way," continues Cyprus, ignoring us and focusing on Sasha. "What do you think of the trial? Should they lock up Augustus?"

"I'm not sure," they say eventually. "The Channel seems committed to defending Augustus. I can't imagine he'll get in that much trouble as long as Ja — the girl he was with, keeps saying love is love and she's in love with Augustus."

"You think it's Jasmine too?" Cyprus seems to be researching it on her phone as she speaks. Personally, I think trying to figure out whose identity is being protected is unhelpful, but I keep that one to myself.

"There's been loads of people claiming to be the girl from the trial," continues Cyprus, "but most of the fandom figures it's got to be Jasmine."

Quinn and Cyprus are both leaning toward Sasha a little. Apparently, my controversy sowing isn't what the two of them are looking for, but I toss it in anyway. "Say Augustus and Jasmine live happily ever after, and eventually they're like thirty-five and thirty-one and the whole thing feels less slimy, didn't Augustus still assault someone?"

I'm not at all certain this is true.

Cyprus looks too pleased. Sex, violence, fame, all the makings of an iconic scandal. "He put Jasmine's older brother in the hospital. That's why people figure it's her, even if the news won't confirm it. They say he was in a coma, but he's come out of it. Otherwise, it could have been a murder trial. *Apparently* there was a big confrontation when the brother found out and Augustus beat the shit of him 'in self-defense.'"

I try to move the conversation back to real music by mentioning that College Collage's lead guitarist just quit. It prompts minimal reaction, so I resign myself to celebrity gossip. "Are you going to take down the old Admirer poster above your bed or what?" I ask Cyprus.

"Maybe I'll just cut off Augustus and leave Alexander up there all sexy and mysterious and unproblematic in his helmet."

Quinn does this thing he's really good at where he notices someone drifting out of the conversation and reels them back in. He takes on a fake interviewer voice. "Sasha, what do you think of Alexander Ash's long media silence? Should he speak out in defense of his brother or should he condemn his actions?"

Quinn holds an imaginary microphone out to Sasha, who takes a long moment before responding. "I can't imagine what Alexander would possibly say."

Then they ask where the bathroom is, and I let them out of the booth. That's the situation I'm avoiding when I sit on the outside of the booth or take the aisle seat. That way if I suddenly need space, I don't need to awkwardly get someone to move or squeeze by them while I'm panicking in order to get out. Even with Emelia, I didn't like sleeping between her body and the wall. Sasha doesn't look panicked, though.

"Do you think we overwhelmed them?" I say to Cyprus and Quinn. "All these moral quandaries and shit."

"Probably more the getting chased out of the Mercury." Quinn gives me a knowing look. "Et cetera."

Et cetera being the part where I grabbed their hand and didn't let go.

I say, "Hey, they were the first one to insist on getting close to the stage."

Before he can reply, I manage to make the College Collage conversation happen, and things feel simple for a few minutes. I love this restaurant, love the venues and their quirks, love all the safe corners of my world where I can grab a breath before going out again. Without Emelia, a lot of those corners are gone.

Cyprus has gotten pretty quiet, which these days usually

means she's texting Emelia. I want to ask how Emelia is. A whole week of school and I haven't run into her. I want Cyprus to text, "We all wish you were here," to let Emelia wonder if I'm part of that. I don't know how things are being navigated. I know she hangs out with Cyprus separately. For something like tonight, I didn't think Emelia would want to be invited. Maybe Cyprus invited her and she said no. What if she'd come to the show? What would I have done?

I have this moment of fantasy that Cyprus sends my message to Emelia and Emelia says, "I love Falafel 'Til Dawn. Would it be okay if I biked over and joined you?" And then she'll arrive and she'll know I don't like to sit on the inside and nothing dramatic will happen but there will be the hint of a thaw. Tonight, late, we'll send a few text messages, just a few. I'll say goodnight then lie awake and there will be a tiny bit of hope.

"Soooo, are you making a move on Sasha?" Quinn asks me. He glances over his shoulder toward the bathroom, but the door Sasha went through is still shut. I've spent my share of time sitting in bathrooms psyching myself up for social things. Their hair doesn't look like it maintains itself either.

"They said they're nonbinary," continues Quinn, "but I'm not sure how you fit into their whole orientation."

If I was to be surveyed in a nicely inclusive way I'd say bisexual. Biromantic too, body and heart, though those don't separate for me. People sometimes project other identities onto me because I only dated Emelia, which … just no. I know myself, and I think some people of my gender are attractive, and also people of every other gender. In Sasha's case, *very* attractive. It's way less confusing than when I assumed I was straight. That never made sense in me.

"I can find out," continues Quinn. He looks off into the distance. "They call me *Le Wingman*."

I try to wave him off, but he says he'll figure it out anyway. Emelia would just be able to tell. It's uncanny.

And now I feel guilty about being attracted to Emelia and about flirting with Sasha. Isn't that just grand.

"Lillian needs *Le Wingman*," says Cyprus. "She was mean to Sasha about locking up their bike, and now they're probably afraid of her."

"I was direct," I say. "And helpful. If they think I was bossy, that's engrained sexism. I'm a goddamn leader."

Quinn smirks at me. "A leader who flirts by pouring salt on their crush?"

"First, not my crush. Second, I wasn't trying to flirt. They had salt on them. I was just casually brushing off the mess I made."

"Smooth," says Quinn.

"Chaotically endearing?" I try.

Cyprus considers it. "Quirky dream girl?"

Which actually hits really close to home, because I hate every single time I'm a cliché. I hate that no matter what I do, I fit into one some way or another. And if it seems new and unclichéd, give it a week and it'll have clichés about its clichés. Emelia once joked that I was a punk bi trope, which basically confirmed the fears I already had. I started dressing more randomly, mixing different styles and aesthetics and mostly getting very unhappy. Emelia tried to let me work my way through it but got tired of how long it was taking me to make choices about literally everything, since I was always worried about whether I was being authentic and unique. She kissed me and she said gooey things that I adored but almost pretended not to in an effort to be tough.

She said, "Express in whatever way makes you feel alive."

She said, "It makes me smile to see you as yourself."

She said, "It's okay if other people dress like you."

She said, "You're already Lillian."

She said, "That's already and always enough for me."

She kissed me again and said, "Love, you're *my* punk bi trope."

Then she sang some awful just-be-yourself bubbly pop song at the top of her lungs and wouldn't stop until I sang along. I used to hate that song, then for a while I smiled every time I heard it. Now I can't listen to it at all.

Sasha arrives back at the table at the same time as the food. They look reassembled with their suit jacket back on and their hair tidied with the couple strays falling out perfectly. They put on ambitious winged eyeliner that I'm honestly kind of impressed by.

"If there's going to be a quirky dream girl, can it be me?" they say. "This food looks unbelievable."

Later, when we drop Sasha off in front of a patchwork two-storey house a few blocks from where I live, I'm still wondering how much of our conversation they heard. They never indicated that they caught anything other than the end. I try not to add that worry on top of everything.

I'm so tired.

I wanted to run all night and I couldn't. The sadness caught up. But it was good. It helped my heart feel reactivated for a little. I grabbed some moments of forgetting.

We've got band rehearsal tomorrow night for the first time since the breakup. More moments of immersion, I hope. It's two steps forward and a step and a half back, but there's an upward trajectory.

I keep picturing Sasha on their tiptoes, reaching for the fire escape.

17

SASHA

When we were out last weekend, I locked myself in the small bathroom at Falafel 'Til Dawn and gripped the edge of the sink until I thought my hands or the sink would shatter.

I don't want to keep the truth from these people, but I can't let them find out about my connection to Admirer. Fame moves me from potential friend to shiny object, I'm sure of it. Even if they kept it a secret, they'd never look at me the same way again.

Then I steadied and reminded myself that no one here has any reason to suspect I'm Alexander Ash. Even though Cyprus is a fan. There are fans everywhere. She was probably at the show we played here last year. But there was no talk of me having gone missing, just going quiet. That's good.

I looked up a picture of me in the helmet and held it beside my face while I looked in the mirror. I wore it from thirteen to seventeen. Alexander Ash is an idea, and I'm a person. A mirrored visor and a face. It's awful, but also a line of defense. People won't connect the two.

I shouldn't do anything risky like sneak into more shows. I want to be independent and free, but I can't afford to get in any sort of trouble. I don't have a fake ID or a fully formed alias. The name on my ID is Alexander Moore. As long as no one says it around Cyprus or Quinn, I'm alright.

I put on dramatic eyeliner for the first time in public. I'm not as behind on gender-coded skills as I might be. Isabelle taught me a lot about makeup, since I'd just go and put on my helmet anyway. She'd help me practice and give me tips while we hung out backstage at charity events or waited for photo shoots.

At the restaurant, I needed a trick to feel invincible. Some days that's a baggy denim jacket or a sweater. Or a sleeveless white dress I only wear around my walk-up. Other times, nothing feels right or everything does. I try to notice what's going on inside me on any given day and follow that.

That night, it was winged eyeliner. It reminded me of Isabelle, of friendship, trust and glamour. Invincibility tricks.

Quinn and I are in chemistry class a few days later when he starts quizzing me about who I'm attracted to, which is tricky to answer.

I shouldn't say it like that. He isn't pushy, and I know I can respond in any way and it will be fine. He makes sure to add, "You don't have to be attracted to anyone."

I am, though I haven't worked out a pattern for it yet. At the Channel, it felt a little secondary, or maybe there was no one around that I was attracted to. Not even Isabelle, one of the sexiest teenagers alive according to several questionable publications that overtly fetishized her. Ignoring that bullshit, she's beautiful and my dear friend and I'm not into her.

I tell Quinn some of the first things I think of. Confidence, swagger, passion. A fierceness of being yourself.

Then I look around the classroom and say, "People mostly seem so automatic. Or unconsidered? I guess I'm not attracted to gender at all. That's how I use the word "pan." But with some people, I sometimes feel like there isn't space for them to be attracted to me. Like anyone who's into me in a totally straight, cis way is misgendering me, which is very not sexy. I just generally feel more comfortable with queer people."

I realize I've been rambling, journaling out loud, so I tag on, "If that makes any sense."

Quinn nods. "Yep. Very excellent. If it's strange, that's where we live. Objectively speaking though, and I'm talking data-driven facts here, you and I are by *far* the hottest people in this room."

"Based on pure analytics," I say.

Quinn starts listing celebrities he's attracted to. He uses a bunch of gay terminology I know and a couple terms I'll have to research later, but suffice to say the list features a lot of facial hair. To my mild discomfort, it also includes Alexander Ash because, and I quote, "There's something so kinky about never seeing his face. Hot take: Admirer songs have smutty subliminal messages."

I genuinely laugh. I also almost throw up.

I love chatting with Quinn, but I don't want that to be where my connection with Quinn, Cyprus and Lillian ends. Now that I'm a bit removed from the high of the night when we ran into each other at the Mercury, I'm worried that getting fully swept along with the group was a one-time phenomenon. They are, without a doubt, my favorite people I've met since leaving the coast. Along with Isabelle, my favorites ever.

Yet despite having acquired great ways to contact all of them, have I managed to send anything to any of them or initiate any ongoing anything? No, of course not. I'm terrified of real people who treat me like a real person. I deliberately avoid being on the apps that would let me peripherally stalk them. It feels opposed to my goal of experiencing life outside of fame. And the digital world is also probably bent on finding out where I am and what I'm doing.

Quinn's the one I've gotten closest to texting. What do I say? Am I just like, "Let's hang out"? I don't know how this works. What do normal people do? How do you get closer to people you think are remarkable?

It's hard to be confident when you desperately don't want to mess up.

And it's hard not to mess up when every conversation is full of lies.

Later that day, I'm on my way through school and I see some bastard who typically has something ugly to say to me about who should and shouldn't wear the clothes I choose. I slip through a side door, going outside to avoid him, and almost trip over Lillian.

She's sitting on the back steps among the discarded cigarette butts and shattered plastic slushy cups. I immediately recognize her jacket from behind (black denim, a thousand patches for bands and activism, random zippers to nowhere, rips held together with pins, DIY spikes on the shoulders). Tripping over her in that jacket would eviscerate me.

She's sobbing so silently that I barely notice in time to stop myself saying hello in a horribly friendly, bright manner. She's curled up tight with her arms around her knees and one hand clutching a green pop bottle so tightly her knuckles are white. There's an open notebook sitting by her feet with heavy, dark, scrawling writing in it. I guess there aren't any good bathrooms here to lock yourself in.

I consider slipping back through the door, but the guy inside is really pissing me off and scaring me a little and confronting him is definitely more of an Augustus move than a Sasha one.

And there's hurt pouring off Lillian.

I think of her pulling me along as we ran out of the concert. Walking away now feels like leaving her behind, even though I barely know her. I go with my instincts. I unzip my backpack, pull out my headphones and cue up Monochrome Stoplight.

Normal ways of getting to know people clearly aren't meant for me anyway.

"Hey." I say it softly.

Lillian still startles, glancing up at me looking ready to rip the head off whoever's found her like this. Her face and eyes have the fatigue of someone who's been crying hard for a long time. She's halfway through telling me to go to hell before she recognizes me.

"Oh, Sasha. Shit. I mean, sorry." Her words are shaky, like she's just managing to stop the crying for this moment, clinging to a place between waves. "Sorry, I'm okay. It's —"

I hold out the headphones, and she grabs them like a life preserver.

I sit on the steps a couple feet away from her and wait while she listens to the closing song on the album — six minutes. Her eyes are squeezed shut. It feels private, intimate, like I should look away even though she knows I'm there. Twice, she says, "Louder," though I could already hear the volume bleeding through the headphones when she first put them on.

Towards the end, her body stops shaking.

Lillian waits for the final synth notes to finish echoing out and then waits another few seconds before taking the headphones off and handing them back to me.

"I have class," she says. Her face looks wrecked, not like someone who's going to walk back through those doors.

"I don't. Want to stay here a little longer?" Anyone who wants their music at that volume could probably use someone who cares to sit with them.

"No, no, I'm alright. I'm sure you've got things to do. I should go too."

She stays sitting, takes a drink from the mostly full green plastic bottle. She offers it to me somewhat apologetically, and when I take a sip, I see why. Warm orange juice and vodka, mixed strong. I wouldn't have stomached much of this either.

"The day drinking is not a normal thing, let me assure you," says Lillian. "I bought it off Logan. It's a special circumstances experiment. Didn't work." She laughs in that trembling way of having just survived something. "I can't move. I actually can't move. See?" She lifts an arm and lets it drop limply. Laughs again, blows her nose.

"What class are you missing?" I ask.

"Language Arts." Saturated in disdain.

"Sounds skippable. We can sit out here …" I gesture to the overcast sky and the filth scattered all around "… in this beautiful place instead."

"And we're doing *Pride and Prejudice* of all things."

"I'm a Jane Austen connoisseur myself." I've learned that

sarcasm is something Lillian reads pretty easily from other people. I'm not entirely certain she knows when *she's* being sarcastic and when she's not.

"Who's Jane Austen? Does she play the boring one or the sexily rude one?"

"She wrote *Pride and Prejudice*."

"So she's dead?" Lillian takes another drink. "What's the actual point? You can forget me as soon as I'm dead. There are people making great art with language right now. Like Monochrome Stoplight, *that's* worth studying. Let me write about Liv James' lyrics all day."

"You know Monochrome Stoplight?" This isn't some band everyone loves. I only heard of them because Isabelle said that an acting coach once used Liv James as an example of how to stand powerfully. "I chose that randomly. Well, not *randomly*. I thought you'd like it."

For a moment, Lillian's distress seems to dissipate entirely. "Okay, so first off, I hate that you read me that easily. But also, top tier choice. Liv James is why I started a band." Then there's something that rattles through her body, like she might resume crying. She drinks again.

"Band trouble?" I have a self-centered moment of sadness at the thought of discovering the people I think are so wonderful are at each other's throats. You find something good and it implodes.

"What? No." She seems surprised. Hopefully that means there's no mess between her and Cyprus and Quinn. "I mean, kind of, but no."

"You don't have to answer."

Lillian rolls her eyes. "If I don't want to answer, I won't answer, no worries." Even in this moment, slivers of bravado. "I had a fight with ... my ex, I guess. It was very not great."

"What happened?" I manage to make it sound empathetic. Which it is, though curiosity is also a significant factor.

"Unreconcilable creative differences." It's a joke that she follows with a sort of sad half smile. "I just haven't seen her since we broke up in the summer. I've been route planning around the school to avoid her. And today I accidentally got into the elevator with her."

"You accidentally —"

"The doors were almost shut! I went running yesterday and today my legs object to stairs. I didn't know she'd be moving a cart of books. She's one of those helpful, good people."

I can't tell if she means that as a compliment or something utterly hateful.

"I tried to say hello and ask how she was doing because I care about her. She didn't take that well. Now I'm drinking on the back steps and I can't move. You need your heart to be working to move."

She picks up her notebook and writes something in it, pressing so hard that the tip of a stubby pencil dents the page. She keeps talking while she writes. "It *does* create band problems. Normally, she's the other singer. We've been trying to rework everything."

Lillian bumps the bottle.

We both watch it wobble and tip and spill and roll down the steps. It leaves a trail of orange liquid on the concrete before landing empty at the bottom.

Lillian closes her eyes tight and swallows. She's working so hard, almost says something, but I guess she's out of quips and flippant comments. I consider trying to set her up for another or trying to find a different way of helping her hold herself together.

"You seem like the sort of person who gets punched in the mouth, wipes the blood off and keeps on fighting. You're not down for the count."

"That's very sweet." That one only *sounds* sarcastic. It's genuine, I think. She's looking hard at the bottle like she's focusing on keeping the tears down. "But today I am. Sorry to disappoint."

There are times when you're done with the show. I understand. It takes guts to admit it.

"Do you ..." There are actual metal spikes on the shoulders of her jacket. Everything about her says, *touch me and you'll die*. "Do you want a hug?"

Lillian leans toward me slightly.

At first, holding Lillian is like jumping on top of a grenade and praying it doesn't explode. I slide across the step and put an arm lightly around her. She grabs the other one, wraps it around her, clings to it. My breathing doesn't want to stay even once her body's next to mine. Hers is split into pieces. I try to take slow breaths, counting them in my mind.

"Keep time with me," I say quietly.

We each focus on this one thing.

On aligning.

We breathe together until we're grounded.

Until we're in four-four time.

Until the world becomes steady.

When the school door slams open behind us, Lillian pushes me away from her like we've been caught in a compromising position. Two guys talking loudly barging past too close to us. There's fratty country music playing thinly from inside one of their backpacks. One of them crushes Lillian's bottle under his feet so the last of the makeshift screwdriver trickles out of the cracks.

"Turn down the rednecks!" she yells after them.

I knew she had too much snarl to stay crumpled.

I have a moment where I almost slip up and admit that I've

met that country singer. I want to tell Lillian about it, because he was the asshole his songs suggest and we could mock him together. I would stay on these back steps and exchange stories if I had any true ones I could tell her. I want to listen to Monochrome Stoplight with her.

Because somehow, despite everything, sitting here with Lillian makes me feel honored. It's nearly impossible to catch people in moments where they aren't performing or running at all. They have to trust you. I trust Lillian, and I was being fully myself with her.

Except for the part that's an international popstar.

Something inside me has stopped running too. For the first time since I texted Isabelle my plan. Or since this spring when I got the call that Augustus had been arrested and I was worried, angry, isolated, under orders to talk to no one. Or since I put on the helmet. Or since I first auditioned. Or since my dad told me and Augustus, "The whole world's going to know you're kings."

Lillian's already on her feet, tucking her notebook into her backpack. "I really shouldn't skip this entire class. I need a decent grade somewhere. I'll see you around, Sasha."

The door swings shut behind her.

I'm not sure what just happened.

Out here, it's gray. There's a distant siren and some wind in the leaves of the trees around the school. It might rain. I hope so.

I think I care what happens to Lillian.

That scares me. I want to chase after her and say, "Wait. I need to know about wanting to be forgotten when you die. I have to learn that. What do you need to do before then? Do you know how to stop running? Me neither."

I'd say, "Want to figure it out with me?"

There's a gust of wind. When I wear types of clothes that are new to me, the air moves differently around my skin.

When I feel new things, the air moves differently around my skin.

18

LILLIAN

I was pleased to have slipped through the gap of the closing elevator doors. I like how it feels to barely make it, even if it's a small thing.

Then I saw Emelia. The doors shuddered into place.

"Hi?" I said.

My body said that I had to touch her face. I had to reach my hands into her hair and kiss her as hard as I could. Desperately. I could hold her and bury my face in her scarf. I could at least brush her hand.

I stepped toward her, saying, "How have you been doing? I've been worried about you."

She shrank away from me into the corner of the elevator. It jolted as it started moving. "*You're* worried about *me*? Really?"

"Of course," I said. "Of course I'm worried about you. I like your scarf."

"Are you worried that I'm not fine? One of us has to be fine."

"I don't need you to be fine."

"Yes you do. I'll be okay. I'm always okay. You know that.

You broke my heart out of nowhere and now you're worried about me."

"It wasn't out of no —"

"I worried about you all the time. I didn't know when you were going to be anxious or ecstatic or in love or afraid. It never stopped. I knew I needed space. I was scared you'd go into some tailspin. Or start a fire. Or disappear."

The elevator had reached the next floor. The doors started to open, but I pressed the button for them to shut again.

"I know," I said. "I know, I know. I'm so sorry, Emelia. You said take a break, and I panicked. I never wanted to hurt you. I love you."

This is something we'd said to each other. Me too quickly and Emelia once she was sure she felt it. I got scared when she didn't say it back right away. She talked me off that ledge.

In the elevator, she was crying. I knew it was frustration, not that my words had worked. I knew as soon as she shrank away from me. I could feel the lights in me flickering.

"What the fuck, Lillian? This is exactly what I'm talking about."

The elevator doors had opened again, and she pushed the cart of books into the hallway. She was leaning on it like everything was too heavy on her. She looked back for a second and said, "You can't count on the people who love you to save you."

Then who will?

No one else got into the elevator. The doors started sliding shut.

I said, "You broke your own heart," but I never saw how she reacted.

19

SASHA

I'm already in bed when my phone vibrates on my nightstand (which in this case is an old stool I found by the sidewalk). My nervous system reacts fight or flight, because the only person with this number who'd text me at this time is Isabelle, and only if something's wrong.

I sent her my new number but told her not to message me unless there's an emergency. I told her that I won't reply, since it's safer for her messages to come to me than mine to her. Heather Erin has grabbed my phone before to see who I was talking to. Isabelle already took a risk for me, and now we have to make sure that risk doesn't put her in a position where she has to choose between her career and exposing me.

Instead, it's a voice message from Lillian, four minutes long, no text explaining it. When I think of her and I on the back steps of the school, pressing play on the recording only makes me slightly less nervous than opening a message from Isabelle would.

"Hey, Sasha." Lillian's talking quietly, and her voice sounds tired in a smoky sort of way. My phone finds my Bluetooth speaker in the dark, so it's like she's in the room.

"I started writing a song on the steps earlier today, and I just finished it. I thought since you were there you should hear it first. Sorry it's so quiet. My family's already gone to sleep so I don't want to plug in my guitar. Okay."

She starts playing a slow part with her fingers on an unplugged electric guitar, then stops. "And, um, thanks for being there. It helped a lot. Anyways, here goes."

This time the guitar part continues. When she starts singing, her voice has a withheld power. The growl is there, but latent. It feels like an amplifier turned all the way up with a guitar being played quietly. Push harder, and it will distort.

I'm in the shadow where everyone smokes
Where the concrete pools the cold
Cigarette butt leaves
Plastic bottle greenery

Please, please
Keep my vices close to me

I have that feeling
When the elevator starts moving
Give me a handrail
The bottom's dropped out
Mix me a screwdriver
For the way down

I'm playing she loves me, loves me not
With no flower petals to rip off
Coke can tabs torn away

Jagged nothings left to say
Please, please
Keep my vices close to me

I have that feeling
When the elevator starts moving
Give me a handrail
The bottom's dropped out
Mix me a screwdriver
For the way down

Give me a minute give me an hour
It takes a heart to get back up
In five or six years
Ask me why
I always take the stairs

I have that feeling
When the elevator starts moving
Give me a handrail
The bottom's dropped out
Mix me a screwdriver
For the way down
Mix me a screwdriver
For the way down

There's a soft scuffling sound and the recording ends.

It was rough, brand-new. She made some mistakes. Yet it held me in place, made me feel known. I want to listen to it again right now, closer, until I've memorized all of the words. She hasn't sent anything else. I should reply right away in case she's nervous of what I think of this rawness. I half-write a couple things, delete them. They're too gushy, but that's how I feel.

Lillian
Spit it out already
Those bubbles have me in suspense

Sasha
I just ... today?
You wrote that today?

Lillian sent a photo

It's four pages of crossed-out words and arrows and chords and tab and circled sections moved to new places and others marked with stars. It's the words all tangled together and smudged.

The last song I wrote on had eight songwriters. It was a number-one hit that got its heart from the people who loved it. This song showed up with its heart on its sleeve.

Sasha
The song's amazing
It absolutely wrecked me
But

Lillian
But?

Sasha
The most impressive part is that you can read that

Lillian
Then the most impressive part is fiction
I have no idea what half of it says

Sasha
So will the words be different next time I listen to it?

Lillian
A second listening
What a tremendous honor
And yes they'll probably change
Want to hear it in person?

I don't know what exactly she means by that. It doesn't give me enough information to jump to any sort of conclusion.

My body has its own thoughts. It responds with a small flip inside me. It's not bad — anticipation, nervousness, curiosity, some combination. I can't tell. My body knows more than I do a lot of the time, so I pay attention to it.

Sasha
It would be a tremendous honor

Lillian
Christ I'm awkward at self-promotion
But Cyprus will kill me if I don't invite you to our next gig

Sasha
Count me in

Lillian
It will be terrible

Sasha
Time and date pleeeeease

Lillian
Those are terrible too
Or the time is
Midnight this Sunday at Initialism
It was the only slot Christensen had this week

Sasha
Initialism?

Lillian
It's a bar
I mean technically it's a "concert venue"
But really it's a bar
You're going to love it

Sasha
Not sure I trust you …

Lillian
When have I ever led you astray?

I've got to do another take of this to send to the band
Goodnight Sasha

Sasha
Go to sleep Lillian

Lillian
You
Can't
Make
Me

I can't make myself sleep either. I lie in bed listening to the song another few times and try to choose an outfit for Sunday. But I don't know the place and I don't know how I'll feel that day.

I pick out four different sets of clothes.

By the time I fall asleep, I've also picked out harmonies for the song.

LILLIAN

I'm wide awake.

I wasn't until I sent the recording to Sasha. Now there's a lightness that I can't waste sleeping. I'm jittery with undirected energy.

I record the song again and send the demo to Quinn and Cyprus. Then I reread my messages with Sasha before powering my phone all the way down.

I go downstairs and eat toast with strawberry jam.

Back upstairs and restring my guitar.

Pick up my phone, set it down. I already said goodnight to them.

I take all my guitar pedals off my pedalboard so that I have to rearrange it. The choice to follow this energetic burst is definitely going to come back to bite me at school tomorrow. I start swapping around the mini connector cables then go downstairs again for cereal. I'm trying to visualize the perfect sequence of pedals. I swear, it's like playing chess. Though unlike chess, there's the possibility of solving my problems with a bigger board.

I like the thought of looking out over the people at Initialism and seeing Sasha there.

In the morning, the only new messages I have are from Jasper, telling me to "Stop galumphing around like a trucker named Duke" and then a surprisingly adept sketch of what he imagines I'd look like as a "trucker named Duke." We sit next to each other at the kitchen counter, me with my headphones on and him with his earbuds in, sending cursed, ridiculous corners of the internet back and forth.

SASHA

Tonight's experiment: the short skirt.

For people assigned male at birth, there's a bit of an uneven record as to whether your thighs should appear in public (actually that's true for everyone, but I'm going to stick to a limited topic). If you're an action hero walking sexily out of the ocean and/or you professionally attend the gym and are essentially hairless, okay.

Otherwise, not so much.

All this fluctuates by era and culture, but where and when I learned these rules, two leg-holes on your garment are generally also essential. But men wearing towels after getting out of the shower? Classic sexy. Kilts, kind of a divisive subject. Still, often considered sexy. Yet skirts are somehow their own category. Of course, I'm not a man anyway, so to hell with all of that nonsense. Though knowing that's how most people will judge me makes it hard to ditch the aforementioned nonsense.

What I'm getting after is that I'm here for anyone's thighs if they want their thighs in the open. All thighs, not just the hairless ones that are a "perfect" shape. Do all the lies I've ever heard about legs worm into my brain as I head to Initialism? Absolutely. The first step is knowing it's nonsense. The harder step is to stop applying that nonsense to myself and everybody else.

I wouldn't have imagined some random bar = safe place for Sasha to experiment with wearing a short skirt. (It's not *that* short either. One step at a time.) But Quinn convinced me it'd be okay.

We were in class a couple days ago, and, as usual, learning our own material while something very power-ballady played from our teacher's stereo. Quinn was wearing his safety goggles on his head. I was wearing mine in the way that protects your eyes because I had no clue what I was doing.

"Want to come see my band on Sunday?" asked Quinn. He shot finger guns that landed squarely between ironic and genuine. "You can watch me hit a bunch of drums to work out my repressed rage."

"I'm already in! Lillian invited me."

Quinn raised one eyebrow. Presumably he ditched the safety goggles to allow him that range of facial motion. "Wow."

"Under no circumstances are you allowed to say 'wow' and go back to reading the textbook."

Quinn made a show out of slowly flipping a page before answering. "Lillian's sure the show's going to be a train wreck. To be fair, she's usually sure it's going to be a train wreck until she gets onstage. And sometimes after she gets offstage. She's the worst at telling anyone we've got a show at the best of times, which band-wise, this … isn't."

"Her ex?"

"Yeah, there's the thing with Emelia. You might have seen her around. Redhead, very adorable, kind of short, excellent ponytail game, usually being nice to somebody? The two of you would get along."

I told him to put his goggles on, because there was a decent chance I'd blow something up with the next step. Quinn seemed mildly disappointed when there were no flames.

"It's at Initialism, though," he said. "So you should come even though we might go down in flames — much as this beaker did not. Initialism is a goddamn queer haven."

From what he told me as we kept talking, it sounded like I could wear whatever I wanted.

I arrive at Initialism at eleven on Sunday night. It wasn't a very long bike ride from where I live, though I still managed to nearly die twice trying to navigate the unexpected challenges of riding a bicycle in my chosen attire through a city that's mostly potholes.

Initialism turns out to be an unpretentious two-storey building next to a board game store. The upper floor looks like it's been empty for a while, but the main one is bustling. The venue's attached to a restaurant with big windows showing a wooden counter facing the street. The air's a little cool, but people are still out on the porch drinking and eating. I lock my bike up the way Lillian taught me. Though there's no shortage of single-speeds and fixies attached to signposts and the patio fence for me to use as examples.

Above the entrance, exposed light bulbs pour warm light onto the sidewalk. They spell out the word *INITIALISM*. There's no lineup and no bouncer out here, but I can hear indistinct music leaking from inside. Just the sensation of the long sound waves of the bass and kick touching the inside of my chest are enough to draw me in.

Inside, it's immediately apparent that there is nothing fancy about this place. It's built inside one large, low room divided in half by a loose definition of a wall (a frame covered in bare plywood).

To the left is Initialism, the source of the music. To the right, there's the food-type establishment called Munchies Arcade and Culinary Delights. It's adorned with an assortment of food-themed neon signs blinking on and off.

I turn into Munchies without taking much of a glance into Initialism.

That's where they're IDing people to get in.

Quinn explained to me that it won't be a problem age-wise. Since Initialism is enjoying legal loopholes surrounding concert venues and alcohol, they'll just put a "minor" stamp on my hand. Quinn doesn't know my particular anxieties around showing people my ID.

On the Munchies side, I'm brought to a full stop.

The restaurant side of the makeshift wall is covered in bright, semi-erotic street art featuring a lot of androids. It's really beautiful and queer in every sense of the word. Most people are ignoring it or leaning against the wall, an android reaching out to embrace them. They're just there, massive and sprawled and undefinable.

I can hear the music coming through it, like the bright world pictured there is churning it out. Electricity and vibration. The deep fryers sizzle. The pinball machines at the back of the room jangle and whir.

Somehow, I know if I stepped inside the art, I would feel completely safe.

There's another thing that's remarkable to me that perhaps I should have noticed before getting mesmerized by the wall. As far as I can tell, there's a whole diverse mess of visibly queer people around. Not everyone, but way more than usual. Also, rather more varied. Since Initialism is all ages, some of them are young like me.

They seem comfortable and free and impossibly cool and leave me with aspirations, inspirations and the sort of crushes that make me wonder if I want them or want to be them. Like four different instances from just the people I can see.

I stall on going into Initialism, people-watching and ordering food off a menu Quinn says gets increasingly random and craving-oriented as the night wears on until it's cereal, macaroni and cheese, or milkshakes.

Eventually, I hear the band onstage finish their last song. Any time before that would have been a good moment to be something like alone when I show my card. Now the entrance gets crowded with people leaving or stepping outside to smoke.

I check the time, wait for a lull. When one hits, it's now or never. I walk up and present my driver's license in a terrified manner that makes the person at the door look more closely at it. Who uses fake ID to be underage though?

"You been here before?"

I stammer my way to saying I haven't, while trying to seem very relaxed.

"Just know it's your space. If anyone treats you in a way that makes you uncomfortable or threatened, even if it seems small, we'll take you seriously. Talk to me or Christensen or Len." They gesture to someone with knuckle tattoos and heavy eyebrows that are dyed pink. I realize the person at the door isn't suspicious. They can see I'm nervous, so they're trying to put me at ease. It makes me want to give them a hug.

"And it's five bucks," they add.

I pay them, they stamp me as a minor, and I'm in.

Truthfully, the welcome was more impressive than the place itself. The entire establishment benefits from the dim lighting. Open room, concrete floor, scattered tables and chairs. Despite the lack of aesthetic, it's busier than I thought it would be on a Sunday night.

I'm standing there feeling disoriented when I spot Quinn onstage. He's swapping out the cymbals for his own.

When he sees me, he hops down and points toward the bar. "Let me buy you a drink," he says. "Something virgin."

From onstage, where Lillian's setting up her pedalboard, she calls after him, "Virginity is a myth that perpetuates a false hierarchy of heteronormative sex acts!"

Someone cheers.

This is a weird place. I like it.

At the bar, Quinn asks what I want, I shrug, and he orders me a virgin mojito. He's wearing a beanie with the same logo as the sweater he wore when I met him, though these waves are all green. His hair's curling out from under the front. His tank top's cut low at the sides, showing a dark gray binder underneath.

"Oi, Christensen!" Quinn yells down the bar. "I want you to meet the amazing Sasha Weaver."

Christensen's look stopped dead in an era — the combo of immaculately maintained beard and suspenders over his plaid shirt. He owns Initialism with his husband, who Quinn is adamant used to be a professional basketball player. Or baseball. Certainly a sport with a ball.

Christensen shakes my hand and does an actual multiple-move-fist-bump-secret-high-five thing with Quinn. I start praising the place to Christensen, saying how comfortable I already feel here.

Christensen aw-shucks away my compliments, but he's clearly pleased. "I figured, rich white gay guy like me, there's space in the world for me now. Lots of places, at least."

He leans on the bar and hands me my drink. Quinn's nodding along like he's heard this before.

"When I was a kid," says Christensen, "there wasn't much, and I remember that. There were people who carved open spaces for me. I owe my life and success to them. You got to take the good fortune you're given and push into the future with it. That's how this got built. It's my responsibility to create a place like this. A safe place where young people like the two of you can be yourselves and there's live music. Every. Single. Night. It's not much, but Initialism is yours. I saw Taylor give you a spiel at the door, so you know I'm not lying."

There's a smashing sound at the other end of the bar. "Shit," says Christensen. "A life of shattered glass. Quinn, you're not going to wear your binder to drum, are you? You know exercise, binders ... not the best combination."

"Do you lecture everyone in heels on the risk of back injury?" says Quinn. "Relax, I did what I need to be safe. And I don't even break a sweat drumming."

"Fair, fair. I've never worn one. I just worry, but you're the pro." He grabs a pen and mutters, "Remember, not expert at everything," while he writes it on his hand.

Someone yells for Christensen and he yells back that he's coming goddamn it. "Enjoy these guys, Sasha. They're the next medium-sized thing."

Quinn takes a sip of my drink once Christensen's gone.

"Does he always give that 'when-I-was-young' speech or what?" I ask.

"Basically. Lillian says his whole thing is a little virtue-signaling.

She loves him too, though. He has really, truly, never given any of us a reason to doubt him."

"Who is he?"

"Big music industry person of some kind. He moved home to be with his dying mother and never left. That's another story he'll tell you if you hang around. It's a weeper." Quinn spins his stool around and hops off. "Now take a seat, Sasha, cuz we're the next medium-sized thing."

I choose a table against the wall, so close that I can faintly hear the pinball machines on the other side over the canned music playing in Initialism. The band's tuning up.

Lillian's wearing her spiky jacket and a matte purple Telecaster guitar with pick scratches on the body from playing hard. Cyprus stands to her right at a keyboard with a two-octave synth above it. She's wearing turquoise earrings that brush her shoulders. They have the visual presence of about four different earrings put together. Quinn is in the back behind the kit, attempting various drumstick twirls and dropping his sticks.

I think I recognize Christensen from somewhere, but I'm pulled away from the thought when the music on the speakers stops. A couple of other teenagers across the room whoop. Lillian glances up from her tuning pedal and squints against the stage lights to scan the room.

When she finds me tucked in my dark corner, she smiles.

The stage lights shift to a blue tinge. Lillian plays a part with an echoing delay, her boot on the pedalboard gradually building the volume as Cyprus's keyboard part comes in. Quinn is bobbing his head even though he hasn't started playing, already locked in.

Lillian leans in the microphone, so close her lips almost brush against it.

"Hey, everyone, we're Wavelength."

LILLIAN

I'm going to kiss Sasha tonight.

It's after the show, and Sasha is sitting on the edge of the stage at Initialism while I coil my cables and someone sweeps up.

"Wavelength is my new favorite band," they say. "I'm not flattering you. I love some mournful, yearning alt-rock, anything that has me wanting to dance in a sad way. But I almost liked the moments of release better, where you were nearly pop-punk. Heavier on the punk than the pop, of course."

"I should fucking hope we are. When we make an album, fingers crossed that you're the one reviewing it."

"It'd be five stars for your songs alone. Did you write them all?"

"Most of them." I unplug the cable from my microphone. "Hey, so you clearly know something about music, right?"

"A little."

"Brutal honesty, how'd we sound tonight? Not in some general way. *Tonight*."

Sasha tilts their head to the side. "Style, great. Individually, great. Lyrics, great. As a unit, like someone was missing."

"That was honest, but I asked for brutal."

"Like a car on three wheels, Lillian."

I'm glad they don't try to pretend otherwise. Emelia normally stands to my left. We reoriented, but all night I felt adrift between where I usually stand and where Emelia should be. It was even worse because we've played at Initialism so many times.

Heartbreak is the familiar made unfamiliar.

"Is that why you didn't play the new song?" Sasha asks.

Quinn's a few feet away, locked in what might be described as a passionate embrace with a guy our age who's often at our shows. His name's Sef, and it didn't take him and Quinn many minutes of banter to get where they are. It isn't helping my loneliness, though it may prompt other thoughts re Sasha.

"It'd be better with another voice," I say simply, throwing a coiled cable on the stage and starting on the next one. Though I'm not sure the new song would have felt any worse than the old ones we played tonight. On those songs, Emelia had always been paired with me.

"Joining in on the second 'please' of the pre-chorus," Sasha says, fiddling with a stray guitar pick from the stage. "I can hear it."

I can hear it too, in that exact spot, but there's nothing there.

I'm standing behind Sasha, and they tilt their head back to look up at me. They sing the pre-chorus in a tenor. "Please, please / keep my vices close to me."

Their eyes look big even without makeup. They make a comment about Initialism that I don't hear, because that's when the thought of kissing Sasha tonight becomes a decision. With their face an inch from my leg and the notes rising up to me.

That's the first chance, and I don't take it.

With the gear packed, we can't fit Sasha's bike in the station wagon. There's no school tomorrow, so we're all heading to

Cyprus's house. Sasha leaves before us, but at nearly two in the morning when we're unloading at Cyprus's, they still haven't showed up.

The night's taken on the stable darkness of everyone in bed, with no headlights disrupting it. I squint down Cyprus's street for a sign of Sasha.

"I think the universe is on our side," says Quinn as he picks up Cyprus's synth. "It's the only explanation for getting Monday off the day after a late gig."

"Or everything is random," I say, "and we're just tremendously lucky."

"That's quite good." Cyprus is videoing me rather than moving her equipment. "'Everything is random and we're just tremendously lucky' is exactly the vibe the fans want from you."

"We have fans?" Quinn pretends to almost drop Cyprus's synth before slinging it over his shoulder. She flips him off and heads toward the door.

"Who do you think you were making out with after the show?" I say distractedly. I'm looking out into the dark street. "Do you think Sasha will find us okay? They're new to the city."

"I quickly realized Sef was a fan of me *personally*," says Quinn. "A little too much so. Too enthusiastic with his tongue. If it wasn't so, I would be off with him right now."

"You would be exactly here right now talking about how Sef was just the right amount of enthusiastic with his tongue and how possibly you're in love."

"Not wrong. But I would have gotten his number." Quinn punches me in the shoulder. "Speaking of love ..."

I try to smack him back, but he ducks out of the way. "Worrying about my queer friend riding home at night in a new city is basic decency," I say.

"Do you usually concern yourself with basic decency?"

"Don't you have a keyboard to carry?"

"Don't you have a keyboard to carry?" Quinn copies me in a fake whiny voice and follows Cyprus inside.

I'm nervous Sasha decided to go home instead. Or got lost. Even though they're going through safe neighborhoods, I'm worried about them.

I see the blinking red safety light on their bike come around the corner. I wave and call for Sasha since I'm sure they can't see the house number. They get off their bike right in front of me. Suddenly my heart quickens a bit. They're taking off their helmet and trying to fix their hair and I say, "Here, I've got you," and touch their hair to make it how they seem to like it, and that's the second untaken chance to kiss them.

Inside, we all talk quietly until we're downstairs. No one wants to wake up Cyprus's parents, but their house is huge and easier to sneak around than mine. Once you're in my house, everyone knows you're there.

Cyprus's place is an old-fashioned upper class house. It's the sort of sprawling, multi-storey monstrosity that has a staircase for servants from the kitchen to the second floor, which her parents think is nostalgic. For them, the good old days also include several administrations that should burn in hell.

Behind the house, there's an in-ground swimming pool and a yard that sweeps down to the edge of the river. *Sweeps* really is the right word. The landscapers made sure of it.

Cyprus wants to get everyone into the basement as quickly as possible, since it remains untouched by the latest renovation. Where modern floor plans haven't knocked out walls and comfort hasn't been replaced with a "tasteful" mix of the old and the cold and contemporary. Expensive yet bland art, gray floors, uncomfortable couches, but with vintage chandeliers and elaborate, garish banisters.

"Please excuse how I'm literally descended from The Man," says Cyprus. She's slightly embarrassed by her family's class, though Sasha takes in all the wealth with a glance and without comment.

"Cyprus is only friends with us to be rebellious," I say.

"Shut up. You know I'm friends with you because you make me feel good about myself."

"Glad I have qualities."

"But will they be … okay with all of us?" Sasha asks me as Cyprus leads us through the house to a door that opens onto a steep staircase. Quinn's already down there. I hear the soft clack of pool balls being set in a triangle.

"Yeah, yeah," says Cyprus. "Confused, but passively accepting. When I told them Quinn's pronouns, they were like, 'That's nice, honey.' They honestly had more follow-up questions when I got everyone to start calling me Cyprus in middle school, and the only reason I did that was because they gave me the beigest name of all time."

"They are prone to absent-minded deadnaming," I say, "and the occasional *very* broad cultural generalization."

"I'm chipping away at them," says Cyprus. "Yesterday, there was a teachable moment about how benevolent racism is *still* racism. Watch your head on that beam."

Sasha ducks under it, then grins as they look around the room.

We're surrounded by wood-paneled walls. Our feet are deep in orange shag carpet. There's a pool table with faded red felt, ugly posters of cult classics on the walls and a pile of partially disassembled electronics in the corner. The couches are worn, striped fabric, and the gaming system is a decade old.

This is Cyprus's space. She crosses the room and pushes a VHS into an ancient TV. A Dropout Burnouts concert video from the early nineties starts playing in the middle of a song.

Here there is no closing time. Tomorrow, we have no clock to punch.

An hour later, Cyprus and Sasha are playing an old racing game while I'm facing Quinn in what is not our first game of pool. I want to be good at it, because being a pool shark seems intimidating and like the sort of skill that a person like me should casually have.

Instead, me and Quinn are both terrible. Me, because I'm trying too hard. Quinn, because he thinks every shot is an opportunity to attempt a trick.

"You're doing it again," says Cyprus.

Sasha crosses their legs. "Well, you're lapping me again."

"*You* asked *me* to help you learn how to not flash everyone."

"I am imagining my knees and/or thighs are attached to each other," says Sasha. "I am imagining that I'm incapable of leaning over."

Cyprus sets down her controller as her car takes itself on a victory lap and Sasha finishes the race. "I presume at this point you'll all be sleeping here? I'm going to go see what sort of bedding I can scrounge from my room."

Quinn accidentally sinks the eight ball long before he was supposed to. "Can we please call that the end of the game, or do I have to pull all my balls?"

Cyprus and Sasha both snort.

Quinn says, "I'm here alllllll week."

"I'm in a basement full of children," I say, cuing up my shot. I scuff it completely and accept Quinn's resignation. He follows Cyprus upstairs, saying he's going to make stealth nachos, which as far as I can tell are nachos made while he sneaks around like a cartoon villain.

I swing myself over the couch and land shoulder to shoulder with Sasha. They smell like a cozy idea of Christmas that I didn't know I had. All pine and sugar.

This third chance to kiss Sasha is when I start to get annoyed at myself.

I should be able to do this. It's just a kiss. A lot of people kiss a lot of people.

I used to believe that Emelia would be both the first and only person I kissed. It was ridiculous to begin that level of romanticism when I was fourteen.

Emelia's probably already done something emotional and rebound-ish with one of her other friends. Margot's a lesbian, like Emelia, and single, and has wavy blond hair that's never a mess and has never involved regrettable undercuts, and she smiles at everyone in a way that makes them feel like they belong, and I bet Emelia's been thinking about kissing that smile for a long time and I bet dating Margot would feel soft, not sharp.

Like how I felt dating Emelia, not how she felt dating me.

The hour has me sad and uninhibited. I should be coming off a performing high that never arrived. One move toward Sasha and I could create a rush in my body that would cover up the grief.

Kissing Sasha would be soft.

The voice in my head calls me a coward when I pick up Cyprus's controller and start a new race. "Prepare to meet Mad Lillian: Fury Road."

"You, competitive? I don't believe it."

"If we're friends after this, we're friends for life." I'm flicking through cars, trying to find one that's the same shade of purple as my guitar, Butler, and trying to ignore that I'm counting chances in my mind.

"But I'm a beginner, so will beating me really be satisfying?"

"Cease your mind games." I shift on the couch, because their mind games aren't the ones they think they're playing. I hope their effect on me isn't something they can guess. That they don't see through me like how they saw that I'd love Monochrome Stoplight.

It's in their shoulder against mine. How they aren't shy after seeing me in ruins behind school and how easily they've settled in with my friends. That they're already making fun of me even though they barely know me.

By four in the morning, I feel like asking for a corresponding fourth chance is too much to ask. I've got an ache growing in me as I lie down on my air mattress between the couch and the TV. Sasha played me pool for first dibs. I won, and I chose the *air mattress*. I said it's way better than the couch, which is a lie that will cost me some sleep.

This crush is getting entirely out of hand.

Quinn turned the pool table into a blanket fort and crawled in a while ago wearing his headphones, while Cyprus has gone upstairs to bed with a promise to leave a note on the basement door so that her parents and her older sisters don't wander down here in the morning.

Cyprus said my performance clothes are so spiky they might puncture the mattress, so I've changed into an orange camp T-shirt of hers. It's that heavy cotton, boxy variety that fits no one. I'm wearing these pajama pants she had that are too long yet too tight at the hips and have something in silver lettering written across the butt. I chose not to read it.

I try to confidently walk to the mattress, but it's hard when Sasha is lying on the couch, looking all tired and gorgeous sleeping in their clothes. While here I am, lying two feet from them trying to decide if I take off these goddamn pants underneath the blanket or try to see out the night wearing them while feeling both crushed and short.

"I've had too many second winds to be sleepy," says Sasha. We're both lying on our backs looking at our phones. "I'm playing space pinball out of nostalgia. I'm still a wizard."

"Does that include real pinball?" I'm scrolling through pictures from last summer, trying to find a single one where I both like how I look and I'm not inseparable from Emelia.

"I've never played." They hum along to a sound effect in the game. "Maybe next time we're at Initialism, you can teach me."

"School you, maybe," I say, though I like all the implications of Sasha's suggestion.

"What's with the robots at Munchies?" Sasha asks.

"You've got to say the full name every time or people will know you're not from here." I turn off my phone. It's making my body ache more somehow.

"What's with the robots at Munchies Arcade and Culinary Delights?"

"Oh, *those* robots. Len and Taylor, the bouncer and the doorperson, they painted them."

Sasha rolls onto their side to face me. "Are they like impossibly sexy or is that just me?"

"I wouldn't say Taylor's 'impossibly' sexy." I can't see Sasha's face anymore now that the glow of our phones is gone. It makes them feel closer.

"You know I'm talking about the robots," says Sasha. "But true. I should have asked Taylor what they put in their hair."

I'm thinking about the androids and what Sasha might see in them. "When I first saw that wall," I say, "I panicked. I was with my mom, and with the mural and all these hot people it just felt like there was *sex* all over the place. And she was comfortable with it all, which was almost worse."

"You were with your mom at Initialism?"

"To my perpetual shame, she found it before I did. She took me there to see this properly heavy band on my thirteenth birthday, like way heavier than anything I listen to. I'd been out for a couple years and I still had this sense I was alone in that. Being there that first time ... I felt almost dazed."

"Like you couldn't blink?" suggests Sasha.

"Yes!" I lower my voice. "Yes. And especially with the androids. It's like that wall is a dystopia for someone, but not for me."

"Or a utopia written by someone who understood me." Sasha's generating this enthusiasm and connectivity in the middle of the night, understanding me like the mural understands them. "I took a picture of the one with the transparent heart. If you get it from the right angle, it's making eye contact with you and it's devastating." They turn their phone back on.

I roll off the air mattress and kneel beside the couch to look at the picture. I'd barely have to move to press my lips to their mouth.

This fourth chance proves Quinn right. The universe is trying on my behalf, gracing me with me another opportunity.

I don't hesitate before taking chances. I'm not afraid to start a song on a big note. I don't usually have trouble committing. Things occur to me and I try them to see what happens. Growing up with Cyprus taught me how. Even with Emelia, I asked her out. Sort of, at least.

Maybe first times are easier because you don't know how much it can hurt.

Sasha's looking at the picture. I'm looking at their mouth. My body breaks through the barrier to motion. It's jumped and I'm going to kiss them.

They go tense.

I think it's something I've done. I've barely started moving, but it's enough for Sasha to know what's going on. They've turned their body away from me. I follow Sasha's eyes to their phone and they swipe the message away fast. Another one appears and they push it off-screen without opening it.

They sit up, say they have to go to the bathroom.

I see another message blink onto their screen as they walk across the basement. They close the door behind them and I can hear it lock.

That's that, then. Click.

I crawl back onto the bed, but I can't get comfortable. I take off these ridiculous pajama pants and wrap the blanket tight around me. There's no way I'm getting out of bed now. I'd wear just my underwear and a T-shirt in front of Quinn or Cyprus, but not with a new person around.

I'm crying in a way where I realize it's happening instead of feeling it build up. There's a well of emotion in me that's brimming all the time. Teardrops are just slipping out. Figures I'd have the ugly cry on the steps when Sasha can see me and (I presume) the less-ugly cry when I'm alone in the dark.

It stops after a few minutes, and all I feel is less. I flip over my pillow.

Sasha's gone for long enough that I pretend to be asleep when they get back. I can feel their energy clenched and awake a few feet away. That may have been because of me.

The crying is still in my voice. I can't disguise it. I won't reveal it.

And I can't stand to hear them say they just don't feel that way about me, so I stay quiet.

23

SASHA

Isabelle

You already know this isn't good news

It's a lot. Stay with me

Okay, here goes

Heather Erin and your security talked to me the day after you left. I told them you seemed restless when I was over. Not like a danger to yourself, just distracted. For a while, I kept posting as if you were around. Then there started to be noise that you'd broken up with me and I was in denial. Since I was romantic about us and your accounts are silent

I'm sort of insulted. If we broke up, I'd go all Princess Di liberated and parade around looking fabulous, not pine. You'd be heartbroken and mysterious and write songs about me. That'd be the best look for us if we need to do that, especially if we plan to get back together later. People are too confused to figure out who to be angry at right now, so it would be good publicity. Except you're trying to disappear

It's quiet for now, but Augustus's court case is going well. Or ... not well. It looks like he might get away with it all. Which means the Channel wants you back

Today, Heather Erin brought me into her office along with some of your producers, the twins and LucSee. We had to sign special NDAs on top of our contracts, then she basically interrogated us. I guess they thought LucSee and you might be close from touring together, or that the twins were friends with you too and not just Augustus. I know it was lonely, but I think the helmet saved you. No one knew anything. I stuck to my story. Whenever you're back, don't talk about me before consulting me

Augustus hasn't even asked me about you. I'm sorry. You know how he is

There's been a deliberate "leak" that says you're taking a break from media scrutiny. Frame it as wellness. People are talking rehab, but that's not from the Channel. When people ask me about it, I've been redirecting. Celebrities are people too, that bullshit. I've got to toe the Channel's line from now on. They're already suspicious of me

Heather Erin is looking for you. She's in the how-could-he-do-this-to-me phase of anger. You should come in. You know she gets cruel. This could fuck up your entire life, Alexander. Maybe you could wait until your contract's done at 21? It's not too late. You'll have to show your face, but people might forget it eventually. Someday

If you're not coming back, lie low. Be a whisper for me, ok?

I didn't realize how much I missed you until writing this. Please be safe

24

LILLIAN

Sasha's gone in the morning.

I wake up to daylight clobbering my eyelids through the basement windows. I remember that I'm not wearing pajama pants when I realize that I'm only half under the covers and only half on the air mattress.

I blink my eyes open to see my undignified self and an empty couch. Hopefully Sasha didn't witness me in this state. They left their blanket folded and the pillows laid out nicely in a way that no pillows are ever organized on a basement couch.

Once I'm up, Quinn says he talked to Sasha briefly. Sasha said being home in the morning would help keep their parents happy. As long as I'm only out with Cyprus and Quinn, my mom doesn't care much. I think I'm pretty mellow compared to the absolute metalhead hell-raiser she was when she lived in the UK.

Quinn says Sasha looked a bit wrecked, which goes for me too, and not in a grungy, alluring, TV-show way. The whole crying and not sleeping enough combination has Cyprus giving me quizzical looks while we eat breakfast.

She picks up that I don't want to talk about it, just like she doesn't want to talk about why she can't hang out this afternoon.

My silence is about Sasha, or Emelia. That's all woven together. It turns out Cyprus's is about Emelia too.

Jasper comes by a few minutes later to pick up me and my gear. I'm putting my amp in the trunk when I see a familiar bike round the corner at the far end of the street. I recognize Emelia's white bike helmet and her white shoes that never seem to be dirty.

She quickly changes course to coast down an alley. I can see the corner of her helmet as she's waiting, watching, thinking she's out of sight. Before she hid, I saw her shape too, her way of moving. In twenty or forty years, I could still pick out Emelia walking across the floor of a crowded room. There'd be the same tug in my stomach as when she first sat two seats in front of me in class. When I paid Logan twenty dollars to switch seats with me. He didn't realize how desperate I was to be beside the new girl. He could have wrung me for all I was worth.

Jasper glances in Emelia's direction as he puts my amp in the trunk of our parents' car. "Girl problems?" He gives me a knowing nod. "Same, same." Which usually means altogether too many girls are interested in him for his own good.

I get in the car so my heart's not out in the open for the world to see it straining at its leash, wanting to run for Emelia. To punch her or hold her.

She'd be more likely to let me do the first one.

She'd say it hurts less.

As we back out of the driveway, Jasper says, "Past Emelia so you can flip her off, or around the long way?"

"The long way."

"Coward," he mocks, but lets me choose the music as we back

out of the driveway. The drive home takes one song, which turns into a few while we sit in the car behind our house. I'm sure Jasper can feel me ricocheting around.

Jasper drums on the steering wheel along to the song. "Do you want to talk? Sit in silence? I'll leave you alone if that's the mood."

Cyprus and Quinn will be with Emelia this afternoon. It's painful for the obvious reasons, then painful a second time because how I feel right now must be how Emelia feels all the time. Not in the band, not at the Mercury, not at Falafel 'Til Dawn, not sleeping over, not even meeting Sasha.

It's absolute rubbish that you can be angry at someone and devastated by them and they can be angry at you and devastated by you and you can both be devastated that the other person is devastated. I have words and blows for whoever invented love.

"Why am I like this?" I ask, which would throw most people off.

Jasper responds immediately. "A total dick? I'd say poor genetics, but look at me." Unhelpfully, but immediately.

"I'm either feeling too much and running from it or feeling nothing and doing anything to get feeling back."

"I diagnose you with being in a band," says Jasper, which almost gets a smile out of me. "Who's this noise that's playing now?"

"Etherealish."

"I hate it. It's the worst. What's the album?"

"*Underloved II.*"

He saves it in his phone. "Do you want a smoothie? I was going to make myself one. Mom's home, but she's buried in deadlines. You'll be able to brood in peace."

A smoothie sounds cold, like it could slow my body down or reinvigorate it.

"I want a milkshake. No sneaking in protein powder or spinach."

Jasper shrugs. "I can't guarantee that."

"Or I'll remind Mom you're not allowed to drive unsupervised yet."

"You supervised me."

"On the way there?"

"You asked me to pick you up! You peer-pressured me."

"You *wish* you were my peer."

We stop arguing once we're inside our house. There are some things I don't want even a laid-back mom to weigh in on.

I'm late for school the next day, but I don't notice Sasha's bike in the rack. Quinn says they're not in class, and I don't see them around school. The next day and the next, Sasha's not there. They're not responding to Quinn's texts either.

I don't send any of my own, because I know it's my fault.

I leaned in too hard. With sending such a vulnerable song. With the encounter on the back steps and then fleeing. With grabbing their hand after the concert and touching their hair and trying to kiss them.

They knew I was about to. It must have been obvious. They could be seeing someone already. Maybe those texts were from them. Or maybe there's someone back where Sasha's from who knows all their secrets. Hometown, grew up together, talk every night.

I want to talk with Cyprus or Quinn about it, but every way my heart is pulled and torn pushes on some other way. I'm trying to remember what Cyprus said and not pit my friends against Emelia. I'll lose Cyprus if I do that, at least for a bit. For all the people she knows, she lets very few know her closely, and she holds them dear. I wonder if Sasha could be a person like that for Cyprus and Quinn. A potential close friend I just drove off.

On Wednesday, a frustrating band rehearsal leaves us all in bad moods. Sasha was right. We're three-wheeled without Emelia singing. Cyprus and Quinn are uncomfortable with the new song. I'm calling it "Elevator," and we all know it's a good one, but I think they're imagining Emelia at one of the shows. They're unsure about being part of her hearing that song.

I imagine it too, with alternating vengeance and hope.

In either case, it makes Emelia cry.

By the time I get back from practice, I'm agitated. I've got a lyric stuck in my head about how death is just a blink where your eyes never open. Usually I can do a breathing exercise and expel that sort of thought. Not tonight. Now it's in my body. Like when you consciously focus on your breathing and suddenly the rhythm won't settle, but with my eyes. I'm fixated on the little dark spaces whenever I blink.

Comfort food, cheese toast in the oven, trying to calm my nervous system, pacing around the kitchen. I check it, look in the fridge for no reason, check it again and the edges are getting too brown.

Then I just grab the glass dish with my bare hands.

I don't mean to. I'm not present, and I grab it and the pain hits me and I pull away fast. The dish hits the open oven door and then smashes on the floor.

I've got my burnt fingertips clenched into my fist. I'm just standing there, glass all around me, the oven door still pouring heat out. Not even a swear available.

My mom looks into the kitchen and says, "Don't move," as if I was going somewhere. She comes back with a broom and sweeps a path to my bare feet amidst the glass.

She's got hints of a British accent. We moved back here to her hometown when Jasper and I were little, so I never picked it up. Her edges have worn down, but she still raised me on maxed-out speakers and atheism and a distrust born out of working as an investigative journalist. She gave me the tools and space to know I was bi when I was eleven and tried to take care of her kids by saving her darkest music for when she took the bus alone.

Sometimes Jasper just hits the dial and lets the radio hand him whatever's playing. Like he doesn't care. That's what really scares me.

My mom insists on taking a close look at my hand when she reaches me. The left took the worst of it. "Dear, how'd you manage to do that?"

I don't think I'm anyone's dear right now. That's sort of the problem.

"I was making cheese toast," I say.

"Well, that is a difficult food. Go run this under cold water. It'll be alright."

"Can I take the toast with me?"

"Lillian, it's got glass in it."

"It's all big chunks. I'll pick them out."

She doesn't sound condescending. I don't know how. "Go run it under cold water. I'll make you more."

"We're out of the good bread." I was looking forward to that bread.

"There's more in the freezer."

"I just wasn't thinking. We had a bad rehearsal."

"I could have guessed."

"It was a new dish."

"I know." She sweeps more glass aside so I can leave. "It's alright."

I want to believe her.

Cyprus says my mom makes her feel safe because of her voice. She can have a softness in moments of care that always makes you feel listened to.

There's never softness in my voice, and I don't think it would help me. I don't make anyone feel safe, it turns out, not even myself.

SASHA

Isabelle said Heather Erin's angry, and that's what scares me most. Her viciousness will extend beyond the consequences of violating my contract.

After I left Cyprus's, I went straight back to my apartment. I've barely left since. I've been ordering delivery and going into tailspins. The uncertainty makes it worse. I wonder how the Channel will treat me when they manage to get me back, how they could harm Lillian and Cyprus and Quinn.

If my friends learn about me, I could lose them. But that's not the worst thing that could happen. Celebrity is a process of collateral damage. They could become part of knowingly keeping me from the Channel, complicit in my betrayal, candidates for vengeance.

I'm immobilized and alone for a week, trying to be a whisper. For the first time since I left, I consider admitting this was a mistake. Isabelle might be right. Maybe the best option is to go back to the Channel and see out my contract.

But today one of my plants died.

When I go outside to pour its remnants into the compost, one of my downstairs neighbors is working on part of the backyard collection of haphazard gardening projects.

I try to hide that I'm carrying a pot, but my neighbor is all friendly and makes me show it to him. Which I do with apologies and expressions of confusion at its fate.

He says no worries. He's more than happy to provide another.

"You just overwatered it," he says, touching the soil.

I touch the dirt myself, where it's soft and the mold has taken over.

"If you try too hard to keep them safe, they get smothered," he says. "They didn't evolve to be controlled. They survive great in the weather. It's a bit nonsensical to try to grow them inside at all."

He carries on with practical plant-care tips, but I have trouble listening.

I didn't run away just to hide out again. If I keep my secret from my friends, I keep them in my life and keep them innocent. And I do have influence at the Channel, my own power, maybe enough to protect some people if it comes to that. I won't be managed by fear.

My mind is out in the weather.

26

LILLIAN

It's Monday night and I can't make my body play another note. I've been working on a guitar part since I got home from school, my half-healed fingertips stinging every time I slide across the low strings, making me grit my teeth.

I love to play guitar. More than singing, more than songwriting. The first love is the truest and all of that. I'm preoccupied with sound, chronically distracted in stores by the distant intricacies of guitar parts on speakers overhead. How'd they get that delay? How can I attain the same reverb? I'm mapping out pedals, different dials compensating and combining and generating new sonic problems. I have to go home and try it.

This is why I didn't stop playing tonight. I'm sure of it. I need to get this part sorted because I love music.

It's about love.

It's about love.

I look at my guitar and it feels like a weapon I'm using on myself. Like something I push against that pushes back. I have the urge to grab Butler by its neck and smash it against the floor. To feel it splintering.

Because anything you can destroy surely has no power over you. As long as I can cause ruin, I am owned by no one.

I stop playing.

What am I doing? This doesn't feel like the tortured artist moments I'm sometimes prone to. It recurs, persists.

For a while, I blamed all the turmoil on being queer and raged against myself. But I didn't believe it. It was a false explanation.

Because I love being bi. To wish it away is to negate one of my favorite parts of myself.

To wish away who I am is to let the bastards grind me down.

Of course it'd be easier and safer if I wasn't queer. Obviously. Someone had the gall to decide research was necessary to prove repression and discrimination and all that ugliness is bad for your mental health. I suppose it's nice confirmation that being queer isn't what hurts you. Being in constant fight or flight, unfortunately, rips you apart.

But personally, I'm fortunate. I'm mostly in contexts where I don't have to hide it. I lost a couple people when I came out, but only ones who were pretty shit to begin with.

Whatever makes me want to smash my guitar started before I had a real concept of sexuality. My dad being in and out of the picture doesn't cover it either, like I used to think as a kid. I still have family who care about me and tell me they care about me and tell me they'll care no matter what. They've shown it time and time again, and the friends I've added along the way have too.

Still, I wind up here, throwing myself at something and unable to figure out why.

Lately, I've pinned it on the breakup, but Emelia didn't buffer against all the moments like this. I know she tried. I think I had to believe she could do it. That she could be a wall between the parts of me that burned bright and the parts that burned dangerously.

I don't know how to distinguish between all the fire. I've lost Emelia, and now most of the things I care about most are getting scorched. From the newest, like Sasha, to the oldest, like playing guitar.

Someone's got to step in. I can't.

I knock on Jasper's door. When he opens it, it's laugh or cry, so I pick the easier one and say, "You're right, I have girl problems."

"What?"

He doesn't remember the conversation, plus some soccer video game is open on his monitor. But I've made it this far. "You said you had girl problems too. We should form an alliance."

"Don't tempt me by making it sound epic."

I take a stab at the deep tones defining every bad movie trailer. "In a world torn asunder by high-stakes teen relationships ..."

He tries to resist for a second before taking on a much better version of the dramatic voice. "... one ruggedly handsome protagonist and his ratty sister will form an alliance to solve their problems and find the answer before it's too late."

"Too late" is a major concern of mine.

Jasper sits in his desk chair, spinning one way and then the other. His room is always tidy in a way that makes me feel like I'm something an animal dragged in. The bed is made too tightly to disrupt, so I take the floor and fiddle with the closest thing I can reach, which makes Jasper twitch a little.

"Why are you the protagonist?" I ask. "You have none of the qualities."

"Well when we were kids it was always you," says Jasper, "so now it's my turn."

"What can I say, some of us were born to be heroes."

"But are you ruggedly handsome enough?" He makes a frame with his hands to look at me. "I'm seeing orphan, street urchin, rogue."

I flip him off with both hands.

"What'd you do to your fingers? Was it toast again?"

Seeing them from his perspective, they look worse than they did in my room. I don't want him to look at me like he's worried. Then everyone in the house will.

"So girl problems," I say. "Or romance problems."

"Ooh, is there a *boy*?"

I give Jasper a look.

He spins his chair around again. "There's no drama like queer drama. Who are they?"

"Sasha Weaver. They just moved here and they've hung out with me and Cyprus and Quinn a couple times. They go to our school. They've got really excellent hair and outfits. They're like friendly, but shy. And also honest. And sort of bold?"

"Yeah, yeah, I know who you're talking about. I can see how you'd be into them. Or you can keep waxing poetic about this dream-person if you want."

I cover my face with my hands because I'm blushing. "They're into good music too."

"Oh dear lord."

"But."

"But?"

Talking through it again doesn't solve it. I hoped it magically would. It's an impossible tangle that starts with how I'm not over Emelia.

If Sasha doesn't like me how I like them, I might have scared them off. Cyprus and Quinn care about Emelia too, and they're also becoming friends with Sasha, and I bet they don't want

Sasha to be scared away either. My singleness is not creating a fun time. I'm sure my friends miss how things were before.

And there's the band.

When I finish, Jasper doesn't even pause before saying, "There's an obvious solution."

"Flee the city and change my name?"

"That would work. And I'd get your bedroom. This idea is growing on me."

"What's the *real* obvious solution?"

"Be patient for once. It requires some background."

I'm not sure where he's going with this, but okay.

"I had a summer thing at camp with this girl, and now we talk all the time. As in, *a lot*. She lives far away, I still really like her, but there's nothing to be done. Tragedy, tragedy."

This is the first time I'm hearing about this.

"I also maybe had a moment with Julia."

"Volleyball Julia?"

"Yes, Volleyball Julia. Now let me tell my story. I like Julia."

"Duh."

"As I was saying, I like Julia. Does she like me? I don't know. Good news is, I don't just like her because she's —"

"Incredibly leggy?"

Jasper stops spinning his chair and looks straight at me. "Do you actually want to talk about how sexy Julia is? You want to have that talk with me, your little baby brother?"

There's a memory from two nights ago, masturbating while my brain made frustrating, confusing jumps between fantasizing about Emelia and Sasha. Known desire, fresh desire. Nothing was occupying enough to pull me away from that confusion. Even recalling it while I'm in Jasper's room is utterly distressing.

"Let's stick to relationships," I say quickly.

"Let's." He leans forward and takes the controller I'm fiddling with out of my hand. "When I'm with Julia, I'm happy. I get home, I'm still happy. That doesn't hinge on whether we hook up or not. Also Calvin's into Julia and he's my best friend and he thinks I'm hung up on Camp Girl, which I sort of am."

"There's no drama like straight drama."

"Touché."

"So, what's your play?" I'm looking for another thing to have in my hands, but Jasper's room is so tidy that I'd have to rip something off the wall.

"Don't say 'play.' You're dangerously close to talking about sports and I can't bear to watch you flounder."

"I know about bases and how they reinforce rigid sexual scripts."

"Please stop." Jasper spins his chair the other way like he's resetting. "So I'm going to be friends with Julia and give it time. If I stay friends with her, then great. If something else happens along with that, also great. Genuinely, either one. I'm not, like, waiting to pounce. I'm serious. I'm not going to use her as a rebound."

I believe him, though I'm also wondering how he went and got so mature on me. It's downright unsettling.

"The point is," says Jasper, "if you're friends with Sasha in the end and that's it, will it be a disappointment to you?"

I'd like to answer no with confidence. I settle for the evasive truth. "I'll be most disappointed if I lose a new friend."

Along with disappointment in myself that I'm not tough enough to simply get over Emelia. I'm not as bold as I thought I'd be. I thought I'd have fun, undirected desire to toss around. Instead the only people I want are my ex and someone who's probably not interested in me.

"Now you owe me a game," says Jasper, gesturing to his monitor.

That's Emelia's favorite game. She used to make me play when I was at her house, and I always seemed to lose. I played with her anyway because I loved her. Also because I wanted to win.

Jasper knows all that, but he either forgets or understands that when your life has been woven together with someone else's you can't go avoiding every little thing that reminds you of them. Soon, you're doing nothing and feeling sad about when you used to do nothing together.

I lose 6–1, but I called last goal wins, and that was me. In your face, Jasper.

Upstairs, Butler is leaning in the corner staring back at me, challenging me. Why did you quit? Why not work on that part a little more? Why not play a chord with your guitar facing your amplifier and let the feedback bury everything else? It offers me something to cling to.

I unplug my amp.

I've found a little focus somewhere else, enough to hold on to.

I'm going to text Sasha soon. Say, "Hey, I haven't seen you at school," or hopefully something better. I'll send them a song by a weird artist they might like. I'll slow the hell down and try to understand that slowing down isn't stopping.

It's hard to learn when your two speeds are sprint and impact.

My phone vibrates. And it's Sasha.

It's hard to learn when the world tilts between crashing and acceleration.

It's Sasha and they've skipped messages and they're just calling me here, now, with their voice in my bedroom. I watch my phone until it stops vibrating. I'm going to give this a minute and see what this is. I'm not going to throw myself in.

One missed call — Sasha.

One unread message — not Sasha.

Emelia

We haven't done the thing where we drop off boxes of each other's stuff. I've got loads of your favorite clothes here. I know your outfits must be in fragments without them. You've got a book of mine in your nightstand that I was halfway done reading and I really want to know how it ends. This doesn't mean I'm ready to talk in person yet. This isn't a way to try to make that happen. I do need to keep that boundary for now, even if I don't always want to. Last time was too much for me. But would you maybe be willing to drop off my things sometime? I can send you a list. Or if you gather them and leave them on your front steps, I could pick them up. I'm around tonight if you want to text or chat about it.

That's too much to hold inside me.

I wish I could damage something and feel the release. Throw my phone across the room not caring about the cost.

As if I didn't know about the book. I know the exact paragraph she's on. I keep ripping back and forth about whether she left it behind on purpose. With its ending that's going to make her cry about us. I don't want to give it back.

I know all the things she's left. I don't need a list. Her pajamas and her sweaters that are too soft for me to wear but perfect for my face to press against. Her scrunchies and the earrings she took out when my hair got tangled in them.

I make a call.

I hear music playing in the background when the call connects us. Blue Cremations, an old album from back when they sounded surprisingly folky for a group that some consider a punk band. I should be listening to something like this tonight myself. I know I'm really out of sorts when I forget to turn on music, or worse when I know it will help and I just don't care.

"You called back!"

Sasha's voice isn't brokenhearted, and it doesn't break mine. There's relief and confusion in me, but all incalculably less than the intensity of talking to Emelia. Here, in this new space with Sasha, there's no old hurt to suddenly sink its teeth into me and pull me down.

Sasha seems rushed, lively. They say sorry for not being around. I tell them it's fine, no explanation necessary. They say tonight they're restless and home is too small. They called earlier because they want to bike somewhere and they don't know where to go. Asking me because this is my city. Do I know somewhere?

"I could show you a place?" I offer, then immediately worry that maybe that wasn't what they were asking for at all. "If you want company."

"I'd love nothing more," says Sasha sincerely, so I give them my address, and they say they'll be here in ten minutes. Ten minutes to think of somewhere.

Emelia's message is on read.

I could leave her like that.

I don't want to make Sasha wait, and I want to meet them outside. I don't want them to interact with anyone in my family because then there will be curiosity later, and I don't need people asking me questions. So what I write, I write fast, before putting my phone on do not disturb and trying to ignore how heavy and alive it still feels in my jacket pocket.

Lillian

Good idea

I'm out with Sasha right now but send me a list and I'll see if I can find what you left behind

27

SASHA

Lillian's working on her track stands on the sidewalk in front of her house when I arrive. She stands on her bike pedals — body shifts slightly, holds stiff, shifts, maintains her balance. Her concentration breaks when I pull up next to her and she's forced to put a foot down.

She pretends to glare at me. "I was on my way to a record time."

"Isn't that true every time you start?"

She takes a second to think about it. "One part math, two parts truism. Everything I hate wrapped together. Are you good to ride far?"

I've barely responded yes, I'll go anywhere, when she's off and moving. Riding fast in the almost empty streets, weaving around potholes and the trash that's swept to the curb. She calls back to me, "We can make this light!" and then digs in a little harder. It's less reckless than it is expert. She knows this city, and I trust her to lead the way.

I have to work hard and stay focused to keep up. The Channel-mandated gym sessions and the personal trainers who got

Augustus and I to maintain "ideal" body shapes are gone. I don't miss it, and neither does my body. Those spaces always disconnected me from myself. But right now, I'd definitely take the cardio and strength that came from hours of training, rehearsals and performing every other night.

Lillian constantly glances over her shoulder to make sure I'm keeping up. She makes turn signals for my benefit. She never races through a light if I can't follow her. She's got me. I know it.

The city starts to thin out to industrial buildings and metal roofs. Here, everything's a little more run-down, and there are too many train tracks. We cross a bridge over the railyards. It's a faded area, rusted out and covered in street dust. We push out toward the edge of the city, where the remnants of an ambitious mall project stand partially completed. The buildings look well over a decade old.

Lillian sweeps into an empty parking lot and makes straight for a multi-storey parking garage. She squeezes through the gap between the gate and the wall without getting off her bike. Inside, there's a cool darkness. We climb in spirals up the ramps. Lillian stands and pushes hard on her single-speed while I gear down to survive the climb. She doesn't stop until she reaches the western edge of the open, empty top level.

I pull up beside her, sweaty and breathing hard. With the breeze up here, I'm glad I dressed warm. I was rushed enough when I was leaving that I just picked black jeans and a hoodie. My favorite green hoodie, and let it be noted that it's coordinated to my lipstick, which is coordinated to my eyes, which is a lot of green overall and may be too much.

I catch the thought sooner than I sometimes manage to. Because when people say a gender presentation is too much, they mean it makes them uncomfortable. I remind myself of how Isabelle once told me there's no such thing as style that's inherently too much. It just shows what someone can't cope with.

Lillian gestures to the chest-high concrete barrier around the edge of the parking garage. "Take a seat, if such heights suit you." She hops onto it and swings her legs over the edge, letting them dangle six storeys from the ground.

I lean on the barrier beside her, keeping the concrete between me and the drop.

The light's starting to fail around us. The sun is sinking down, though there aren't enough clouds for a dramatic sunset. We can see out over the failed mall to the edge of the city, where the fields and tree lines begin. I haven't been out there yet, but I've crossed the prairies in Admirer's tour bus.

Augustus said it was a godforsaken lack of topography.

I felt like the world opened up, nothing rising around me. Half the world was sky, not just slivers above you like where I grew up. Even facing the ocean, humanity was pushing against my back in high-rises.

"Do you take all the enbies here or just me?" I ask.

She holds her legs straight out, revealing enough of the hangman tattoo on her leg that I can read it. There's a blank, then lowercase *o*, another blank, and a lowercase *e*. There's a crossed out *a* too, but no parts of the person. "I wanted to show you someplace you couldn't find in a tourist guidebook."

"This city has tourists?"

"And a long and fascinating history which I will now summarize. Hem-hem." Lillian takes on a chipper, informational tone. "After a long period of dubious colonial activity, which you will find conspicuously absent from school textbooks, the railroad arrived. Its construction remains a hallmark example of racist employment practices. The railway marked an increase in capitalist industrialization and a redoubling of most bad things, especially colonization. Then, in short order, airplanes were invented, and the city became irrelevant. Visitors can still enjoy a vibrant arts scene, with great local bands such as Wavelength, as well as tour buildings that are nearly one hundred years old, which means in one hundred more years, they might be considered notable. But you get to see them first!"

I break off a loose concrete fragment from the parking garage. "Is this one of those buildings?"

Lillian keeps up with her tour guide impression for a sentence. "There's no way this cheap structure survives that long." When she goes back to normal, it reminds me how much I like the timbre of her voice, with her singing power hidden just behind it. "Bet you can't hit that fire hydrant."

I throw the piece of concrete as far as I can, but it plummets before the hydrant and shatters in the empty parking lot.

We're quiet for a while, watching the day fade out. It's one of those moments where the last trace of summer stops clinging on, which would normally be melancholy.

To my summer, I say good riddance. It was the fallout of scandal and disaster. I was shifting back and forth between fury at Augustus and some corner of me that wanted to justify his actions so I could believe my brother was good. I spent too many days locked in the beach house wondering if Augustus had cost me everything I'd worked for and if there was something I could have done to stop it all and protect the people who got hurt the most.

Kicking Jasmine's brother in the head when he was down wasn't Augustus defending himself. That's just the violence of someone who's too powerful to believe in restraint. No one says no to Augustus. How could his relationship with Jasmine be anything but wrong?

When I eventually take my helmet off as part of Admirer, and people see who I am, the first words I say in public will have weight. I'm not going to burn them in support of Augustus's crimes. But I can't stand for them to be condemning my brother either. I just can't.

I'm still not sure what those first words will be for. I hope it's my choice.

The silence has turned into a long one, where my thoughts drift away and then return to watching Lillian silhouetted against the dusk. She seems solid and relaxed here. Occasionally, she closes her eyes and her fingers move slightly. I imagine there's a storm of notes inside her head that need to pour out.

I recognize it. It's started happening to me again for the first time in a long time. There are melodies popping into my head that I record on my phone. Often there's no words, just runs of notes and rhythms. I keep thinking of them as being for Admirer, but they're all mine. They may never mean anything to anyone beyond myself, never see the radios and playlists. I could write them by myself without an army of professionals working and reworking every detail.

I can't say they'd be better, just that they'd be mine.

I climb onto the barrier, take a deep breath and let my legs hang over the edge. Now I'm sitting next to Lillian with a long, straight drop below me. My hand grips the concrete too tightly, an inch from hers. She barely seems to be holding on.

"It's better here, right?" she says. "The first time I found this, I couldn't sit on the edge at all."

"You're not afraid of falling anymore?"

She turns to me, and I feel her slightest movement in my

stomach. Because she's so high above the ground, or because she turns toward me. And her hand gets close enough to mine that I swear I can feel the warmth off it and I remember how it felt when she grabbed my hand at the Mercury.

"Of course I'm still afraid of falling. Aren't you?" Lillian seems concerned, and I guess that surprises me. I read her as flippant about death.

"Definitely afraid," I say.

"Good." She's looking right at me, and I turn my face to meet the intensity of her gaze. "I don't want you to fall. I'm just getting to know you."

It's only occurring to me now that possibly she was worried about me when I disappeared for the week. I know Quinn definitely was. His messages stayed upbeat, but the concern snuck in. I just responded to them all tonight. I owe him many apologies for ignoring him.

Lillian didn't say anything, so I thought she probably didn't care. Not in an unkind way. We've only known each other for a couple weeks.

Yet there's a memory of right before I saw Isabelle's texts, when I was showing Lillian a picture. Her face near mine. Then the rest of the night is overrun by lying awake, trying to decide what to do.

There's an alternate next that's missing. A scenario where Isabelle doesn't text me right then, and I want to know that other timeline. A deep wanting, radiating through me, curved after something that might not have been there at all.

"It was weird not seeing you around at school. Have you been okay?" Lillian asks.

"I think I am now," I say. "I just had to lay low for a while."

I'm scared she'll ask me why, and I'll have to lie. I didn't leave my apartment with a lie planned. I like that she's been looking for me, that she's looking at me now. In the half-light, with her eyes focused on me. They're not eyes I want to deceive.

Instead, she asks, "What got you out of it?"

Even if I could tell her the truth, this would be the perfect question.

"I overwatered one of my plants," I say.

"Yeah, that actually makes sense."

I look back out at the darkness past the city. "It's beautiful out here … not like glossy beautiful, but the kind that cuts you open. Does that make any sense?" I say, unsure if I mean the view from this parking garage or the entire world. I believe Lillian will understand.

The edge of my hood is blocking my view of her face, but I think she smiles. "I'm glad you like it. The closer we got, the more I thought I should have taken you somewhere pretty, like a cute park or something."

I get stuck on why she'd want to take me somewhere pretty.

I'm used to people flocking to me, to being an object to project desire onto. The concept of Alexander Ash is something people want. The Channel used Isabelle to ensure that, and vice versa, though what with not showing my face, I needed the boost in desirability more.

This oh-my-god attraction is what I'm used to, and it's very easy to recognize. I also know the use-me-to-advance-their-own-career attraction — a slimier, less innocent industry by-product than fandom. Alexander Ash experienced plenty of that.

I don't think anyone's been attracted to Sasha before.

And I have no idea what to do with it.

I'm not even sure I'm reading it correctly. It seems real. I almost definitely want it to be real. I'm not simply drawn to the concept of someone desiring who I actually am, though that's an ecstatic thought.

It's that it's Lillian.

When I was in Admirer, I used the helmet and being with Isabelle and the sheer relentlessness of my life to deny most attractions. They were hypothetical, distant. Lillian is not hypothetical.

"Have you ever noticed," she asks, "how being on the edge of something high feels the same way as the second before you make a big decision? Like it's the same as when you send a message and you're not sure what's going to happen, or you buy a plane ticket without a plan."

My hood's still blocking my view of her face, so I have the courage to say, "To me it feels almost exactly like the moment you're deciding whether to tell someone you like them."

I only know this feeling from right now, this second. I'm setting myself up and I don't even mean to. I'm being honest and it's happening.

"The moment before you kiss someone for the first time," says Lillian. "Or I guess any sex thing for the first time. Not the warm, we've-been-together-forever feeling, but new and unknown."

I'm definitely blushing. Thank god for this hood.

"I've never kissed anyone."

Wait, what the hell? Why did I say that? It just spills out.

"I've only kissed one person, so you could surpass me with a good game of spin the bottle." Lillian means it like a joke but says it too flatly.

It reminds me of how she sounded on the back steps of school. Right, that. She's just out of a big relationship. Admitting anything right now isn't kind to her. That's what I tell myself. I won't admit anything now because I'm being kind.

Lillian picks a piece of concrete off the edge and lets it slip out of her hand. I follow the piece all the way until it clatters off the pavement.

"If I fell, they'd blame you," I say. "It'd be a murder case."

"As if. Most people don't care if people like us fall, Sasha."

For me, there'd be tribute concerts. That's the imbalance of the world. There'd be headlines for months. It'd put this city on the map. There'd be a shrine built at the base of this parking garage with flowers and posters and helmets. Augustus and Isabelle would do teary-eyed interviews that would mix genuine with performative, because there's no way to stop the show from creeping in when there's a camera in your face.

I'm suddenly aware that I may be in the least safe place I've been in my entire life. That for all its warm corners, the world is a more frightening place without a security team. I say something about how dark it's getting.

Lillian responds by singing the soft chorus of a song about nightfall, the notes drifting into the void in front of her. I take the first lines to learn the melody and grab a quiet harmony when she repeats the last one. It doesn't show any of my full singing ability, just that I can pick it out.

She punches my shoulder, which, given the distance between me and the ground, is terrifying. "Not too shabby, Sasha. Have you considered a career in music?"

Then we both laugh, her at the absurdity and me at the truth.

28

LILLIAN

It's confirmed: Sasha isn't attracted to me.

We're out late together, alone for a long time. We sit watching something resembling a sunset. We're vulnerable and open. Everything is right for them to admit feelings, to say that they only turned away in the basement because they were distracted by the message, or because they haven't kissed anyone before. It would have been easy for them to take my hand or kiss me if that was what they wanted.

Not that I'm keeping track anymore. I'm taking my time and being friends, like Jasper suggested. I can't make another move only to have them let me down gently.

I won't ruin it when we're way out here with no party for either of us to drift away into. I don't want to ride back in silence, only sticking together for safety. This, right here, is already good. This closeness to Sasha is what I want. Part of it, at least.

SASHA

We go back to Lillian's house at a less frantic pace, close together on the empty sidewalks. She talks about her memories of the places we pass. Little things, details, not what you'd tell to make yourself look interesting.

When she asks where I grew up, I find some slivers of reality for her. Some of my stories are off-limits because they're famous, ones I always tell the same way. About Augustus and I putting on musicals together as children and how my dad knew right then that we were destined — he always used that word — *destined* for stardom. I can't tell her any of my touring stories. How Augustus and I were once so behind schedule we took a helicopter to the stadium and had them lower us onstage. Augustus was too shaken up to sing, so I did a solo song. I can't tell her my fake stories about Isabelle and I falling in love, and if they were true, I wouldn't want to.

So I tell her one I've never told before, that I couldn't tell anyone else.

I tell Lillian about meeting Lark.

When I was eight, there was a fair set up on the beach near where I grew up. This was before we signed with the Channel, before me, my dad and Augustus moved down the coast to be closer to their studios. It was before my dad's brain tumor took him away. Unlike Augustus, I've been outspoken about the cancer. I've started a foundation. So I leave these things out of what I tell Lillian.

I wanted to ride the Ferris wheel, but Augustus claimed Ferris wheels were boring. That disdain was the stage he was at — one he never grew out of. Augustus went to find a roller coaster so that later he could pretend it hadn't scared him.

I called Augustus my older sister when we talked at Falafel 'Til Dawn, but I don't remember what name I gave him, so I simply stick with "my older sister." The fragility of these deceptions frightens me, but I don't know what else to do.

Dad got a phone call that was relevant to his efforts to make me and Augustus famous, so he sent me alone. It was crowded and anyone who wanted to ride alone got paired off, and I wound up with someone who made me do a continuous double take.

Gender performance seems to inundate beaches. It's narrowing in the most literal sense, all bodies cut down to a few select pinnacles of desirability. It drives away people who don't slot in smoothly. It perpetuates itself with polished skin and whatever fashion the clothing industry handed down to beachgoers that summer.

This person, Lark, didn't fit into most of the performances. And those were the systems all around me, so Lark didn't make sense to me. There were cis gay characters in movies and on TV, and there were pride parades around the city. My dad would complain about them blocking traffic and say, "Now there's an example of celebration without accomplishment." Yet he liked celebrating birthdays just fine.

These are the things I tell Lillian, that no interviewer or show host has ever gotten out of me.

Lark was friendly and pointed out landmarks down the coast while I was confused about their face and their shoulders and their makeup and how the hair on their sunburnt, white chest spilled out over their blue bikini top. I couldn't speak at all as my mind tried to figure this human out. I was confused by the stories I'd been told about how there's types of humans.

Halfway through, I interrupted them midsentence and said, "What sort of person are you?"

"My name's Lark. I'm the sort of person who loves how puppies always step higher than they need to. Who still listens to loud music when my parents fight even though I'm twenty-four and I'm only home for the summer. I'm the sort of person who spends hours playing with the magnet words on fridges."

"Are you a boy or a girl?"

"No," Lark said matter-of-factly, not reprimanding. I'd asked a multiple-choice question and the answer wasn't A or B, it was False.

"I'm genderqueer," they said.

Clearly, I looked baffled, because they explained.

"That means I'm not a girl or a boy. Or at least that's what it means to me. Those feel like very small boxes I don't fit in. It's like if someone said you're either a square or a circle, but you're a triangle. But they don't believe in triangles. So they say that's just a funny version of a square. That's not true, is it? Triangles are a different thing entirely. So are hexagons, or ovals. You might pretend to have four sides. People will probably make you try to have four sides, but you're still a triangle that's being squeezed and torn up and pushed around."

That made sense to me, though I was iffy on what a hexagon was.

Lark waved at a friend far below us, smiling. "Today, I'm winning. I've got my own number of sides. I've got people on my side. What sort of person are you?"

Kids mostly know what sort of answers they're expected to give. It's part of surviving. I remember thinking they were asking the same thing I did, boy or girl, but then suddenly I could tell I didn't have to say I was a boy. This was the first time I had been given that permission. So I didn't say it.

"I like to sing," I said.

"That's one of my favorite sorts of people."

Lillian and I pull up at a crosswalk and she tries to track stand while she punches the button. The yellow lights start flashing, though there are no cars out for them to stop.

"Did you already know then?" she asks as we cross.

"Not at all. It was just one of those memories that stayed clear in my mind that I kept replaying, and I didn't think much of it. I assumed I remembered some things better for no particular reason. Seven or eight years later, I slowly figured out why it had stayed with me."

When I started to sort it out, I dedicated a song to Lark that I usually dedicated to Isabelle. Apparently, it caused a bit of a murmuring among the most committed cohorts of Admirer fans. Who was this Lark? Was I cheating on Isabelle? But Lillian doesn't even listen to Admirer, so there's no way she'd know an obscure fan theory based on one incident.

We're getting close to Lillian's house now, riding slower and slower through the night.

She's holding one hand out to coast along like it's out the window of a car. "It's like when you're younger and you're obsessed with being friends with someone and only later you realize you had a crush on them."

"Yes! Except not a crush in this case. At least I don't think so. If I met them now, I probably would. But Lark gave me words for a feeling. And they were the first person I ever met who didn't automatically assume I was male."

There are still lights on in Lillian's house. I can just see her mom through the plants that are either hanging in baskets or growing upward to cover most of the glass. She's curled up on the couch watching TV in the living room.

"That was one of the best stories I've ever heard," says Lillian. She hesitates, like she's about to invite me in, then just says, "Goodnight, ride safe."

That's best. Her mom's around, and I want to avoid personal questions. Or if I can't avoid them, I at least need time to prepare.

I thank Lillian for the night, for showing me somewhere remarkable I never would have found on my own.

She's already opened the porch door, carrying her bike expertly up the steps, when she turns back to me. "I'm going to see you at school tomorrow, right? You're not going to vanish again?"

30

LILLIAN

Emelia hasn't responded.

That could mean a thousand different things. Terrible or lovely or some without much meaning at all.

I gather up all her things anyway, except for the book, which I leave in my nightstand. If she asks, I'll say I couldn't find it.

I just don't want her to believe in sad endings.

SASHA

I sit on the edge of my bed, turning over a small piece of concrete I took from the parking garage just before we left.

Lillian asked if I was going to vanish again.

I said, "Definitely not. I promise."

Every promise is just a hope, though.

32

LILLIAN

I love having Sasha back at school this week. Each time I see them, I feel a spark that makes me want to rush across the room to talk to them, to chase them down a hallway. I don't, of course.

Quinn's better at friendship than I am, and he gets Sasha to start sitting with us. They disrupt some of the sad patterns we were falling into, infuse some brightness into our worn-out group.

Today, the four of us are laughing and carving a cityscape into one of the picnic tables.

"This is you," says Sasha, carving a tiny stick figure in a window and giving them a straight line for the mouth.

"What are all those lines through my head?" I ask.

"Piercings," says Sasha.

"More importantly," says Quinn, taking a break from his argument with Cyprus about "visually balancing" the skyline, "how did you so accurately capture the hate that burns within her, consuming her, driving her to ever angstier depths?"

"Minimalism?" suggests Cyprus. "Make it a little more obvious and I'll post it."

Sasha adds what I think is supposed to be a tiny skull to my T-shirt.

That's when I see Emelia watching us. Just half an entirely disruptive second where our eyes meet before she's out of sight.

The shortness of the glance lurches inside me.

When Emelia and I first started dating, we'd lie around and look at each other's faces, smiling. For minutes and minutes, not saying anything, just soaking it in, memorizing.

I'd like her at the table with us. She could fit in. It's strange, but I have a moment where I want her to meet Sasha. She said she couldn't see me in person, wants her things back, isn't ready to talk about it yet. I don't have a clue where to rest my belief. Knowing Emelia, if she were here, it would only hurt anyway. Awkward sad pleasantries and the devastation of her being close but feeling distant.

My favorite people belong together, and lately that's been a whole mess. A compounding, snowballing, god-awful mess. The original band hasn't all been in the same place at the same time since the middle of August.

It was the day before Emelia and I broke up. Me and Quinn were having our annual-and-often-more-than-annual day of taking scissors to old clothes and seeing if we could make something cool. We met Emelia and Cyprus at a movie theater to go see some big-budget affair about a famous band. We sat in the back row and ate popcorn and critiqued the musical inaccuracies and bad lip-syncing.

Why is everyone disregarding the rhythm of the song? This is supposed to represent the *first time* he played guitar? He just got really motivated and wrote the whole album in one night, did he? And where are all the cables? It was the seventies in the film, yet not a cable in sight. Or worse, cables clearly plugged into nothing at all.

I could rage on, but what matters is that I rested my head on Emelia's shoulder.

Did she already know we were done? Did she just let me go along loving her anyway? Sometimes people who are only able to be kind wind up being cruel by accident.

Cyprus claims she has to get to class early, which is something I've never seen her do. I'm proven right when I find her sitting on the hood of her station wagon fifteen minutes later. She seems too tired for the blue thigh-high boots she's wearing. I think it's about Emelia, though I'm not sure she'll want to talk about it.

I sit next to her, both of us stalling on going inside. She puts her arm around my waist and pulls me close.

She seems to need this, and so do I. I'm used to having lots of warm physical contact, and lately there's been a deficit. And while Jasper's surprisingly decent for advice-giving, our relationship isn't what you'd call touchy-feely. Sasha or I keep passing up on all the opportunities and Quinn's never been inclined to sit still for long enough to settle into comforting contact. Though as his body becomes more his own, he keeps getting happier to exist physically in the world.

When I first told people I was bi, I had some friends who

immediately thought I liked them that way. They stopped being comfortable around me and started constantly thinking I was flirting with them. They read everything I did toward everyone like that, just applying their ludicrous systems around boys to my interactions with every person on earth.

I mean for fuck's sake. We were all eleven years old. Also, they seriously overestimated their own allure.

Cyprus was never like that, even though people lumped her into the non-desirable social pool of Lillian Finley. She told me that if I liked her, she'd be able to tell long before I did. She told me I wasn't subtle with my heart, and as soon as Emelia came along, all of that proved incredibly true. Cyprus let me keep saying, "I love you" to her and knew it was friendship. All along.

I know that standing by your queer friends isn't something that should be heroic so much as a base expectation, but when we were in grade six, it felt pretty damn heroic.

Cyprus is one of mine, and I'd take a bullet for mine.

"You just had to invite Sasha to the showcase," I say eventually. "Any other show, it'd be fun to have them there again, but the *showcase*?"

"We'll sound better in two weeks."

Her encouragement doesn't have much conviction behind it. Industry showcases are uninspiring at best. An opportunity for an opportunity for an opportunity.

And it's another thing I'd planned on having Emelia with me for. I thought the two of us singing together could make at least some sort of impression, even though we aren't the most marketable band.

"I just want to have enough fans to fill somewhere tiny," I say. "People who care enough to sing along."

"You write the songs, and Quinn and I will cover merch and

promotion. We'll get there." With her close to me, I believe it a little more than before.

"I guess you went after Emelia," I say.

Cyprus nods. "It seemed right." She pauses, considering. "Being in the middle has me all strung-out feeling."

I start saying, "Does Emelia ..." then stop. I've been trying not to contribute to Cyprus being pulled in all directions by my breakup.

"Ask me anything," says Cyprus. "I'm very capable of telling you that I won't answer something."

Deep breath. "Does Emelia talk to you about me?"

"Yes, she does," says Cyprus. "Her other friends don't really know you as well as I do."

"They're probably good for when she needs to hate on me, though."

"Definitely."

"Does she hate me?"

Cyprus holds me a little tighter. "There's a big gap between being angry and shattered by someone and hating them. I mean, it's not like you hate her."

She's so sure about it that I can't even argue with her. I want to push back and say she's wrong, to try to convince myself that I do hate Emelia.

"It'd be easier if I did," I say.

"But the songs wouldn't be as good."

"True."

"We should go in," says Cyprus, unmoving.

"Yep."

"Got more questions?"

"Yep."

"Want to ask them now in the name of, you know, graduating?

I refuse to spend another year in this place."

"Do you want Emelia and I to get back together?"

Cyprus hops down from the hood of the car, her boots crunching on the leaves in the parking lot. "We should get to class," she says.

33

SASHA

It's a Tuesday near the beginning of October. And it's six in the evening, which is too early for live music to really be kicking off unless you're at a festival.

Yet here I am, sitting in the sparsely populated main hall of the East Side Performing Arts Center, waiting for Wavelength to come onstage and play their three songs to the bottom-tier industry people who attend events like this.

The houselights are on with no intention of turning them down. It's a showcase for young musicians, so the people who are supposed to be listening seem even more slimy and/or condescending than usual.

I haven't been at this level of the pyramid for a long, long time, and even when I was, it was in a place where entertainment was big money. Especially after Augustus and I got picked up by the Channel as kids, the grimness had a veneer over it.

But there were still auditions and sweaty desperation and trying too hard and dreams of fame hanging on incalculably thin odds. There was still passion worn down to the bone and various types of predatory behavior from those who held the keys.

Isabelle dealt with a lot more of that than me. Augustus did too, though not to nearly the same extent. From some of the things he's mentioned offhand as if they're light stories, he sheltered me from some powerful creeps when we were young.

I wanted to thank him or ask him more. Someone should have asked him if he was okay, but those weren't the sort of words we traded. Heather Erin took us on and transferred us from acting to music only. From then on, it was constant coaching and rehearsals, then eventually recording and tours.

When we broke out, my dad helped restructure the contract to make us Admirer, to make us aim ever higher. I was just thirteen. My dad knew about the tumor then — an inoperable, obscured hourglass — though he hadn't told us yet. That contract was his last supervising act for Augustus and I. The business he had to finish. Things went downhill really quickly for him after that. Metastasized, endless treatments, pressure on his brain. A distant, foggy version of himself.

All the while, Admirer's star rose.

Toward the end, he only remembered Augustus. If I visited him by myself, which was most of the time, I'd say I was Augustus, because I wanted him to know one of his kids was still there for him, not some stranger he forgot ever naming Alexander.

Admirer fans like Cyprus or even Quinn have heard parts of this story. Here I've told them my parents are still alive. It'd be easier to maintain that they're dead, but when we were back at Falafel 'Til Dawn again a couple days ago, someone asked me about my parents and I answered without thinking.

While the first bands cross the stage, nervous and dressed to be whatever they imagine is most appealing, I go through the lies in my head, trying to keep them organized. It's driven me to keep my circles small. Already, what I've told Quinn, Cyprus and Lillian over the weeks since I met them clashes with what I've told my downstairs neighbors and what I've told the school.

Example: the school thinks I have a rich family who basically bribed them to get me in at the last minute and that I live with my aunt, the family on the main floor thinks I'm a college student, and my friends think my parents own the entire house. I guess they rent some of it to the people who actually rent to me. I haven't figured that out yet.

My friends also think my parents are overworked, exhausted, jet-lagged professionals who don't like it if I have anyone over. My older sister (who I'm still not totally sure what I've named) goes to college back on the coast. So they're all pretty absent, though I say they've found their way to accepting or affirming my identity.

If I'd said otherwise, my friends would try to take care of me, and I don't want them to support me based on lies.

At the Performing Arts Center, a man who I resent for bringing too much false enthusiasm to the showcase, steps up to a microphone and says, "That was Angelica Richmond. Give her another round of applause!" Only a couple people do. "Next up, we have Wavelength."

He proceeds to do that horrible thing where he reads the bio out loud as if it's a casual introduction when it was clearly not written to be read out loud. I can see Lillian cringing as she plugs in and whispers a few final things to Cyprus and Quinn.

As I try to ignore the emcee, I have an awful moment of realizing how everyone would pander to me if they knew who I was, or who I used to be. How all that desperation would be heaped on me for a chance to get ahead. I don't have a helmet anymore, or a security team. I'm only invisible by allowing myself to be seen.

I'm afraid of being viewed as nothing more than a ladder. I'm afraid of the mob and all the hope they tie to me. I'm afraid my friends would be among them. Dear god. I don't think my heart would ever go out into the world again.

So I can't let my friends find out until I'm gone. The big secret, that I'm half of Admirer and I'm on the run, can't reach them. That's the end. They'd never look the same at me again, because celebrities aren't people.

Cyprus hits record to start filming, Lillian nods at Quinn, he counts them in — and from the moment Lillian plays the opening riff, I know something's wrong. They're too good to be off the rails, but they get rattled at the start of the first song and they can't seem to shake it. Leading with a difficult song was a gamble that isn't paying off.

I believe on another day they'd recover and bury the mistake in the confidence of the rest of their songs. Not today. I can see them all trapped in their heads. I think I know why.

34

LILLIAN

I hope no one knows why I'm so distracted tonight. Cyprus might, but if she does, she's kind enough not to mention it. I'd die of embarrassment even more than I did when the emcee read our bio or when I made the mistake that messed up our first song.

I avoid eye contact with Sasha. At least they don't have a clue. Of all the ways I want them to feel toward me, pitying is not one of them. Which they would, if they knew about yesterday.

SASHA

For Cyprus, she's doing too many things at once. The keyboard and bass and samples and occasional backup vocals. She's the one who screws up initially.

Before the showcase, she was noting who the people in the room were. Such and such knows so and so, they produced this person, this person manages this band. All that must be in the success-driven parts of her mind too. She's got two phones set up taking A- and B-roll. I'm taking video for her too, though eventually I stop. We both know she's not going to be using any of it.

For Quinn, it probably started at school today. He gets a lot of shit from a few people at school. Not most, but a few. I can't imagine my presence helps, since I'm visually a bit less low-key. This afternoon, some guy I won't honor with a name was harassing him.

Quinn takes the clown approach to shrugging things off, while I take the time-honored tuning-out strategy. I've got practice ignoring what people are yelling at me. I pretend I'm onstage and I'm focused on hitting the high notes, or I'm being moved through a crowd and I'm about to enter the insulated silence of a limo.

I pretend I'm wearing my helmet.

This guy used a slur for Quinn that I won't repeat. Quinn made a quip, but my ability to tune it out broke. I stood up so fast I knocked a chair over. People were calling for a scene, and for that second, I forgot that I needed to stay out of trouble. I was scared to be who I am in the world.

I grew up with Augustus — someone whose fear blended angry and could leap straight to eruption. Responsible for dents in walls and wrecked gear. I looked up to him for a long time and learned to see the ways he acted as toughness. Like the rest of it, I'm trying to shed that.

I unclenched my fists. I'm not that kind of fighter. Augustus was enough fighter for two people. My plan didn't go past getting between this guy and my friend. Then a teacher was there. Things defused. She told me and Quinn to settle down, not the person who started it.

Quinn prefers to sit behind a drum kit. He's most comfortable with people only noticing him when he's making them laugh and then letting the attention slide away. He didn't need me to leap to his defense. With all eyes on us, I could see his claustrophobia.

We went for a walk. The air was crisp in a way it never is where I'm from.

Quinn kept checking if I was okay rather than letting me check on him, and I didn't press him for his feelings. He says he's dealt with this for his whole life, starting long before he came out. I know it's true.

Lillian uses the term *intersectionality*. For example, being trans and gay and having brown skin. Quinn experiences triggers and dangers that never reach Lillian or me.

Quinn didn't use that word. He said sometimes people hate you from four different angles. Terminology is more Lillian's domain.

In the end, one result is that Quinn's head isn't in the game at the showcase. He's a little shaky and has no panache this evening. It'll be back, just not right now.

For Lillian, she hates losing at anything, even pool and racing games, but I don't think that's all of it. I heard the band talk about the showcase, and she insisted on doing the hardest song first. At the end of the set, I see Cyprus and Quinn trying to apologize to her. Lillian gestures that the blame is on her. I'm sure the others are quick to say she didn't let the band down. I imagine, like Cyprus, the lost opportunity will hurt Lillian, but not as much as the fact that Wavelength didn't make good music. And not as much as believing she didn't take care of her friends.

Lillian missed the incident at school, which is probably for the best, because when she heard about it, she made a big pitch for firebombing the guy's car. At least slashing his tires. Every now and again she'd mention another idea without context.

"Sugar in his gas tank?"

"No, Lillian."

"What happens if we plug the exhaust?"

None of us knew anything about cars, even Cyprus and I, who own them (though mine is still at the beach house, so I don't mention it). We agreed that retaliation would probably make him lash out at someone else. Which is to say Quinn, Cyprus and I agreed, and Lillian begrudgingly promised not to crawl under his car and start drilling holes in things.

Lillian's brother, Jasper, who's on the basketball team with the asshole, has vowed to never play a good pass to him again.

Lillian mimed strangling me when I suggested that her and her brother sounded kind of similar. But she looked pleased to have rubbed off on him.

I think there are other things too, lurking outside the periphery of what Lillian likes to bring up. Sometimes she's panicked, though from what I know of her, she seemed more preoccupied than anything else during the set.

Emelia's absence would be enough to account for the whole state of the performance. It's a huge hole musically — the drive of an actual bass player and a layer of vocal sound that I can imagine filling out their sound, lifting all the emotions of their songs. But there's also a gap whenever someone mentions her name. Nobody seems to quite know what to say.

And this place has a growing fatigue about it. From the third act on, you can see musicians realize they're not good enough or right enough or being listened to carefully enough. And the industry people know, once again, they're not discovering anyone. They know the business doesn't have the same potential it once did, and nobody's getting a big record deal.

No one's in the mood to stick around for the other performers, so I meet Wavelength out back to help load the gear. It's that awkward time of day where evening and energy are too spent to do anything else, but it's not late. Like stepping out of a movie theater too early.

We haven't even finished loading up the station wagon when Lillian announces that there's no practice tomorrow.

Quinn leans against Cyprus's car wearily. "Yeah, I was going to suggest that."

"Did your band ever play like that?" Cyprus asks me.

Yes, we did. I wish I could tell her, because it'd make her feel better. She's a fan, so she probably already knows about it.

Admirer, in Madrid, in front of sixty thousand people. Normally, if Augustus or I messed up (and it was very rare), the other one could smooth things over.

Our adoring audience would laugh away a lot, let us restart a song, sing part of a song if one of us forgot a line. Even if we were playing passionlessly, we put on a good show. Fans deserve that regardless of how you feel any given night, and if you stop believing that, you should quit the business.

That night, no one was picking up the pieces.

There were mistakes and technical glitches and a weather delay. We couldn't get in sync, culminating in Augustus transitioning to the wrong song at a crucial moment. I decided to follow along instead of catching it, but Augustus realized this was a bad moment to be winging it and stopped. He tried to make it a joke, something for the audience to feel close to us about, while I was still going for the song.

Then all the pyrotechnics went off at entirely the wrong time, no big musical moment. Every time we set those off, it cost an obscene, disgusting amount of money, and that night the sequence started as the song fizzled out.

I turned to watch the display with the audience, hoping to make a moment out of it. Augustus left the stage.

Later, he claimed there'd been a missed cue and he only left the stage because he thought we were right before an encore. LucSee, who opened for us on that tour, told me he flipped a table, put his foot through an amp, and asked her if she wanted to get out of there. Then he said what was the point of her being such a slut and stormed off when she said she didn't want to go anywhere with him. She said he apologized later, as if that fixed it.

"We had some pretty rough shows," I say to my friends. "Like how it was tonight, just nothing settling right and nobody in the right space to fix it. Also, I once fell into the drum kit and got all tangled up."

"Please say there's video," says Cyprus. "Like Alexander Ash that one time on the All My Love tour. Have you seen that?"

That was the exact time.

I say, "Everyone compared it to Admirer when I did it."

The strongest lies are the ones you play closest to your chest.

"I should hope it's been censored," says Quinn. "Potential damage to drums isn't something to laugh about."

Lillian slides her guitar case into the trunk and slams it shut. "What about potential damage to Sasha?"

"They're still standing here," says Quinn. "The drums, though, who knows?"

"The drums survived," I say. "The video, scrubbed from all platforms. All our recordings too. My guitarist wanted to become an actor, so she had anything potentially embarrassing about her taken down."

"But you kept a secret backup of everything and we can watch it?" asks Cyprus hopefully.

"I did not."

This pattern of digging a hole for myself and clawing my way back out is unsustainable.

Cyprus sighs. "That was the last hope of rescuing tonight. I've got a family thing, and I think I've stalled as long as I reasonably can."

Another band leaves early, looking defeated. By the time it's done, there will hardly be anybody left. At least Wavelength played close to the start.

In the car, I check if Quinn wants to do anything tonight. He says a bit of space would be good. That he might watch a movie with his dad, which seems like a safe space for him to recharge for tomorrow.

"I'd watch a movie too if you want to come over, Sasha," says Lillian from the front seat. She'd claimed shotgun with conviction. Even in a low moment, she takes control of the music, rewinding the cassette so we start from the beginning of the B-side.

When we drop Quinn off, he leans back through the window and says to me, "You should play us some of your songs sometime. I'd say we aren't judgmental, but Lillian …"

Lillian twists in the front seat. "Okay, have you *heard* yourself complain about drummers in music videos?"

Quinn's already halfway up the front walk, mouthing "I can't hear what you're saying" at Lillian.

36

LILLIAN

Best-case scenario, maybe Sasha thinks I blew the showcase because I was obsessing about how to enact some form of justice, or at least revenge, on that human dumpster fire that harassed Quinn and them earlier. Though it isn't my place to be the angry one.

But that's not the main thing that threw me off. Fucking yesterday did.

I know, at the very least, that Cyprus and Quinn want Emelia and I to be friends again. Or just make up already and get back together. They're both too kind to put pressure on me or Emelia. I split into fluctuating thirds on this. I draw pros and cons lists of identical lengths.

I want her back, I just want to be friends, I want nothing to do with her.

It changes minute to minute. Sometimes having Sasha around makes it better, sometimes worse.

That whole confusion is coming up again as Sasha and I slip into my house through the back door. To watch a movie. Movies are long. Physical contact has a way of gradually building. I'm very drawn to Sasha. They're not to me.

Stay friends, don't screw it up. You've got this.

In my head, it sounds sarcastic. Pep talks aren't my strongest suit.

It's all frustrating and confusing and Emelia never did send me a list. Which is sort of what started everything yesterday. In a particularly weak moment, I slipped a note into Emelia's locker. Written impulsively, yet in my prettiest handwriting rather than my usual scrawl because Emelia likes pretty things.

Pathetic, my brain said to me as soon as I did it. Be tough, move on, aloof is sexy, aloof is powerful.

Not that I could get the note back.

Dear Emelia,

Meet me after school today at the birch trees? I'm ready to talk now.

Lil

It was the "dear" that really haunted me. I shouldn't have written that. It felt too formal and yet too warm. And the nickname. No one else calls me Lil. Emelia started doing it early on and I hated it and I told her so and she said, "If you want the name back, you'll have to steal it from my mouth."

So I loved the nickname from her and only her, along with countless other words.

I almost didn't go to the trees. Quinn had rambled on about how he's a gelati connoisseur, so him and Sasha were leaving to get gelati from this adorable place with a red-and-white tile floor, but I stayed.

By the birch trees, the wind was cold and blunt. I could have worn a warmer jacket, but I wanted to look a certain way. Tough, moving on, aloof. Aloof doesn't dress warm, and I know this is basically toxic masculinity and emotional repression. Still, maybe Emelia would think I looked attractive.

I don't know. I never saw her.

I'd been there for longer than I should have waited, bolstering my continually thinning hope by attaching some love story to it. Using some of my need to make it seem possible, to convince myself that if I walked away to see if her bike was already gone, that would be the precise moment she showed up.

My phone vibrated and most of me sank. Slow to check it. I told myself it was probably Cyprus or Quinn. Maybe I'd forgotten something, or I was supposed to be somewhere else.

I'm only punctual if I'm waiting beside a tree for a girl I adore who almost definitely isn't showing up.

Emelia

Please please don't do that again

It wasn't cute

I am not charmed

There was a minute where I could see that she was writing, but I stayed there. I'd already waited so long. What was a little more?

Emelia

I know you remember asking me out for the first time by leaving a note in my locker. Don't pretend you forgot, because that would be worse. All you've done today is make me cry. I told you I'm not ready to talk in person yet. Just because you suddenly are doesn't cancel out how I feel, Lillian. I've dropped your things off at your house. Please leave my stuff on my back deck. I'll send you a list

At least I didn't punch the tree, because I'm not a shitty person who hates trees.

At least I didn't tell anyone.

There's nothing as vulnerable as showing people your foolish hopes. It's really best to keep them to yourself.

She's right that I remember the note from three years ago. She used to have it pinned up alongside concert tickets and Polaroids.

Emelia + Lillian + a quirky coffee shop tomorrow?

We already talked in class, since I negotiated, aka paid, for a seat beside her. It wasn't exactly asking her out, but I hoped it was.

That's why you hope. Sometimes you get years with a beautiful person. Sometimes you hope and people say yes.

I put my phone away when we got to the showcase. The hundred times I read Emelia's messages yesterday were enough to have them echoing around. I tried to focus when we went onstage, home in. Then I gave a tiny miscue that made Cyprus screw up more noticeably, and there was this thought that I couldn't get rid of.

I wondered if Emelia told Cyprus about the note yesterday. It'd be fair if she did. It's not Emelia's role to keep my secrets now. Cyprus could be sad at me too. Or disappointed. Like how she's disappointed we're blowing this showcase, I thought, how I'm blowing it.

I went adrift. No one onstage pulled me back to shore.

Somewhere on the drive away from the showcase, I started feeling a little better. Not somewhere — exactly when I asked Sasha if they wanted to come over to watch a movie and they said yes. Not everything is the band or Emelia. There's this too, this uncertain thing, and I'm excited for it, however it may be.

Now we're inside my house. Sasha's curious, going through a little too slowly and looking around as we head through the kitchen and up the stairs. I'm deeply wishing I lived alone and that there was no possibility of running into anyone in my family. I texted my mom to say the showcase was not great, so she'll know I don't want to talk about it, but I didn't mention Sasha was coming over.

Luckily, it seems like no one's around. But at my bedroom door, I realize there's an entire box of Emelia's things on my bed. I was going to do like she said and drop them off tonight, be respectful. But now Sasha's here. I'll do it another time.

She returned my stuff in a backpack that I left there. It's still got dried grass stuck to it from the festival we were at. I started emptying it before I left for the showcase, and it's spilled out all over my bed.

"Can I just ... put away a couple things?" I say.

I managed to make that sound like I've left sex toys lying all over my room. Should probably check that they're all stowed away in their very inconspicuous and boring-looking shoebox under my bed, though.

"Of course," says Sasha. "We can watch somewhere else if you'd rather."

"I would *not* rather. My mom and brother manage to be everywhere else all the time, so, anyway, one second."

I take my gear into my room, which is respectably tidy. Representatively untidy. I'm not going to go way out there and pretend to be someone like Jasper who makes his bed *every day.* I put the box of Emelia's things in my closet, push everything back into my backpack, put it on top of the box, and close the closet.

I open the door to let Sasha in. "Welcome to my humble abode."

37

SASHA

On the main floor, Lillian's house is the opposite of Cyprus's parents' place. Semi-deliberate choices without the need to pretend that no one lives there and it's being prepared for an open house. It's like a grown-up college dorm, where there are posters for bands most parents do not endorse, and these posters are nicely framed.

There's a clutter of memory all about the main floor, like every random object might be explained with a long story. The fridge is fully covered in pictures, every inch of it. I could stand there and see Lillian's life stretch back.

Furniture somewhere between vintage and old, with an emphasis on comfort. The coffee table (and several other surfaces) are spilling over with books and magazines and none of them seem like prototypical coffee-table reading material — either very academic or very activist looking, or both.

I feel comfortable here the same way I feel at Initialism. Like I'm not a disruption. I've dropped in at Initialism a couple times in the past few weeks just to feel like I unquestionably belong. Just to exist and to listen and to drink something sugary while I learn how to let my body dance without performing for anyone.

When Lillian lets me into her room, it provides stiff competition for the title of my new favorite place.

It's a lot like the rest of the house, but more on the music. It would be a big room if the ceilings didn't slant every which way, making half of it impossible to stand in. Where the walls aren't covered in signed T-shirts and pictures that Cyprus took and drawings that Quinn made, there's sound baffling. With all the cables and her gear from the showcase, there isn't much of Lillian's floor available to step on. There's a desk covered in recording equipment, computer in the middle, speakers on either side. They seem to be hooked up to devices to play everything from vinyl to CDs to ... 8-tracks? There are dried flowers hanging over it, multiple bouquets upside-down and dried out.

I sit beside an acoustic guitar on a low, striped couch. I used to play a fair bit, every show on the wave-your-phones songs. I pick this one up — old strings, worn wood, capo on the headstock — and strum a few chords.

"I didn't know you played," says Lillian. She unplugs five different cables from her laptop so she can bring it to the couch.

"Not like you," I say. "I'm more in the hum-and-strum variety of guitar playing. Three chords and the truth." I realize I'm unconsciously playing an Admirer hit and switch to something else before Lillian notices.

She's got a sea of movies open on her screen. "What do you want?"

"High school, dark comedy maybe. *Juno* or something old and deeply defined by an era that isn't the one we're in."

"Please, *Juno* is for the weak." She definitely loves it. "It's got to be eighties, it's got to be *Heathers*," she continues, pulling it up on her screen.

All I really know is that I want to wear what Winona Ryder is wearing, and that's enough to have me convinced.

Lillian slides closer to me, behind the neck of the guitar. As close as you can sit without it being notable.

Though I do note it, ringing out in me.

"You play the right hand and I'll do the fancy chords," she says. "What should we play?"

I name a Monochrome Stoplight song, one where I've got the fingerstyle sorted but my chord changes are slow.

"The acoustic EP version?" she asks.

"Obviously."

"Is it sacrilege to say it's better than the original since it's basically Liv James playing by herself?"

"If it is, it's my kind of sacrilege."

Our attempt at the song is out of sync, playful, broken by laughter. It's a mess, but we're not trying to be anything else. I should look at my right hand and Lillian's left hand, but I mostly watch her face. I sing with her, just the simple backup parts and a little high falsetto above her on the chorus.

When we hit the end, she's grinning at me. "I forget that most music isn't the scramble of that showcase stuff. This is music too. Now, have you considered guitar lessons?"

"Come on, I did good."

Her look says, *as if.* "You showed potential."

I tell myself that some people just have a generally flirty demeanor. Not Lillian, though. She's more for throwing dirty looks at strangers and looking angry until she's talking to someone she likes. Like the way she's talking to me.

She jumps up so quickly she almost hits her head on the slanted ceiling. "Popcorn! A movie needs popcorn. I'll be right back."

"Do you have honey?" I ask. "I've got a great popcorn recipe I can make."

38

LILLIAN

So we head downstairs. Together. Which is a problem.

Because if I sat next to Sasha for another second with their voice mixing with mine I was going to kiss them and I said friends friends friends and they don't like me that way and I've got a box of my ex's things in my closet. I thought I'd go downstairs, clear my head and then put the popcorn in between us.

But I just know it'd be the warmest, softest kiss. Sasha's wearing leggings and fuzzy socks and a huge gray Wavelength sweater that they saw and immediately wanted. They wouldn't let us give it to them for free even though it's a misprint that says *Wavelenght*. Sasha said merch is the real way you pay bands for music. Since we thought no one wanted it, Quinn had been doodling Wavelength logo ideas on the sweater.

Sound waves lapping at the shores of a city.

A microwave with a face on it.

Rulers growing out of the ocean like trees.

When we get to the kitchen, my mom's standing at the counter, just back from work. She's still dressed professionally, suit jacket and such. She's scrolling on her phone and eating leftovers straight out of the container.

"Hey, you two," she says, like it's normal for Sasha to be over even though Sasha is the first new friend of mine to enter my house in some while. Possibly years.

Sasha's looking at the fridge, which I'd prefer covered in a sheet. Or shot into the sun. Every picture of me on there features a previous version of myself whose look I like less than the version now.

After going through most of the cupboards, I turn to my mom. "Popcorn kernels?"

She points to literally the one cupboard I haven't looked in.

"What else do we need?" I ask Sasha.

"Um, honey and cinnamon and butter, or coconut oil, and vanilla and maple syrup and nutmeg." They smile at my mom. "I'm Sasha. Sorry I'm stealing all your ingredients."

My mom looks up from her phone, deadpan. "You've a very demanding guest, Sasha."

"I'm Lillian's high-maintenance friend."

Even Sasha says "friend."

"Will you be needing cassia or Ceylon cinnamon?" my mom asks.

I'm making a little row of ingredients on the counter. I look in the spice drawer. I only use the cinnamon shaker that Jasper mixed with sugar.

"I can make do with cassia."

"That's very decent of you," says my mom.

Then she leaves. That's the whole conversation. Goddamn it, why did Jasper inherit all her effortlessness and not me? It's insufferable, and I aspire.

Even though it's my kitchen, I'm not much use except for trying to find things for Sasha to make food with. They don't seem to mind.

"It's been a while since I've been in a real kitchen," they say. "It's so spacious."

"Does your house not have a full kitchen?"

Sasha checks if the honey in the microwave is melted enough. "No, it's tiny and weird and partially renovated. Neither of my parents are much for cooking."

I'd like to come up behind them and wrap my arms around them and kiss the back of their neck. I would like to be a snuggly, distracting, sexy nuisance while they're trying to work in the kitchen instead of sitting on the counter talking. Not that I mind that. It's just that I like the way they move, and I'd like to move with them.

I didn't ask for this heart.

Some people have casual hearts.

Hearts that hook up and never think dancing-in-the-kitchen thoughts.

"If I ever write a song where people are dancing in a kitchen," I say out loud, "you've got to have me put down. I've gone country, and there's no saving me."

"I dance in my tiny kitchen every day," says Sasha. They twirl around, a demonstration, a laugh, a blur, something I want to catch and hold on to.

The back door slams — Jasper back from running. He comes into the kitchen wearing shorts and my headband and gives this little nod to Sasha as if they've already met.

To which I give Jasper the look of *you talked to the person I told you I have a crush on?* He gives me the innocent *who, me?* look back. He asks Sasha how their test went and takes some popcorn on the way by. Declares it a blessed gift to humanity and heads off to shower.

"The stamp of approval," says Sasha. "Anyone else I should

meet? Godparents, music teachers, pets?" They point at a picture on the fridge. "Maybe I should meet this weird cousin."

"That's me."

"Wow."

"Is that wow like 'hot damn,' or wow like 'you poor thing why did no one tell you those bangs were a bad idea?'"

"Sooooo, how about that movie?"

Cyprus should have stopped me. The blame for that haircut is squarely on her shoulders. But I lead the way back up to my room rather than focus anymore on my past hair regrets.

We put my laptop on an old speaker, and I hold the bowl of popcorn in my lap instead of using it as a barrier. I tell myself that I have to sit close to Sasha for strictly practical reasons. That laptop screens are small and that's why the bowl isn't between us. Sasha's already enjoying the start of the movie while I'm feeling a whole wish-wash of things. Nervous? No. Adrenaline? A bit of that. Anticipation and excitement, I think.

My fingers are sticky with the popcorn, which helps keep me away from Sasha for the first part of the movie and doesn't help me with thinking about how their mouth would taste right now. I can feel a slight pressure every time they grab some popcorn, one step away from touch. I last for half an hour.

I pause the movie.

Sasha glances over at me.

I could say I have to go to the bathroom. Makes sense. I need to wash my hands, though honestly we've both licked the honey off our own fingers. Like in a normal way. Silly, not porny.

And I felt dirty for thinking there was anything sexual to it, but I like people kissing my fingers. That's allowed. I'd like Sasha to kiss my fingers. There's a lot of nerves in fingertips. It doesn't have to be about penises. Hands are very sexual without any phallic connotations.

That's a demonstration of how I do have a filter. I didn't relay that whole thought process to Sasha. Some people may think I say everything that pops into my head, but they don't know all that happens in there.

"I don't want to make this weird," I say, which is the very best way to make anything weird. "But do you want to cuddle? Like platonic cuddle? If not, that's all good. No pressure."

"Doesn't everyone want to cuddle all the time?"

"So, yes?"

"Definitely yes."

I press in close to their side, my face against their sweater, my legs swung over top of theirs and our arms around each other. I'm not going to side-hug cuddle. Cuddles should be entangled. My body is starved for this, and now that I'm here and settled and the movie carries on and Sasha doesn't act any different and gradually, gradually my heart rate slows to normal, it doesn't feel like a trick. I thought it might be me suggesting one thing and feeling another. This warmth surprises me, more intimate and natural than I thought it'd be.

I feel safe with Sasha. I trust them.

The way their body relaxes into me tells me they feel the same.

Possibly, there's nowhere I'd rather be.

At the end of the movie, the streaming service could let the credits roll by. Instead, it starts playing something jarring and fully unrelated. It doesn't want to give us the moment where we're still touching but without anything we can pretend to be focused on. It forces me to shift from Sasha's arms enough to close the lid and break the moment.

This is why I hate corporations. They're never on the side of love.

Not that love has anything to do with this.

I stretch and offer Sasha a ride home. It's not because I'm tired of having them here. I suddenly feel exhausted, a bit empty, far away.

As soon as the cold air in my room hit where my body had been warmed against Sasha's, there was a switch inside me. Like a circuit breaker tripped by feeling too much. It snapped off. It could be to protect me, or it could be a malfunction. Either way, the lights go out and I need to be alone.

They say they're okay to walk home since it's not that late or that cold yet. They say, "I'll see you tomorrow" like it's a guarantee. I didn't really want to ask to borrow the car or talk to anyone else tonight. Sasha saves me by saying they'll show themselves out. Maybe they could feel the shift in me.

They hug me goodbye. It's a nice development, but in this moment, I don't feel it at all.

"Don't worry about the showcase," they say. "The world forgets most things. It gives a surprising number of second chances. I'll leave you to put away your gear." They close the door gently, as if a loud sound might be too much for me.

Little does Sasha realize that dumping my gear on my bedroom floor *is* putting it away. There's nowhere else for it to go. And nowhere else for me to go besides bed.

I'm under the covers before Sasha's left the house. I hear voices, the sound of Sasha saying goodnight to my mom. It's a brief exchange, too short for anything mortifying to be said. Then the back door opens and closes, softly again.

Sometimes a presence brings an absence back, and my bed feels emptier than it has since the night Emelia and I broke up.

39

SASHA

I genuinely believe there doesn't have to be anything sexual to cuddling, no matter the combination of bodies and identities and orientations involved. Friends can cuddle. Friends who are in categories of potentially being attracted to each other can cuddle.

I grew up socialized in a type of maleness where cuddling orbited sex. I'm happy to tear that all down any way I can, and if it's a queer way, then that's just another gift from queerness to everyone.

With Isabelle, I could hold her hand on the red carpet, snuggle up to take cute photos, and then when we put the cameras away and I took off the helmet, we could stay like that. It was safety, never anything else, but it wasn't lesser.

Great, delightful, an excellent, articulate theory backed by an example.

The problem is that I'm very much attracted to Lillian. Not in a slight hmm-interesting sort of way that I guess I'll ignore. I mean, I did try to ignore it. She said platonic and I agreed, so suggesting anything else would be unfair, right? And unwise and unkind.

I could hurt her, and I could lose her and these friends.

If I lose these friends, I slink back to the Channel and beg forgiveness. I'd like to believe otherwise, but if my heart's broken, I'm going where I can pretend to fill the emptiness with stadiums of screaming adoration. Enough decibels to hide under.

Or what if Lillian likes me the same way, but the Channel still catches me someday? She won't have tours, the endless running, available to her if I break her heart. Just showcases and gigs at Initialism on Sunday nights and a city full of places that remind her of hurt.

I walk home from Lillian's house slowly, letting the coolness sink in and push away my desire. I kick up leaves, imagining I'm in a music video with my face in the open. A music video I direct where I decide how my body should be portrayed.

It isn't distracting enough, not nearly. My skin remembers Lillian's warmth soaking into me, how she moved near to me like she wanted as much of her touching me as possible. I think that's the truth. I know I drew her close to me. We seemed synchronized, like our voices blending perfectly in some of the moments when we sang together.

I'm overcomplicating. It's only desire. Probably only my desire. No one's thinking about heartbreak, though Lillian's heart already is broken. I could see it at the end of the tonight, like she'd poured herself out and realized it too late.

The next morning, I'm late to school because I take so long deciding what to wear.

I put on eyeliner and take it off and change the color and leave a pile of clothes on my floor. There's a whole world of ways to present that's wide open when I'm not trying to be anyone's idea of an attractive boy.

I want to be more put together than the night before. Sexy, not snuggly.

Instead, I can only hope my rushed bike to school leaves me windswept and attractively flushed. But I've seen a team do that look to Isabelle, and it seems ambitious to have it happen to me naturally.

When I run into Lillian at the bike racks, she seems softer, like she's slept properly for the first time since I met her. She says her family likes me and they're being insufferable about it, which makes me happier than it probably should. Parent issues, et cetera.

Lillian says last night was exactly what she needed.

"Someone to make you snacks?" I say. I fiddle with my hair, trying to repair the damage my bike helmet did.

"Someone to melt into," she says.

She walks into the school before I have time to try to come up with a perfect response, leaving me to think about those words oh say a million times.

Her softness lasts until noon.

By then, Lillian's fired up about "recapturing the spark" of music. I've lost that connection to sound for months at a time and been listless, hoping it'd wander home eventually. It takes Lillian less than twenty-four hours to need to revive it for herself and her friends.

She says she made a plan while she was taking notes, but when she shows us, the plan is written in the center of the page with a few lines of English notes in the margins. She's done the title in big loopy letters with what I think are supposed to be ironic sparkles around them.

40

LILLIAN

Recapture Your Spark in Just Six Steps!

1 — skip tonight's practice

2 — Saturday night concert video viewing party (Quinn's?)

3 — Monday protest march attendance because voices aren't just for singing

3.5 — before next week, each go down musical rabbit hole and discover a new band we've never heard of

4 — next Wednesday, instead of practice, live band karaoke at Initialism

5 — band meeting the following weekend

6 — book a gig so we've got something to aim at

SASHA

Cyprus flips the list around to see it after Lillian reads it out. "Shame you got rid of all your gel pens last year."

"When I was eight, Cyprus," Lillian says.

"You know you kept the black ones," says Cyprus.

"Did you try to hide research homework for us by putting it in the middle of the list as a subpoint?" asks Quinn. "Also, did you volunteer my house?"

"I would've volunteered Sasha's place, but their parents hate young people," says Lillian, half a question. "By the way, Sasha, you're included in steps two through four. You're emotionally in the band."

I'm beyond pleased, but I try to downplay it. "Thanks for incorporating me in your great methodology. Isn't that basically what you'd do anyway?"

"But as a list!" Lillian's immensely proud of her organization.

Cyprus has taken out a bright highlighter and started "improving" the list decoration situation. "And we couldn't possibly have other plans?"

Quinn bumps her so she squiggles a line. "Do you have other plans?"

"Not really. No. None. I'm not too sure about karaoke though."

"We don't even have to sing," says Lillian.

I immediately see what she's doing. Just generate the situation, get everyone there, and we'll all get into it and wind up involved.

Not me. No stages for Sasha. People might figure me out and then I bring a huge media frenzy on this town and this school and Initialism and my friends and wind up back at the Channel and they'll probably make a feature about it or something horrible.

The homework takes me to a lot of mediocre music and a bit of truly remarkable stuff. Every time I think I find a new band, I text Quinn and he's already heard of it. So I go further down the rabbit hole and eventually get drawn into clickbait about Admirer.

I try to avoid this. I mostly do. Because when you're famous and you start researching yourself, you never hit the bottom.

I become glazed over, obsessive, reading half an article and getting disgusted and moving to another and another and desperately trying to avoid logging into my accounts to see every post and comment. I hold out on that one, but I do learn some things.

People hate me.

Not everyone. Not even a tenth of our fans. Some people, though. They feel betrayed that I haven't spoken up for Augustus. Or betrayed that I haven't spoken out against him. Some people are pointing to when I fell into the drum kit as a sign that I've been needing rehab for a while now.

The trial drags on, and as much as I try to avoid it, there are moments where I can't look away. I read half an article about what's unfolding before stopping myself. Everywhere it's Augustus and people defending him and despising him. Legal technicalities and loopholes, rich men getting out of all sorts of trouble, and pictures of Augustus with Jasmine. Whatever remnants of anonymity she had are done for. The internet's dredging up hints of their relationship and creating stories. It seems like she's supporting Augustus's side against both the stat rape and assault charges. I've never really met her, and I didn't know much about their relationship until it all came crashing down, but I know that thirteen was too young to be with Augustus. She shouldn't have her life publicly ruined by this.

I start thinking about what the Channel could do to me for breaking contract and running. How the nearer my friends are to me, the more they're at risk. The less they know about my life in Admirer, the safer we all are.

I have to stop researching. I never do find a new band for everyone to listen to.

The protest march takes me off guard. I didn't give it much thought until I left school with Quinn, Lillian and Cyprus. I don't know what I was expecting, but I didn't expect to feel so much. I've been to other protests. I guess it was different now that no one recognized me and I was allowed to be simply one voice among many.

It's for the rights of trans youth. It's against legislation that's about erasing queer kids no matter how it harms them. Kids younger than me. Pretending it's about anything else is where the lies start. It's not the worst right where we live, but it's pressing all around us.

I don't know if I feel more anger or hope. I know when I get home, I go straight to bed in the afternoon and don't get out for a long time. The march shouldn't have to happen. These rights shouldn't be up for debate. I don't want my existence, Quinn's existence, to be a protest.

But there were people there. Lillian with a cardboard sign and chants she knew. She fucking cared. For most of the people there, it wasn't about protecting themselves. That gave me hope. And I remembered that getting onstage is one way of tearing these systems down and marching is one way and staking out space for yourself is one way. Sometimes the only safe place to stake out that space is inside yourself, and sometimes it takes a long time to even be able to do that.

Every time, it's a sledgehammer to something that should never have been built. It shouldn't have to be that way, but every hammer blow gives me hope.

It's that hope that takes me to Initialism the next Wednesday, more or less recovered from both the research and the protest. I believe in this place and feel safe with these people. Listening to my friends sing karaoke can't do anything but help.

42

LILLIAN

I sign up right away. "It's going to fill up," I claim. Whether that's true or not is entirely beside the point. No one will regret singing.

"Oh *no*," says Cyprus sarcastically, then five minutes later she leaves to sign up once she sees the list of all the songs the band knows. "For general morale," she claims, but I think it's just an excuse to belt out a sparkly pop hit from our youth.

There are lots of people here. It's happy noisy. Everyone loves this karaoke night, and why not? The chance to sing your favorite songs backed by a real band who changes keys on demand. Uninhibited, cheered on by your friends. It doesn't much matter how well you sing since no one cares or remembers.

"Do you sing?" Sasha asks Quinn.

Quinn stirs his drink with a straw. "Sasha, Sasha, Sasha, let me tell you a story about taking T and voice changes. I'm happy it's hitting me that way, but singing in public? Big-time hiatus. But you should! Lillian says you've got chops."

"Not my exact words," I say. "I just said I liked your voice and that I'd love to hear you *really* sing. That's all I said. No pressure. You always seem to be holding back, and I think it's time you cut loose."

"Footloose!" sings Cyprus.

Sasha admits they've never seen it, and now a group viewing of the original *Footloose* is nonnegotiable.

"It's basically the moral center of all eighties movies," I claim.

"You said that about *Heathers,*" says Sasha. "Clearly we shouldn't listen to you."

I kick them under the table. "Except about signing up to sing."

"There's not a chance," says Sasha, "not even for you."

SASHA

So I'm onstage at Initialism.

This is, in short, all Lillian's fault.

Indirectly, inadvertently.

It's her fault for existing.

I shouldn't have cuddled with her or paid so much attention to how she takes care of her friends or fights for what she cares about. I definitely shouldn't have focused on how she said she'd love to hear me really sing and then secretly signed myself up and chosen a song that pushes the edges of my range and singing ability. A song that shouldn't be a karaoke song. It's too hard. It doesn't hold up well when it's sung badly, but it doesn't get funny either.

There's a microphone in my hand for the first time in months. Even dented and chipped with a smudge of lipstick on one side, it has that familiar weight. The bandleader is asking me if the original key is okay.

I nod yes. It's hard, but I can manage it.

Below me, a couple tables back, I can see Quinn and Cyprus and Lillian. Quinn gives me a thumbs-up.

Lying low, zero stars out of ten.

Maybe I get half a star for insisting that Cyprus doesn't record it.

When I signed up, I told myself that I'd sound very different singing this emotionally fraught song than Admirer's peppy music, that none of the handful of people who can recognize me will ever be at Wednesday night live band karaoke, that Initialism makes me feel safe and I can't stay in the Channel's cage.

But really, my reason is Lillian, who's been barely containing a grin since Christensen called my name from the list.

At the microphone, Christensen says, "It's time for Sasha Weaver with a weeper. Best of luck with that bridge."

The band's counting in.

LILLIAN

Sasha's drawing eyes to the stage. Not as many as Cyprus drew with her combination of knowing half the people in the room and choosing a beloved pop hit. It's not the universal appeal of a sing-along, but Sasha has total command of some people's attention. They halt a couple of conversations.

It's not raucous like the two-minute punk song I did. Which I absolutely nailed and which was possibly too intense for the occasion. In that way, Sasha's song selection and performance are the same as mine. We both lack the ability to read the size and mood of the room.

We both sing like we want the world to listen.

Like we need it.

Sasha has talent. And actual technique. But what's attractive is the passion.

Onstage, they're completely present. This isn't the Sasha who's always friendly and nice. Sometimes hesitant or embarrassed. Who occasionally feels like they're in no way prepared for the world. This isn't the soft, cuddly, popcorn-making Sasha who often seems slightly distracted.

For three and a half minutes, they exist on the stage, at the microphone, and nowhere else.

Sasha hasn't even hit the big part of the song when Quinn taps me on the shoulder. I lean over to hear him, my eyes still on Sasha, who's wandering around the stage, leaning on the guitarist's shoulder, full of gesture and performance, brimming with music.

"Do they play bass too?" asks Quinn.

"What?"

"Do they play bass too?" he repeats louder.

"I heard you. But why?"

Sasha reaches the bridge and my attention snaps back. I can imagine my own voice rising parallel to theirs on this stage at Initialism where I've been so many times. I imagine what my songs would sound like with the two of us, and I get what Quinn's suggesting.

45

SASHA

The most common question I used to get asked was, "Why did you put on the helmet?"

It got to the point where the origin story was practiced. If I told it when Augustus was around, I even knew where he tended to jump in. I'd downplay certain things because I knew he'd exaggerate them. I had to start them off small or else he'd grow them to impossible proportions.

As part of Heather Erin's plan to transform us into popstars, we were on a glorified musical talent show. One of those ones that thrives off reaction shots and judges being cruel to children and then passing it off as doing them a favor. A show premised on throwing people into a multi-round grinder, and whoever comes out alive is held up as worthy.

I'm somewhat more charitable when I describe it in interviews. Those judges are famous, after all. Surely they're not needlessly sadistic. Surely.

I was thirteen years old. I was hyperventilating backstage, certain I was going to be sick and absolutely terrified of one of the two men sitting on the left. I couldn't make eye contact with him. He kept saying good things about us and looking at me like he hated me. In interviews, I leave that out. I talk about being nervous to perform because it was the final round.

The thing is, the final round of that show is prerecorded. The headset mics are for show. People don't like to know that. Augustus saw that I'd be a lip-syncing disaster if I was panicking. He saw his career in trouble, though in interviews he puts his arm around my shoulder. "Couldn't stand to see my little brother suffering," he says. I'd like to think there's some truth to that.

He grabbed the nearest thing that could save us, a motorcycle helmet that belonged to our security guard. Full visor, dark and reflective. He named some famous musicians who wore masks and helmets and put it on my head. It was massive. The Channel always uses the only photograph from that performance where I don't look like a total orb.

But I could see the judges' faces and they couldn't see mine, and that was enough. We won while I was wearing that helmet, our biggest spike in fame prior to Augustus's trial.

I felt safe, invulnerable. I refused to take it off for days. The Channel saw an opportunity and made it my brand before I had time to consider whether I wanted to live like that.

As my face changed behind the visor, the idea of getting away started to form.

On tour, I sang everything live. Always. For me, it's integrity and spontaneity. And it'd break my heart to do otherwise. As much as the helmet the Channel made for me was an expensive technical marvel with amazing internal microphones and sound technology, singing full voice without it on is a completely different experience. I only used to do that when we recorded, and now I'm on a stage with nothing between my face and the faces looking back at me.

I try not to spend the whole song looking at Lillian. She's got a smile at the corner of her mouth. I understand. I loved seeing her jump around stage like she owned the place. It made me pull out all the show I've got stored inside me.

After this, no one is going to tell me what to change. No one will make me switch my clothes or tell me how to use my voice. I'm singing whatever I want. Singing for myself and whoever I want.

I hit the last note, and there's a round of applause and a few cheers. Mostly from my table, mostly from Quinn.

That's it — on to the next person. I leave the stage.

I used to be able to get the crowd to start singing something as I left, and they'd keep going even after the houselights came on. I imagined their voices echoing mine on the buses and cars as they went home, onward and outward, extensions of me sitting alone on the floor of a hotel room shower trying to feel connected to something.

I thought this would seem like less, but as I squeeze between people to get back to my friends' table, I feel like I've done the performance of my life.

Cyprus points at her phone face down on the table as proof that she didn't video. "Only pictures," she says, which wasn't exactly what I asked for. For her, that's pretty big though.

"Incredible. Fabulous, even." Quinn sways to imitate a way I moved that I didn't realize. The effects of wearing a dress and my head feeling weightless and not performing the male popstar.

Lillian says, "Well damn, Sasha," when I sit beside her. She's smirking at me, has to lean close and talk loud to be heard over all the voices. "You do realize we're at a bar, not Live Aid?"

"Do you?" I say back.

She shrugs. I can feel it because she's so close she's touching my shoulder, justified by the noise around us.

She says, "The room's as big as you make it. You broke the walls down."

I'm soaking in the moments before. Seeing her face made me want to sing my best, more than a stadium full of Admirer fans did.

She's the entire crowd, all the voices carrying out into the world. She's the one I want with me afterwards, backstage, in the taxi, tangled in the white sheets of a hotel bed.

After introducing the next singer, Christensen handshakes and hugs his way over to our table. "I knew you kids were prodigies," he says. "Is there already a band named Punk Prodigies? There should be."

"But subversively," says Cyprus.

Lillian says, "Because punk destabilizes the concept of 'good' music, rendering the category of prodigy without meaning."

"That's got to be from a book," I say.

Cyprus shakes her head. "Nope, Lillian can just talk like that."

"And *you*," says Christensen, looking right at me, "you can sing like all hell. Wherever you blew in from must have been sorry to lose you."

Then he's back to milling about, and I realize where I recognized him from.

Christensen worked for the Channel.

46

LILLIAN

Sasha's coat is hanging on the back of my bedroom door. It's long, pale pink, clearly out of place in my room. They wore it at Initialism on the karaoke evening. They find it colder in this city than I do, and our table was in a bit of a draft from the door. Before they went onstage, they took it off and handed it to me. It smells like a mixture of new clothing and the very unobtrusive perfume Sasha sometimes wears.

That scent has been soft in my room for a few days.

Underneath, they wore a white sleeveless dress with a V-neck. It ended just above their knees, pretty and full enough for them to sway in, to feel it moving around them. I've always hated that sensation, but I could see them loving it onstage.

There's a lot of talk about gender and body dysphoria, feeling like your skin isn't a place you belong in. There's not enough about the opposite, about ecstatic belonging. I see the euphoria on Sasha or Quinn most days. They'll look at themselves in a window we're walking past, and they'll walk a little slower, turn at a certain angle, watching themselves.

That's not always good, but sometimes it is. More and more for each of them, I think.

Sometimes, Quinn says he looks in a mirror and he actually sees himself looking back. He can't even find the words for it.

"Hyped to the max," he said once. "Stoked, pumped, high on life. I could write an eighties hit about it."

Seeing my friends feel like that may be my favorite thing to witness in the entire world.

At the end of the karaoke night, Quinn draped Sasha's jacket over my shoulders because I hate wearing pink and Sasha pulled my leather jacket on. No spikes on this one. It's plain, a bit big on me — perfect on Sasha's shoulders.

They were laughing and spinning every chance they got because their dress spun with them. I felt like a cupcake at a wedding photo shoot, but Sasha was still wearing my coat when we dropped them off.

I liked that, so I didn't trade back.

Now it's Sunday. I've accomplished every step of my list. We've skipped two band practices, watched a concert video together (very distracted by Sasha next to me, did not cuddle, haven't told Cyprus about that because reasons blegh I don't know). Found new bands, except for Sasha, who said they tried but we're just such nerds. We did our karaoke.

Cyprus got us into this triple-header local band scenario that's happening in a few weeks at a little venue called the Pilgrim. She saw a link between our acquaintances and Quinn's dad's music scene connections, did the follow-up, sent about a thousand messages, "accidentally" ran into the organizer at his work, and now Wavelength is on the bill. Together, the three bands can fill this place up. It'll be a great time, and we're playing second, which is ideal.

Tonight, the band meeting is starting any minute. I've got a bonfire blazing in my small backyard and chocolate chip cookies, which I'd love to claim credit for. In truth, Jasper stress-baked them and then got all athletey and said he shouldn't eat three dozen cookies on his own, so now there's cookies for me and my friends.

I take one last look in the mirror. I can't get my beanie to flop just so, but I hear a pebble hit my window (which Quinn finds an endlessly amusing alternative to doorbells) and I know my friends are here.

Time to make my case.

"No, absolutely not," says Cyprus. "This is your worst idea."

The three of us are sitting close to the fire. I'm going to bring out the cookies later and use them to make s'mores. Clearly, I should have used them earlier as a bribe.

Quinn moves his shoes off the edge of the firepit. It was starting to smell like burnt rubber. "Strictly speaking, it was my idea. Credit where credit's due."

Cyprus turns to Quinn. "Quinn, this is *your* worst idea. Sasha can't join the band. Lillian's obsessed with Sasha."

That gets me to cut in. "I *like* Sasha, okay? I'm attracted to them. I'm attracted to lots of people. Or at least a few. Sasha's not the only one. Have a little faith in me."

It's good I didn't mention the whole snuggling with Sasha thing. When Cyprus asked, I said nothing happened at our movie night. Did I consciously define "nothing" differently than her? Yes, absolutely.

Some sparks jump from the firepit and Quinn stamps them

out when they land in the leaves beside his lawn chair.

"I have so much faith in you, Lillian," says Cyprus. "Sappy amounts of faith. But our band's literally in trouble right now because Emelia broke up with you."

"*We* broke up," I mutter instinctively.

I've been doing the gestures of moving on, though. I dropped her things off yesterday and only wrote two horrible, unreadable songs about it in the twenty-four hours since. I didn't ring the doorbell or anything. She didn't meet me at the trees, and I haven't texted her again.

Sometimes, when I have the compulsion to, I send a message to Sasha instead. They send me pictures of outfits they look beautiful in, and I can't tell what it means.

Cyprus is looking into the fire.

"Emelia said she'd rather have friends than a band," says Cyprus. "And I feel the same. People who really know you and care about you are so rare. But also this band has been with me for a long time. And what if they're the same? What if the band keeps us together and if there's no band we graduate and we become people who run into each other at concerts and are like, 'Hey,' awkward pause, nothing to say."

Quinn takes several moments to hop his chair over until he's beside Cyprus. He slings his arm around her shoulder. "There will never, ever be an awkward pause. I'll fill it with inane chatter no matter how disconnected we are."

"You're stuck with me," I say. "First dance, last dance, with or without the band. Ride or die and all that."

Cyprus is a little teary, laughing a little. "I'm serious."

"Me too," I say, but I'm thinking of us sitting on the hood of her car and how she didn't answer about whether she wanted Emelia and me back together and wondering if the breakup started us drifting apart too. Wondering if she's right, that the band is what ties us together now.

I leave that thought be. I pretend there's no way that could be the reality.

"Bands don't last forever," I say. "I know it. Notes fade out."

"You should write that down," says Quinn.

"Shut up, I'm trying to make a point." I should write it down though. "And that point is that Wavelength is already in trouble. *We're* not, just the band. So there's no risk to adding Sasha. Emelia could still come back if she wants, since Sasha doesn't play bass. Maybe it revives Wavelength. Maybe we crash out."

I gesture to Quinn and Cyprus. "Us, we'll be fine."

"With Emelia though —" starts Cyprus.

"We'll be fine," I repeat. I try to say it hard enough to make it true. "So that's a yes, right? You know Sasha and I are going to sound heaven-sent together."

"Yes," sighs Cyprus. "But only because I want to hear it and you said nice things and I know you're withholding cookies."

I check the clock on my phone. "Good, good. It would have been super awkward if you'd stood by your initial reaction."

Quinn and Cyprus both give me quizzical looks that are so very satisfying.

"I may have invited Sasha here and told them our meeting wouldn't be long, with a plan to actually make them a part of the meeting?"

Cyprus rolls her eyes at me. "Oh my god, that is so needlessly risky."

"It's called confidence ba-by."

Sasha rides up the back lane a minute later. "Sorry I'm late," they say. I was counting on that too. They lean their bike against the fence and grab a lawn chair. "How was your band meeting?"

"The council has come to a consensus," I say. "Sasha Weaver, do you want to join Wavelength?"

47

SASHA

At the Channel, Heather Erin taught me to never pause when I was asked a question in an interview. Not for a moment. She told me to treat it like being onstage. Start right in answering, talking, playing the next song, interacting, laughing. Fill the space even if you don't know what you're going to say.

Otherwise the pause becomes the first response. The pause means something. Don't show you're thinking. Don't show you're taken aback. Don't let the energy drop. The immediacy will make people believe you're genuine. It will make you seem alive and engaged.

You're fun fun fun, no one wants your consideration. No one cares what you have to consider. If you pause, that pause happens inside them too.

They snap out of the moment, and outside the moment, it's just fear. That's what Heather Erin said.

Then she laughed and started talking about something else. Her laugh is a foreign language to her, like she learned how to do it from watching TV.

When Lillian asks me to join the band, I stop dead.

I'm taken off guard, but I'm not silent for a lack of words. I know exactly what to say.

No.

No is absolutely what I should say. For a thousand reasons. For myself. For these dear people I've come to adore.

Normally, I might go with the ever-reliable pretend-you-don't-know-they're-serious. What? Really? No, surely not. Hahaha.

You can create a lot of space to think like this if there's anything to think about and if the person asking you the question isn't Lillian. Sometimes, when she's joking, I can't quite tell. But when she wants to be serious, there's no doubting it. It's locked in.

I should sit down. I've just stopped in my tracks, and even though it's only been a half-second that means I'm only a half-second away from the pause becoming the answer, and to them it's not a big question. It's a why-not for a high school band. Something to give a shot. We'll be queer and joyful and play at Initialism and know we belong in the world.

Only I don't belong. Alexander Ash shouldn't be here, and neither should Christensen.

I didn't have to look up his name to confirm it. Quinn said Christensen used to be big in the music industry but moved home because his mom was dying. Once it clicked, it was obvious.

Back then he had buzzed hair and a gym-rat body instead of a beard. He was called Chris, lord among the Channel's talent scouts. He was behind the scenes, only known in select circles, not in the album credits and not on the cover of magazines. He was a gatekeeper who "discovered" a Top 40's worth of musicians. He fed the machine.

I know of him because he brought LucSee to the Channel, and years later, she opened for the entire North American and

European legs of an Admirer tour. She must have been one of the last people he scouted before leaving the Channel and opening Initialism.

Here, I haven't heard anyone talk about him having connections they could use. He runs Initialism and gives a lot of young queer people a safe place to see music and a safe stage to play on. That seems to be all. Even Cyprus hasn't said anything about him knowing people.

But still, I don't trust him. The Channel is always hungry. Maybe he watches some of these musicians and thinks now is the moment for the Channel to elevate someone queer to show that they can keep up with the times. Now that there's money in it.

Maybe he considers turning me in as a way to get back into the business.

As Sasha Weaver, I fear he'll make me back into Alexander Ash.

Though the longer I'm Sasha, the more I realize this is who I've always been. Alexander Ash was the part and Sasha was the actor. Despite all the pain, I don't think I'd trade my life story away. The role was wrong. But I love the lights too much, even though I only felt them on my face through a visor.

With all my heart, I want to plunge in. Goddamn recklessness and Lillian and Quinn looking hopeful and bright. The pause has stretched. I can see Lillian start to wonder. It's so slight, a hint in her eyes. Her walls of confidence stay up.

"What do you say?" she asks. "We've got sex, drugs, and rock and roll."

"We do?" says Quinn. He turns to Cyprus. "I know I'm personally a sex symbol, but are drugs part of Wavelength's deal now?"

"We'll add it to the talking points of the meeting." Cyprus is watching me very closely, in a different way than Lillian and

Quinn. It's more cautious even as she jokes, "Maybe if we get an official sponsorship."

They've given me the moment. As always, they're more generous with their judgment of me than I expect. The world isn't out to tear my every pause to shreds anymore.

I must believe this.

I sang in this city without my helmet on. Christensen didn't report me, no one else could have recognized me, Isabelle hasn't texted me again. As long as Augustus is on trial, the Channel doesn't need me for Admirer. For now, I can live freely here.

I must believe this.

"Well, so long as it's corporately sponsored, I'm sure it isn't dodgy," I say. I open my lawn chair and join the circle. "That was my concern. Now that I know Wavelength isn't a bad influence—"

"Rude," says Lillian.

"—I'm in."

Whatever happens, Lillian's face makes it worth it.

As the evening goes on, we make band plans and eat s'mores made with cookies. Lillian notices I'm cold and lets me wear her beanie and gloves. I'm not prepared for the weather, and I'm overwhelmed by what I've just committed to.

It's not that I've got to learn and modify parts for an entire set of songs in the next few weeks. After listening to some demos around the fire, I'm realizing just how good of a singer Emelia is. I can do it technically, as in I can hit the notes, but can I hit them in the right way? With shadow in my voice and a fuller commitment than Admirer's songs ever required? Though my voice will be clean and clear compared to Lillian's no matter what I do. In every aspect, I want to meet Lillian's standard for being ready to perform, which is high enough that it'd impress the people I worked with at the Channel.

I'm overwhelmed to hope this could work.

I feel barely afloat and more excited for life than I've ever been.

"I started my first band with Cyprus when we were thirteen," says Lillian.

"Twelve," says Cyprus.

"Mechanical Heart," continues Lillian. "We thought it was pretty edgy. I had a hair situation which I can only describe as substantial and wore my guitar far lower than anyone should ever wear their guitar. All remainders of that era are in a guarded vault in a secret location."

Cyprus takes a nibble of cookie. She's eating her way around the edge. "That'd be my old laptop I spilled sangria on."

"I was already doing their artwork," says Quinn, "but I joined when Lillian started Wavelength. Her and Cyprus really needed someone to help them keep time. Then Lillian seduced Emelia to get her on board." Quinn beckons me from across the fire. "And now, I've seduced you. It's a vicious cycle."

Lillian's shifted to squatting by the fire, adjusting the logs with her bare hands.

"I mean, it wouldn't *not* work," I say. "You're by far the hottest guy at school."

Cyprus has her camera on Lillian. "Jasper will be heartbroken to discover it's not him. He seems so certain."

"You're … meh," says Quinn to me. "Okay-ish, I guess. I'd hook up with you to save the band." He routinely tells me I'm a fifteen out of ten when I see him at school.

A log falls, showering Lillian's arm with sparks. She swears and jumps back, waving her hand.

Cyprus pans with Lillian. "To our legions of fans, this is how little Lillian cares about Wavelength. Do you remember Wavelength, Lillian? You need your fingers."

"My line between badass and self-destruction is just really thin." Lillian takes a close look at her hand. "I'm alright."

"Well," says Cyprus, "her body's alright. Emotionally, she's using humor to deflect attention away from real problems."

"You're posting this?" asks Lillian.

"Some of it, probably. I'll save the rest as unseen footage for the documentary I'll make about us in forty years."

"'Her body's alright'?" repeats Lillian.

"Of everything she said, that's the part you're worried about?" I use the fire poker that's sitting *right there* to adjust the logs. I'm pretty invested in drawing more warmth from the fire.

"Aaaaaand, meeting our newest band member." Cyprus sweeps the camera over to me. "This is Sasha, who's going to be singing."

"I can play tambourine too," I say. (That's true.)

Then I remember why I thrive on this kind of attention, why I feel entirely familiar with it. "Actually, can you not video me?"

Cyprus pockets her phone. "Of course. Probably better if the news spreads in person first."

She means Emelia, who I've never met. A peripheral ghost whose chair I'm in right now.

Later that night, when I'm sitting close to Lillian on her couch after Quinn and Cyprus have gone home, watching the pilot of *Twin Peaks*, that feeling flickers again.

Do I belong here? Is this ill-fated from the start?

But where I'm uncertain and afraid, tonight keeps obscuring it. Everything is campfire smoke and music plans and my head resting on Lillian's lap. She touches my face like it's absent-minded, and I have to work not to shiver.

I close my eyes.

48

LILLIAN

Let's play hangman forever
And I'll make you
Guess "December"
We'll pretend that Christmas lights shine
And we're not kissing under
The exit sign

Holding you is already goodbye
I can't draw stars
On our midnight sky
So wrap me up in your arms
While we wait for
The fire alarm

Where's the light switch in this room?
I need to be
In the dark with you
Just to see the exit sign glow red

And the round clock
Wish us dead

All these orange bottles in a line
I'll take a few
Then I'll be fine
I'll put my last breath into this song
Come closer, love
Prove me wrong

Seventeen, why do I think like this?
Like a teardrop
A mascara drip
Never enough to make our eyes strong
Wish we'd known that
All along

I'll teach you telephone and SOS
Let me win
So we can rest
We can sit on this empty stage forever
And play hangman
All December

SASHA

It's the weekend before my first show with the band at the Pilgrim, and Lillian and I are in Quinn's basement, where Wavelength rehearses. We're working on vocals in a spare bedroom while Quinn and Cyprus hash out some drum and bass parts. When we hit a roadblock, she plays her new song for me.

"Hangman Forever."

I must look slightly concerned when Lillian finishes singing, because she says, "Don't start worrying about me. You've written songs. You know they're an accumulation, not a moment."

She's right about that. Songs are exaggerations and calculations and passions combined. I should know better than to worry.

But my songs for Admirer were pure shimmer and romance. I don't know how to lay my hurt that directly on a page. I'm more comfortable with the talk of forever than the talk of goodbyes and endings.

When a fear's that close to me, I can't speak it like Lillian can.

LILLIAN

"December's an idea," I say to Sasha. "It's a celebration, but melancholy. We all party and pretend to know the future and sink ourselves in love to feel alright. But there's always a moment on the thirty-first when you feel alone, no matter what. The countdown on New Year's Eve hides the human condition."

"Loneliness?" Sasha suggests.

"That we all die. So yes, maybe loneliness." I feel my breathing tightening just talking about it. I want to reach out for Sasha, so I quickly grab for the way I can be closest to them.

"Want to sing it with me?" I ask.

51

SASHA

Three weeks after I joined Wavelength, we're backstage at the Pilgrim, where our set is next. The guy on sound, who looks like he's only a couple years older than me, sticks his head into the greenroom.

"You guys good to go?"

Lillian tells him to give us a couple minutes.

I'm ready, buzzing, not sure what we're waiting for. We set up our gear after the last band finished a great set. I'm already covered in sweat from dancing.

The Pilgrim's built in an old movie theater with a concrete floor that slants just enough to be very uncomfortable. I have firsthand experience from a show we saw here a couple weeks ago. And we joined the crowd for the first set tonight. People don't care how the venue is. It's packed and alive out there.

In theory, the first band was too explosive to be a good act to follow. But I love being after excellence, and that's not unearned confidence. I've had some great openers. It's a young crowd, but we're still the youngest band here. I'm used to that too. I'm wearing tall boots and a short dress and I'm ready to tear this place down.

"Bring it in," says Lillian, drawing us into a huddle.

Quinn has to spin his hat around so we can all press our heads close together, arms around each other's shoulders, strong against the world. This is being part of something like I've never been before. You can't be this invincible alone, and with Augustus, I always felt alone.

Lillian's in leader mode. I've seen this part of her since I joined the band. Whatever inconsistency and chaos chase her around for much of her life, she sets it aside when she runs Wavelength. In rehearsals, she doesn't like to stop until things are perfect, and neither do I. She doesn't mind telling me to sing better, to change a part, to make us all quit goofing off because we've got a show in three days.

In the crowd during the first band, she pulled me close enough to hear her between songs. "I changed my mind!" she yelled as people cheered around us. "Come in on the first 'please' in 'Elevator.'"

I nodded back. I've got it.

Since the night I joined the band, it's been relentless. Three weeks where every conversation between Lillian and I has been about music or Wavelength. Getting me up to speed, working on how I fit in vocally, sorting out parts. Lillian will send me a song at two in the morning by a band who existed for six months in a city I've never heard of. She'll have a suggestion. How on one verse of a song I should try doing the timbre thing that the singer does in the bridge of what she sent me. I've been practicing on my own too, memorizing the set and getting my voice back in shape.

I love it. It was never the music I needed to get away from.

Lillian's reinvigorated. Or she has something to latch on to. It's hard to tell the difference. Either way, I'm in.

Personally, I'm throwing myself at this like the rest of the world doesn't exist. Cyprus has kept becoming more invested in Augustus's trial, and every time she mentions it I have to push down a clenching inside me. She'll wonder aloud if Admirer's tour will come back here if Augustus gets cleared. She's up to date on all the lawyers and every person who testifies and the delays the trial keeps hitting, each one sparking hope in me.

But slowly, inevitably, it progresses. Today Cyprus told us it had resumed again. Lillian grinned at me when I followed her cues and steered us back toward Wavelength like I've been doing since I joined the band.

I put up walls of sound against realities I can't stand.

"Whatever happens," Lillian says in the huddle backstage at the Pilgrim, and her eyes are blazing close to mine, "it's on me. Especially for you, Sasha. I brought you in on belief and didn't give you much time. We've put this together fast. Don't worry if it's a little rough. There are going to be nights when we play better, when we're tighter. But let's set a high bar for passion. Let's set a high bar for sheer fucking noise. We are here and present and powerful in this world."

Cyprus holds out her phone in the midst of us. "A hype tradition," she says, and starts playing a song I recognize from watching TV on Lillian's couch.

It's the raucous, campy nineties pop-punk theme from *Buffy the Vampire Slayer.* I feel my energy rising. I want to do this with these people and listen to this theme a hundred more times, until the song brings a rushing sense of belonging and readiness for anything.

The song crashes to an end and we move through the ratty back hallway of the Pilgrim toward the stage. Lillian's talking right up until we're there.

"Remember, unless Sasha's singing lead, you're following me. If I repeat or skip a section, follow me. I'll get us to the end or die trying."

I stop hearing her the moment I see the first sliver of the audience from side stage. It's new and it's home and I'm the last to step out, taking the mic stand to the left of Lillian as the lights go down.

Quinn counts us in.

There were shows with Admirer that blurred by, highway driving, reaching the final song and not remembering how I got there.

With Wavelength, I feel awake for every moment.

The lights in my eyes, unfiltered by a visor.

Taking my microphone off the stand.

Never putting it back.

Crouching at the front of the stage.

Reaching out to touch people's hands.

Laughing with eyes I meet.

Because who am I to reach toward?

The weight of sound around me.

The unfiltered kick drum beating across the stage.

Cyprus.

Quinn.

Lillian.

There's Cyprus playing a synth part with one hand while panning her phone across the stage, across the crowd. She only appears still because she's doing too much to bother with extra performance.

Her head's bobbing slightly as she triggers a sample to start us off, adjusts a dial, her hands adorned with rings big enough to catch the light. Sunglasses inside. Behind them, I know her eyes never stay focused on one thing for long.

There's a moment when I stumble in my boots. It's not a very high heel, but it's more than I'm used to. A panic inside me. What am I doing? To walk out and sing and perform and be seen by all these people when I'm dressed like this? A moment where I feel certain someone watching me right now hates me and the stage is louder than I'm used to and maybe I've lost my place and I glance back.

And there's Quinn. He knows where I need to be, has the whole song held together. Plays a part and gives me the smallest shrug to say *what does it matter, you tripped in your boots*. He mouths something at me that I can't understand. Smiles. Whatever it was, I know it means he has my back.

The first song is a little bit sound check part two, with us hammering through it as the guy on sound gets the levels sorted out. That's what you get for being one of the openers. At a converted movie theater.

With Admirer, they mixed the opener worse than us on purpose until I put a stop to it. I'm not for depriving anyone of beautiful sound.

By the second song, I can really hear my voice blending with Lillian's. She doubles some choruses, cranks up the intensity, takes it down. We all stay with her. She plays solos, homed in on her strings at times, and likes to be facing Cyprus or Quinn when she starts a song.

She makes a lot of eye contact with me. It reminds my body of a vibration between us, something that's been set aside for a future record while we work on Wavelength and this show.

But there was a second when we were sitting on her floor with our backs against her bed listening to something for the fourth time, trying to get a sense of it. She was leaning against me, and one of her hands brushed my chest. I willed my body not to respond, not to gasp or curl toward her or pull away with surprise. Her hand stopped, rested there, gripped my shirt, then moved to hit play on the song again.

I remember that all the time.

The show builds toward the first time Lillian and I will sing a big note together live.

We reach the end of our third-last song, and she lets her voice carry before the final chord falls. My voice rings with hers, holding a high note above her until I feel like I'm about to give out. Watching to see when her hands will drop across her strings one more time to bring it to a close.

The crowd hears it. They cheer louder for that song. That note. Augustus and I sang together our whole lives and I never felt the power of our voices merging the way I feel this.

Where the whole world gets suspended.

A song later and we're about to start the last one of our set. We're in the mix of applause and talking that seems to happen between every song at a show like this. Grab their attention, lose it again. That won't do at all, not for this song.

I look over at Lillian and say, "I'm going to make them quiet to hear you."

LILLIAN

I think I just fell in love with Sasha.

53

SASHA

Alexander Ash could do this with tens of thousands of screaming people. Surely Sasha Weaver can do it with a couple hundred.

I step to the front of the stage and bring a finger to my lips.

54

LILLIAN

Sasha was letting me know as bandleader before trying something, giving me a chance to tell them the obvious: it won't work.

But Sasha said it like it was a fact, and I believed them.

They stood at the edge of the stage with a finger against their lips, their other hand with its palm flat to the floor. It took a few seconds, just long enough that I started to doubt it. A few laughs, loud voices coming from corners of the room. Sasha turned toward each sound and it fell silent. I've never heard the Pilgrim like that.

Sasha drifted toward side stage, giving me the floor. When I started the song with my best and hardest guitar part, it had a different impact than ever before. Volume crashing straight into the silence.

And yet that's not the moment that's still reverberating in my chest. At the front of the stage, I saw a command radiate from Sasha. An infectious joy that the crowd picked up on. It said, *listen to me, and we'll make something together.*

So I fell in love with them.

And I desired them.

55

SASHA

The song ends and we wave goodnight. Lillian holds up her guitar, Quinn his drumsticks. It's over and we're off the stage talking over top of each other saying *oh my god holy shit*. The people won't be quiet. The houselights are back on, but they cheer enough that the next band, the one running the show, says we'd better play one more.

Lillian agrees now and worries later.

"That's all the songs," says Quinn. "All the good ones we've all rehearsed."

The lights are going back down and the tone of the cheering has shifted.

"Do 'Hangman Forever,'" says Cyprus. "You two go out there and start it. Share the microphone. Me and Quinn will join in partway through. It'll look great."

Lillian starts to say it's not ready, but Cyprus pushes us back out onstage.

Lillian picks up her electric and gives it a strum. Her and I have sung this song together a handful of times with her playing acoustic guitar. Only a couple times for the band. I'm still sketchy on a few lines of the haunting lyrics.

The levels get turned back up halfway through the chord ringing. Lillian presses some pedals to change the sound and it becomes as acoustic as it can be.

When we sing, Lillian's mouth is inches from mine. I can feel every one of her notes. We sing of coming closer in the dark and wrapping in each other's arms and kissing under an exit sign, and it's not hard to make it feel intimate. I think anyone watching us could see it.

It's not a fake gesture like Augustus and I performed to look like best friends onstage when we barely spoke to each other off it. It's not like Isabelle and I in public, always touching, her ability to switch on adoration in her eyes. Maybe it looks like the same theatrics, but my heart is racing.

In the middle of the song, Quinn makes his way back to the drum kit and Cyprus comes in with an ethereal synth part. It stays quiet to the end, never escalates out of its sadness.

We all take a bow at the front of the stage. It's over for real, people scattering to buy more drinks, line up at the bathroom and talk over the transition music while we hurry to clear our equipment and make way for the last band. Amidst coiling cables with Wavelength's blue tape markers on them, all four of us keep catching glances from each other. Because we know we've done well. We've made something.

Then, instead of going backstage, we plunge into the crowd and scream, dance and sing along with the final act. So the post-show low gets pushed later and won't be as heavy when it finally hits. We give and receive from the stage, then reverse it and receive music and give our love back.

After, our ears ringing and bodies thrumming, we join the press of people going into the lobby. That low can wait a little longer, because there are people my friends want me to meet. I tell myself no one recognizes me. I have a new story, and it only started a few months ago.

I work on a catalog of faces, names and connections. I'm good at this, though I don't track a tenth of the people Cyprus greets with hugs and specific questions about their projects. It helps that I genuinely like people and want them to feel liked. Plus these people are pretty likable and give me lots of validating compliments on my outfit.

I even see one of my downstairs neighbors and almost wave at him, then remember I've told different versions of my story to everyone, that I can't let separate parts of my life cross. Luckily, he's on his way out.

Quinn goes to check on the merch table, where Wavelength stuff is being sold along with the other bands' merch. Cyprus leads us toward a group in the corner, saying, "You've got to meet Jemma."

"Jemma's the best," says Lillian, with a look that indicates that she thinks Jemma's considerably less than the best.

Lillian has a bold way of finding her way into closed circles of people, holding my hand to guide me around another cluster and then sweeping me in with her, making me feel welcome and known. This is her terrain, and she's suddenly more social than I've ever seen her. Unthreatened and unshaken by everyone until she sees the last person in the group we just joined.

She shuts down, can't speak. Her hand tightens on mine.

Cyprus bails her out.

"This is Sasha," she says. "Sasha, meet Jemma, TJ and Emelia."

LILLIAN

Emelia's hair is in a ponytail, some falling around her face, messier than she likes it. She looks flushed from dancing, and I know exactly how her mouth would taste right now. I know how her shoulder would feel against mine if I was standing beside her and that she'd complain about the spikes on my jacket. Not serious complaining, but she's short and the spikes are in her face. I know that she needs a glass of water but doesn't want to leave her friends to get one. I'd normally go get it for her without her asking, and she'd smile at me.

It's a smile I'd die to have turned my way.

I did not start dating Emelia because she played bass and sang and leveled up Wavelength substantially, I swear. I started dating Emelia because she was the loveliest person I'd ever met.

Now I'm still holding Sasha's hand, not sure what it means or how I want Emelia to feel about it. I can't let go without looking guilty and giving her some stab of hope or satisfaction or pain. With her just a few feet away from me, I can't stop myself wanting her in my arms, wanting Sasha in the same place. It's cacophony inside me, like I'm a record someone's trying to play forward and backward at the same time.

People are talking, Cyprus, TJ, Jemma, even Sasha. But not Emelia, not me.

"You guys sounded great."

"I love your boots, Sasha."

"Thank you. I'll trade you for yours."

"That last solo though."

"Orgasmic."

"Eww."

"It's sex-positive."

"It was a guitar solo."

"Solo?"

"I love the new Wavelength beanies."

"Quinn made them."

"Sh… *he's* so good."

"Does he design for other bands?"

"Noah wants pins for the new EP."

"I'm pretty sure Quinn could do that."

And the whole time Emelia and I are pretending to follow the conversation while watching each other. I'm soaking up her presence. My body screams.

Safety.

Heartbreak.

Home.

Emelia recovers before I do. She has more social grace in just the way she stands than I've ever had altogether. But when she speaks now, her voice is the draft from the door. Slight, only a moment. Then she closes off her hurt to keep the warmth in.

She talks right past me to Sasha, which there's nothing wrong with except everyone here knows about me and Emelia. There's six of us and we can all see she's not talking to me. It's like she's grabbing Sasha by the collar, interrogating them.

"You can really sing. Where'd you learn?"

"There was a great music program in my old school," says Sasha, which I've never heard them mention before.

"Did they teach you to be a rock star too?"

"Hardly. Just musicals, mostly."

"Don't be modest. When you made everyone be quiet? That was wild. You must have learned somewhere."

"I doubt it'd work again," says Sasha. "I just had a good feeling."

"I didn't even know you'd be playing."

Emelia says it like it was a pleasant surprise and like Wavelength isn't on the event page or the poster. She says it to Sasha but means it for me. To hide that she came to see me? To demonstrate that she wouldn't have if she'd known?

"I'm glad you were here," I say, but it comes out wrong. It was supposed to be to everyone, but it sounds like it's just to Emelia. She can't ignore me anymore.

All the eyes on us, expecting something gladiatorial, and I'm remembering our last conversation in the elevator and how she heard me sing the song about it tonight.

Cyprus checks the swarm of messages on her phone. "Quinn says Noah wants to talk to us about opening a show." I can see there's nothing from Quinn. "Noah should open for us, am I right? We'll bury him if we go first. Jemma, I'll text you about that festival. Good to see you guys!"

We're out of the circle.

To me, this is the equivalent of diving into traffic to push me out of the way of a speeding car. Saving me and Emelia before one of us made things properly awkward or ugly.

"I am so sorry about that," I say to Sasha the instant we're out of earshot. "She's a bit much." I hate that expression. It's almost always sexist and I'm using it to brush off Emelia. I add, "I should have gotten us out of there quicker."

There, I've released Sasha's hand. Mine are both in my pockets now. I'm willing myself smaller, done being somewhere where everyone knows me. Done being seen.

"It wasn't bad at all," says Sasha. "I've been in worse."

I feel like I want something from Sasha. For them to say either cruel things or charitable words about Emelia. Or maybe to not have been so friendly.

"Still an awkward situation," I say. "You replacing her in Wavelength. I pushed for that. I shouldn't have frozen up."

Maybe I want Sasha to hate Emelia because they see how remarkable she is. Because her and I used to be together. I want all that could come with Sasha feeling that way.

Sasha just says, "We've all got skeletons."

"Not invertebrates," says Quinn, joining us from the merch table.

Cyprus says, "Lillian ran into Emelia."

Quinn feigns astonishment. "But, but … she survived."

Cyprus puts her arm through mine without making me take my hand out of my pocket. "Nope. This one's dead on the inside now."

I mean, true, but it annoys me.

"Don't patronize me."

"I would *never*," says Cyprus.

Sasha laughs.

"What?" I say. They're all smirking a bit.

Sasha explains, "Last rehearsal, Quinn said that there are five guaranteed ways to kick-start Lillian. One of them is patronizing."

Nothing will embarrass you and make you feel safe like being known. I'm in that space between wanting to be mad and wanting to hug everyone and cry. It's time for me to get home.

"What are the other four?" I ask.

"So we got paid." Quinn waves a packet around. "In a classy envelope of cash. This is the big time."

"What are the other four?"

"And we sold merch," continues Quinn.

Cyprus looks up from her screen. "To who? Who bought shirts?"

"The new smoldery guy who just started shooting music videos for all the good bands."

Cyprus stands on tiptoe, which really puts her a head above the people milling about. "Where is he? I've been meaning to say hi to him. Are you into him, or are you saying I'd be into him? Either way I want a look."

"Maybe I'd be into him," says Sasha. "I like some smoldery guys too. Lillian, you interested in a smoldery artsy guy?"

Which reminds me that Sasha's not mine, not like that. Other people must have noticed them onstage. I've seen some people check them out tonight. Before the Pilgrim finally starts to clear out, a friend of an acquaintance asks how long Sasha and I have been together. Sasha says, "Tangibly or spiritually?" and sidesteps the whole question.

When I look back for Emelia, she's already left. Eventually, with the lobby cleared and the venue winding down, we do the same.

In the back seat of the station wagon, I say to Sasha, "You're not going to tell me the other four, are you?"

They shake their head. "To the grave."

This is legitimately going to keep me up at night.

SASHA

Our next gig is even better.

We repeat the show from the Pilgrim when we play at Initialism a couple weeks later. But this time, it's all on purpose and planned, from quieting the audience to ending with "Hangman Forever." I don't stumble, and I don't try to forgo my cut of what we get paid, which I tried at the Pilgrim. That was highly suspicious.

At the Channel, I was surrounded by wealth. Here, being paid is like a happy coincidence, the amount determined at the end of the night. Half of the musicians who are older than us are still living in their parents' houses, and none of them are doing music full-time. Or they're doing music full-time and then also working somewhere else full-time. It doesn't involve a lot of sleep.

Lillian complains about the Initialism show afterwards, but anyone who knows her can see she's glowing. She just expects more now that we've had another two weeks of rehearsal.

I doubt that will ever really stop. It doesn't for me. As unforgiving as it was, I'm a person who loved rehearsing every day for weeks and putting little bits of tape all over the stage, choreographing the show song by song.

Emelia isn't at Initialism. I can't tell if that's better or worse for my friends.

Last week, waiting together for a bus on a slushy day when I knew I'd die if I tried to bike, Quinn asked me how it was meeting Emelia. He looked at me doubtfully when I said it was totally fine.

"She's Lillian's ex."

"I know."

"I thought maybe with you and Lillian ..."

I elbowed him. "Don't trail off at me. You'd know if we were together."

"I know she finds reasons to touch you with a very non-Lillian cuddliness. And I know that when you described who you're attracted to —"

"That was ages ago. I'm a quickly evolving person —"

"— you literally described Lillian."

"I'd just met all of you."

Quinn started counting on his fingers. "Confidence, swagger, passion, *fierceness of being yourself.* Oh, and queer, and not automatic."

I looked over at Quinn, who seemed prepared to keep listing things until I got the point.

"Well shit."

"Well shit indeed," agreed Quinn.

He must have seen I was a bit rattled by this realization, because he laid off on the teasing once the bus arrived.

My mind was skipping through tracks.

Lillian doesn't think of me sexually. At least, I don't think she does. I see myself that way though. I feel the most attractive

I've felt in my entire life. Except sometimes I feel ineligible, too strange and hard to pin down to be anyone's crush or desire.

Platonic, Lillian said.

All the times we've been close. In her room alone, Cyprus's basement, the edge of the parking garage. Lillian's not a coward. If she had a move to make, she would have made it by now.

When the bus stopped by my house, I wanted to show Quinn where I live. I'd love for him to see the space I've made, but I couldn't. I claimed homework and my parents — always blaming my parents. I wanted to talk to him about Lillian, but what was the point?

I can't tell him the main reason it's all a bad idea.

I was Alexander Ash.

Though I'd die to see Quinn's reaction.

At Initialism, Christensen wasn't there for our show, though he asked Cyprus to video it for him. I guess he takes nights off too. It made me more nervous. I'd rather have him in my sight and be able to see how he looks at me. Now I know who he is, I can monitor for recognition. Watch for whether my singing and movement tip him off.

Isabelle's been silent. On the tabloids in the grocery store aisle the other day, I saw she's pregnant and it's Augustus's baby. The sheer absurdity of that concept almost made me laugh out loud. I started reading other gossip magazine covers, and they seemed stretched to manufacture decent lies, which is good. Maybe it means the initial breaking news of Augustus's scandal is losing momentum and a verdict is too far away for people to care. Maybe it means my absence is becoming less notable and there's no official info being released by the Channel.

I could be getting away with it. Every day, that old life gets closer to the horizon line.

Then a splash of red writing caught my eye. A cover with bold letters across a paparazzi picture of me in my helmet looking away from the camera.

WHERE IS ALEXANDER ASH?

I tucked it behind a magazine with reality TV stars on the front and checked out.

Here, with Wavelength after our show at Initialism, we're all embedded in the present.

We're inside live music. We focus on who's here and who's not and what choices to make right now. Cyprus is talking about who's following us and how the streaming numbers for Wavelength's music are up. Sef slipped Quinn his phone number. Quinn's saying he might call it, and Lillian's writing lyrics on napkins.

So Emelia's the past too. She's not here right now, and her and Lillian aren't together right now. That's what counts. If any part of my past shows up here, there will be more than some awkwardness. But that's not the present.

Let us scream "I am" and turn away from "I was" no matter the cost.

I say that part out loud and it goes on the napkin of Lillian's lyrics with my name in brackets beside it.

"In case you sue me for royalties," says Lillian.

"For you," I say, "all my words are on the house."

She kicks at me underneath the table. "That sort of mixed metaphor is why I'm the main songwriter."

Then Lillian looks right at me, turns the rest of the world down to a backing track.

"To hear your words," she says, "I'd spend a fortune."

58

LILLIAN

A few days later, it snows heavily in the way that builds up on the picnic tables in mounds. Snow that will last all winter. We finally have to give up eating outside, but we survived November and were the last ones left. Sasha was keeping a blanket in their locker to wrap around their legs just to stay warm.

In fairness, it's worth going to lengths to spend as little time in this building as we can. There's nowhere good to have a breath of space.

We've taken up residency at the far end of the second-floor hallway, sitting on the floor. There's a stairwell closed for "safety reasons," creating a forgotten space nobody moves through. That's what we've claimed as our own.

In the inside pocket of my jacket, I can feel my present for Sasha. I asked when their birthday was, and they said it was a secret, which makes me think it happened on a night we were doing something else and they didn't say anything. So I've got a present for them now.

"Listen, my parents are out of town this weekend," says Cyprus.

We just finished eating Falafel 'Til Dawn leftovers I brought from home and Cyprus is scraping out a hummus container with a spoon and eating it straight. Clearly, she has no one to kiss right now. None of us do, though if Quinn ever calls Sef he might.

"Empty house," Quinn says. "Are you thinking what I'm thinking?"

"Say it on three," says Cyprus. "One, two, three —"

We get a disjointed combination of "dance battle" (Quinn), "baking show" (Sasha), "house concert" (me, and it's a great idea), and something Cyprus says that I have to ask her to repeat to hear properly.

"Swimming pool." She eats a spoonful of hummus. "My parents are still keeping it heated, but they usually close it by mid-December. This is last call to use it while they're not around being you know, themselves."

"Bland and befuddled?" suggests Quinn.

"Watch your mouth, boy," says Cyprus. "That's my family you're talking about. I prefer the words *awkward and clueless*."

It pains me to give up a house concert, but to say public swimming pools are not the most queer-friendly locations is an understatement. I'll take what I can get.

I throw a loose fry at Sasha, missing. "Why aren't your parents ever out of town at the same time?"

"The real question," says Sasha, "is why don't they have a pool that's still heated in December?" I can see them considering. "I'm going to have to get something to swim in."

Cyprus is quick to add that it's not like we have to swim if people don't want to or don't feel comfortable. "I just love having you guys over, whatever we do."

"I think I want to swim." Sasha adjusts their skirt. "It's fun picking outfits to be around you three. You give me all the space to be experimental, playful, catastrophic, whoever I am."

Quinn, possibly to ward off things getting too sincere, declares that in the spirit of being experimental, playful and catastrophic, he's going to call Sef for real this time.

We all want to be on speakerphone, but Quinn takes just Sasha with him into an empty classroom. Since Sasha won't give away that they're listening in. Unlike some of us, apparently. I can see Sasha and Quinn sitting on desks through the narrow window beside the classroom door.

I pull out my wallet and wave a bill in front of Cyprus. "Five dollars he doesn't actually call Sef? No, five dollars he doesn't contact him in any way."

Cyprus is looking at me evenly, like she's waiting for me to run myself out of energy. Mixed patient and impatient. She's got something she has to say, and it's not for Sasha and Quinn to hear. These are the things you learn from knowing someone your entire life.

"Yes?" I say.

She exhales. "You're not going to love this."

Her face already has that please-forgive-me vibe.

"I invited Emelia tonight too."

"You were there at the Pilgrim, right?" I'm still holding out the bill. "Standing beside me? I'm quite certain you were there." Emelia must not have told Cyprus about the note I left her, how she wasn't ready to be anywhere near me yet.

"You two weren't altogether hostile. I said she can bring a friend or something. Margot, maybe?"

"I hate Margot." I used to like her just fine actually, before I thought about her comforting Emelia and Emelia spilling all of my secrets and mistakes to her.

I manage to keep my voice down, but what I say is, "What the actual fuck were you thinking? There were buffer people at the Pilgrim too."

"I'm thinking it's been shit trying to be friends with both of you without making one of you feel abandoned, and I hate it, and I need you two to grow up because me and Quinn don't care and I'm pretty sure Sasha doesn't either. It's going to be awkward, and we're going to be okay."

"No," I say. "That's not fair. You don't talk to Gabriel at all. I'm not here calling you childish and inviting him to things behind your back."

"You once told me you 'loathe his very aura,' so not really a fair comparison, is it? He wasn't friends with any of you. He wasn't in the band."

"But with Emelia the situation's somehow better?"

"It's more nuanced."

"It's a dumpster fire."

The present for Sasha suddenly feels less like it's waiting to jump out of my pocket, ready to be given, and more like it's digging into my side. It feels too bulky, all angles and errors.

"I thought maybe you'd be happy," says Cyprus.

"Why in god's name —"

"I thought you'd be happy because you're still in love with her."

In the classroom, Sasha turns their head at the initial outburst of my reaction. I try to stay quiet when I continue.

"That is the single most ridiculous idea you've ever had."

Cyprus looks me dead in the eyes. "That you'd be happy or that you're still in love?"

I get so quiet I can't say anything at all.

A part of me is choking. Realizing there may not be an end to this, no surface to break through. I may be underneath the cold water from here to the end, snatching at light cutting through from above, cradling any tendril of warmth that reaches me.

Cyprus is backtracking, sort of. Saying Emelia will probably say no anyway. Saying it's a start to ask. Especially if she can tell Emelia I'm fine with her being around.

I am, I think. Or I want to be. Yet there's how things were at the Pilgrim and that message I put in her locker and the one she sent back.

There's Sasha.

But I don't say any of this.

And Cyprus already asked Emelia. I'm cornered.

Cyprus is an absurd, foolish optimist, and I want to yell at her and tell her that she has nothing to apologize for all at the same time. There are simply too many moving hearts to avoid some collisions. It's a mosh pit out here.

Sasha and Quinn emerge from the classroom. Sasha has their arm around his shoulders. "Your boy Quinn's going on a proper date, and he's probably going to wear a goddamn suit, and he's definitely going to be the handsomest bastard you've ever seen."

"You owe me five dollars," says Cyprus.

Transitions are the parts of it all I'm the worst at.

When the song's over, I can't let the echo die.

At home, I find the book of Emelia's I've been keeping.

I gave it to her freely. It isn't mine to take back or to choose which endings she sees.

I use a pen to put words on the inside of the soft cover where it feels like cardboard instead of paper, where there's nothing else to see and no one else's dedication in my way. I write the truth, or the echo of it. I'll bring the book along on the weekend. I'll hand it back to her and if she doesn't say anything, I can imagine she continued reading from where she was or gave it back to goodwill.

I put the book in my bag.

Even if she never sees what I wrote, it was still written. Sent up to the surface to float where it may.

59

SASHA

I run barefoot across the snow-covered deck, Lillian right behind me. The cold burning my feet and then gone as I throw my body into the steam rising off the deep end of Cyprus's swimming pool, a shallow cutting dive with water rushing around my face. In the warmth, my feet are on fire.

I open my eyes underwater.

Lillian dives deeper than me and pulls a few strokes to take her deeper still. Now she's curving upward to take a breath. She said she hates swimwear, swore off buying it a long time ago. She's still wearing her baggy black jeans and a long black T-shirt billowing weightless around her.

Quinn hits the water, all cannonball and bubbles swarming. He's wearing a two-piece like me — his light gray and high compression, mine less on the compression and more on the bright stripes.

Cyprus is last in, dressed in a statement of asymmetry and fluorescence. She throws a large inflatable in above me and slips into the water with more dignity than some of us.

Everywhere I move in the water, I feel like I glimmer. Like my skin is sparkling with life. Like I've arrived home in my body now that I've exhaled the rigid gender I got handed without consideration.

Lillian curates the music while Quinn and I string up an unseasonable pool volleyball net. Her selection's surprisingly summery in a seventies new wave sort of way. The water's warm, and even the air above it if you stay toward the middle of the pool. Quinn and Lillian keep saying it must be costing a fortune to have it open in December. It hadn't even occurred to me.

Cyprus texts her older sisters to bring us drinks, waiting to see which one will respond. Victoria (law school, spectacular manicures, suit jacket aficionado) comes outside in a bathrobe with a tray of margaritas. We nestle the glasses in the snow beside the pool. Victoria throws snowballs at Katherine's window until she joins us, and we all play something approximating volleyball. And nobody's bothered that my swimsuit covers part of my chest because it feels right.

There's a few big sing-alongs after Victoria usurps the music selection for pop songs. Lillian says she'll wait it out at the bottom of the pool, but she winds up singing too. It's not something she can really resist.

Chart-topping music flickering by, a rainbow beach ball overhead. I've hit so many of them back into the audience at festivals. It was only a matter of time before an Admirer song came on. An older one, the lead single from our second album.

"Turn it up!" yells Cyprus, because even with Augustus on trial and Alexander nowhere to be found, a great hook is a great hook and this song was written by an army of the best in the business, even if the people singing it were kids at the time.

Live, there are parts of this song I never sing. I just hold my microphone out to the audience and let them carry the load.

Tonight, I don't let a word slip by. I take all of my own parts amidst the other voices and Victoria's persistent tonelessness. I want to understand what it felt like to have these songs at the backbeat of my youth without the burden of creation. I imagine this song is just a song, that I don't remember the pressure of making it in a studio when I was fourteen and everyone was treating me like I was far older or far younger. Forget that my helmet hid a lot of tears when I was out of the isolation booth between takes.

Sometimes, having cried helped me sound older.

Tonight, I pretend I don't know my unspoken stories. I sing along. A great hook is a great hook. You know it when you find yourself humming your own songs.

At the edge of the pool, Cyprus takes over the music, and the era shifts back to before Admirer had broken into the mainstream. Before we became the whole damn river.

Lillian and I are the last ones to leave the water.

For Cyprus's sisters, it's back to studying and keeping up with their incredibly high standards. Cyprus goes inside to make snacks, and Quinn follows not long after with plans of using the fireplace because no matter how warm it is in the water, there's no way to get out without freezing again. Quinn's goal is to cook some type of food over the fire indoors. It's a good thing Cyprus is in there with him.

"Too cold to leave?" asks Lillian. She's balancing on her tiptoes, holding her chin up to keep her face out of the water.

"Too warm in here," I say, treading slowly, farther out.

"I'll give you motivation. I've got a present for you. Come on."

She breaks into sloppy front crawl, hacking her way to the edge and leaving me no time to ask why she got me a present.

LILLIAN

This afternoon, Cyprus told me Emelia was coming over earlier than the rest of us. That she'd probably be gone before me or Sasha showed up. She hadn't decided yet. Maybe she'd stay for a bit.

I wanted to ask more but couldn't bring myself to. I just said it sounded good as if I was relaxed about any plan, and I left Emelia's book in my backpack. Then I put a bow on Sasha's present and added it to my bag too. I filled the rest with different sets of clothes to insulate against the whole thing. It gave me some sense of being prepared, like I'd have what I needed no matter what.

But when I arrived, Sasha's bike was by the door and Emelia wasn't there. Nobody said anything about it beyond Cyprus smiling a sad smile at me and saying, "Maybe next time. Time breaks down everything, right?"

Which was precisely the problem between Emelia and me.

Perhaps also the solution, but I'm not patient. I'm one of the angry waves that throws itself at the cliff face believing my sole effort will smash the whole thing down.

I had no idea what I wanted if we got another chance. I had

this picture of kissing Emelia underwater and my fingers in her hair. I had a picture of us carefully being friends and of giving her the book and our hands touching. A hint of hope at the corner of her mouth.

I had a picture of us entangled, sinking, but I didn't know if it was good or bad.

I did feel relief when I saw Emelia was already gone. Then again, half the time relief is just a sign of cowardice.

All the things I really want are terrifying, from stages to bedrooms to living forever.

I didn't realize what time had done until I went to put my backpack in the changeroom and saw Emelia's swimsuit hanging there.

There are dedicated rooms for going to and from the pool. A space with dark tile and a bathroom and dry sauna attached. I'd gone in alone to take a moment before we went outside. Somehow the house felt very full. Emelia's swimsuit was hanging on the last hook, deep yellow, almost orange with the water clinging to it, dripping onto the floor. It looked limp, half-covered by a towel. I wondered if Emelia left it uncovered on purpose. I'd never seen it before, but I knew it was hers, and I wondered if she'd thought of me seeing her in it and chosen it with my eyes in mind.

And then, I didn't wonder anything.

All the need washed out to reveal a clean surface with only melancholy curiosity. Something like nostalgia. In a few months, I've gone from knowing every detail of her life to not knowing when she'd been here or what she'd looked like or where she'd gone. I don't know the girl who chose that swimsuit anymore.

I felt like I was going to cry, then it faded without ever streaming down my face. I was exhausted in the way you are when your chest has been ripped open and sewn back together.

I cuffed my jeans and put on a shirt I didn't care about over my sports bra and said some very Lillian-consistent bullshit about the swimwear industry even though I'd brought proper things to swim in. Today, I defend myself with heavier clothes and let the water drag at me.

Every stroke to the surface was hard. And it was good.

Amidst Quinn's easy, self-assured movement, Cyprus bright enough to be seen from space, and her sisters in their expensive bikinis, I couldn't take my eyes off of Sasha. I haven't been able to for a while. They're more dazzling with each day their expression gets freer.

My eyes ache from floating underwater with them open, taking in the blurred edges of Sasha's form. The way their feet shift on the pool floor like they're wearing heels, the muscles in their legs, their hips and their hands and their softness and the way they seemed weightless that makes me want to touch them and send jolts of feeling through them.

My desire hidden under the water above me. Hiding me thinking of my mouth all over them, leaving marks on their exposed stomach and their neck. Of peeling everything off them and falling onto a bed with both of us entirely naked, laughing the way we've been laughing all evening, but alone. The wondering gone, replaced with wonder.

So as people left one by one, I stayed in the water even though my limbs were tired. I watched Quinn run across the frozen deck and through the door.

Until it's just Sasha and me in the steam off the water with the night wrapped around us. It's true I want to give them my present, but as I swim past them, it's all I can do to stop myself taking the few strokes that would get me close enough to wrap my legs around them.

61

SASHA

I'm barely out of the water, trying to get to the door as quickly as humanly possible without slipping on the ice from all the water people have tracked in and out. Then Lillian turns and tackles me, low and hard. Unstoppable, which I always suspected about her. I don't have a chance.

We hit the snow together, tumbling, my bare skin grabbing it up. I swear my heart's never accelerated this fast. Lillian's still holding on to me, her arms wrapped around my bare stomach and one hand hovering on me.

I'm immobilized by the cold. That's what Lillian must see, not me totally still under her touch. I'm willing to lie here if her momentum slows and she meets my eyes.

Her skin's warm when everything else is ice. Yet all my senses have latched on to her hand touching the bottom edge of my top. Her hand that I want to slow down, to keep tracking upward, to press me into the snow.

LILLIAN

In the snow, they look brand-new. In the snow, my eyes lock on their mouth grabbing at the air. Every part of me is cold except where I'm touching them.

63

SASHA

But Lillian's already scrambling to her feet. "To the pool!" And she throws herself back in with a twist, looking at me as if she's pulling me with her.

When I hit the water, the snow clinging to my skin dissolves around me. My skin falls asleep all at once, wakes up, gets reborn.

Lillian's laughing at me. "You *had* to have been able to see that coming."

"This is like the second time I've ever been in snow. I don't see *anything* coming."

"I'm sorry, I'm sorry. You're used to golden beaches I'm sure."

She's the least sorry person I've ever seen. She's crackling with energy right now. It's been growing all night, though I'm not sure why. Like she's nervous but excited. Like it's keeping her afloat.

"This time I'll go inside," she offers. "No more tackles. Cross my heart and hope to die."

"Because I'm sure crossing your heart carries so much weight for you."

"I'll have your towel ready and waiting."

When I make it inside, Lillian's thrown a hooded bathrobe on over her soaked clothes. It's white with gold embroidered letters on it, and it's too big for her. She's wearing it like a boxer, untied, hood up. She's holding out a fluffy towel for me.

"See, I can be trusted," Lillian says as I dry my hair and wrap the towel around me just under my armpits. "I'll prove it."

She rummages in her backpack on the floor, around a change of clothes and a book and a quarter-to-quarter cable that lives there just in case. She emerges with a small rectangular present wrapped in heavy cream-colored paper with a big purple bow on it that she has to poof up.

"It was better before. I should have put the bow on after I put it in my bag. I'm usually more of a wrap-it-in-duct-tape-and-laugh-as-they-struggle sort of gift giver. Anyways, happy birthday."

"It's not—"

"Well you wouldn't tell me. Last time it was your birthday, I didn't know it was. So this is to make up for that."

"You hadn't even met me."

She sings, "Happy birthday, dear Sasha / happy birthday to you" and hands me the present.

I'd like to always be her dear Sasha.

Inside, there's a mix CD in a clear plastic jewel case. She's made liner notes, a little booklet with a drawing on the cover of a skyline at night and swirling letters above it.

If I Fall, I Blame You

I handle it like treasure, looking at the stars on the CD and drawing out the liner notes, flipping through them and stopping for a long time on each one.

Every page is for a different song, each with a sketch to go with it.

Her figures are stick people drawn with bright pencils. Black outlines with splashes of color.

And each song is about me. About us.

The song she sang on the edge of the parking garage paired with a drawing of us sitting side by side, our bikes leaned against the concrete and our feet dangling. Her and I on the back steps of the school, with her wearing my headphones, listening to the same Monochrome Stoplight song that's on the CD. There's us on her couch with a song from a movie we watched together, and one labeled *Bonus Track* with a picture of Wavelength in a huddle. I know what that is. There's the acoustic EP version of the song I played for her on guitar. My pink jacket hanging on the back of her bedroom door with the karaoke song I sang. And a few songs we've sent each other with drawings of each of us lying in our beds, listening to what the other person chose. Packing Boxes, with her holding my hand, leading me off the floor, the only figures drawn in color.

LILLIAN

On my desk, there are five earlier versions of the CD. They're missing songs or in the wrong order. Ones where I messed up the cover. There are pages of attempted liner notes and a notebook with crowded sketches and potential track lists.

I kept thinking of more songs for the soundtrack of every hour we've spent together. Some I adore, some I emphatically don't but they've found a spot in my heart. They come from listening closely to Sasha and asking about what they hum along to. Learning what's playing in their head so I can sing along.

All around, crumpled wrapping paper from my numerous attempts to make it pretty and fold the corners tight. It's the late-night wreckage of wanting to get this just right for Sasha. They deserve something perfect, and I wanted to be the one to put it into their hands and see their face respond before someone else did.

How could I possibly think giving the book back to Emelia was anything like what I made for Sasha? In my backpack, I touched the book and pushed it farther down in shame. A snap mistake compared to a gift I worked on night after night, that made me smile and didn't fill me with dread.

When I give Sasha the music, it means what it says at the end of the liner notes.

Love, Lillian

They take a long time to get to that part. People are noisiest about presents when they have to prove they like them. Sasha's quiet, flipping forward and taking in each page while I take them in. Their towel tight across their chest and the beads of water on their shoulders and the way they cross one foot behind the other.

It was always this, fighting helpless against a riptide, pretending I wasn't getting carried farther and farther out. I am that sort of fool.

SASHA

I say Lillian's name softly because I love how it feels in my mouth. Because I don't know what else to say. Because of how close she's standing to me.

One of her hands brushes against my thigh. On purpose, lingering, tracing my skin with the calluses on her fingertips.

I make a sound, I think. A small involuntary inhale that Lillian responds to by pressing up against me. Reaching around me, one of her hands gripping at my towel and the other strong on the back of my neck, pulling me toward her until our faces are nearly touching.

And I've set the CD aside, fumbling, trying to be careful with it when what I want is to move fast. All they've said about urgency is true. All I've said. The imaginary kisses I've written songs about and the flirty lines I've sung without feeling a thing are moving through me now, words I'll never sing the same again.

She's breathing harder. From the cold, from treading water, from feeling me racing against her, like we've just gotten off-stage before the encore. She contains all the withheld power before the drums and bass come in, and I want to drown in it when it does. I want to feel it so loud that it fuzzes out the rest of the world and leaves my ears ringing for hours afterward.

"Yes?" she asks.

I push her hood back, and she pulls me in closer, my forehead against hers. We're going to sing like this someday.

In that moment, everyone will cheer and scream because this is a story the Channel would tell. They'd suspend every corner of their suspicion and cynicism and say it's perfect. A fifth, a clean harmony making you certain that love reverberates across time and circumstance and improbability. People need those stories.

And my heart will feel settled as I look directly at her. The crowd will be roaring but I'll be able to make out her voice amidst it all. Live, from her mouth, not amplified and not affected for the world. I'll know it isn't a story. I'll know it isn't make believe.

"Can't you tell?" I say.

We are equally in this. We're both the sea relentless and consuming and the ships reckless for setting sail on it, for throwing away caution and navigating by the stars.

I whisper yes.

LILLIAN

I can feel their anticipation everywhere their body touches mine, where my hand is on the back of their neck and my fingers are gripping their towel, one move from ripping it off and starting to undress them.

"Yes," they say. A little like a plea, almost relief.

So I pull Sasha to my mouth, push Sasha against the wall.

Every fragment of them is response and breath. Their lips are soft. Their sounds too, the ones that I'm too shy to let escape until I'm so overcome I can't control it anymore. I feel the noises against my lips, from their tongue through me. I consume each one. Melodies to replay alone in my bed. To memorize note for note.

The towel's crumpled around their feet and their hands are on my lower back, drawing me in closer even though all the ways I want to be closer are not for this room. Not right now. All of my desires whisper the word *later* in my mind. All of this is reverberating inside me when I entangle their fingers with mine and I press the back of their hand against the wall.

"Sasha," I murmur through it all, their name. "Sasha, Sasha."

They break away, only so far that I can focus on their eyes.

"I thought ..." they say, stop. "When did this start?"

Their mouth looks kissed in the way that brings the pink out in their lips and matches it to their flushed face. It looks kissed in a way that will melt and sigh if I kiss it again.

Beside us, sitting on their bag, the liner notes are open to the first of two Packing Boxes songs. A drawing of them reaching for the fire escape.

"Since then," I say. I touch their face, suddenly allowed to feel them react as I trace beside their eye. "Or since you sang with me. Or since right now."

That's all true at once, which may make it all a lie.

"It doesn't have to be a moment," they say.

They take my hand and kiss the back of my fingertips, on the verge of slipping them into their mouth, and I don't know how I'm supposed to speak.

I hear the door unlatch. It's feels loud, triggering part of my brain I didn't know was on edge and listening closely. I snap away from Sasha, almost slipping, portrait of suspicion, but the door closes again quickly before I can get a look at who cracked it open.

"Shit," I say. "Did they see us?"

Sasha looks flustered and chagrined in the sexiest possible way. "Does it matter if they did?" they ask.

I'm listening for the cold in their voice. Or accusation, or doubt, or the staggering step backward that says this was a mistake. But it's not there. They're just asking. I trust them.

I tie the front of my bathrobe shut.

"The band," I say quickly. "It's the band. When I made the big pitch for you to join, they, well, Cyprus, was worried about me liking you. People in band sleep together, band implodes. Not that we're ... anyway. So us, whatever this is, yeah. It's tricky. Right?"

I'm suddenly acutely aware that Emelia's swimsuit isn't hanging on the hook anymore. Did Cyprus put it away to look out for me? Or was she the one who left it there to try to bring up something inside me?

I think of her saying I'm *still* in love when what I really feel is something that's fresh. I don't want Sasha to think I regret this. I must look like I'm panicking.

And I am, but only because sometimes the world tilts too quickly. I want to hold on to them and tell them I'm just dizzy. I just moved too fast for my own good and if we weren't here, I'd move even faster to stop the spinning.

"Just for now," I say, "can we hide this?"

They pick up the CD. "'This,' being what?" they ask.

I feel like I can see through the booklet to where it says *Love, Lillian*. They say it smiling, though, not afraid.

"I don't know," I say, "but I want to find out if you —"

They kiss me again, envelop me. It's tender, like we've been kissing for years. It makes me less overwhelmed. It makes me want to cry and to build a blanket fort and to wake up beside them for the hundredth time in a row and notice their eyelashes in a way I've never noticed before.

"Me too," they say when they break away. "Very, very much so. Now let's get it together. I'm going to get changed and go in first. I can put on a show anytime I like."

"An expert, I'm sure. But I'm the pro of pretending."

"Is that so?"

They kiss my neck hard for a moment, flooding my mind with the thought of them underneath me, and I find that it is in fact a good idea if I take another minute before acting like nothing happened.

By the time I emerge, Sasha's crouching in front of the fire with Quinn wrapping frozen pizza in tinfoil, talking about how to get a smoky flavor. Cyprus is watching something on her phone with one earbud in, leaning on the counter while a food processor full of fresh salsa churns on the counter beside her. Victoria has profoundly not gone back to studying. She opens a bag of chips and adds a few more spices to the salsa.

Cyprus slaps her hand away. "Not all of us have your tolerance."

"I thought you were too distracted to notice."

"I perceive all."

I must look desperately guilty at Cyprus's word choice. For a second, I'm sure she was the one who opened the door. I need to figure out what this is before I let anyone know. I want her to find out from me, not from me trying to hide it.

Revealing you've been hiding something looks heroic compared to being caught in a lie.

"Oh, you're done in there," Victoria says to me. "I keep meaning to get my phone from the bathroom, but it was locked before." She gives me the world's least subtle wink as she goes by, and I know I'm in the clear for now.

A couple hours later, I've figured out the way I'm actually most likely to give something away is by the sheer amount of time I spend watching Sasha. Their mouth has become somewhat more mesmerizing than before.

It's what my focus keeps slipping back to as Cyprus rambles about the Admirer trial while we play pool. Sasha and Quinn are sitting on the other side of the basement loudly singing along to old music videos and making Wavelength spray paint stencils but mostly making a crafting mess.

I track the broad strokes of what Cyprus says, enough to *mm-hmm* and *oh wow* at the appropriate moments. A bunch of Channel musicians are now testifying on Augustus's behalf

(Cyprus thinks some of them must have been forced to) and there's mounting pressure on the Channel to present Alexander Ash.

Cyprus's words lull for a beat. I miss a shot while looking at Sasha's lips, and I'm still not fully tuned in to Cyprus when she says she's sorry Emelia didn't stay.

"What?" I say.

Cyprus is standing close to me while she chalks her pool cue. "Emelia was in a better space about you. She's figuring stuff out. She felt really bad about how cold she was to you at the Pilgrim. I bet she would have stayed, except she got called in for a shift." Which could be real or an excuse, but Cyprus reads it honestly, adding, "I just think it could have been fun to have her here tonight."

She takes a perfect shot to delicately send a ball sideways into a pocket.

"Tonight was already pretty good," I say, focused on Sasha carefully cutting out a letter.

"It really was. But I know it still hurts." Cyprus understands how echoes remain in me. It's like she can see through my backpack to the words I wrote in Emelia's book. See how things linger even if I think they're gone.

But Sasha glances up at me with the slightest of smirks, and I have to tear my eyes away from them. I'm sure they see me hide my smile.

"Less this evening." That's true, even if she reads it wrong.

"Next time we see Emelia, will you try to talk to her? I think it'd go better."

"I don't know."

"For me, Lillian."

"I'll try."

Cyprus hugs me from behind while I try to take my next shot, resting her head against my back. She stays there for a while afterwards.

"I'm okay," I say. "I really am doing okay. It's your shot." She's beating me three games to none. I can't stop playing now.

"I know." She doesn't let go. "Do you think there's a chance everything works out?"

"Like cosmically? You know I don't."

"No, just that each tomorrow is better. Do you ever think back to who you were and realize how far you've come? I know our hearts won't stop getting broken. But maybe looking back could always be hopeful. We could be glad we found our way to where we are."

"We could," I say, and Cyprus asks when I became glass-half-full. She says I've been replaced by a clone, but both of us are glad to see the other one seeming alright.

I fall asleep on the couch and wake up to the smells of breakfast food cooking upstairs and a warm murmuring of voices. The sort of music where every song sounds a little the same and it's comforting. Someone covered me in a blanket, but I don't know who. Each one of them cares enough to do it, so maybe there's a chance everything works out.

SASHA

Lillian
So

Sasha
So?

Lillian
Um

Sasha
Um?

Lillian
You're being no help at all

Sasha
Such accusations

Lillian
How's the mix CD?

Sasha
I had to borrow a CD-playing stereo from my neighbors. We had an adorable interaction where I told them a friend made me a mix CD
And they were like a friend or a "friend"
At which point I just turned pink and ran, boom box on my shoulder
The CD is perfect. I've listened to it a thousand times

Lillian
Back up to friend or "friend"
If you want to just be friends that's okay I swear
Like at school and Wavelength practice, I can't tell what's going on with you

Sasha
You said to hide it for now

Lillian
It's been days! I can't skulk around for days

Sasha
Good word

Lillian
I know thank you
Don't think you can distract me with compliments

Sasha
Quinn and Cyprus have always been around. Or other people

And there is an amazing deficit of convenient closets to pull you into

Lillian

I see I see

You should have told me you were looking

I'm great at finding closets

Sasha

Sorry

I know you've done this before but I'm really new at it

I felt so confident at Cyprus's place

But then I panicked after and wasn't sure what any of it meant

Lillian

I'll tell you

Sasha, do you want to go out with me?

Sasha

I thought I made that super clear

Lillian

You really are new at this

Sasha

So you're asking me out?

Lillian

For fuck's sake yes!

Sasha

I'd love to

Lillian

I'll borrow the car and be by in ten minutes

Dress warm

Sasha

You're asking my queer ass to choose how to present in the next ten minutes?

I am only a person, not a god

Lillian

I'm willing to debate that point

But I have to be outside by the time Lillian shows up. She can't come knock on the front door and have people answer it who aren't the family I described. My downstairs neighbors are so friendly that they're bound to mention the true nature of my living situation and blow my cover.

It's evening, and the weather does the work of choosing my clothes. I dress warm with all the thermal layers. At the store, I said where I was from and that I needed to not die this winter. They were more than happy to help.

I've got this beautiful white parka with fake fur around the hood. Light pink lipstick that I think will look good when my face gets flushed from the cold. Which I may regret if I have to cover my face. Or if we kiss, but it's too late to change it. Lillian's pulling up in front of my house.

I run down the outside steps to meet her before she gets out and rings the doorbell or something disastrous like that.

This is why I've been a little too good at hiding things between Lillian and me since the weekend at Cyprus's. Putting on a show is my default. Saying how I really feel and what I really think isn't something I've ever been supposed to do, even less so now. It's something my heart tricks me into doing like it's tricking me into going along with Lillian in the cold.

Some part of me keeps locking down, and I keep unlocking it and throwing away the key. Then I find it, throw it farther out. Hoping it will get lost forever, knowing I'll need it back.

I just threw it again.

"You have your own entrance?" asks Lillian as I slam the passenger door behind me, trying to keep in warmth that hasn't built up in the car yet. The windows are frosty except for a patch where Lillian scraped the ice off.

"It used to be a walk-up. It's great for not explaining where I'm going." Even my small lies stack up piece by piece, precarious.

She turns the music down even though it's a great moment I know she loves. Each of the escalations in intensity. Right when it's about to get louder, that's usually when she turns it up.

She looks like she's about to say something, but she starts driving instead. One hand on the top of the steering wheel while the other spins the volume knob a notch lower so it stops on fourteen instead of sixteen. Back up to fifteen. That's the one. She skips a track, killing it right at the pinnacle. The next song is lower and steadier. All growl.

A block later, she turns sharply down a back alley and pulls just off to the side. She puts the car in park, moving the gearshift hard as she undoes her seat belt.

She's on top of me, legs spread around me, both hands behind my head and kissing me like everything hinges on it, like she's been caged all week, like a chord that was ringing and now someone's stomped the volume pedal down. She's moving against me, and my hips are rising into hers. Everywhere, our hands, fumbling at zippers and getting our jackets undone to get closer. Her hands are cold underneath my shirt, where I can feel every one of her rings against my skin as my hands search for the lever to push my chair back. It moves suddenly, but she kisses me harder instead of breaking away.

All of me blends into her, and I belong here. I make a whimper, and she responds to it by slowing down, which somehow feels like more. She places her palm on my stomach with her fingers spread out. She softly bites my lip when my hands settle on her hips.

She touches me like I am the exact and only thing she wants.

With her, I don't feel like a concept or a fetish or something she's pretending is male or female to be attracted to. I'm met, matched. I'm swept up in her power and hunger, and it brings out the same things in me. They're new in my chest and my hips and under my tongue. They're fascinating and igniting.

"Is this good?" asks Lillian between deep kisses.

"This is perfect," I say. "For now."

"I like both parts of that."

Lillian's lips and hands are noting my body. She's paying attention, learning me and overwhelming me by touching me the exact same way again, noticing where I sigh when she traces her fingers down the side of my ribs.

She is devastating. The most beautiful and fierce, the song that comes on insisting it's alive and carrying you with it. We aren't sexy like a catalog, a checklist, an anatomical paint by numbers. Tired scripts entirely beside the point to me.

The point is that she's devastating, and I'm overcome.

I used to wonder if desire had any strength in me. I thought I should desire Isabelle. I flipped around different words to describe not feeling much, tried to accept them because I truly believe them to be real and good. But they didn't fit me.

For me, this was waiting until I found out who I was. As Alexander Ash, there was no home for these feelings, no bed for them to lie in.

As Sasha, I'd like to let these feelings burn me down.

They will, but not all at once. We read this from each other as the fire shifts to coals, something we could build back up at any moment.

By the time we stop, the car's blowing warm air onto us. Lillian's headband is crooked, revealing the ear piercings she likes to keep out of the cold. There's lipstick all over her mouth that she wipes off with limited success. The pink clashes with the red bandanna tied around her neck.

She climbs back into the driver's seat and puts the car in gear. Each of us is quiet for a moment, both of us smiling. She puts her arm on the back of my headrest to reverse out of the lane, lets her hand linger on me on the way back.

Lillian's having trouble keeping her eyes on the road instead of me as I zip my jacket back up and flip down the mirror to fix my lipstick. It's a mess of evidence on my face. I'm not used to thinking of these things yet. Each newly discovered aesthetic and expression creates a set of curiosities now that I allow myself to be anything that might feel right.

I turn the music back up and skip to a fast song to match the way my heart is still hammering. "You make me feel like I'm in a storm," I say.

"Thunder or snow?" asks Lillian.

"I mean where everything is changing and uncertain, but I want the windows open. I want to go out and dance in it and be scattered."

"So you *don't* want to know where we're going?"

"It's not a principle I apply equally to all things."

"Too late. You've spoken, and now you live in mystery."

I pester her about it for the rest of the drive through the city in the early winter darkness. Look for hints, steal her headband, plant a kiss on the back of her hand that looks more like a smudge than lips. Every time I think she's going to tell me she comes out with a different ridiculous suggestion and tries to convince me with all seriousness. Roller rink. Poetry slam. Strip club. Polo match.

"I'm just such a horse girl," she's saying when we stop at a quiet community center by the river. "Cowboy boots, stable boys, banjos … um, saddles?"

"You're really selling this with your encyclopedic knowledge of all things equestrian."

"Mane, hooves," she continues. "Ooh, horseshoes!"

"Now you're just picking things with the word *horse* in them. Where are we?"

Lillian hands me a pair of ice skates from the back seat. "We're on a wholesome first date."

She's serious, I think, but says it like she's sarcastic, so I respond in kind. "Everything we've done in this car has definitely been one hundred percent wholesome. Not a single dirty thought."

Lillian tilts her head back and forth considering. "Wholesome compared to some things."

"And your thoughts?"

"Yeah, those were filthy."

Lillian brought Jasper's skates for me. I tie them once, then she helps me tie them again tight enough before we go out on a long skating trail on the frozen river. It's clear and cold with air that feels like it's the cleanest I've ever breathed. High on the banks, the biggest, oldest houses in the city have impressive facades facing the river. If we skated far enough, we'd arrive at Cyprus's.

It took several attempts from Lillian to convince me that the ice is safe, winning out when she started going on about how cute it will be when we held mittens.

It is that cute. Cute enough to venture onto the dark ice. Love-story cute that I snapshot to keep with me for when I'm back at the Channel someday, to hold on to in a greenroom in a city I've never been to before.

I'm wobbling at first, but I gradually smooth out and stop windmilling my arms. I skated once with LucSee and Augustus in northern Europe somewhere. A photo op, but Augustus and I stayed for hours as he taught me to stop and turn and not fall on my face.

He'd be like that, suddenly patient and present. A fragile belief would rise in me that this was his underlying nature. But I always sent the first text and last text, and he always ended the phone calls and conversations. He was always the one who had somewhere else to go that was more important than me.

Lillian and I glide down the river, seeing the city I chose as my home from a different angle than I knew existed.

Sometimes we clasp hands, going slowly, talking. Or Lillian skates backwards in front of me saying she likes to be able to see my face. She gives me tips. Her rusted-out thrift store hockey skates leave marks on the ice for me to follow.

"You're just showing off now," I say, as we round a bend in the river and she executes some backwards crossovers that are fifty-fifty sketchy and impressive.

"It's the only way I can think to seduce you." She settles in beside me again, bumping up against my shoulder and nearly knocking me sprawling. "Got to show my exceptionally pretty date how cool I am."

"Where'd you learn?" I look at her through the fuzzy edges

of my hood. "Was it the hockey or the figure skating?"

We both start laughing too hard to keep moving. It's only partly about the image of Lillian participating in either of those sports.

Mostly it's a haze of disbelief that we're here, getting high on the warm space we create when Lillian's face is shielded inside my hood and we kiss. It's me almost tumbling into the snow from Lillian's enthusiasm and her having to catch me. Other people skate past us as we stand on the edge of the river trail, lost in our own capsule of time. Then we stretch it out by skating farther, knowing we'll have to skate all the way back to the car someday.

As for her skating skills, she says she practiced because she didn't like being bad at it. And that the cold sometimes brings balance rushing back through her. It helps kick her body into presence, remind it that it wants to be alive.

"It's an alternative to feeling like nothing is real," she says. "I get scared everyone will leave, or that they're already gone. When it's cold, you can't think you're anywhere else or worry about reality. It's like getting slapped in the face. In a wake-up way, not a kinky way."

"I love that those are the two options."

"Okay, well, glad I was vulnerable with you. Never again. You'll probably just leave." She grins at me, but she's even closer to the truth than she believes she is. "Tell me something about you I don't know. Am I the first person you've dated?"

68

LILLIAN

For some unsettling reason, that question makes Sasha laugh.

"Define *dated*," they say.

No one could miss that evasiveness. It's fully obvious in their words, but not in their manner. They don't seem like they're pulling away from me or lying. At least I don't think. My analysis of these things tends to be fear based. In cold air at night, I know this. But that was very dodgy.

They pause for too long, but then say, "You're my first kiss and first real date. I have a really close friend from where I grew up that I used to fake-date as a popularity move. We looked good together, prince and princess sort of vibe, and beauty is power. That's what the 2000s high school movies say, and surely they wouldn't lie to us."

My doubts rose up too quickly. There's no trick from Sasha.

"I was only asking for my own protection," I say. "I want to make sure no gorgeous, angry person with perfect teeth who surfs and has strong arms is going to sweep in from the west coast to hunt me down."

"Do you want to have a threesome with the imaginary ex you've created for me?"

Sasha, they make my face ache from happiness. I want to be laughing and flirting on this river from here on out. I don't want to go back.

"Do your parents care?" I ask. "About her or me or that you're in a lightly angry band with queer friends? That should make any parents' blood run cold. We might turn you into an anarchist."

Sasha's quietness stretches out for too many moments. I consider adding that we can talk about something else. Or suggest we turn around. Maybe pretend to crash on the ice. I'm about to try the last option when they start talking.

"My dad would care in his own way. He's gone all the time now, but when he was around more, he maybe would have sat me down and asked a bunch of questions about the music. He loves music. Or he used to have moments where I could see he used to love it. He'd want all the numbers, the sales, the audience engagement."

"Sounds like he'd adore Cyprus. They could talk marketing strategies."

"He'd be over the moon. Otherwise, it's ... hard to tell with him. But I think he was most interested in the fake-dating thing once he knew it was fake. With you, he'd be worried about how it affected the band. And he's sort of fine with all the queerness. Except he'd be sure to say that it doesn't make me special. He says it's what you do that counts. And he definitely wouldn't count everything I do as important."

"And your mom? When you get dropped off late at night by some girl who looks like a punk to her and your lipstick's all smeared."

"I've got my own entrance to avoid any and all questions tonight."

"But let's say you couldn't."

We keep skating farther out. I sense that the moment we turn around, this conversation will be over. This is all so new. I want to cup the whole thing in my hands and press it close to my chest. Sasha and I.

All Sasha says is, "I like to think she's glad that I'm choosing how I live for myself."

We've hit what amounts to the end of the skating path. I hold Sasha's hand as high as I can and spin them around a couple of times, trying to catch their face as it goes past, wondering how I ever thought I was anything other than infatuated with them.

On the way back, I tell Sasha about working at the drop-in rec center where we started skating. I tell them about how I became friends with the meanest, strangest, angriest, scariest, snarkiest kids and probably made them even snarkier and stranger. I sing Sasha bits of the first songs I ever wrote.

I suppose this means I'd rather hear them laugh than hold on to my pride.

I remember this feeling. I've missed it so damn much.

Sasha tells me their older sister, whose name I'm embarrassed to have forgotten, is always in trouble. The getting-arrested sort of trouble. The kind that can't be ignored. So Sasha always has to seem okay. Someone's got to be the easy child.

"Do you think Jasper feels like that?" I ask. Shit. Hearing about Sasha's sister made me furious at her. What if Jasper hates me for all the space I take up? For the years when my panic attacks were more frequent, more immobilizing, preoccupying our mom. "Like he's got to be perfect to make up for me?"

"Let me assure you, you've got nothing on my sister."

"I'm serious."

"Say Jasper stopped communicating with you, full radio

silence, how long before you'd kick down his door? Or give him a call?"

"I want to say two weeks. Honestly though, a couple of days? He's the same with me. When he's at camp, he texts me all the time. Ridiculous stuff, not a word on how he feels or what he's doing. If I don't respond, he starts leaving me pretend-sad voice messages saying he feels like we never talk anymore."

"And if Jasper told you something personal or secret, you'd listen?"

"We're averaging once every five years for that. But yes."

"And if he disappeared and left you no way to contact him, you'd talk to Jasper's friends and try to make sure he was alright?"

"They're so sporty and intimidating though."

"But you would?"

"Of course."

"Listen, you're a great sister. Basically an angel."

"If you ever call me an angel again, I will kill you."

That night, I don't have a hope of sleeping after the last of the late-night texts are sent. I zoom in close on pictures of us, and I can see what had our friends mocking us and people asking if we were together. We're perpetually angled toward each other with our eyes and attention.

All the best pictures are with Wavelength, since Sasha typically doesn't like having a camera pointed at them. It was like that for me too when I first came out.

Not that they necessarily just came out. I don't know that whole story for Sasha, but I do know that they seem to have been discovering themselves very quickly over the past few months. I never like a lens aimed at me when I'm trying something new.

So next time I see them, I'll tell them it's all a beautiful wonder. The elegant and the sexy and the clothes they haven't figured out how to wear yet. The lace peeking out, the heels they have to concentrate to walk in.

I lie there imagining Sasha's breath slowing to a steady rhythm, their eyes shutting. When I first met them, I thought they were shy, someone who glances away from intensity. Now they can look right at me, unwavering.

I would skate backwards from here until the ice ran out to keep looking into those eyes. I could read everything, steady and expressive. There was desire, play, joy, surprise, tenderness, and something else that terrified me.

The look that said they trust me completely.

The look that said I won't hurt them.

The look of following me to whatever end.

Adoration.

Then we kissed again and I wonder why on earth we ever stopped.

It's six times we've kissed now, or seven, running off of one hand and across the other toward a number I forget, where times stack up until some disappear, even some of these first ones. I'll remember a few forever.

At Cyprus's. Reverberating inside me for days.

In the car. Fire in my body.

On the frozen river. Ice in Sasha's eyelashes.

I've done this before. And it goes …

The first: fourteen years old, late fall, too cold to have a picnic.

Emelia and I were out there anyway, lying on a blanket with as much of it folded over and wrapped around us as we could.

We'd been to a coffee shop, and another time we went to a movie, and those felt like dates. That day, she'd dragged me into a deep corner of the park where no one could see us.

We were on our stomachs, shoulder to shoulder, silently taking turns writing words in a notebook. A game of bad songs, one fragment at a time. Me putting a melody to it at first, lost in the music until I saw where the rhyme scheme was going.

L—so

E—I

L—was

E—wondering

L—how

E—to

L—tell

E—if

L—you

E—want

L—me

E—too

L—I

E—was

L—wondering

E—if

L—I

E—could

L—kiss

E—you

E—Lillian?

E—Lil?

E—can I kiss you?

In the hundreds: backstage at Initialism.

We'd just finished our first ever set there, which was also our first set with Emelia. We were so young and playing to the scattered people who were there early before the proper bands arrived.

We were really too young to play there at all, but I'd asked Christensen and given him the demos and he'd given us a shot. He said I burned too damn bright to be anywhere but on a stage.

I remember Cyprus and Emelia hugging and all of us jumping up and down and talking at the same time. Given the choice, I would have stayed out there and played until I dropped dead of exhaustion, even if it was only for my mom and a few friends and a dozen random people half-listening.

Then Emelia kissed me hard, right in front of Cyprus and Quinn and the band that was moving their gear onstage. Hand in the back pocket of my jeans hard. She didn't like to kiss when there were people around, full stop.

We always argued about it. I used to think it was all flirty bickering, but it was really that we were no good at fighting. So it was arguing. I knew she wanted me and loved being with me, but sometimes it felt emotionally restrained. Like she was holding something back. She said she wasn't. Whatever idea I had of what she was holding back, I've never seen from her.

Or it was like I was too much. With the spikes and opinions and breakdowns and my will to light the world on fire. My need to be desired without caution. To have her declare us fated and challenge my hatred of clichés by kissing me like no one's watching.

I never managed to tell Emelia about it that way. It just didn't seem like how I should feel.

The thousandth or millionth: in Emelia's bed.

Sometimes I forgot how remarkable it was that she was mine and next to me every day. I don't recall the day or month or even the season, just that it was morning and we hadn't closed the blinds and there was sun on her face while she slept.

I'd woken up early. Early morning is usually my darkest time because I know what I need to do is get out of bed and get moving, but I can't. The hour pins my body down. It requires necessity to throw the covers aside. I can't seem to teach myself that getting out of bed *is* a necessity.

I was thinking about time with this huge, pressing fear that I might waste it all, or that I already was. My brain was scrambling through decades toward my deathbed. Imagining lying there, an emptiness creeping up on me. Looking back and crying inside, *No no no, what have I done? Let me try again. Please, reincarnate me as me. Please.*

But as much as I want to, I don't believe in that sort of thing.

Then I saw Emelia's face in the sun. I knew I'd made it past sunrise again.

I kissed her awake, and she curled her back into me. I buried my face in her hair.

How could this be a waste?

Our last: outside the drop-in center.

A Friday morning in August. The center opened in the morning, but it was always dead for the first few hours. I wrote songs and did yesterday's cleaning and played arcade games. Sometimes alone, sometimes with Emelia.

That day she had a shift, but there was time to walk me to work. She said she'd pick me up later, and we'd go spend Friday night at my place like we always did.

It could be like this and be alright, I thought. It could be enough. If this girl walked me to work, I think I could set aside the dream of rooms full of people singing along to my voice. I saw the next decades and for once, I didn't feel the rush to the end.

I kissed her outside the doors, because we had made begrudging progress on that. It was a quick kiss, light, a see-you-after-work kiss. I thought I'd save all the deep, long ones for later. She must have seen in me that adoration I saw from Sasha today. She put in her earbuds as she walked away.

What song was that? It bothers me all the time, because if it were a movie, it would have played over it all.

I don't see Emelia online. Ever. To Cyprus's disappointment, I have no digital influence. Everything gets downloaded then deleted in cycles on my phone.

I say it makes me an enigma.

She says it makes me irrelevant.

So it's deliberate to seek out Emelia's face. Redownload an app, watch it refuse my face ID, reset a forgotten password, log back in.

She hasn't done anything to stop me from seeing this. There are photos of her in Cyprus's pool that I want to go past quickly instead of lingering on. The lingering wins. Digitally, her whole presence is careful and curated, nothing left in view she might regret. No moment of video that's truly candid. None of her goofiness and grinning and ridiculous dancing is on display.

She's making something timeless and with an interest in framing that's improved in the past few months. Look at her, being all productive and learning photography and giving off this air of undamaged calm.

I'm scared it's all true.

Further back, there's a series of pictures from the show at the Pilgrim. The hands of the crowd reaching up in front of her camera as she stretches to capture the moment. A shot through the throngs of feet, focused on a bottle lying on the concrete floor. The garbage swept up to the stage after the show.

TJ with his shaggy hair and Jemma with her another-era bangs up on his shoulders. Margot and Emelia wearing matching pins in support of something I care about too. The first band onstage, the last band leaving.

And one picture of me. Tucked in the post at second last.

It's taken from a low angle, up close, so she must have snuck near to take it. She let the bodies hide her, because I didn't see her face until we were in the lobby afterwards.

I've got my guitar slung around my back, headstock pointed at the floor, microphone off the stand, feet planted wide, chin up. I can hear that picture.

I stop there. I don't go farther back to see whether she's scrubbed me from every corner of her gallery of self.

I wish I'd glanced down to see her.

69

SASHA

Quinn figures it out before Lillian and I have decided how to tell the rest of the band.

The next week, Wavelength's rehearsing in his basement. Everyone except Lillian's slacking off a little since we don't have a show scheduled until early February. It's opening for a band none of us even have any friends in, which is a big step, though it's at an ill-reputed venue called Brickworks. Lillian's mom said she thinks she's still banned from there, but she refused to tell Lillian and Jasper the story no matter how much they bugged her.

Now that I'm a regular in Lillian's house, I get to witness these exchanges. I'm friendly and polite and in the band, but according to Lillian's mom, that's not what clinches how comfortable she is with Lillian and I being together.

"Even if you were altogether rude," she said, "if Cyprus trusts you, the highest standard has been met."

Not that Cyprus always looks at me like she trusts me.

In Quinn's basement now, he's watching me and Lillian with his own brand of suspicion. Every time her and I get close to each other, he gives me a look. Or when we sing something remotely about love or sex. Which happen to be two of the main topics of music, so all the time.

It took Quinn less than two weeks from that night at Cyprus's to arrive at this realization. To be fair, I did give him a couple fairly sizable hints.

I told him about the mix CD Lillian made for me. I was humming a song off it at school, and when Quinn asked, I figured I could make it seem like a friendship thing. It could have been, no reason why not except for maybe the words at the end.

I mean, *love* is a friendship word. And romance and friendship aren't mutually exclusive. Friends love each other. Still, I didn't mention those words.

"She drew pictures?" asked Quinn. "Were they deliberately bad? Because normally Lillian works out her insecurity about her drawing abilities by drawing bad on purpose."

I described the drawings with the color thrown in and the lyrics worked around them. Outlines of people with defining features and pieces of clothing.

"Um," said Quinn, "that's not a usual Lillian mix CD. Usually it's no-nonsense. Music-focused. A scrap of paper with the track list if she's feeling kind."

"Maybe your artistic prowess is rubbing off?"

"Trust me, it's not. I've tried." He threw a campy, overplayed shrug at me. "I wonder what other explanation there could possibly be?"

"You hopeless romantic."

"Sasha, babe, no romantic is ever without hope. That's the very nature of the thing."

Then last night I answered a call from him when I was in Lillian's bed with her. Clothed, and strictly speaking on the bed, not in the bed. Though my version of clothed would be called skimpy by some. Our legs tangled, our music suspiciously loud. Leaving kisses along each other's collarbones.

It wasn't escalating, just hovering there. I could feel us both wanting to move quickly and both holding back a little. Both a bit scared of the abandon we wanted.

This tension has to break soon, somehow. We both know it.

I promised to talk to Quinn after his date with Sef. But I figured Quinn might not call until the next morning. Or deep into the night, past when I could reasonably stay over at Lillian's without there being some discussion with her mom. Lillian's mom keeps her assumptions to herself, but apparently she's not a morning person or a fan of unexpected people around in the a.m. Though Lillian says her mom is mostly just happy Lillian's out of her post-breakup spiral from earlier this year. She doesn't want to disrupt Lillian's trajectory.

When my phone vibrated, it could really only be a couple of people, and one of them was Isabelle. The spike of fear in me was enough to break the moment and have me check.

When I saw Quinn's name, I answered the call without considering calling him back or letting him wait. I turned off the video fast before it grabbed the background.

I could see Quinn wearing a suit with a bow tie undone. He looked charmingly ruffled. Sexy ruffled.

"Hey, I can't see you," said Quinn on speakerphone.

"I just got out of the shower, but how was the date? Tell me all."

Lillian, lying on her back and listening, murmured something about how she liked the image of me in the shower, and I swatted her away.

Quinn gave me the short version because he said he'd tell the band tomorrow at lunch anyway. He said it was fancy, for sure. Sef's family is rich, and he tossed that around to make a big show out of things.

"Don't get me wrong," said Quinn, "I love expensive food. There was this dessert ..."

"I sense a 'but'?"

"If you breathe a word of this to Sef I'll think of something unspeakable to do to you."

"Sounds kinky."

"Okay, well, I'm not very threatening yet." Quinn dropped his voice as low as he could. *"Me and the boys will mess you up.* Better?"

"The voice, definitely. But the boys are who, Jasper and no one?"

"I was including my dad and Lillian for threat purposes."

"Now that is terrifying."

"Rude," muttered Lillian, loud enough that Quinn asked who that was. I said I'm not sure what he meant. I suggested it was the music and turned it down.

After a series of jokes and sidetracks, Quinn found his way to the point. There were good things, simple acceptance, fun for a while, but he aspires for *spark*. Also true love. He was being more serious than usual. Lillian mouthed *oh my god* at me.

"So you're looking all undone because of a cute peck on the cheek, right?" I said.

"Your audio's breaking up. What was that?"

"What's got your bow tie undone?"

"I'm going through a tunnel. I can't hear you."

"How was the S-E —"

Quinn covered his face for a second then reemerged grinning at me. "If it's this fun now, think how it's going to be with practice and being in love."

"Don't forget the spark."

"If only I could. Even without that, all the firsts in this body … it's so good, Sasha. Though a little overwhelming."

"You okay?"

Quinn waffled for a second then nodded. "Yeah, I really, really am. I mean, I'm the same. Fundamentally unchanged. I'll keep you posted. What are you listening to?"

I took a guess confidently and Lillian rolled her eyes at me.

In rehearsal, Quinn drops another beat and Lillian stops the song. "Get your head in the game, Quinn, my friend. You know you're all that keeps this whole thing on the road."

"I'm just so distracted," says Quinn. "There's this earworm I can't shake that Sasha was listening to on the phone last night." Quinn starts drumming and sings a little bit of what Lillian and I had on. "I can't remember what it's called."

I know my original guess was wrong. Lillian mocked me roundly for how far off it was and how the band I named was "loathsome, but not in a fun way." But I stick with it.

"It's 'Amber Bottle,' by Lockpick."

Cyprus has been watching this unfold with a composed expression that makes me think of how Lillian's always more cagey about us when Cyprus is around. Cyprus is holding her phone like she's using it, but her hands are still.

"Lockpick, niiiiice," says Quinn. He's looking straight at Lillian.

She breaks after about two seconds. "Sasha, I would never in a million years put on Lockpick. They're misogynist trash, and that's an insult to trash everywhere. It was 'Crueler Still,' by Artist Pickup."

Quinn looks smug beyond belief. "Sasha was just visiting and then showered and was getting dressed in your room?"

Now Cyprus sets down her phone.

"They weren't showering," says Lillian.

Quinn spins his drumstick to point at Lillian. "So why'd they say they just got out of the shower?"

Lillian looks so scrambled and guilty that I start laughing.

"Well, I did my part trying to keep it secret," I say. "Your music snobbery won out."

Lillian steps back to her mic and plays a chord. "Glad we got that sorted out. Everyone's in the know? Can you focus now? Great, good. Okay, from the top. One, two, one two three four."

Only Lillian starts playing.

Cyprus gestures back and forth between me and Lillian. "So you two are ...?"

I say, "Together."

She says, "A thing."

For the joy of making everyone cringe, but somehow ultimately dispersing awkwardness, Quinn says, "Banging it out."

Cyprus and Quinn bombard us with questions. I've never met a gossip columnist who was more persistent than these two.

Then, I suppose I've never had a group of friends. The top young Channel actors were friends with each other, not with someone like me who went from being a quiet extra to living a life on the road. Who hid in closets and helmets.

"I should have put money on it," says Quinn. "Cyprus, get this, Lillian made Sasha a mix CD with *nice* drawings."

"Oh, wow," says Cyprus. "I thought maybe this was a hookup situation. I'm cautious to say it, but this sounds like ... dating?"

I can't speak for Lillian's heart, but I wouldn't characterize what's happening in mine as cautious. We both make it out to be very casual, just seeing what happens. We skip over a lot of gazing into each other's eyes. I'm not sure anyone's buying it.

"How long has this been going on?" asks Quinn.

"Since we were at your place a couple weeks ago," I say.

Watching Cyprus very closely, there's a second where the playfulness is gone. A second where if I could make the shutter snap at the perfect moment, she'd look sad.

LILLIAN

I have to talk to Cyprus before we head out for the night. It's been all joking, pestering and prying from her and Quinn. But as the evening went, Cyprus got incrementally more distant. When I put my jacket on, she's leaning against a wall watching something on her phone with a bunch of images of Alexander Ash in that weird helmet while a voice fires off a barrage of hot takes.

"How's the trial going?" I ask as a feeble icebreaker. I can do better than that. "Have they gotten the younger brother on the stand yet?"

Cyprus puts her phone in her back pocket. "Not yet. Looks like they might not need to. The Channel lawyers are pushing really hard to have things wrapped before the new year. They must be confident."

"That soon?" I say. Is it soon? Maybe that's slow for this sort of trial.

"That soon," echoes Cyprus, adding nothing more.

I guess I'll have to plunge in. "Look, I'm really sorry. Not for being with Sasha, but I could have —"

"It's okay, Lillian. You're good." She takes out her phone again but doesn't switch it on. "Just remember how this stacks up. You said there was no risk to adding Sasha. I can't go through this all again."

"*You* can't?" I say.

"Maybe none of us can. Maybe we can't."

"I do remember. It's friends then lovers then bands."

Cyprus pulls on a big fur hat. "I'm not sure you've got those last two in the right order."

"It all bleeds together."

"I've noticed that," says Cyprus. "I'd rather it didn't bleed at all."

SASHA

Lillian drops me off at my place. The main floor lights are on. There are a few cars and bikes outside and people milling around in the kitchen.

"Well this is unusual," I say, though my downstairs neighbors seem to know most of the city.

"Your parents are going to let us all come over yet."

"I wouldn't hold out hope."

"Cyprus will manifest it into being. You heard how curious she was about if I'd met your family and what I thought of them. Not that I like formally introduced you to mine or something. They're just kind of around. We just started *dating*-dating."

"Quinn put it so artfully though."

Lillian laughs, but she flushes a tiny bit too. "There's no rush is my point." I hate to have let her ramble herself out instead of telling her the truth. But now she shifts her tone and looks at me in a mischievous way. "Your parents *do* seem very busy. Let me sneak upstairs with you. Just for a minute. I want to see your bedroom."

It's clearly its own suite. It'd give me away.

I'd love to return Lillian's look of trouble. I often do, but not as much as I'd like to. The secrets keep me a little farther from her.

Outside of this house, I'd like to imagine my family lives there, and this is my home.

Secrets are the loneliest thing in the world. No one can tell me otherwise.

"I'd say yes, but when they've got people over they're guaranteed to come and get me and be like, 'you've got to meet so-and-so from the firm.' I can't drag you into that nightmare. We've been vulnerable enough for today."

Lillian leans into me. "I'm glad we're done lying though. I'm not sure you noticed, but I'm not the smoothest criminal."

"You were doing admirably until there was an implication you'd put on Lockpick."

"I'm never forgiving you for that."

I rest my head on top of hers and squeeze her. There's a spot for her in my bed, one that's never belonged to anyone else.

On tour, I'd lay my guitar there, the headstock on the pillow, so the bed felt less empty. So I could reach for it if I woke up in the night.

Lillian says, "I guess we're in this now."

She kisses me before I can say we always were.

LILLIAN

It's snowing outside my bedroom window.

It's a few days after we let our secret out, a few after I asked to go upstairs with Sasha, meaning everything I could think of. Thoughts that have only grown. Sasha does that to me.

There are times like yesterday, when the band was watching gorgeously sensual, ragingly queer performance clips from one of our favorite musicians. Sasha said queerness is when all the rules and definitions lose meaning until you're free to create your own meaning. You're free to discover what's constantly shifting or what's always been there.

They said, "There are a thousand things that count as sex now that no one's telling me what counts and what doesn't. We get to make it and name it ourselves."

What's sexier than a revolution?

Now my house is empty. This snowstorm has Jasper stuck out of town at a basketball tournament. My mom's at her office working toward the late night while she waits for the worst of it to die down and the plows to start clearing.

A snowstorm and an empty house and Sasha here and

beautiful and I want them so desperately. But even more desperately, I want to be *here* like they are. I'm tired of glancing at my guitar.

Because once, when I took it apart, I hid something inside and closed the guitar up again. So it'd be surgery to get it back out. So the love would be underneath my right hand while I played every note.

It's the paper Emelia and I wrote on before our first kiss. I took the string of words and folded it away beneath my pickguard. Even Emelia doesn't know it's there.

I wonder if I should dismantle Butler again to rip it out. Crumple it up, recycle it, use it for fire starter. The thought exhausts me. It feels like keeping it is clinging on but throwing it out is pretending I haven't loved before. Or pretending the past doesn't catch up.

I need something to be true. I wish I knew what.

There's the shift of the mattress as Sasha moves even closer to me. We kiss again, deeper, and it turns out the truth is hungry in me. Sasha said I made them feel like they were in a storm, everything changing and uncertain, wanting to dance and be scattered.

Something true is that I want to scatter them.

All the rest of the noise slips away when I take off their dress and leave it crumped on the floor beside my bed. Flowers amidst a mess of black cables.

SASHA

Above me, Lillian's laughing. Pouring off her in response to how I'm so caught up I can barely speak. In how she can interrupt all my sentences with her mouth on my chest.

I say, "If you listen, this is magic." I mean that in the sound of every syllable when she says my name and every way she touches my body, I know I'm seen. Not as a boy or a magazine cover. But as a harmony lining up perfectly.

"Should I get my wand from under the bed?"

"Not that sort." Though not *not* that either.

"Aren't you sentimental. It's a rally cry and you know it."

We mean the same thing.

When I met her, I didn't know she had so much joy in her. I'd chase her around the world trying to lure that joy from wherever it's buried. I want to bring it to her voice and the corners of her mouth for me to gather with mine.

Then all my words and ideas are smudged across the page, lost to her eyes fixed on mine, tender and intense. Lost to every sound that escapes my mouth until Lillian covers it softly with her hand and absorbs all the waves through her skin.

I'm fragments of white lace and skin underneath her covers.

"Are you nervous?" she asks a minute later. "Is this too fast?"

"Is it for you?"

Lillian seems surprised when I ask. It isn't for me and I hope it isn't for her either, because my heart's racing when her lips press against my neck before she responds.

"Of course it is. Most things are too fast for me, Sasha. The world usually scares me."

Her breath breaks up her words. So does her mouth.

"But less right now. All my favorite moments are like this. They wrap me up in time. You know the memories that feel safe because they'll always have happened, no matter what happens next? I want this to be one of those with you, if you do."

She once told me we can't change the past, and that's lucky. What a mess we'd make if we could.

I kiss her back and draw her into the rush with me.

LILLIAN

At first, I thought I'd do this with someone else right away. Then it seemed like it might be a long time before I was ready.

Now I look down at Sasha curving their entire being up to me, and I can't believe how they were just suddenly here. They were like some lyric rushing into my mind when I'm half asleep that I have to write down before it's gone. I got a few words on the paper, unsure what they meant. I knew they were important, but I was too removed to piece it together.

I think I'm sorting it out.

They mean I'm fully here. My questions and memories and glances at a note buried in my guitar fade out. My world becomes our bodies together.

This is outrageous fortune. Absurd, horizonless, sun-kissed. Let the waves crash on me. Let me be torn to pieces by every feeling I hold.

And when we're finally too tired to do anything but crumple cozy into each other and soak in the warmth of each other's skin, I bite my tongue instead of telling Sasha I love them. I'm saving it. Tonight is already a lot.

Some chorus is starting to take shape.

SASHA

Repeat and repeat and repeat until you can't get it out of your head.

76

LILLIAN

"I felt like I recognized you when I met you," I say, "like I'd known you all along."

The snowstorm's slowing down. I hear the distant beeping of plows starting to clear the city. Sasha, their back against my chest, pulls my arms a little tighter around them. It's late, and we both know they should go soon.

77

SASHA

I wake up early on Christmas morning and press play on my one and only mix CD. I wear a red satin jumpsuit I've been saving for today and spend a long time on my makeup. I put on delicate pearl earrings and look at myself in the tilt of my full-length mirror.

The second half of December's been a soft blur of times with my friends and times alone with just Lillian, wrapped up in each other in every possible way.

Wavelength is in a lull where even Lillian's resting a little on rehearsal intensity. My friends all have cynical and accurate things to say about how Eurocentric it is to have our school schedule determined by Christian holidays, though Cyprus really leans into decorating for someone who says she hates Christmas. Quinn sings parodies of carols and Lillian declares that "all Christmas music is postcolonial noise pollution." Even though she says you can't be anti-capitalist and love Christmas, she still got me these earrings from a pawnshop. And when I gave her a discontinued guitar pedal she's been trying to track down, she said it was the most romantic gift she's ever received.

She said love is distortion.

This December made me get what she means.

It's in a memory of one of our practices when Lillian and I were sharing a microphone. I was close enough to touch her. To me, this is always remarkable, whether it's on a stage or in Quinn's basement. I'm a fan, a friend, a parallel heartbeat. Anywhere I go with her, it astounds me that I get to be beside her and see her face.

Everyone can see my face now too. I could feel Lillian's hair brush against my cheek when we stepped up to sing at the same time. An ordinary moment preserved perfectly, and unlike with Lark, I knew why right away. Because in that moment, I knew an era was done.

I won't ever be putting the helmet back on.

Another was when the four of us were lying on our backs on Cyprus's basement floor with all the lights off a few days ago, looking at the sea of glow-in-the-dark stars we'd stuck to the ceiling. It was like staring at the embers of a campfire, talking about things that are easier to say from beside each other.

Cyprus started talking in a way where we all listened quietly, even when she'd pause for a while then pick up somewhere else. At first it was about hanging mistletoe, then about how it confounds her how much people seem to think about sex. How she thought she was supposed to want it or feel repulsed by it, but she's been realizing it's not either one for her. She said maybe she didn't notice because she's all about romantic love and always wanted it. For her, with a man. And is she a bad feminist for not loving sex? And she wanted to bring this to us more sorted but here it is and also would Lillian stop looking at her like a proud parent?

Lillian sat up beside Cyprus and pulled her up into a hug that seemed like it was entirely about this while also holding a hundred other things. "You don't need to have it sorted for me," she said. "I don't require any certainty from you. People's certainty changes all the time. You can bring me all your half-baked maybes and perhapses."

"Thanks," murmured Cyprus into Lillian's hair.

"Always, I told you. Also, there's an album about this you should definitely listen to."

"Is it *Teleprompter Classroom*?"

"It *is Teleprompter Classroom*."

A few nights after that, me, Lillian, Cyprus and Quinn were at a show at Rolling Way Alleys, which is the sonically overwhelming combo of run-down bowling alley and music venue. We were lounging around eating fries between sets when I clenched inside.

My downstairs neighbor, the one who gave me advice about overwatering plants, was walking toward our table. He said hi to me then turned to Cyprus like he knew her and asked how that synth was working out for her. When she said she bought the synth from some local guy, I never thought of this. This scene is too small for my secrets.

Cyprus started into a technical conversation that stayed away from my living status at first. It sounded like she's had it for a while, so she could forget the house. Then Cyprus asked about his daughter. It was getting closer, a sharp shock I've been afraid of since I met Wavelength.

Of all people, Emelia saved me.

Maybe this scene is just small enough. She came out of nowhere and slid into the booth to give Cyprus a hug. "Look at you with a synth pretending you're a bass player."

My neighbor glanced down at his phone, out of the conversation. He waved at someone across the room and was gone. Not that I was without problems, but Cyprus was sitting between Lillian and Emelia, so that was something.

"I'm just heading out before these guys start," said Emelia. "Me and TJ. He's here somewhere." She reached across the table and took some fries.

The most remarkable thing happened. A minor miracle.

Lillian glanced at Cyprus, then looked at Emelia and said, "It's nice running into you here. Maybe I'll try to get Wavelength a slot sometime." Like it was a test.

Quinn intercepted it. "There's nowhere with a more fabulous aesthetic. That certain murdery appeal."

But Emelia responded. "I'd come see you guys play here. Wavelength's my favorite band. This place ... more Lil's dingy vibes."

"You calling my vibes dingy?" said Lillian.

Quinn said, "You insulting my favorite dive?"

Lillian was almost smiling. There's a framework that says this development should have made me jealous and then anxious and then angry. Augustus would say, "Are you just going to sit there?"

That's exactly what I did. What are the classic alternatives? Emotionally punish Lillian? Fight someone? These are Augustus's ways. I don't dislike Emelia. I don't hate her for having been with Lillian. Of course I'm jealous, but I can keep an eye on that and talk about it with Lillian if I need to.

All relationships create some tangled messes. Romantic, sexual, platonic, passionate. There are threads everywhere.

Love is distortion. I love Isabelle. I love Augustus, for fuck's sake. You don't have to have dated someone to hurt them, and people you've dated aren't in some unique and unforgivable category. It's not like all your love gets entirely fixed to a person you're sleeping with then entirely ripped away. No clean transplants. Love is in lots of places at once.

There was some small talk. Comfortable-ish, less and less cautious. Lillian and Emelia showing hints of how well they know each other. A couple old band stories for my benefit. Emelia seemed to know Lillian and I were dating and didn't make any direct comments about it.

Before she left, Emelia invited us to a big New Year's Eve party her and TJ are throwing at his place.

"I hope all four of you can be there," she said. "It'll be good."

"No doubt," said Quinn.

Cyprus, sarcastic. "I hate parties. I always spend New Year's Eve at home."

I would go too, but this wasn't my heartbreak or my friend. I gave Lillian a look that said this was her call.

"We'll be there," said Lillian.

But New Year's Eve isn't for six days. Today, all my friends are busy, and getting dressed up is as far as my plans extended. I take some pictures of myself. Some like I'm showcasing the outfit, some like I'm showcasing how sexy I look.

A part of me wants to call Augustus just to hear him say merry Christmas. I go into my contacts and remember I don't have his number anymore. I can't even make a gesture at family. When I chose this, I never imagined I'd make it this far. I never considered this day and being alone in this room.

But I do see Isabelle's number. I haven't sent her a single thing. She should be off today, not around industry people, so I attach a picture without my face in it along with a merry Christmas for my oldest friend.

I send the sexy ones to Lillian, who responds with some explicit words she definitely shouldn't be texting from her grandparents' house.

I'm trying to figure out what to do now when Chrysanthemum

knocks on my door and comes in at the same time. She's been sent by my downstairs neighbors to invite me to have Christmas brunch with them, because they know my family doesn't live here. I try not to tear up, tell her of course, say I'll be down in a minute.

Before I go, there are two messages on my phone. The first is from Christensen to me, Quinn, Cyprus and Lillian.

Christensen

Have I got a gift for you four!

Got to discuss details. Come by Initialism at noon tomorrow?

Then there's another, an almost instant response I open thinking of the banter and affirmation in the messages Isabelle and I used to send.

Isabelle

Emergencies ONLY

Things here are beyond tense

The Channel's leaning hard on Heather Erin to find you

Think about what I said before ok? It's only getting worse the longer you're gone

Got to clear these messages out quick

I stare at the two sets of texts.

In the one with Christensen, Quinn sends a series of question marks, and Christensen says he'll have to wait until tomorrow.

I swipe away Isabelle's texts and open the chat with Christensen.

Sasha

Can't wait to find out!

78

LILLIAN

Initialism has been rearranged since I was last here.

The makeshift wall has been moved, connecting Munchies Arcade and Culinary Delights to the main area, making the venue larger. Too large for normal shows there. And the pinball machines are now in the same room as the stage. It doesn't make sense.

The mural of the androids has been put as the backdrop for the stage, blazing color across the room, which is one change that seems perfect.

Christensen's behind the bar, where my friends are already sitting, drinking a variety of brightly hued drinks with sugared rims.

My eyes go straight to Sasha. They're wearing a black dress, tights without runs, and heels that would leave me flat on my ass. They have a poise about them today that I both want to admire and to dismantle with my hands and my mouth. There will be time for that. Time isn't running out as fast as I always believe it is.

"The prodigal daughter arrives at long last," says Christensen to me. He hands me a bright drink with a swirly straw that I wish I could pretend isn't delicious.

"I'm not late," I say. "The rest of you are early."

Quinn spins his stool around. "I'm anxious for this news. Was that wall load bearing? Is the news that we're all going to die?"

"Good people, youths, my friends." Christensen pauses for drama. He's a ham, but he's my favorite one. "This upcoming year, on January fifteenth, Initialism is going to be hosting the next surprise show by the one, the only ..."

My brain is scrambling for who this might be. I feel like I know. Someone who's been doing a surprise concert tour, just appearing and disappearing.

Cyprus gets there first. "Wait, Monochrome Stoplight is playing here? At Initialism?"

Christensen nods and the next couple minutes are spent trying to get us to calm down and stop hyperventilating and talking about setlists and outfits and how Liv James is probably some sort of supernatural being. Liv James is going to be here, and I know about it before almost anyone. I've always been scared Monochrome Stoplight would finally come to my city and I'd hear too late and not get in. Now it's guaranteed.

"Save your pandemonium!" says Christensen. "I'm not done. Monochrome Stoplight has been doing the entire Whisper Campaign tour with local openers. They asked me to send them recordings and live footage of some younger acts that I know well and can count on. People who might suit their feel."

My heart skips straight over probability, leaving my rationality behind.

"Now, I sent them a bunch of bands. They were very certain about who they wanted opening at Initialism. They chose Wavel —"

At which point everything descends into chaos that Christensen has no hope of reining in. He's trying to tell us details, but I only catch half of them. How it's a big enough show to rearrange the venue and it's a huge responsibility and something about sound check times and if we so much as breathe a word of this before Monochrome Stoplight announces it we'll all be disappointments to Liv James. But don't put too much pressure on it. But also don't screw this up.

I'm counting days until January 15, thinking how many rehearsals we can fit in before then, what songs to choose, which ones Christensen might have sent to Monochrome Stoplight. I'm wondering what to say when I meet Liv James, thinking how I've seen her bring openers onstage to sing with her at the end of shows.

In the midst of miraculous news, I can't help but dare to dream.

Everyone's talking at once except Sasha. They've gotten quiet. From their face, they may be sad, or bemused, or have simply regained the poise they had before the news broke. Mostly, they seem a little elsewhere. It happens sometimes, but they always come back. I'd like it to be soon. I want Sasha here for this moment.

I want Sasha here for every moment.

"People are going to notice us!" Cyprus is saying. "Fucking *Liv James* noticed us! I always listen to artists she recommends."

Meanwhile, Quinn's going on about how he needs a really, really excellent haircut and I just want everyone to open their calendars and schedule some practices.

Sasha kisses me, quick and bright. Celebratory and familiar. I'm with them and they're back again, grinning at everything around them.

They reach into their purse and hand me a spiral notebook opened to a new page. "Let's get planning," they say. "Is there anything we can do to promote ourselves around the event? We've got to see if there are any particular songs that made Monochrome Stoplight interested in us, make sure to meet what they're looking for. But still sound like us."

I lean close to their ear, whisper, "I love you, Sasha."

Because everything's happening.

The others have joined in, and I'm dividing the paper into columns before Sasha has time to respond. Sasha's right there beside me, all of us leaning over the table. I know I say that too soon. I know it.

But the world is short on truth. If I've got a beautiful one, I want it out there.

Under the table, Sasha takes my left hand and presses a pen into my palm. They draw twin lines, curving up and away and then back down to meet.

Over the next days, whenever the heart starts to fade, Sasha traces over it again.

SASHA

In fifty-seven minutes, it will be the new year.

I'm going to start it as Sasha, start it with my new friends. Start it by kissing Lillian. I'm going to start it without a helmet on. I'll start surrounded by people in TJ's living room. Start with a good secret inside of me for once, two weeks out from the show I'm anticipating more than any stadium I've ever played.

I was dancing a moment ago. My body is beginning to understand how to move by listening to itself instead of by following instructions.

Soon, I think I'll dance again.

We all needed a party after the relentless last few days.

I've been practically living between Quinn's basement and Lillian's bedroom, preparing for the show. I've slept over at Quinn's twice, dozing off partway through listening to something for the hundredth time. We're changing lyrics and designing new Wavelength shirts. We're cutting and modifying all the old ones to sell as one-offs. I've spent hours with scissors and fabric markers watching old sci-fi shows with Quinn.

We're trying to have a single ready to come out the day after we play at Initialism with Monochrome Stoplight. It will be the first Wavelength recording featuring yours truly as half of the vocals. It's really revealing how badly we need a bass player. But it's a great recording of "Elevator," or it will be once we get it done.

There's an obvious problem.

Someone else owns my voice.

Based on what I understand of my contract at the Channel, I'm not allowed to release this song. They decide who I'm paired with. If it's not Augustus, it'll be another Channel product or a major celebrity. A single with LucSee. Maybe a big British artist.

No matter what, they will choose. These are suits who will tear apart people's lives over bus money just so they can accumulate it without purpose. Who have strategic meetings about how to portray Jasmine to ensure Augustus gets away with everything. No consideration of his guilt or what it will all do to Jasmine's life, or what the fans will do to her.

I doubt the Channel's lawyers would settle for Wavelength's single being taken offline. When they perceive a threat, they don't stop until they've salted the earth. My influence at the Channel won't be enough to stand in the way of that.

Releasing this song would put the people I care about most directly in the line of fire. There's no denying it, and I won't allow that to happen. Before January 15, I'll find a way to make sure I'm not on the recording. I'll generate a new falsehood that means we have to cut my voice out of "Elevator." I'll keep my friends safe. I'll stay undercover and stay their friend. I can do it.

But I don't have to think about that until after tonight.

Lillian and I arrived at TJ's New Year's Eve party late and together. She's wearing one of Quinn's suit jackets over her absolute rattiest band shirt and jeans. Because looking clean-cut is for people with picket fences and Lillian would be more comfortable in a picket line. I've got fishnets and a leather jacket and a white skirt because it's not a funeral.

Emelia answered the door. She was out of breath, barefoot, a drink in her hand, talking over her shoulder until she saw who it was.

"I wasn't sure you'd make it," said Emelia. To Lillian, not to both of us.

"I said I would," said Lillian.

"And here you are."

There was telepathy between them. A whole conversation happened in a quarter note rest while the warmth from inside was hitting the icy night. Steam filling the air around us.

Then Emelia welcomed us in and pointed to the drinks. She was already a couple in, enough that she said we looked cute together. Either she forgot to give it bite or she genuinely meant it.

I closed the door. Lillian and Emelia seemed unaware of the draft.

Emelia hugged Lillian for a beat longer than a normal greeting hug. But then she hugged me too and went on tiptoes to whisper in my ear. A little too loud for how close she was.

"Please watch out for Lillian's heart."

As in take care of it, or make sure it doesn't hurt me?

She broke away and moved cleanly into, "There's people you should meet. Come in."

The house sprawls and absorbs people. It's dated, with spaces dropped by two steps and separated by ornate railings. Thick cream carpets that don't stand a chance once things pick up later. In the room with the best stereo, there's music playing loud enough to fill the house. When we arrived, people were just standing around and talking and drinking, but there was a restlessness growing wilder.

Half the people we walked past warranted hugs from Emelia too. Lillian casts around a lot of those greeting nods that I could never get the hang of. Emelia introduced me to a couple of friends by saying, "This is Sasha. They're in Wavelength." She said it like it was a great thing she was happy about, which generated confusion, especially when she wandered off.

One of the guys in the couple we met said, "Didn't Emelia used to be in Wavelength?"

His boyfriend looked at Lillian holding my hand. "Didn't you used to date Emelia?"

The two of them attributed the whole thing to the oddness of band relationships and neither Lillian or I was in much of a position to challenge that explanation.

After a couple drinks, I was feeling more uninhibited than anyone with my scale of secrets should feel. I went to find Cyprus. She was high and using two croissants to explain, in great detail, the relationship between punk, new wave and the original *Mean Girls*.

"Can I talk to you?"

She took a bite of croissant and closed her eyes. "Like *talk*?"

"Just quickly."

"I'm bringing Gretchen and Karen." Based on context, I assumed those were the croissants, not who she was talking to.

Once I got her into a quieter hallway, she offered me half of Gretchen in exchange for my aid, though I'm not sure with what. I accepted. It seemed like the thing to do at the time.

"Cyprus?"

"Yes, babe."

I actually like that, but anyways. "What is going on with Emelia? Is she going to murder me, or are we friends now?"

She stares lovingly at Karen. "It's like eating butter, but hills."

"Cyprus."

"What?"

"What is Emelia doing?"

"She's done being sad. Friends, envy, pssh." She made a vague hand gesture. "She loves Lillian. You're sharing the load. Emelia works like she's happy she's happy. Like a, what's that thing?"

I could only shrug. "Empathy?"

"A carousel! The old-school rave. Carousal? That has the word *arousal* in it." She snorted and took out her massive feathered earrings and gave them to me. "Wear these. They'll bring out your eyes. Not the birds. Let's dance, babe."

"I like that."

"Everybody knows it."

We danced ourselves slightly more sober, settled on the floor. It's less than an hour until the new year and we're talking about our heroes and working very hard not to mention Liv James and spill the secret show. All us Wavelength people are here, Emelia too, and Jemma and someone with a blue mullet named Denis who took all of ten minutes to hit on every person in the circle. In other circumstances, perhaps. It'd be despite the blue mullet though.

"It's got to be Elliot Page," Quinn's saying. "I mean, king of heart for always."

"Too easy," says Lillian. She's lying on her back with her head resting on my leg. She found a green plastic ukulele somewhere and she's trying to play along to the song in the background. "Narrow it down."

"Elliot Page, in *Hard Candy*, when he takes off the red hoodie and he's wearing the gray tank top. Not the seduction stuff, the vigilante stuff."

"Something for everyone," says Cyprus. "For my hero, I choose Lillian."

Lillian's trying to play a solo over the song outro. "Because I'm a fashion icon?"

"Because you care so damn much."

Lillian says, "How dare you insinuate I care about anything? God is dead, life is meaningless, rage rage rage." She looks quite pleased.

Denis says someone who seems like more of a hair inspiration than anything. Jemma says LucSee.

I say, "I can actually really see that," but can't elaborate on it without revealing that I've spent a fair bit of time with her idol.

Emelia picks an old film star, because of grace and the way she walked and her composed strength. A quiet invincibility.

It's reached Lillian and I. Lillian says, "This ukulele is my hero. I'd make a pinup calendar of it. Stalk it, worship it, marry it."

I know I should be silly like her, laugh off things close to my personal life.

Instead, I say, "This isn't someone famous, but I met this person named Lark as a kid. It was for like less than ten minutes. But they let me talk about myself without assuming anything. Their whole existence opened up gender space for me, and they told me there are more than two options when no one had ever told me that."

"What did you say their name was?" asks Cyprus.

"Lark."

Emelia's tearing up a little. "That is the sweetest." She raises her plastic cup and says, "To Lark and all the queer people before us!"

We all toast enthusiastically to that.

As I swallow, feeling the heat of the alcohol down my throat, I remember Lillian saying December is when you feel alone. New Year's Eve. Celebration tinged with sadness. My heart's exploding because I found my way here, breaking because I wasn't in this place all along.

Lillian was right about feeling loneliness, but it's something I'm remembering, not feeling. It can't touch me right now.

LILLIAN

I play a fragment of my newest song on the ukulele and hum the melody. Sasha catches it and hums along for a bar or two before the music playing from the other room interferes.

They recognize it even though they've only heard it once. Last night, lying in my bed.

Put your heart on my hand
Some kind of promise
I'm nonsense at those
But I'm proud

What I know as honor
Is being willing to die
For what not everyone
Will believe in

What I know as honor
Is loving the fight

Whether or not
You can win

I keep my fists up
For what makes me
Drop my guard

For the mosh pits
For the protest forests
For the aging punk bands
For all the brave plans

And for your heart on my hand
It's all for your heart on my hand

I keep my fists up
For what makes me
Drop my guard

"I liked that." Sasha's voice was sleepy and warm like their skin. "What was it?"

"New words," I said. "Just some words."

SASHA

Cyprus and Quinn say they have to go find food, though after all the croissants, I'm surprised. Where did Cyprus even find a box of croissants? Did she bring them?

The room we're in is one of the quieter ones, away from the dancing and general revelry. Denis produces a deck of cards. Once we get him to stop attempting magic tricks, we wind up playing hearts. Closer to midnight, we'll rejoin the center of chaos. Recharge now and then cycle back in for countdown and liftoff.

Emelia's friend Margot just arrived at the party. She took over Jemma's hand so Jemma could go take a hit of something. Margot doesn't drink. Consequently, she's wrecking us all at cards and seems genuinely apologetic for it.

The combination of losing and losing to someone who doesn't care if they win would usually make Lillian infuriated or hyper-focused, but she doesn't seem to care.

Emelia gathers the cards and tallies the scores. There's a peace here — maybe what Cyprus tried to explain. They're each happy the other one is happy.

"Quinn said you could really use a bass player for the new single," says Emelia. "For 'Elevator.' He played me the demo."

We'll need another singer too, once my voice is out of the recording, but I'll deal with that in the new year.

Lillian picks up the ukulele and gives it a strum before answering. "No one misses a real bass player more than a drummer."

"It's a good song," says Emelia. "Is it about me?"

Jemma staggers back into the circle, partially sitting down on Denis's lap before settling beside him. "Oh damn, what's happening?"

I say, "We're discussing how art is a reflection of aspects of broader human experience."

I don't know how to feel about this except that my first concern is for Lillian. And she seems more settled since she stopped avoiding Emelia all the time, like her world is safer. I want that for her. It's a good thing. I'll help resolve an awkward moment if I can.

Lillian says, "Yeah, it's a little about you."

"The risk I took." Emelia deals out another hand, cards gathering in front of us. Margot's picking hers up, but her eyes are on this. "I could play on the recording," continues Emelia. "If that would be alright?"

"It will be," says Lillian. "It'll be more than alright with you playing on it."

"I came back for *this*?" says Jemma. "If anyone writes a song about me, it's fight or fuck. Both. That's the dream." She tousles Denis's hair. Based on how he tenses up, it was previously tousled in a very specific way that's been disrupted. I feel that.

Margot gives Jemma a cup of water. "How about you keep that dream to yourself for tonight, okay, Jem?"

I foresee Margot driving a lot of people home later.

"I'd like to hear more, Jemma," says Lillian. "Maybe I will write a song about you."

Jemma starts saying something, but Margot makes her drink the water first. Jemma slams the cup upside down on the carpet when she's done and raises both arms in the air. "Let's fight!"

I say, "Of all days not to wear your spiked jacket."

Lillian fakes bad old movie feminine distress with a swooning gesture. "If only I had a man who could only express emotional connection with me by enacting violence on my behalf."

She kisses me, then walks over to Jemma and gently tips her over.

"K-O!" declares Denis.

"Has it been this weird all night?" asks Margot.

"Earlier Cyprus said these earrings may or may not make birds attracted to me." I've swapped back to my silver hoops and hung the ones from Cyprus from the zipper of my jacket pocket. "And something about a carousel."

Margot sighs. "So it's going to get weirder?"

"Most definitely."

When Denis reaches for the cards Margot's dealing, he knocks Emelia's cup of water over, leaving a dark spot where it soaks into the carpet. Emelia asks if anyone else has water because the kitchen is a whole maze of party across the house. Lillian cuts Margot off before she can offer to get some. "There's a bottle in my bag right there. You're welcome to it." Emelia wanders off to grab it.

We're chatting and sorting our next hands of cards, except for Lillian, who claims she plays better when hers aren't sorted.

I push her cards back. It's partly so I can't see them all but mostly to touch her hand. Because I want to find someplace upstairs with her, and I want her to know it. To place it in her mind to flip around and around.

I envision my hand staying a moment, her glancing up. All things known in each other's eyes. The same telepathy between us as between her and Emelia, where we know exactly what the other's thinking.

Lillian pulls her cards farther back. "Have you been cheating?" she asks. "I think we've got to restart the round."

Denis says, "Keep dreaming."

I think Lillian didn't notice how my hand stayed or what it meant. It was too small. Then she asks what's upstairs. Jemma, still lying on the floor, says bedrooms upon bedrooms.

Lillian reaches over and pushes my cards back. "Now I can see *your* cards," she says.

There's the look where we both understand. Twin minds turning things over, distracted from the game and from midnight.

I lead with the two of clubs.

Margot says, "We've got to wait for Emelia."

"I'm back, I'm back." She rejoins the circle holding a paperback book with a crumpled cover. "I found this in your bag," she says to Lillian. "I've been looking for it everywhere. I still don't know how it ends."

Lillian folds her cards into a tight little stack. For a moment, as the music changes in another room, we can hear everyone talking too loudly.

"Oh my god." Lillian's talking quickly and brightly, some new way of being I've never seen before. "It'd fallen down beside my bed and I just found it the other day. I totally meant to give that to you tonight. It's the drinks. I forget everything."

"Poor cover," says Margot, taking the book out of Emelia's hands and folding the cover back and forth, trying to get it back into place.

Lillian reaches across the circle. "Let me try to fix it. It's my fault for stuffing it in my bag like that."

Her hand's there, waiting, but there's no book being placed in it.

"Emelia?" Margot asks.

She sounds anxious in the way you are when you've seen something that makes you afraid and unsure at once. You don't want to ignore it or leave it. You need everyone else to see it and tell you it's made up. You want them to arrive and explain the distress away.

You don't want to see the same disturbance cross their face.

Margot hands the book to Emelia. She's reading something off the inside cover. Her hands are tight, the whole book bending in them.

Lillian slowly pulls her hand back from the center of the circle. She's clutching her cards the same way Emelia's gripping the book.

Emelia reads one more time. "You wrote this tonight?" she says. Jemma's sitting up again, because Emelia sounds dangerous in a way I didn't know she could, a cutting windchill. "If you wrote this tonight, I think Sasha needs to hear it."

"I didn't ..." starts Lillian. She's looking around like there might be a fire alarm she can pull to drown this all out.

"Every time I hear your voice," reads Emelia, *"I'm bent around the sound / Time bends, for a second I'm fine / while I'm bent around the sound."*

"They're just words," says Lillian. "There's just some lyrics and the book was there to write on. You know how I am when I've got an idea. I'll buy you a new copy."

She says it to Emelia, to me, to Margot, to herself and whoever's listening. Which is no one beyond this circle, but still too many spectators. Jemma and Denis and Margot looking horrified and intrigued. I want to hush the whole thing away. I can't stand for my private life to be on display anymore.

I can't stand to hear what's next. Our heartbreak shouldn't be anyone's reaction shots.

Emelia reads Lillian's words.

"I kept this book because the ending isn't for you, it isn't for us. Because whenever you speak, I know I still love you, Emelia. Darling, I'm still bent around that sound / even now."

I knew this. Somehow that makes hearing it out loud even more painful. Sometimes when no one knows how to solve a thing, we all pretend our hardest that it's not there at all.

Emelia choked a bit on the last words, but she's not crying. She looks far too angry to cry.

Lillian's agitated, shifting, unsure of who to focus on when everyone's either angry or doesn't care. I want to tell her to look at me. I want to say I could tell she felt like that about Emelia and it hurts and we can solve this. I'm torn open, but I'd still put my fists up for us.

"I didn't write that tonight," says Lillian. "I wrote it to give you at Cyprus's like a month ago."

I can do the math on that. She wrote that note and *Love, Lillian* inside the mix CD at the same time, then she brought them both there and chose me last minute. Chose me because Emelia wasn't there.

Emelia says, "So you've been using Sasha to make me jealous? Huge improvement."

Jemma says, "Claaassic bi shit. Just insatiable little —"

Lillian stands up like she's going to fight Jemma for real this time. Me and Jemma are on our feet too, because Lillian's going to rip Jemma's arms off unless Jemma runs or I hold Lillian back.

"Do not," says Lillian, "pretend this is some simple thing you can pin on a lazy cliché."

Emelia beats Lillian to it. She pushes Jemma awkwardly, like she's never hit anyone before. But Jemma's barely standing and she stumbles and goes down and her face hits an end table. Through all the yelling and the music from the other room, I think I hear the sound of her nose breaking.

Everything's noise. Jemma screaming and the circle of attention exploding outward. There's blood on the light carpet, on Jemma's hand holding her face and on Margot as she tries to give her something to stem it. All while Margot tells Lillian that she doesn't care *when* Lillian wrote it.

In the midst of it, Emelia picks up the book from the floor and flips to the last page.

"We should talk," I say to Lillian. It's broken, not beyond fighting for.

"What's there to say?" asks Lillian. She's watching Emelia reading. "You're gone. I know you're gone."

"No, I'm still here," I start. "We can ..."

Emelia closes the book and throws it on the floor at Lillian's feet.

"Lil, that, right there, that's our ending. This is the ending for us."

I don't want to watch Lillian's heart shatter. Nothing she could do to me would make me want to see it.

Emelia disappears toward the music. Margot leads Jemma away toward a bathroom and flips off Lillian as she goes by. Denis's gathering his cards and getting out of here.

Quinn and Cyprus must have followed the commotion back into the room. They brush past Margot and Jemma going the other way and don't seem to care. I'm certain Quinn's going to say this is what happens when he leaves us unsupervised, but he's frowning, troubled. One of the faces he usually keeps locked away.

Cyprus takes Lillian's hand. "We need to talk now."

"Can it wait?" I ask.

Cyprus starts to pull Lillian away. She follows like it's only her body they're taking, like most of her is still standing in this room.

"It really can't," says Quinn.

When I take a step after them, Cyprus says, "Not you." It's decisive, not up for negotiation.

Quinn shrugs at me. "Give us a minute. I'll text you."

In the other room, they're counting down.

There's the loneliness.

LILLIAN

"What happened?" asks Quinn. "Why's Jemma bleeding?"

Cyprus leads us up the stairs and into a bedroom with a huge window overlooking the frozen river. She locks the door behind us.

I stammer something, unable to capture it all or explain why I chose those words to put in the book or why I let it ride around in my bag. Those reworked lyrics from when Emelia and I were together, ones I never sang for her. Call it hope, call it love.

"Sasha's breaking up with me," I manage.

They are definitely, definitely breaking up with me. No matter how kind they try to be. It's what I'd tell them to do. This is how I am. I dig a pit of my own aloneness then throw myself down it. So why suffer through the gestures? It's enough to know it's over without the part where they say it to my face.

Cyprus takes a deep breath. "That's not Sasha."

"You don't know how bad it was," I say.

"No," says Cyprus, "I mean, that person isn't Sasha Weaver."

Quinn's looking at the window, facing away. There are skaters on the river. "They're Alexander Ash. Sasha is Alexander Ash."

"Don't deadname ..." I start, and then the syllables he just said land on me. It doesn't snap into shape, doesn't fit.

"You're right, you're right, sorry," says Quinn. He manages to get me to sit down on the bed. He stays close beside me. "Their name is Sasha and they're nonbinary and they're my friend. And they're also half of Admirer. We figured it out."

"They don't look like him. Or like the person from Admirer," I say. "They aren't the person from Admirer. Augustus is on trial and the other one's in rehab or whatever. You've been talking about it since the summer."

Cyprus is finding something on her phone. "The one in the helmet. You're telling me Sasha doesn't look like a reflective visor?"

"This is ridiculous! This is Sasha we're talking about."

These people don't lie to me. I trust both of them — from the stage to my secrets. I trust Sasha. It's all fucking incompatible.

Sasha who just heard what I wrote to Emelia and still wasn't cruel. Who didn't seem angry or threatening. Sasha who I wanted to undress with in one of these same upstairs rooms who I wanted to kiss at midnight who makes me drop my guard.

"Lark," says Quinn.

"I know about Lark," I say.

Cyprus sits on the other side of me. They're both touching me, softly holding me in place. That's how I know it's bad, like they're bracing me for collapse.

"I didn't," says Cyprus. "I heard them say it tonight and it made me think of this fan theory going around a year and a half ago. When I was obsessed with Admirer."

"Clearly you still are," I say sharply. I try to shrug off her arm, but she keeps holding on to me. "This sort of thing doesn't happen."

"The theory was that Sasha was in love with someone named Lark," says Cyprus, "because they once dedicated their song for Isabelle to Lark. And when they mentioned Lark tonight, I had this absurd idea. What if it's Sasha? What if this is where they've gone? Why not here?"

"It's literally the worst city and Admirer is famous," I say. "That's why."

"Exactly," says Quinn. "This is a place to disappear. It's nowhere, Lillian. Sasha was at the point where they either had to speak up for or against Augustus."

"Sasha has an older sister."

"Ava," says Quinn.

"Adaline," says Cyprus.

"April," says Quinn.

I remember a couple of those. They're not nicknames. Sasha mixed it up. It's why I couldn't remember.

"They lied about other things," says Cyprus. "They don't live with their family at all. That house, it's the one where I bought my synth. I just texted the guy I bought it from, who talked to us at Way Alley the other night. Him and his partners rent the suite to Sasha and say Sasha's a college student. I knew I recognized that house. The Lark thing put it into place. After Sasha mentioned it, I grabbed Quinn."

"It occurred to me once," says Quinn. "I told Sasha that Alexander Ash's helmet act was sexy and they laughed in a weird way and I thought, wouldn't it be the wildest thing if Sasha was from Admirer? Like a silly meeting-a-celebrity fantasy. But since then, I haven't been able to get it out of my head. Because of how Sasha sounds."

"Admirer's a pop band," I say. "Sasha's not a pop singer."

Cyprus is cuing something up on her phone, taking her

earbuds out of their case. "Wavelength sounds so different from Admirer. It hides it. Listen to this."

She slips the earbuds in for me. I try to watch the video, but she tells me to just listen.

I hear the audio from the night we were at the pool. There's music playing, an inescapable Admirer hit I remember from a couple years ago. We're all singing along, but I'm only focusing on one voice. Sasha, closest to Cyprus's camera. They're nailing the parts like I'd expect them to do. Flawlessly, but Sasha is a good singer. A great singer. The best singer our age I've ever met.

Then Cyprus plays the original recording. The voice younger, but there's some innate resonance between them, one that meshes perfectly when Cyprus plays the two recordings stacked one on top of the other.

I think of the command they had over the Pilgrim.

How they got everyone to be quiet.

I think of how easily they recorded their vocals.

Of how I've never met their family.

I've never seen a picture of one of their friends.

And they keep us away from that house.

I've never seen any of it besides their bedroom on video.

Never from a different angle even.

Their own entrance.

Their stories from the west coast.

How they spoke about Augustus's trial.

Their older sister, always in trouble.

They didn't want money from the gigs.

And they were nervous to have pictures taken of them.

Their hesitancy to join the band.

When they disappeared after getting close.

What it took for them to walk into school.

"Now watch," says Cyprus. "The All My Love tour. Remember Sasha saying they once fell into the drum kit in a show?"

In the video, there's music building, a huge crescendo, lights sweeping and flashing all around. Both Augustus and Alexander, or Sasha maybe, are running. They're going from the heart-shaped B-stage out in the crowd back to the mainstage. Augustus at the very edge, hands reaching up toward him. Making it back for the big start of the song.

The one in the helmet overshoots when they try to jump onto the huge monitors in front of the drum kit. It sounds like a cartoon when they hit it. The voice laughs and says, "Ta-da!"

I can picture Sasha smiling as they untangle themselves.

I close my eyes, try to take even breaths. Quinn's holding my hand in both of his. Usually, an obvious solution is true, a plausible explanation. Sasha must have some other reason for lying about so many things.

The next thing has played automatically. It's Sasha introducing a song. I hear it and that's immediately what I think. I don't think it's Admirer. It's Sasha with a sea of voices interacting and responding.

"I admire every one of you," they're saying. Huge applause. "I love you, each of you. No matter what anyone else says, you're my brave souls. Whoever you are. Here, here, can I borrow that for a minute? Thank you."

I open my eyes, and on Cyprus's screen, I see someone in a helmet reach into the crowd and emerge with a pride flag. They drape it around their shoulders. Then they put one finger to their visor and hold their other palm down and gradually, gradually, they make the entire stadium silent.

"Anyone who tells you there isn't enough love to go around is lying. This is for all of you, and this is for Lark."

Sasha starts into a simple love song and everything in me wells up toward crying. I love them. Then and now. I've got to sob about it.

My body won't let me.

It goes totally flat, and it's so much worse. I'm watching this happen in third person, like I'm a security camera in the corner of the room. Pixelated, choppy.

I see Quinn comparing pre-helmet headshots of Alexander Ash to current pictures of Sasha, and I know that face. Even young, it's the same. I've held it in my hands. I see Cyprus explain the timeline of Sasha's appearance alongside Alexander Ash's accounts going quiet.

I see myself knowing it's true, but I don't feel it.

I need something.

Noise.

Comfort.

Chaos.

Pleasure.

Anything to detach further or have a feeling — because I just watched Sasha come through the bedroom door and Cyprus say we figured it out. From far off, I hear Sasha talking. They're saying it's true it's true it's all true. Apologizing. Everyone's confused and doesn't know how to interact anymore. Cyprus angry, saying how could Sasha get into a relationship with me while keeping that secret. Quinn unable to make light of it. Sasha's said sorry a million times now. They're saying we have to be careful. They say they can't let the media do to us what it did to Jasmine, which just makes Cyprus more furious at the risk they've taken.

Death will be this distance compounded.

That fear, these far-off voices and this room, it's all claustrophobia pressing down on me.

Kick-start or drown it out.

I stand up. I look Sasha in the eyes, but I see it from the wrong angle. So I miss what might be my last chance to get a good look at that beautiful face. I'm holding out my hand, the one with the heart on the palm.

"What's this doing here? Whose heart is this?"

"It's mine," says Sasha. "It's there because that's the first place it's belonged."

"Not anymore," I say.

I follow myself through the door, down the stairs. Getting farther into the house, more lost, telling Quinn not to follow me. I grab a bottle from someone, glare off their objections. Lock myself in the basement bathroom. Finish the bottle. All in my body. Scrub at the palm of my hand. The heart outline is imprinted. Stained.

Back porch, the wind not enough.

There's a bicycle. Maybe if I move fast enough. Maybe if I get cold enough.

Wake up. Numb it out. I'll take either.

83

Just in time for the new year, Augustus Ash has been acquitted of all charges. It brings an end to what many have called the celebrity trial of the century. For the past months, the older half of pop phenomenon Admirer has been on trial for statutory rape and aggravated assault. Today, jurors found him not guilty.

In a post celebrating the news, Augustus Ash called it a "triumph for love and justice" and thanked the fans who have stood by him throughout the ordeal. He was photographed leaving the courthouse with Heather Erin, Admirer's manager, and Jasmine Hill. Despite initial attempts to keep her anonymous, the fifteen-year-old Admirer fan has been rumored to be the pop star's illicit girlfriend since the beginning of the trial. Jasmine Hill, who is four years younger than Augustus Ash, seemed to confirm this in her own social media celebrations today. She also opened up about the threats she's received and has asked for privacy for her family during this time. Her older brother, Dylan Hill, age twenty, continues to recover from the injuries jurors are now saying Augustus Ash inflicted in self-defense.

The end of the trial marks a huge victory not only for Augustus Ash, but for the Channel itself. Their star factory has generated many of the country's most well-known young celebrities, including the Ash brothers, and actress and model Isabelle. The Channel has been outspoken in their support of Augustus Ash since the charges first came to light. As a long-standing giant of children's and teen entertainment, many considered the Augustus Ash trial a referendum on the entire Channel. While they've come out on the right side of the law this time, the organization remains under scrutiny for its contract practices with young talent.

Augustus Ash wasted no time in hinting toward what's next. He posted that he's "excited for Admirer to get back on the road and reconnect with fans around the world." Plans for another global tour remain uncertain, however, as enigmatic younger brother Alexander Ash continues his months-long silence. At this time, Alexander Ash's representation declined to provide comment on the situation.

SASHA

Lillian vanished into the party after I tried hopelessly to apologize. She wasn't crying. But she was shaking, edge of hyperventilating, unfocused panic-attack-agitated like some deeper version of how she'd been on the back steps in September. Quinn started to follow her, and she told him to fuck off. As if discovering my secret was something he had done to her.

"I'll go after her," I said. "Let me go after her."

Cyprus stuck her arm out to block me stepping through the doorway. "Not a chance. If she doesn't tear into you, I will. Get your ass home." All of this from someone who gave me her earrings and called me babe a couple hours ago. "Nobody wants you here right now."

Quinn put a hand on my shoulder. "I'd listen to Cyprus on this one. This is a lot to process. It's probably best if you leave."

I couldn't tell if they meant leave the party or the city, go back to my apartment or get on a plane and put half a country between me and ever seeing them again.

But I couldn't leave. Not before I'd had a chance to say goodbye.

As soon as Cyprus and Quinn were out of the room, I went

down a different staircase and plunged back into the party. Things were swirling, all the music too loud, impossible to get people to listen to me. I was driven by a desperate focus. Lillian was somewhere here. And she took part of me with her. A type of love that was new to me. If I didn't find her, it'd just be gone.

The longer I couldn't find her, the more the other thoughts filtered down and my worry ramped up. There was a clarity in having no more lies to track. I had one job: find Lillian. I'd figure everything else out from there. I kept asking and asking, then I tried to think like Lillian. She seemed absent when she found out. She'd want something to snap her back or blur it out.

And she needed to get away from people.

So down the basement steps. Eventually, I found someone she took a bottle of tequila from. Then the empty bottle in a bathroom he gestured to. Asked how much was left when she grabbed it. He held his finger too far up the side of the bottle. Years with young celebrities being run into the ground meant I knew what that could do to her. But either Lillian didn't realize or didn't care, because what she drank was too much.

If she needed to be by herself.

If she was alone, no one would call it in.

I was acting too frantic for anyone to want to point me after Lillian. So I pressed a suspicious amount of cash into the hand of some guy whose eyes flicked toward the stairs when I asked the first time, and he said she headed for the back porch.

When I got there, the door was hanging open, letting snow blow in. Through the frame, I saw her already distant form biking away from the house.

Into the killing cold wearing only her suit jacket and her jeans full of holes. Looking like something the night would eat, the same way I looked standing on the porch calling after her.

Maybe she aimed for home. Maybe she somehow would make it and maybe someone else finished the bottle. Or she was dying alone in the cold and dark. I couldn't let her slip away inside her worst nightmare.

I could see Cyprus's grip tighten on her cup as I walked toward her and Quinn in the kitchen. "Was I not fucking clear? I'll get TJ to throw you out if I have to."

"You've got to stop asking everyone where Lillian is," said Quinn. "You're making people nervous."

I was seconds from having Cyprus's drink in my face. "I know you've been trying to find her too. You're too good of friends to let her be by herself right now." I told them tequila and bike and killing cold.

"I don't care how you feel about me or if you never want to speak to me again!" I managed to say it without a sob breaking from my chest, but my raised voice was drawing attention. I saw Emelia and Margot across the kitchen watching it unfold. "We'll deal with it later. Right now, we've got to find Lillian. That's all I care about. I'll go out by myself if you won't come."

Cyprus nodded and slammed back the rest of her drink. Margot said, "Like hell I'm letting any of you drive." So it was Cyprus's station wagon with Margot at the wheel and me in the passenger seat because I'd seen Lillian leaving. Quinn, Cyprus and Emelia in the back seat. No one was talking to each other.

There was no music on.

Headlights and driving in a grid pattern.

Quinn calling Lillian's mom.

Though it's a long way to Lillian's house in the cold anyway.

No answer, calling Jasper.

Lillian wasn't home.

There was snow on Lillian when we found her. A dark lump on the sidewalk beside a bike. Crashed or collapsed.

Either way, she was too still and pale.

That's the moment that's haunting me. Not Lillian's shallow, flickering breathing. Not Quinn and Margot rolling her onto her side. Not following the ambulance to the hospital.

It's before we got out of the car. Because when the headlights first caught her form, she looked like an object, not a soul hanging on.

I'm sitting next to Emelia in the ER waiting room.

On the TV across from us, they keep cycling back to the same picture of Augustus leaving the courthouse with Heather Erin and Jasmine. The sound's turned off, but it's clear.

Everything feels clear.

How's that for timing?

I should have told my friends as soon as we got close. Before I joined Wavelength. Before Lillian and I first kissed. All my reasons and rationalizations, and I left it and left it and left it.

But in the end, these people deserved to know. There's really nothing else to say.

"She doesn't look happy," says Emelia, pointing at Jasmine.

It's the first time she's spoken to me in the past two hours. It's pretty busy at the ER with all the party-night casualties, but there were other seats. She could have sat next to a stranger. Or tried to sit with Quinn and Cyprus in the row across from us, or with

Lillian's mom and Jasper a few seats over. Margot would have stayed all night, but Emelia convinced her to go home an hour ago.

Emelia chose this spot next to me, both of us still in our New Year's Eve clothes. The sexiness and warmth gone.

We're cold and washed out underneath the hospital lights.

"It ruined Jasmine's life," I say, "like flying too close to the sun. That's how stars work. They're only bright by having things to burn."

She doesn't know Augustus is my brother. I thought the fewer people who knew about me, the fewer melted wings. Now it's all down in flames anyway.

"They might love each other," says Emelia. "I don't believe it, but you can't see into people's relationships. Either way, I feel like Jasmine didn't have any choice but to defend him. They probably put her on trial more than him anyway."

"If she hadn't been on his side, Augustus and the Channel's lawyers would have used every ugly way of throwing her under the bus," I say.

Augustus simply went with the best plan to save himself. His moments of protectiveness and presence aren't enough to convince me otherwise.

He won.

To some, he looks like the good guy, but goodness isn't why people walk free. Power is.

"I hope she leaves him," says Emelia. "I bet she'd be the first person to say no to him in years."

"Sometimes it's too late to get out. I hope it's not for her," I say.

The TV's shifted away to something else. Quinn's fallen asleep on Cyprus's shoulder. She's alternating between her phone and looking at me. I keep expecting her to show the anger she had at the party, but all I see is worry and confusion and tiredness.

Emelia quietly says, "I still love Lillian."

"Me too," I say.

"Our timing is the worst."

"Right?"

"If you got here a year earlier, maybe we're all friends. A year later, Lillian and I are mostly over each other."

"Is that what you think would have happened?"

Emelia sighs. "We have different ways of moving on. Mine is more steady, and Lillian's is more like … cardiograph spikes. I thought breaking up with her meant I wasn't allowed to love her. But when has anyone ever been right about who we're allowed to love? So I do love her, just the romance is done. When we broke up, I couldn't even let myself know that's what I wanted. But ever since, I'm less anxious. Being with Lillian was mostly amazing and sometimes awful and now that part's done. We'll date other people. We'll move on."

Unless she's dead. Or going into a coma she never pulls out of. We don't talk about it. I don't think I'd move on from that. It would stick in me until I died, wondering if I had just told Lillian earlier if it would have been a less heavy blow. If she would have rolled with the punch and carried on.

Across the row, Cyprus is watching closely as Emelia and I talk in hushed voices. She reflects the strangeness of it all back to me.

"Is this my fault?" asks Emelia. "I could have just kept quiet about the book."

"That wouldn't have been fair to expect."

"No, it wouldn't." She doesn't sound like she believes me. "It's infuriating that she'd write that. Lillian's kind of an infuriating human."

Lillian's my heartbreaker. I'm hers. Her note filled me with the sudden sense of being her second choice. I want to be someone's love, not an alternative or backup plan. I thought I knew the arc of our story so far, and then all I was certain of was a pressing sadness and a desperation to save what we had.

When Emelia told me to watch out for Lillian's heart, she meant both ways. Now I've been shattered by it and done worse to her.

"She found out something about me too," I say. "I think it tipped her over the edge."

"Lillian's always been careening toward one thing or another and never given much thought to why it's happening or how to stop it. Mostly, things trigger it. They don't cause it."

"If it's not my fault," I say, "it's not yours either."

"Thanks." Emelia shifts a little, crosses her legs. "Though it depends what you did."

"How much do you hate me?"

Emelia seems surprised. "I don't hate you. I'm very fucking jealous sometimes. Do you hate me?"

"Not at all. I wish I'd gotten what you had, the growing up together."

"It's not like the growing up ends."

In a place like this, the secret seems smaller. So I tell her what Quinn and Cyprus figured out, what Lillian learned. And when I'm done, she starts laughing. It's a hospital laugh. Quiet, a little unsteady. Now Cyprus is giving us a really weird look.

"I'm not lying. I can call Isabelle if you want."

"The pop star going to finish their last year of high school in a nowhere city and making new friends and falling in love." Emelia takes a second and composes herself. The laughter snuffed out. "Other than all the queer shit, it's exactly like a story the Channel would tell."

"This part isn't," I say. "None of those stories end like this."

85

Fortune's Waltz

Fortune sits on a spinning stool
In a run-down bar
Starting on Thursdays at noon
Since nobody listens to you

More than that lonely song
On the jukebox
But unless you're alone
Some party boy turns it off

Says here's one for the lovers
And the lovers to be
Fortune orders another
Because they've seen everything

They've seen heartbreak and healing
Drink side by side
Might go home together tonight
Fortune wishes them the best
Whatever that is
Some nights you're lucky
Just to get out alive

Fortune's not Lady Luck
Don't presume Fortune is straight
Fortune's seen every side
Of every spit in the face

Because few love you adrift
Few love you washed up
Most smoke cigarettes
As you cough water from your lungs

Fortune spins on the stool until
Until everyone blurs
It's the clearest of views
Where nothing's quite sure

They've seen heartbreak and healing
Drink side by side
Might go home together tonight
Fortune wishes them the best
Whatever that is
Some nights you're lucky
Just to get out alive

Some nights you're lucky
Just to get out alive

— Lillian Finley

86

LILLIAN

I'm bleary for a while, in and out and in some sort of pain. Disorientation, time stretching out. But eventually, I wake up properly. Enough that what happened feels clear.

I'm so relieved to be awake that I sob alone in my hospital room.

I tell my mom and Jasper I don't remember anything after I crashed my bike. It bothers me to see my mom worried when she's usually so unflappable. I joke about how I never fixed the brakes on my bike at home, so I wasn't ready for these ones to actually stop me. Over the handlebars.

I was just trying to escape myself. I didn't mean to get into danger. I tell them the second part of that, and my mom seems less afraid for me knowing it was nothing worse than a drunken mistake.

When it's only Jasper and I, my attempts to make light break down. I'm crying. He says, "You know you can tell me anything. Whatever it is, we can get you help without Mom knowing if that's what you need."

"Don't worry," I manage. "I don't want to die. I've never wanted to die."

He rolls his eyes at me. "I know you well enough to know that, even if Mom doesn't. But it seems like the world cuts you really deep."

"It was just love stuff," I say.

"There's no drama li—"

I hit him with a pillow.

"I only occasionally want you to die," he says.

"Maybe next time." But when I see his face, I take his hand. "There won't be a next time. There really won't."

Because I do remember.

I remember lying on the sidewalk in the snow. I wanted Sasha's heart on my hand. I wanted to look at it, and I couldn't figure out why it was gone. I remember being colder than I've ever been and being scared that if I didn't stay awake, I'd be this cold forever.

I have trouble sleeping, so there's a lot of empty space at the hospital even though my mom and Jasper are with me most of the time. They don't like to leave me alone after having almost lost me, and I don't want them to. While my brother plays games on his handheld console or my mom dozes off in the chair beside my bed and then pretends she wasn't asleep, I learn about the character of Alexander Ash.

I watch the interviews Sasha did without Augustus. When they were together, Augustus did most of the talking, but alone, Sasha was advocating for things. They made more noise about more causes than anyone at the Channel could have possibly wanted them to.

I loop the video of Sasha singing the song for Lark. Things like that save people's lives.

Sasha visited sick fans and sent them Christmas gifts. They joined protest marches and did charity shows. They were always good, yet they always pushed back at the Channel's definition of good. In a video of one of these charity shows, I see them onstage with Isabelle.

Anyone would be jealous of her. Stunning, talented, kind. Wealth and a crew of people to turn her into some pinnacle of perfection. There are infinite adorable, sexy pictures of her and Sasha together. Loving captions, the perfect couple.

I can see it. Sasha with romance and all the right words and a sweetness that only got sweeter when there was no one but her to see it. It seems real, but despite everything, I find myself desperately hoping she's the close friend Sasha said they only pretended to date.

Because if that was a lie too, my heart's never leaving this hospital.

My friends stayed at the hospital most of the first night, including Emelia. They didn't go home until they were sure I was alright. By the second morning, I'm basically recovered. I'm only still here so the doctor can monitor and retest some numbers that marginally worry her. Cyprus and Quinn come back to visit now that the situation is less dire. Quinn starts a bit where he describes the grim little room as if it was a trendy, contemporary interior design.

Cyprus and Quinn tell me how Sasha wouldn't stop worrying about me and looking for me. How Sasha must have talked to every person at the party and how they were ready to put on a jacket and search the streets for me on their own if no one else thought I was in danger.

Cyprus won't say it, but Sasha saved my life. Even after what happened with Emelia and telling Sasha their heart didn't belong with me, they didn't give up on keeping me safe.

Sasha and Emelia are waiting, unsure if I want to see them. Neither of them wants to upset me. But they came along with Cyprus and Quinn for emotional support anyway.

Few love you adrift. Few love you washed up.

But there are a few.

More than I thought.

I talk to Emelia first. She sits on the edge of the bed by my feet. "Do I have to forgive you now?" she asks.

"I wouldn't say no." I must look terrible and tragic, because everyone is being kind to me.

"The note was from before you were with Sasha, right?"

"Yes, that's the truth. I can't say sorry enough."

"If you're really, really sorry, you'll stop saying you're sorry and start accepting that we're actually broken up. That's what it's going to take for us to be friends, Lil. It's going to be the absolute worst. But you're clearly in love with a popstar."

"They told you?"

"I think we're friends now?"

I cover my face. "What is my life?"

"Queer," suggests Emelia. "Very queer. Lil, sometimes you're unlucky and two people you love arrive too close together and you don't have the right heart for it. Now it's clearing. You and I aren't getting back together. I can say that. It's certain in me. You're not the love of my life, and I'm not going to pine over you for the rest of my days."

"You'd look great in a sapphic Victorian tragedy though."

"That's *true*, and —"

"Like it's raining —"

"— *and*, Lillian," says Emelia. "It's pretty clear that your heart is with Sasha."

"I ruined things though."

"I think we can safely say you two collaborated to ruin things. You're actually really good together. Rebuild some trust and stop giving romantic presents to your ex at parties where you're drunk, and you'll be alright."

I don't tell her about the lyrics inside Butler. I think I'll leave them there forever, the way Emelia chose to leave the book I gave her in the hospital library.

And then, I talk to Sasha.

The moment they walk through the door, I know this is going to hurt. Because on the surface of everything, I'm furious and shattered at what they've done and the lies they've told. And I'm guilty about Emelia and the book. I still have the urge to pull away to protect myself before they can break up with me. But then there's the undertow that wants to wrench me out of my fear and my hurt and my hospital bed and straight back into their arms.

It pulls at me with every step they take toward my bed, remembering how I was attracted to them from the first time we spoke and how every interaction from then until New Year's Eve only made that feeling stronger.

Part of them must still be my person, right?

Sasha sits in the chair next to my bed and wipes away a tear from the corner of their eye before they even say anything. It leaves a tiny smudge. I would have reached out to clean that up a couple days ago. Then they skip the hospital and the ER and all the things that they know feel like small talk to me in this moment.

"Lillian, I'm so, so sorry. You should have learned the truth a lot earlier, and it should have been from me."

This time they don't talk fast or add anything. No warning to be careful with their secret. There's no excuses or trying to justify the lie they told, but then in the tilting memories of the party, I realize they didn't do that before either. They apologized and went straight to looking out for me and Quinn and Cyprus.

I want to brush it all away at the same time that I want to scream at them to get out. I want to tell them to come here and kiss me on this bed as much as I want to be the one to say this is over and at least have that pitiful comfort to hold on to.

I just say what I thought when they came in. "This is going to hurt, isn't it?"

Sasha sighs and rests their head in their hands. "Yes."

"Well then, I think we should hold hands for it. You hold on to me through it all and I'll hold on to you. If that's alright."

They nod silently, and I reach out and tangle my fingers through theirs. Fuck, I may never feel their hand paired with mine again after this.

"Can you go first?" I ask.

They squeeze my hand and start in.

I was right. It's worse than crashing my bike on the frozen pavement or burning myself on hot glass. It's awful both ways, with me talking about Emelia and my whole mess, and Sasha talking about the life they kept hidden from me. I learn about their contract that still has years left on it and Heather Erin and why they left.

All through it though, I notice each little glimpse of hope and store it in my chest. That we aren't cruel or indifferent. How each of us fights to understand how we got here. We each ache for having caused the other pain.

And that we hold hands through the whole thing, even when I say I need a break from dating them. I'm ready for them to react how I did when Emelia told me the same thing this summer. But they tell me they were going to ask for the same thing. I quote Emelia about rebuilding trust for each other, and they don't think I'm abandoning them. We agree to talk about it again after opening for Monochrome Stoplight, because we both care about that show even if we can't release "Elevator."

We talk for hours and hours, and when they leave, I just want them to come back so we can talk for more hours. That's hope too.

I miss Sasha's body, but I need time. I need so much more time than I ever thought I did.

Once I'm out of the hospital, we visit their apartment. I can't believe all along they've had an empty apartment with a big bed and downstairs neighbors who didn't care. My mind goes straight into the gutter looking at their bed as the need for that closeness overwhelms me. But also.

"Did you cheat on Isabelle with me?" I ask, standing in their apartment.

"Oh," says Sasha. "Oh my god, no. Isabelle and I have never been together."

It's like this. So often, Sasha told as close to the truth as they could while still maintaining their biggest lie. I learn about Sasha and Isabelle's fake relationship and how it's held like a state secret. Sasha's trusting me with things that would destroy their career, and Isabelle's too.

Everything I learn fits with Sasha. Sasha colored in all the way to the edges. Sasha complete with tour stories and accidentally mentioning celebrities they know by their first names and being embarrassed by our reactions. I'm settling into it.

"Why here?" I ask as we walk through the snow back from their house to mine. "This isn't exactly one of the great cities."

"I'll tell you, but then you owe me a question. We went through here once on tour."

"I remember. The hysteria was insufferable."

Sasha rolls their eyes. "I blame Augustus's hair. Anyway, everyone said it was a nowhere city. I looked out at the crowd, and I imagined I was from here. It seemed happier. Not glamorous, just happier and simpler and without the desperate need to be of consequence and relevant every day. So after the show, I got someone to drive me all over the city. We drove through this neighborhood. I probably saw your house. I imagined I lived here with my parents and I went to this school. Sometimes I'd click through the street view. It's taken in springtime."

"You made it," I say. "And you'll see it like that soon. There's no reason for the Channel to look for you here."

"Soon they'll want me to record and promote and tour. Admirer's more famous than ever. Every day Augustus is free and I'm not there, they lose money. And that really upsets them."

I can't think of Sasha leaving. I'd never have a reason to walk down this precise street again. It'd be Sasha's street — empty. So I ask what their question for me is.

"What's the tattoo on your calf mean? The *blank-O-blank-E* hangman."

"It symbolizes the incompleteness of thoughts and dreams and how time essentially operates as a closed loop which is in itself enclosed within emptiness. And also an *E*."

"Wow," says Sasha. "That was some pretty articulate bullshit."

"A friend of Emelia's did it at a party, but we didn't finish the game. It doesn't mean anything. I didn't even have a word in mind, so it could still spell lots of things. Or not. Long *O* sings well on its own. I like it this way."

"Yet," says Sasha, "paradoxically, within its meaninglessness, it represents a form of meaning, a type of potentiality defined by its undefined —"

"I will push you in another snowdrift."

87

Isabelle:
January 15th, 3:47 p.m.

What the fuck are you doing?

You try to disappear and then you join a band?

Doesn't that violate every single part of your contract? Couldn't you get in huge trouble? Couldn't you get your new friends in huge trouble?

Heather Erin's been looking for you twice as hard since Augustus got cleared. Monochrome Stoplight posted a video of you playing at some place called Initialism. The guy who owns it apparently scouted LucSee for the Channel, so people here still follow him and the clip found its way to Heather. She knows you're there. I'm going to see where she is …

Though the band does sound great. I've never heard you sing like that before

Also I love your new presentation. Very you

I feel like I should check in about your pronouns?

Shit. She flew out today. I don't know when. I just found out

I'm sorry. I think it's over. We'll sort out a way to explain the whole disappearance. I'll be here for you, ok?

But I think it's time to come in

I know you said no replies, but please send me something when you get this so I know you're ok

Isabelle:
January 15th, 6:52 p.m.

Where are you?

Heather Erin's flight just landed

She's coming to collect you

SASHA

MONOCHROME STOPLIGHT

with special guests

Wavelength

January 15

Initialism

7 p.m. doors / 8 p.m. music

The posters appeared all over town yesterday. Now we've done our sound check, ready to go, full of jittery energy. We're not scheduled to be onstage for another thirty minutes, but Initialism is already packed. We can hear the crowd's anticipation from backstage. The show only got announced twenty-four hours ago, and it's like their fans still can't believe it.

Everyone's caught up in the rush. We knew ahead of time, and it still feels like we've been scrambling all day to get ready. Emelia's coming to photograph the show, and we keep texting her all the things we forgot. An adapter of Cyprus's, my purse, Quinn's "luckiest drumsticks."

Monochrome Stoplight has spent most of the day appearing

without warning at local music stores and venues. Doing signings, playing an acoustic song, then popping up somewhere else not long after. They were only briefly at Initialism before heading out on their quest to cover every corner of the city, so we haven't had the chance to meet them in person yet.

We did talk with their guitarist and their sound person a week ago to make sure we were on the same page about some details. I've never seen Lillian take so long choosing her clothes.

Partway through talking, Liv James wandered through the back of the frame in her pajamas. Just when we were all barely holding it together, she ducked into the call.

She said hello and that she was looking forward to meeting us. That it was going to be a great show. Pleasant and unthreatening, without the intensity she radiates when she's onstage. Like she'd rather be kind than worshipped, and like she was genuinely surprised and pleased that we're such big fans.

It made me glad to see she had a line, the ability to turn off the ferocity she brings to her performances. Whatever unattainable standard fans think Liv James achieves all the time, she didn't seem to have to meet it. I tried to internalize that.

You bring part of yourself to the show, but it is a show. No one else will remember that for you.

After, Lillian said, "I didn't expect Liv James to seem so … alright?"

"Wasn't she really messed up a few years ago?" said Quinn. "Like having big breakdowns and missing shows and they thought the band was done?"

Cyprus shrugged. "Maybe she got help?"

Lillian made a dig at the institutionalized wellness industry. Then she got quiet. A few minutes later, once the conversation had moved on, she suddenly said, "I could do that."

We all looked at her.

"As you were," she said.

"Want to talk about that epiphany?" asked Cyprus.

"I was thinking I'd talk to someone else."

Quinn raised his eyebrows. "Were you thinking maybe Liv James could *teach you her ways*?"

"I'm not commenting on that," said Lillian. "Cyprus, be the mature one."

"Getting help is fucking scary, and I'm proud of you," said Cyprus.

"For real," said Quinn.

"If I didn't know you hated the word," I said, "I'd be tempted to call you brave."

"You wouldn't dare," said Lillian.

Cyprus tilted her head back and forth, considering. "To be fair, Liv James does seem very *experienced*."

Lillian threw a handful of guitar picks at her head.

Nobody on our end of the call with Monochrome Stoplight fainted or embarrassed themselves too badly, so it was a huge success. It's killing Lillian not to constantly text Liv James for advice on everything under the sun. Sometimes I catch her with the contact open, just looking at it.

Cyprus took on part of the role of announcing the show locally and spreading the news, therefore the rest of the band and Emelia got recruited to help poster the city.

When we got to the greenroom, there was a note written in permanent marker pinned to the wall. It was on the back of a crossed-out setlist.

Hey Wavelength! Sorry we haven't gotten to see you yet. We'll be back before you're on. We can't wait to hear you! And if you're down, you're very welcome on our traditional post-show food expedition. Recommendations welcome!

Then a huge black heart and Liv James' signature.

The note's definitely going to wind up framed in Lillian's bedroom. Or maybe our rehearsal space. And the consensus food recommendation is Falafel 'Til Dawn.

Monochrome Stoplight's gear is all over the greenroom. Eventually Quinn psychs himself up to move someone's leather jacket so he can sit down. He touches it like it's sacred.

Everyone's rattling with excitement about sharing the space and wondering if they'll be here soon and talking through setlists and cues and pretending not to be nervous about how many people are out there.

Cyprus is touching up her dramatic makeup, making me think I should do the same. But I left my makeup in my purse along with my phone. I'm beginning to see that I really undervalued pockets. Cyprus comments offhand that it must not seem like too many people to me.

These things keep coming up. How different my life has been from my friends' lives. Suddenly, a gulf opens, and they don't know how to look at me anymore. This stranger is standing with them, this celebrity who's on a screen or the radio.

It's improving, little by little. They're figuring out that I'm not two people, just Sasha. They're giving me more kindness than I ever thought I deserved, but I'm still scared.

Because we don't know about anything after tonight. I don't want to be a part of their past. A story to remember, a moment that doesn't seem quite real looking back, someone none of them have heard from or contacted in a long time because it's too weird, because our worlds are too separate.

They'll have each other. And I'll have the Channel and a private jet and empty hotel rooms and media attention. I'll have a fake romance to boost numbers. I'll be going from city to city to city, wondering where I left myself.

If I want to come out, it will have to be to the entire world in a maneuver vetted by people at the Channel who will try to make me the most acceptable version of myself. Until I'm twenty-one and my contract's done. By then, my friends' lives will be far away from mine. A few months of knowing won't stretch across four years.

The helmet will have to come off.

Once that happens, I'm embedded in the world. I've gotten famous enough to never not be. To never be quite the same as other people. To never be able to live this normal exceptional bizarre confusing crisscrossed life out in the open with these people.

In the greenroom, I say, "This actually feels like the most exciting show of my career. Opening for Monochrome Stoplight? At the best venue I've ever been in with the best friends I've ever had?"

"Aww," says Quinn. "I'm a puddle." He's air-drumming, only half there.

"I really mean it."

Lillian sits beside me on the back of the couch. "Don't tell Christensen you think so highly of Initialism. It'll go right to his head."

"Being friends with a major celebrity hasn't affected my ego," says Cyprus. "It remains at a healthy stable level oh my god Liv James just texted me I am an insider fear me love me. She says they're on their way over."

"Why not tell me?" asks Lillian. "I'm bandleader."

"Because I text right back instead of overthinking it and replying eight days later," says Cyprus.

"At least I don't make euphemistic mistakes," says Lillian.

"That was *one* time!"

We really are ready for this show. I can feel it. Everyone's relaxed enough to be joking around. When Emelia ducks in to drop our things off, she says no matter what happens, the crowd seems thrilled to be here and we've got their hometown mercy.

"Should we tour?" asks Lillian. "We could tour once we're out of school."

"If we toured," I say, "I'd be ready to throw you all off the bus within an hour."

"Love you too," says Cyprus.

"The van," says Quinn. "It'd definitely be a van. Cyprus, how many miles does your station wagon have left? We could all wedge in there."

They understand I'm afraid they'll use me to get famous, so they don't mention it. They pretend we can carry on in our obscurity. But we all know at some point either everything will change in their lives, or Wavelength will be without me. It's all too much uncertainty. Something to worry about later.

While Quinn and Cyprus get into a vigorous debate about the station wagon, I move closer to Lillian. Not touching. We agreed that was too confusing for right now, yet not reaching out to her is something I feel through my entire body.

Around that circle at the New Year's Eve party, before Emelia picked up the book, that might be the last time Lillian kissed me. Already it's faded, a little hazy with alcohol.

I don't want all this to be the past decaying. I want to keep making this story every single day.

"I can't wait to be onstage with you again," says Lillian. "And you look gorgeous."

"You too."

"You know that's not what I'm going for."

"You look fearsome."

"Thank you kindly. I've got something to show you."

She pats down her jacket's innumerable pockets and eventually emerges with a crumpled piece of paper. It's a medical form that she stole and covered in her own words. At the top, it says *Fortune's Waltz.*

Once I'm finished reading it twice, I look over at her. Her face has the apprehension of artistic vulnerability. It tells me that the song came from right inside her instead of from careful consideration.

"You wrote this in the hospital?"

"On the second night, once my family had gone home. The doctor kept saying how lucky I was to have come through alright. And I was thinking about how maybe Fortune is queer. And maybe Fortune's tired and they love us and good luck isn't as glamorous or as clear as we think. I got another tomorrow. Maybe that was Fortune."

"It's my new favorite. I'm not just saying that."

She pulls the sleeves of her jacket over half her hands. "I know. I can see when you're telling the truth."

"And have I been?" I ask.

I want to earn that trust back no matter how long it takes. And as quickly as I can, because time isn't infinite and I miss it desperately. I want to have eyes people look into and know they're safe with, a voice they hear and know things will be alright.

She's about to say something, stops, considers. Maybe taking back scathing words I deserve.

"Yes," she says eventually. "The first fifteen days of this year have all been true. And the more I think about it, the less it all feels like a lie before. You're not a lie."

"Admirer is a bit of a lie."

"I meant Sasha," says Lillian. "Sasha's not a lie. To me, you feel like truth. I'm not done learning you, but you're my kind of truth, the way other people believe in religions or love songs."

There's nothing I can possibly say to that except that I feel the same, and if I say that, then I will say I love you. Now isn't the moment. There's the show and Emelia and Admirer and the heart that Lillian scrubbed off her hand.

"Are we playing this new song tonight?" I say quickly. "I'll learn it right now."

"There's not even a melody yet."

"So ...?"

"We're not going to write it in the next twenty minutes," says Lillian.

"I'm game."

Lillian genuinely considers it for a second. "This one's going to take some time. I was wondering though if you'd maybe want to write it with me? If you want. The Channel will never know. With this song, it seems right, and I know you come up with great melodies and —"

"That's the easiest yes I've ever given," I say.

Lillian bumps my shoulder. "The easiest one?"

Quinn calls, "I thought you two were on a break."

"Stop this flirting or get a room," says Cyprus.

We hear the back door of the venue open, and we all stand up, as if sitting down is too casual to meet Monochrome Stoplight. I grab my purse so I can at least fix my lipstick.

"Deep breaths," I say to Lillian.

"Deep breaths yourself," she mutters. She does take one though.

I pull my phone out of my purse and immediately see a stack of unread messages from Isabelle. Lillian's too focused on being moments from a face-to-face interaction with Liv James to notice how my body tenses when I open them.

Isabelle's texts — frustrated, worried, caring, always on my side.

But from the first sentence, I already know what the last will be.

Her words are the end of inevitability tearing through me, hollowing out everything I was going to use to sing. I once wrote *I'm safe. I'm gone.* But there was never a corner of the earth far enough or a new home dear enough to stop them kicking down my door. The terror of going back catches up and crushes me.

I can hear Monochrome Stoplight talking down the hallway, and in that moment, I can't disrupt Lillian's joy. I want to hold her in my mind like this.

I take my own deep breath. "I'll be back in a second," I say, and slip out the door to the stage.

89

LILLIAN

Sasha's lying. Somewhere in me, I know they're lying.

But I want to believe they'll be right back.

So I just ignore it.

90

SASHA

I look out into the crowd. Christensen's busy at the bar. There are excited people everywhere wearing Monochrome Stoplight merch, with a few wayward Wavelength shirts. Emelia's close to the stage with an Initialism lanyard and a heavy camera around her neck. She's talking to the handsome guy who's taking video. I see Jasper in the crowd leaning close to a tall girl with a low ponytail to hear what she's saying. I pick out two of my downstairs neighbors at the bar.

All around me, backstage and in front of it, there are people I'm excited are here.

By the entrance, Taylor is IDing people and checking tickets.

But no door is closed to Heather Erin.

She sees me first. I can feel her eyes on me. By the time I find her, there's no pretending we haven't made eye contact.

She's standing by the Wavelength merch, not wading into the crowd. If I make her come here, she'll do it with her elbows up and apologies that make people feel like it's their fault for blocking her path and getting hit.

She's proof that beauty standards are about selling things. No part of her is inexpensive or accidental. No part is left to chance.

She points at the Wavelength shirts and shakes her head. And I know I was wrong. I can't shelter my friends. I know if I perform tonight, she'll find ways of ruining everyone in Wavelength. Then she'll ruin Christensen and Initialism and see if she can hurt Monochrome Stoplight too.

She gestures toward the door with her head and mouths, *Now, Alexander.*

It's worse than I imagined. It's colder and more threatening. I will not be forgiven for the trouble I've caused her and the Channel.

So I leave everything behind, even my phone lying on the stage. Nothing to tie me to my friends. A clean cut to keep them away from this ruthlessness. I love them too much to do anything else. There's only one last thing.

I step down from the stage beside Emelia.

"I need your help," I say. "Do you still know the parts?"

"Most of them. Why? What's happening?"

"I have to leave," I say. "But this is Lillian's dream, and Wavelength needs another voice. Sing for me?"

"Sasha, where are you going?"

I'm crying now, my makeup getting washed to pieces.

"It's time," is all I can manage. "Please sing for me."

I push into the crowd, heading for the door. I'm up against a power you can't fight or run from.

I try to picture Lillian's face as she meets Liv James. Quinn's smile. Cyprus's energy. I take that much of them with me.

91

LILLIAN

Monochrome Stoplight greets us like we're already friends. Liv James hugs me and I'm sure she can feel my heart hammering. With her boots, she's tall like Cyprus. Tall like the perfect height to hug you. Even the way she opened the door was perfect. And the texture of her speaking voice has this unbelievable timbre.

Before I can bury Monochrome Stoplight in questions about themselves, they start asking about us. How'd we get the band name, how long we've been together, our band history, our everyday lives.

Quinn's got someone laughing and Liv James and Cyprus are standing with their heads together comparing something on their phones, probably promoting up a storm. Their guitarist says she wants to see my pedal setup and I start going on about the new pedal Sasha got me.

The side door opens. That should be them coming back.

"Sasha," I say over my shoulder. "Veyda wants to know where the hell you found that pedal. She's been looking everywhere."

But it's Emelia. She looks the way she looked before we broke up. She's carrying bad news, and she's scared how I'll take it.

"One second," I say, even though I've never been in a conversation I wanted to stay in more. I'm keeping everything smooth, being a professional opener.

Emelia doesn't even wait for me to reach her or talk in hushed tones. "Sasha's gone," she says. Now I see Sasha's phone in her hand. "They said it was time, and they were crying, and they asked me to sing for them. They're gone."

92

SASHA

Some nights there is no luck. Some nights you've used it all up.

93

LILLIAN

Liv James starts trying to solve it, because Wavelength is shell-shocked. "We can push the opening back a bit more." She turns to Emelia. "I saw you in the older band videos Christensen sent, right?"

Emelia nods.

"Good, that'll work. You can borrow Marky's bass so if you don't know the words you won't seem useless onstage. It's mostly set up already. Does Sasha pull this sort of shit a lot? Because you can't have that in a band. Remember when I was in bad shape?"

"Wish I could forget," says Veyda.

Quinn answers. "This isn't like Sasha at all. They're here for the people they care about. And they were excited to meet you guys."

"Very invested in this show too," says Cyprus. "Almost as much as Lillian."

Sasha wouldn't leave us here.

Unless. Augustus off his charges and promoting Admirer. Monochrome Stoplight posting about Wavelength. The Channel.

"Is Isabelle like *Isabelle*?" asks Emelia. "Someone called Isabelle just texted Sasha."

Cyprus says, "Fuck, what if she's here?"

"Isabelle?" asks Quinn. "That'd be amazing."

"No, Heather Erin," I correct him. "What does the message say?"

"It's locked."

"Wait," says Liv James. "Heather Erin, the Channel manager?"

Christensen comes crashing through the door. He's out of breath, barely balancing a tray full of empty glasses and bottles. "Did you guys know Sasha and Heather Erin just left in an airport taxi together?"

Liv James is looking from Christensen to me to Emelia. "Anyone, please, catch me up."

I can't figure out who knows what. "Christensen, who do you think Sasha is?"

"Sasha Weaver, Wavelength member." His eyes are darting all over. The man can't lie to save his life.

"Did you know?" I ask. "Since when?"

Christensen is still holding the tray. "Do *you* know?"

"Know *what*?" asks Liv James.

A lot of looks get exchanged between me, Quinn, Cyprus and Emelia, ending with Quinn saying, "Sasha's somewhat more famous as one half of Admirer."

Liv James' eyes widen for a second. "The helmet one or the douchey one?"

"The helmet one," says Cyprus.

Monochrome Stoplight is taking this news surprisingly well. I guess they've seen some shit.

"I like the helmet one," says Liv James. "Why are they here exactly?"

"Long story," I say. "I'll tell you after the show."

"Taylor IDed Sasha the first time they were here," says

Christensen. "It's right on Sasha's license. Alexander Moore, west coast address. The name felt familiar to Taylor. It was bugging them, so they mentioned it to me. But Sasha seemed to be getting along fine. I let it be." He picks a drink off the tray and finishes it. "I'm pissed they'd just head off with Heather Erin before a show. Leaving you guys out to dry. Why would they do that now that they've terminated their contract?"

"Sasha's contract isn't terminated," says Cyprus. "Sasha can't terminate their contract until they're twenty-one."

Christensen looks confused. "Together, Sasha and Augustus can terminate that contract anytime they want. It's not even that hard. They lose the band name and the rights to the songs, but their dad negotiated with the Channel and Heather Erin so they could leave. I've read that contract. He left Sasha and Augustus a way out."

Quinn sets down his drumsticks. "Sasha doesn't know that. Heather Erin never let Sasha read the whole contract. They told me."

Christensen takes another drink. "That's very illegal. Also, evil. What are you doing?"

Quinn is rummaging in Cyprus's coat pocket for her car keys. "We're going after Sasha, right? We've got to get to the airport and let them know."

Inside me, it clicks. That Sasha wants to stay. They don't want to leave us and they don't want to leave me. And whether that means we're lovers or friends or bandmates or something else or some combination, I don't know. It doesn't matter.

But even more than Sasha wants to stay, they want to keep us safe. They don't play the show. They don't take anything with them. If they're good and obedient to the Channel, maybe the Channel leaves Wavelength alone.

"If this is some leftover tragic masculine silent self-sacrificing hero bullshit," I say, "I am going to kick Sasha's ass."

Cyprus is already checking the route. "The airport's across the city. We won't ever make it back in time."

I've almost forgotten that Liv James is standing right next to me until she says, "Are you sure Sasha wants to stay? Or that their brother will agree to terminate the contract? Or that you'll make it before they leave? That's a lot of ifs."

"They've done the same for me with a lot of unanswered questions." I put my coat on, zip it up, turn to Monochrome Stoplight. "I'm really sorry to bail on you. But Sasha's in the band."

"You're right," says Cyprus.

Quinn holds up Cyprus's jacket. "Where are your keys?"

"Victoria dropped me off!"

Liv James sighs. "You're the best openers we could have possibly picked. I don't even have to hear you play to be sure of it." She presses a bundle of keys into my hand. "Take our van."

LILLIAN

I accelerate to beat a light. Christensen's in the back seat on a call with some contract lawyer buddy at the Channel. Quinn and Cyprus are trying to unlock Sasha's phone. Emelia's beside me figuring out which flight Sasha and Heather Erin might be getting on.

"If it's this one, we've got …" Emelia checks the time again. "We could make it in before it boards." If things happen quickly at the airport, but I can't think of another way.

"We need tickets to get to departures," I say. "Just any cheap flights."

Cyprus is on it.

Too many minutes later, I slam on the brakes, bringing us to a hard stop in the airport loading zone. Emelia says she'll take care of the van. That she hopes we get Sasha. I want to thank her, but we're already rushing out into the wind biting across the concrete.

Inside the airport, our ragtag group stands out against the sterile blandness. We're spikes and concert clothes in the midst of white floors and automated ticket stands.

It's a quiet night, short security line. Christensen's trying to wrap up his phone call before we reach the checkpoint. He's got this smooth-powerful-businessperson mode he's switched on from his past life. I can only hope it's as effective as it is slick.

Quinn holds up Sasha's phone. "Two guesses left."

"It was a new phone," I say. "So maybe it's a Sasha password, not from their Admirer life. Day they left? Month and day?"

"We tried it," says Quinn.

I lean over the screen. What would matter to Sasha? Sasha who wasn't tied down by the Channel anymore, who was done being who anyone had told them to be.

"Try 5-2-7-5," I say.

The screen opens up.

"What?" asks Quinn. "You've been psychic this whole time?"

"It's the numbers for L-A-R-K," I say.

The line creeps forward a step. I'm willing it to go faster. I've got everything that needs to go in the bin ready.

Christensen says, "You're one of the good ones, Doug, seriously. I owe you twice." He hangs up and looks at us. "It's set to go. We just need Sasha and Augustus to agree to sign it."

"So, problem." Quinn's scrolling through Sasha's contacts. "Sasha has great nicknames for all of us, but they don't have Augustus's number."

"Isabelle's?" I suggest. "She could get us to Augustus."

Quinn hits the button to call a global celebrity. Someone with red carpet looks who wins popularity TV awards and gets voted on to lists of the sexiest hundred. A person whose fame we've grown up with who gets gossiped about and modeled after.

"Can I?" asks Cyprus. "If she answers?"

Quinn rolls his eyes and hands her the phone. "Urgency, remember urgency."

Cyprus mouths *holy shit* at us when Isabelle answers the call. "Hey, is this Isabelle? Wow, alright. My name's Cyprus. Yeah, I *am* in Wavelength. You saw our video? Thank you. Aww, thank you."

I make a speed-it-up gesture at Cyprus.

"We're in the airport trying to get Sasha back from that manager. Yes, same person. We've found a way to get Sasha out of their contract. Really. It's there, but Heather Erin never told them. They / them, yeah. We need Augustus on the phone, but Sasha doesn't have his number. You would do that? You're my hero. I mean, you were before too —"

The security guard waves Cyprus in, and she has to hang up. "Isabelle liked my earrings!" she says, but then she's being processed, so I don't know how the rest went until the other side.

I get through pretty quickly, though of course the guards "randomly" check Quinn. Christensen's keeping an eye on that situation.

"Isabelle sent me the number," says Cyprus on the other side of security. "She's texting Augustus to tell him the call he's about to get is an emergency. And she said I had style!"

We're the call he's about to get.

We're an emergency for Augustus Ash.

There's a holdup in Christensen's line, but by some miracle, Quinn's through already. I put the call on speakerphone between the three of us.

There's music playing in the background when Augustus answers. It's loud for a moment, then fading away. I can hear him excusing himself from a room full of people.

"What's up?" Augustus asks. "Isabelle said you're in trouble? Please say you're not going on trial for anything. The Channel will not love that."

There's a breeziness about his voice and manner even though he hasn't talked to Sasha in half a year. He doesn't sound remotely concerned. Like not caring is the correct position. Like I should feel guilty for hating him and Sasha should feel guilty for being in trouble.

"I need your he —" I start.

"Yeah yeah, tell her I'll be right back," Augustus says to someone else before switching back to me. "No big deal, just a tour question."

I resist hanging up. I have to have this bastard on my side for a minute. "I need your help," I say again. "Sasha's in trouble."

"Who the hell are you?"

"My name's Lillian. I'm a friend of Sasha's."

"Who now?"

Cyprus cuts in. "Your sibling, the pop star, the good half of Admirer."

Augustus laughs, assuming it's a joke rather than be insulted. "My brother doesn't really do friends. Are you his first groupies? Has this whole vanishing bit been a fling? Isabelle will be pissed." I definitely hear a hint of pride.

Cyprus can see me losing my temper. She knows she should stop me but doesn't bother. Someone has to stop pandering to people like Augustus.

"Is there anything," I say, "that you're not entirely ignorant about? Let me straighten some shit out for you."

I'm surprised to find Quinn fired up with me. "First, it's Sasha, they / them," Quinn says. "They said they came out to you quite a while ago, and I want to hear you getting it right."

"Who are —" starts Augustus.

"Second," I say, "Sasha left the Channel because the trial about *your* crimes forced them into a bad spot. They don't want to come back. That life has always worked better for you than for them."

Christensen's through. He looks up at the baffling diagram in front of us. "Our gate is … left. Are you scolding Augustus Ash?" he asks as we start moving through the airport toward the gate.

"We are," says Cyprus. "It's awesome."

Thankfully, Augustus doesn't hang up. "Lillian, you don't seem like *Sasha's* type." He puts emphasis into the name like getting it correct is some act of unnecessary political correctness.

"And why's that, Augustus?"

"You're deeply bitchy."

"You don't seem like Sasha's brother," says Quinn.

"You're an insolent prick," I add.

"Date me instead?" says Augustus. "I'm recently single."

If he was closer, I'd either knock in his perfect teeth or throw up. I'm ready to rip into him again, but I don't bother, because we're at the gate.

It's mostly empty, and boarding hasn't started yet. We've made it. But when I look around for Sasha's hair, their posture, the straps of their dress and their earrings dangling, I can't find them.

They could be at the other end of the airport, a different flight, already gone.

Quinn's giving the space the same once-over. "Sasha!" he calls.

They're sitting facing away from us, head down. When they hear Quinn, they lift it and turn and I see their face. They've been crying, and they've taken all their makeup off. Their earrings are nowhere to be seen. A hundred emotions cross their face as we rush toward them. On the last one, they lock eyes with me.

I think it's fear. It's a look that means *run*.

Beside them, Heather Erin follows Sasha's gaze. If she's surprised to see us, she doesn't show it. Her makeup is very much intact, and her entire manner is composed even as we gather around her and Sasha, taking the seats across from them and beside them, surrounding them.

A voice comes on, announcing that first class boarding is about to begin.

Heather Erin stands, her hand tight around Sasha's elbow, pulling them to their feet. "Presuming you're the band," she says, "this is when you should turn around and leave. Like we talked about, right, Sasha?" Any semblance of warmth or care in her voice sounds rehearsed.

Sasha's still looking at me. "It's for the best," they say blankly.

Cyprus stands up in front of Heather Erin, several inches taller than her. "Sit your ass down," Cyprus says. "We know about the contract. We've got Augustus on the phone. We've got everything Admirer needs to terminate it. Sasha has the right to know. The actual, legal right."

Heather Erin sits back down.

"What's going on?" asks Augustus on the phone. "This makes no sense."

"Be patient for once in your life," I say, but I switch to video so we can all see each other.

"We can get out?" asks Sasha quietly. I can see their fear flickering toward hope. Maybe Augustus sees it too.

Christensen explains, looking back and forth between Sasha and Augustus. "When your dad negotiated your contract, he made sure you weren't trapped. It costs you Admirer's songs and name, but if you both agree to leave, you can get out anytime."

For the first time, I understand the weight of what Sasha's

been carrying. When the inevitability lifts off their shoulders. They realize they may not always have the Channel at their heels. Their joy may not always be hunted down.

"Does the Channel want another crisis?" Christensen asks Heather Erin. "If this comes to light, that you willfully misled Admirer about their contract for years, it will be a catastrophe, Heather. The Channel will need someone to take the fall. Don't pretend they'll defend you like they defended Augustus. People like you and I have always been replaceable."

Heather Erin doesn't look as unsettled as I want her to. "It's irrelevant," she says. "The boys aren't going to give up the band."

Sasha takes Heather Erin's hovering hand off their elbow and turns to her. "I'm going to make this as clear as possible. I want to terminate my contract and leave the Channel. I want to be left alone, and I'm willing to give up Admirer to do that. The only reason I was going with you was because you threatened my friends. Where do I sign?"

In my hand, Augustus's voice jumps. "Hold up. We've both got to sign this, right? Alex, are you an actual idiot? You're killing me here. This is Admirer."

Sasha's having a hard time holding their voice steady. "I never realized we could leave. If I'd realized we had a choice … who knows? But we don't have to stay, Augustus."

"Very heartfelt," says Heather Erin, "but Augustus won't sign."

"How do you know?" I ask.

Heather Erin is holding back a smirk. "Because Augustus found out about the contract years ago."

Overhead, the boarding call repeats.

95

LILLIAN

We've all stopped dead. Even Christensen looks shaken.

"Augustus and I agreed not to tell you," Heather Erin says to Sasha. "You wouldn't have gotten to where you are now if you'd known. You wouldn't have committed yourself to Admirer."

Sasha crumples. Set up, knocked down. I want to wrap them in my arms. I want to crush the phone in my hand and watch Augustus's face flicker out.

"You fuckers," says Cyprus.

"Hold up, hold up," says Augustus. "Alex—"

"Still Sasha," says Quinn.

"I was just looking out for you," says Augustus. "It would have been a distraction. I didn't want to give you false hope. And it's not what you really wanted anyway. Remember how it feels to have a hundred thousand people scream your name? The Channel gave you that. They've got your back. I've got your back. Brothers to the end, right?"

Heather Erin gives the slightest nod to Augustus. Good dog.

Her and I both know that Sasha's waited their whole life to hear some part of those words. Heather Erin says Sasha can't expect Augustus to make the biggest decision of his career on a whim. Let's get on the plane. We'll all sit down at the beach house and sort out what you need. Augustus and her and the entire Channel.

Manipulation I'd ram back down their throats.

These posers of empathy.

"Shut. Up," I say. When Heather Erin doesn't, I snap the words at her. Give it authority, conviction, too sharp for an airport. I just play louder than her.

And I look her in the eyes so she knows there's no limit to how far I'll push this.

I set the phone on the arm of a chair so I can see Augustus properly and put my body between him and Heather Erin. "Forget about 'the biggest decision of your career.' Sasha's your family. You can be a solo act. You'll still be famous. You'll lose millions, but you've got millions to spare. Someone will write new hits for you. But you've only got one sibling. From everything Sasha's said about you, I've taken away two things. They love you. And you've treated them like trash."

"Sasha, what have I ever done to you?" Augustus gets their name right when he wants to.

Sasha pauses so long that I'm scared they've bought the deceit. "It's more what you haven't done," they say eventually. "It's that you don't even know me well enough to know I've never heard a crowd scream my name. Or to realize how you've hurt me."

"It's all the chances you've had to be good to Sasha," Quinn says. "Somehow, my friend still cares about you. No one gets it. I'd talk them out of it if I could. Because you've let those chances slip away."

"Don't do that this time," says Cyprus. "You won't get another chance to start treating Sasha like they matter."

In the background of the call, someone tries to say something to Augustus, but he brushes them off. To us, he says, "That's what I'm trying to do. Leaving Admirer isn't the right choice."

"You took my choice when you kept the truth from me," says Sasha.

There's a spark in them I'd dedicate my existence to breathing life into. All our eyes are on Sasha.

"I can't let you throw away our future like I almost did," says Augustus.

"You and I don't have a future if you choose this over me."

Augustus stammers, peters out. He's pushed Sasha and they've pushed back, and I see on his face that he's glimpsed how badly he's broken this. That it might already be too late.

Sasha's still got the sort of words they've used to connect to every person in a stadium. They step away from Heather Erin and pick up the phone. "Dad built an escape in case one of us hit a breaking point. I'm there. If I go back, it will break my heart every single day from now until the end of that contract.

"I've needed a family to look out for me for most of my life. Not one who was trying to make me famous or use me to get famous. I've got that family now. They're here. They gave up something that meant the world to them to come get me. Today, you can be my family by helping me stay with them. It's that simple."

It's quiet then. More encompassing than when Sasha silences a crowd.

"What do I need to sign?" asks Augustus.

I could throw my hands in the air and start crying all at once.

Then Sasha looks down at Heather Erin. The spark aflame, threatening. "Don't try to expose my identity. If that happens, it will be on my terms. People love Admirer. Not you. Not the

Channel. I have the followers, the fans, the platform. You gave them to me. Don't make yourself regret giving me that power."

Heather Erin starts to say how she could make us all famous, but Cyprus shushes her.

Sasha looks from me to Cyprus to Quinn. They've got tears in their eyes. "Can we go now?"

"We've got this from here," says Christensen, holding his hand out for the phone. "Maybe you can still catch some of Monochrome Stoplight."

Sasha doesn't say goodbye to Augustus. They see Quinn's open arms and hug him. Then the rest of us join in until Wavelength's huddled like we're about to play a show. We're close together standing in departures. I don't even know if I'm crying. Some of us are.

I just know Sasha's here. They're close to me, and they're not leaving.

Sometimes, you can count on the people you love to save you. They can't keep you from diving in or protect you from the waves, but they can stop you from drowning.

I hold Sasha's hand as we head toward the exit.

They're trying to say they're sorry we didn't get to open the show and we're trying to find a way to explain it. We're a band and a family.

"Remember when we sat on the edge of the parking garage?" I link my fingers with theirs. "That's when I knew I wanted you in my life. Somehow. Someplace. I knew that if you fell, I'd start missing you before you hit the ground."

96

SASHA

The automatic doors slide open with a rush of cold air, pulling us back into the city.

Back toward dancing. Toward our heroes playing our favorite songs. Toward singing along and merging into the sound.

And I'm crying. I get to give all of my voice to the people who came back for me. Who surround me, who make me realize this time I'm not just trying to disappear, I'm coming home.

Together, we're going to catch the noise we've been chasing down, and we're going to scream for an encore.

Don't turn on the houselights yet. Our show isn't over.

LISTEN TO "ELEVATOR" BY WAVELENGTH

ACKNOWLEDGMENTS

To my agent, Amy Tompkins, for believing in this story when I was nearly done believing in it. Having you in my corner has changed everything, and your endless willingness to answer my questions about all things book industry has taught me more than than I ever knew there was to learn.

To my editor, Emma Sakamoto. From the first time we spoke, I knew *Wavelength* was in safe hands with you. This whole book thing is terrifying, but your care in every conversation about *Wavelength* and every round of edits put me at ease. Thank you for being in the absolute weeds of editing details with me, for talking about breaths and sentence rhythm, for finding every single line that was never quite right, and for being willing to put "commas idiosyncratic but intentional" on the style sheet.

To the entire rest of the team at Groundwood, I'm so lucky and honored to get to work with you. I couldn't have dreamed of a better home for *Wavelength*.

To Bhavna Madan, for designing this gorgeous cover in all its queerness and chemistry. I stand in awe of your art.

To the friends who read the book first and helped me hack it into shape. Elyse, for being there from before I remember. I'd trust your opinion on truly anything, including editing, of course. Alen, for describing *Wavelength* as "queer Hannah

Montana." Teresa, for telling me to rewrite that part because there are no drugs that work that way. Nina, for turning this book from draft to pitch-ready manuscript. And Kay, for being in my life for more stages than I can count and for starting this whole thing off by suggesting that maybe, possibly, the experiences I was describing might be genderqueer. I started writing *Wavelength* the next month.

To my mentors Darcie Little Badger, Katherena Vermette and Tanya Boteju. I want to be each of you in a different way when I grow up.

To my dear pals. For the ones I grew up with, none of these characters are you, but your fingerprints are on the heart of this book. Jesse, thank you for a million games, for always being interested, for listening to me ramble about my latest half-baked ideas. If you find a friend like Jesse, hold on to them for life. My 2022 Banff Centre and 2024 Lambda Literary cohorts, you lit fires in me about writing and being alive. You gave me the sorts of moments of belonging you spend your whole life chasing after.

To my family. Mom and Dad, for filling our house with books and music and for extending your love to everyone and everything I care about. You make writing kind parents easy. And again to my mom for proofing a truly unbelievable amount of my terrible early writing. To Dasha, for paving the way and for teaching me how to write grant applications. To Tirian, for all the late-night talks in the kitchen at our parents' place. To Tayah, for singing songs and nerding out with me. You three are the wacky siblings of my dreams.

To Carly, for being the queer love story I always imagined.

To Waffle, for being the pet love story I never imagined.

To all the musicians I've seen live, and to Winnipeg's incredible music scene. This city isn't where *Wavelength* takes place, but there are bits and pieces of its venues and shows all through it.

To the Winnipeg Public Library staff, especially at the Cornish and Henderson branches.

Special thanks to Canada Council for the Arts and Manitoba Arts Council and the amazing people at each who've answered so many questions for me over the years.

And you always seem to get thanked last, like an encore. Thank you to everyone who read this book. I've imagined you every step of the way. Anyone who tells you there isn't enough love to go around is lying. This is for all of you.

CALE PLETT is a nonbinary, genderfluid writer who lives on Treaty One Territory in Winnipeg, Manitoba. Whatever genre they're writing, they try to create spaces where queer characters can exist safely within their identities. Their karaoke is tuneless, and the last time their car was broken into, the only thing that was left behind was their mix CDs. *Wavelength* is their debut novel. Their second YA novel, *The Saw Mouth*, is forthcoming in summer 2026.